MAJESTY AND
PERNICIOUS TEASER

Annette Carolyn Ely

UPFRONT PUBLISHING
LEICESTERSHIRE

Published in paperback 2002 by
UPFRONT PUBLISHING
ISBN 1 84426 142 5

First Edition (Hardback) 2003 by
UPFRONT PUBLISHING
ISBN 1 84426 223 5

MAJESTY AND
PERNICIOUS TEASER

*To Mr. Allan Paul Wane, resident of the Vineyard Precincts,
Peterborough Minster, Peterborough, England, who so graciously
escorted me to the places I longed to experience, where the footsteps of
medieval characters depicted herein seemed recent, and with whom he
joined the ages, suddenly and without warning in September of 1999.
May his ashes rest in peace beside the cathedral he loved so well.*

This royal throne of kings,
This scept'red isle
This earth of majesty...
This other Eden... demiparadise...
This blessed plot,
This earth, this realm
This England...

Richard II (Act II, Scene I)

Acknowledgements

Sir Henry and Lady Bedingfeld, Oxburgh Hall, Norfolk.

The Right Honorable Douglas Hogg, QC MP for providing from Kettlethorpe Manor Rectory, Lincolnshire, England, copies from *On Lady Katherine de Roet Swynford Lancaster* by R.E.G. Cole, MA, Prebendary of Lincoln.

Lovely Mrs. Ella Garn, Thorpes Gate, Peterborough, England, for knowledge, wisdom, wit, charm, and her love of P'boro Minster.

Professor and Mrs. Robert Rathburn for the use of their library, encouragement and fun.

Professor Margaret Boddy for the use of her exquisite volumes from medieval England.

Sherie Ann Abbasi, Law Librarian, DOT, Washington, D.C., my cousin, for providing additional information regarding the Hope Diamond and for accompanying me to view the same at the Smithsonian Institute.

Betty Anne, Librarian, Alexandria Public Library, Alexandria, Minnesota, for assisting in research regarding England's elite security forces and other matters.

Mr. and Mrs. Graham Cornelissen, Peterborough, England, for making my research trips possible with great hospitality.

Foreword

Aside from well known public and historical figures, all characters in this book are fictional. Interaction with current, real persons did not occur. The heists did not happen. The author has taken the historical accounts of a Stuart Queen and her one girl babe over whom historians disagree as to even having existed and invented a story. Having already written that section of the manuscript, and hoping I'd find one more Stuart Princess, there she was, listed as at least having been born. Overjoyed, I felt that perhaps between the lines within the heart of that closely knit family, such things as I'd written could have transpired. You may decide. God bless the Queen and her family. Please remember that dreams contained herein are exactly that – dreams.

Prologue

Could ever a poem be more appropriate regarding August 31, 1997; or September 8, 1649?

Earth Moaned her Loss
(On Lady Jane Maitland)

Like to the garden's eye, the flower of flowers
With purple pomp that dazzle doth the sight,
Or as among the lesser gems of night,
The usher of the planet of the hours,
Sweet maid, thou shineds't on this work of ours,
Of all perfections having trac'd the height:
Thine outward frame was fair, fair inward powers,
A sapphire lanthorn, and an incense light.
Hence, the enamour'd heaven, as too, too good
On earth's all-thorny soil long to abide,
Transplanted to their fields so rare a bud,
Where from thy sun no cloud thee can hide.
Earth moan'd her loss, and wish'd she had the grace
Not to have known, or known the longer space.

William Drummond
of
Hawthorndon
(1585–1649)

Chapter One

London, England, January 30, 1649. Outside Whitehall's magnificent banqueting hall, the executioner stepped forward to King Charles I.

So ended a life.

Nearby, a thirteen-year-old princess lay weeping, for the life which had been stilled was that of her beloved father. Under close, but gentle house arrest, her sorrow was respected. For little Elizabeth Stuart's mild nature and gentleness toward her father's enemies had gained her the name of 'Temperance'. Those characteristics came of majesty within her young being, an attribute of which only she seemed to be unaware.

Seven months later at Carisbrooke Castle, where she and her father King Charles I had tearfully embraced goodbye, the sweet princess died of fever, having never recovered from so great a loss. For she had always known what historians, including Sir Winston Churchill, later concluded: her father's private life and character bespoke 'a man above reproach'.

So ended two lives.

London, England, August 31, 1997 and the U.S.A., August 30, 1997, respectively.

Television anchorpersons stepped forward, and with emotion announced the death of the world's fairytale princess, England's lovely Diana, Princess of Wales, aged thirty-six. She was beloved by many who described her as 'real'. As the tempestuous nineties had battered her marriage, people around the globe found room in their hearts to understand and love not only Diana but her husband, the Prince of Wales, and their sweet sons as well. Wisdom dictated skepticism when the media was used as the method of duo character assassination before the lovely lady's demise.

So ended three lives... prematurely.

Chapter Two

The second millennium in an unprecedented electronic age was drawing to closure in an ever-changing world. Sorrow ignited via satellite-fed, instantaneous global television. As events occurred, live action could be seen by everyone and anyone with a television set. Universal sadness gripped a universal world over a universal beauty renowned for her public compassion.

In America, characterized as a forgiving nation through its few centuries of discovery, birth, and gigantic leaps into astonishing adulthood, public majesty had crowned Diana's good works. Therefore, on this horrendous day, American women were gripped in grief as they watched a courageously caring ex-husband escort the coffin of his sons' mother from the hospital chapel in Paris.

Damned if he did and damned if he didn't, creditably he did.

Those who knew heraldry and the place of a Crown Prince/husband/father/son of a reigning Queen, recognized the significance of Prince Charles accepting his mother's Royal Standard with which to drape the casket in dignity. Honor befitting the deceased's good works; and place in history as the mother of a future king was given.

'And a *good* mother!' one imagined the Prince shouting at her detractors. (If princes ever shout, that is.)

No one born and raised in a kingdom could miss the silent message that their sense of loss was shared. The Queen of Compassion was carried in quiet dignity back to the sons and people who loved her.

Never before had anyone other than a member of the Royal family in good standing or an honored head of state been decorated in such fashion by the British monarchy.

To Christiana Deerfield, watching it with her great, green eyes from Midwestern United States, the gestures were obvious. The song 'And his banner over me is love...' went through her grieving mind as tears coursed through black lashes down her youthful face. She realized that the Prince's immediate response in gathering his former love back to the scept'red isle bespoke reawakened, tender memories as he responded with compassion and majesty to their finest moments together in a long ago. To his only bride, he was again speaking the language of love.

To one American, possibly more, the Prince's feelings were obvious. 'Many American anchorpersons seem to be missing the significance of both Prince Charles being there and the Queen's Royal standard covering Diana as if to protect... yes, even as if to forgive all the unhappy past!' Christiana wept in frustration. And if she could have been omnipresent, she would have seen three-quarters of her countrywomen and many men weeping at the same time. Christiana brushed her soft, black hair back into place as she and others around the world watched a kingdom dissolved in tears, carrying flowers in their arms to Kensington Palace in London. Silently, they saw the British waft their Princess toward heaven's gates upon a sea of fragrant blossoms; not one petal more beautiful than she.

For one terrible week, it seemed as if the world stood still. The majority of women and young mothers in the United States wished they could join their sisters across the Atlantic to show admiration for one whose self-chosen privilege in life was to love the unlovely. That God-like quality which had graced her life had been infectious after all.

As it should have been, Christiana and the rest of the world felt for the Princess, the sorrow of her young boys and their daddy, as her three men led the way to self-discovery of the majesty within every saddened heart around the world. Global willingness to serve and comfort others surprised Royal and commoner alike; and the impulse to be merciful came fast upon its heels. Together, people everywhere felt majesty's rebirth within their own hearts and minds as they subconsciously held the three valiant princes in sorrowing arms.

Chapter Three

London, England, August 31, 1997

On Jermyn Street in the Mall district of London, an impeccably dressed middle-aged American man stood in the mist, dressed in a black London Fog coat, smoking a fashionable stogie in a ritualistic manner which said, as did Mark Twain, 'If I cannot smoke cigars in heaven, I shall not go.'

The man about town's salt and pepper-colored hair was getting curlier by the minute as he felt the airborne moisture infiltrating every shaft to the very roots. Wisps spilled onto an intelligent-looking brow, hiding an abrupt ridge in his scalp from crown to the tanned middle of his forehead where a Vietcong bullet had more than grazed his head. Surgeons had implanted a steel plate to replace the blown-away bone, hiding it under his skin. It hadn't ruined Old Blue's looks. He was tall, lean and slightly round-shouldered, but not enough to make his figure unimposing nor unattractive. Brown eyes sparkling with mental brilliance belied occasional disguises as a street bum. Even when he was off duty on a drunk, one could see unusual intelligence lurking there.

Liquor was his favorite relapse into fun followed by all the vices of blackout – women, marijuana and an occasional snort of cocaine. But even while spending three weeks trying to forget what he had just had to do to secure an innocent's life in the shadowy world of espionage, the guy never touched the hard stuff. Reason? He didn't want to fry his brain into resembling an overdone egg on a grill in some sleazy diner.

He was particular about his beer and his women. Basically, he preferred the beer; and would say of his underlings who wallowed in a haze of white powder, or grass and women after completion of a tough assignment, 'Let the fools be fools! I don't need it to have fun. Where's the Pabst?'

He was known as Old Blue because not one tip of the bottle ever reached his lips until the blue ribbon was flicked off the brown glass neck. The fingers tearing off the azure paper ribbons were as long, lean and hard as the rest of the human machine. Almost fifty-six years of age, he had the hard, tall body of a twenty-three-year-old – tight stomach, skinny, hard hips, muscle everywhere in a svelte way. That understated elegance of large cats as they walk nonchalantly hummed like a fever radiating from his persona. He could outsmoke, outdrink and outmost anything, especially outthink the majority of people... and outkill if need be to save a government figure or an innocent child held hostage.

Oddly, into that leathery, scarred-beneath-the-trim-beard and moustache of the brown-eyed man, compassion often stamped its presence when he saw suffering humanity. He hated oppressors of freedom with a passion beyond his love for beer. His dresser drawer held a purple heart, medals of honor and other decorations from his Presidents for responding to that compassion under fire. He was quite a man, with a mind like a steel trap, and a heart of gold.

There were only two things which could undo Old Blue: the smile of a child, and innocence in a woman. But beware to the female who ever pretended such virtue, for then he could be ruthlessly sarcastic and physically abusive in exposing her wiles. He hated women who lied just as much as he hated men of the same stripe. In his mind, all skunks and polecats were related, and to that fraternity, he relegated all deceivers. Perhaps it was because he was a highly trained master deceiver himself and a teacher of the same.

In his type of business where deceit was the name of the game, he took pleasure and pride in being able to spot a liar 'one hundred miles away'. He took even greater pleasure in annihilating them if their falsehoods caused the loss of life. These things transpired during the course of his workdays and nights. Yes, his success rate was one hundred per cent. He was in great demand, for no one enlisted by free world governments could equal the work Old Blue put out, whether it was by way of his attorney-honed skills fashioned at Oxford's school of law in Queens College on a Rhodes scholarship, or at the end of his lean arms and long fingers when disengaging an attacker's esophagus.

But his conscience screamed out many a night as he lay trying to sleep after completion of assignments. Tears coursing down his battle-scarred face where no one could see him, he would wrenchingly ask, 'Why me, oh God, why me? Why was I asked to be a Joshua for my country? Why me?' Rolling over to bury a wet face in the pillows, he'd mutter, 'Why didn't I say no the first time!' He could not forgive himself, therefore into every happiness that came his way, he would mentally castigate it, or her, into non-existence in self-chastisement and guilt.

Unworthy. He had stamped his soul with big, red letters: UNWORTHY.

Old Blue came to the corner of Jermyn Street and Bond Street. If he went right, he'd walk automatically onto, of all places, *Old* Bond Street.

Ruefully smiling at the 007 reminder to his right, in whose movies his kid brother had basked whenever big brother was home from college or the service to take him, OB stepped neatly around the corner to the left where he was supposed to walk. He was expected to keep an eye out for unusual behavior around St. James Palace and the Mall.

The city, teeming with subdued party goers from Piccadilly just a few blocks to his left, was filled with groups standing around crying silently or just staring into space, dumbfounded. As Old Blue walked around from Bond Steet to St. James Street, he was engulfed by droves of what seemed like the walking dead for no one spoke; no one sobbed as tears, shot into amber-like iridescence by the yellow bulbs from lamp posts high above their heads, slid slowly down faces.

'Eerie!' Old Blue muttered under his breath, simultaneously noticing that his stogie had gone down as if at half mast. 'I've never seen the masses cry without making a noise before.'

Passing opposite the understated elegance of historic White's Club, the Tory's lair, he eyed it with an appreciation for the spirited political discourse, insults aimed at their opposing party and impeccably covert gaming which had taken place between many of the nation's crème de la crème beneath its sheltering roof down through the centuries. No matter that the establishment had zigzagged across the street from three doors south of St. James Palace since its inception in 1693. Mr. White and his wife's business sense had been right on in acquiring a larger space to provide for highbrow conviviality. Eventually, roasting Whigs at White's became a popular diversion, sending that political party's permission down the street to Boodles Club for the tearing of the Tory's by the Whigs who frequented there. Just as prestigious as each other, the gentlemen's clubs flourished, and continued as the playground of the eighteenth-century elite, such as the unflappable Charles James Fox who loved to play at the third part of the Triune of Clubs, The Brooks. The year of our Lord, seventeen seventy-four, knew the likes of him.

Old Blue grinned. 'What a bunch of rowdies they all must have been without their women along, except for Mrs. White who sold tickets to the opera and such as a cover to hide the gaming!' That was right up Old Blue's alley. 'Too bad only White's and Boodles remain in business nowadays,' he said in South Dakota slang.

He stepped into a little side street directly opposite White's to light his stogie. Looking at Boodles down the street half a block away, he could imagine the whole building indignantly shouting political insults back up the hill to White's for all past injuries. No matter that the red brick building had once been White's Chocolate House before they moved up a few doors when it changed hands in 1920. Old Blue chuckled imagining the incendiary remarks one might hear if walls could talk. The white, low-slung elegance of the Tory club serenely basked in the mist behind its black wrought iron fence and lamps, contrasting with the richness of Boodles' rusticated red brick. Both dignified clubs had no signs posted.

'Oh, the illustrious Royals, aristocrats and politicians who have had a thing or two to say in there!' Old Blue mentioned to a tuxedoed gentleman who had just come out from White's and crossed the street to the little alley which sheltered OB as he lighted his balking cigar. Taking a big puff, blue smoke filtered into the misty air overhead. 'Are you a Tory?' he smilingly inquired of the man who was obviously in his prime.

Startled by Old Blue's impertinence, but warmed by his

friendly tone on such a soul-chilling morn, the man replied, 'Truth be told, I am actually half-and-half. A Tory aristocrat married a Whig and eventually spawned me a few generations this side of Brummel, Selwyn and Walpole.' He chuckled good-naturedly. 'I'm a bit of a lord in my heart and mind, but am an earl with a great love for commoner and Queen alike.' He suddenly became somber. 'Poor Princess.' He looked down the hill at St. James Palace, a block away. 'Poor boys... and poor Prince Charles for that matter. Just look at the people!'

He paused, looking up and down St. James Street to the Palace. 'They are like gentle, wounded sheep who have lost their shepherdess.' The young man dug into his coat top and extracted an enameled Fabergé cigarette case and flipped it open, its priceless latch silent in the night. He proffered to a declining Old Blue, and took a slender brown smoke from the burnished interior. Closing the box, which again made no sound as it closed, he slipped it back into his breast pocket. Quick as a wink, the American had a light waiting for him in a cupped hand. Bending into the flame, refined features of the black-headed, green-eyed English tribes of old were exposed as a moth to the flame.

'Thank you,' the gentleman breathed as he inhaled. 'Mind if I walk with you? You're an American, I take it.'

'I'd be honored.' Old Blue smiled, exposing a set of unusually white teeth with a charming chip off the left front tooth beneath his expertly trimmed salt and pepper mustache. With an elegant move of the hand and wrist, he put the stogie back to his mouth above a tidy, short beard. The tip of his stinky smoke glowed in the early morning darkness.

The men started to walk slowly down the hill toward St. James Palace. Before them, Prince Charles' residence seemed to be kissing the skies with its sober walls of ancient brick.

Seeing the Prince's home prompted Old Blue's compassion. 'I feel sorry for Charlie. I'd hate to be him right now. If I had loved a woman no matter how long ago, her death would be such a blow... especially if she was an exceptionally good mother to my children.'

'Wouldn't it matter – the bitterness which developed later?' The Englishman looked over at his companion as they descended the hill and took a drag.

'Hell, no!' Old Blue softly answered. He looked up above St. James Palace at the hint of dawn in the sky.

'How so?'

'Well…' he cleared his throat, 'I've dated many a fetching woman. Set my heart on one or two as potential wives. But something was always lacking. I just couldn't quite put my finger on it, for there was always an emptiness lurking behind a locked door in my heart.' Pulling another mouthful off his cigar, he continued, 'Now, it seems to me that Prince Charlie experienced the same thing before he fell in love with Diana.'

'I see. Yes, I suppose you are correct in assuming such a thing,' the friendly Englishman conjectured. 'Go on.'

They took a left at the bottom of the hill to skirt the Palace walls and Queen Henrietta Maria Stuart's little chapel where the present Queen sometimes worshipped of a Sunday morn.

Old Blue continued, 'My first love slipped away, too. Being young and lusty, I dated and dated and dated. No one interested me enough to actually marry.' He sneezed. 'Pardon me!' Whipping out a white handkerchief (a Walgreen's special from Indonesia) he tidied up his well-groomed face.

His companion noticed the lean, mean-looking muscles rippling across the back of the hand which held the handkerchief; tendons and bones which looked a bit bent out of shape, yet not quite. The man involuntarily shuddered.

'You cold? Want my London Fog?' And before the gent could respond, Old Blue had whipped his coat off and was holding it out, spread wide, for the fellow to slip into. 'You can't have it, but you can wear it and send it back to me later. My card is in the pocket. I'm staying at The Savoy.'

'You keep nice company, then,' the astonished Brit remarked as he slid into the coat. He saw that nothing would deter this stranger's kindness, so he decided to luxuriate in it instead of freezing to death and catching cold.

'One might say so,' Old Blue smiled, 'at least sometimes.'

'Look at that sign on this seventeenth-century chapel which the first King Charles built for his sloe-eyed, creamy-skinned beauty of a bride.' Old Blue had stopped dead in his tracks facing the white miniature elegance where the French princess turned English Queen had worshiped as a Catholic by special treaty.

'What about it?' the sojourner wanted to know.

'Well, it says that the public is welcome to come attend service with the present Queen if they have a mind to.' He shook his curls. 'Hot dog! I just might do that when she gets home. I feel rottenly wretched over the accident and consequent demise tonight, too; and, there's something motherly about Queen Elizabeth. It would feel good being near her in such a setting right now.'

Old Blue turned to his new acquaintance, brown eyes searching green. Caught off guard, the man from England was surprised by the moisture gathering in Old Blue's eyes. Snuffling a bit to check the catch in his own throat as he was impacted by his new friend's words, he put his hand to one eye as if to rid it of a speck of dirt. Digging around for a handkerchief, out came a white linen monogrammed with a golden crown beneath which a royal blue 'W' was embroidered in the finest of satin stitch. Coughing and sputtering elegantly, quietly, a runaway tear didn't escape Old Blue's notice as it soaked into the unusual identification of the man who stood before him. He also noticed how lengthy the coat was on the diminutive man. Oddly though the sleeves fit, as did the shoulders.

The steel trapdoor of Old Blue's mind clanged shut. 'I've seen this guy before. He's born and bred a commoner about as much as my Buckskin horse in South Dakota!' Old Blue's muttering was lost in the sound of good English shoe leather which respectfully kept filing past the two men toward Buckingham Palace where the wearers would fill the Mall to the Palace gates and beyond in all directions.

Compassion for the chilled man filled Old Blue's psyche. This man had known the deceased. His feelings were as obvious as those of the multitudes who thronged to the Royal residences for solace and to show their love in the sunshine and shadow of the ancient homes. Symbols of solid continuity, the timeless splendor of the majestic palaces brought to mind their equally beautiful princess.

Old Blue patted the man's shoulder and said, 'Come on. It's

getting light.' He let his stogie go out as, deep in thought, they resumed the walk along the gardens to the elegant street leading to Buckingham Palace on the Mall, where the Queen and Queen Mother's homes were set like white diamonds midst the emerald trees. Around them, adults and children were silently gathering as far as the eye could see.

'Isn't it something that during times of crisis throughout this century it has been natural for the people to turn to the Crown?' Old Blue looked at his Royal companion.

'Yes, for the Crown itself signifies not only the monarchy but all who are attached to her as are our British people, their House of Commons, their House of Lords,' the handsome young fellow softly added as he gazed compassionately over the thousands who stood weeping before the great Palace and houses which lined the elite street. '"Noblesse Oblige", to serve, has always been, and must always remain the sole intention of the heads who wear a crown in this country.' He turned to gaze at Old Blue. 'And now the people are here to accept that offer from u...' he stopped short, and smiled.

Old Blue smiled. Eyes met with full knowledge of identity.

'Now I must go.' The man started to take off the London Fog wrap.

'Hey man. Keep it on. If you're headed where I think you are, you'll need it a little while longer. Just send it over to the hotel when you're finished with it... or to Charlie's.'

It was then that the goodness in both men was apparent to the other. The younger took leave of the older. Old Blue started toward Queen Victoria Memorial while his companion walked through the wrought iron gates leading to the night guard of Clarence House. Passing the guard on duty whose left leg came stiffly up with the right arm at the turn of the minute, he warmed to the sight of the soldier as he had when playing in the nursery years earlier. Smart-looking this man with his firearm upon the left shoulder, and exquisite uniform.

Old Blue's companion rang the doorbell in the stone wall at the wooden gate. He would be needed upon his grandmother's tomorrow.

Grey dawn was making it easier for Old Blue to see as he

looked at the magnificent Lancaster House opposite that of the Queen Mother's residence.

'It's a far cry from the windswept and barren hills of home,' he mused, suddenly wishing for the comfort and isolation one could reach on horseback when descending into the coolies on a hot day. Shoving thoughts of the Little Sioux River away, his boots hidden by sharply creased gray slacks, carried him along. He shivered under the Harris tweed of black, white and gray. Pulling the collar higher against the misty fog of the early morn, he thought of the Prince and his mother whose safety he had been called from Madrid to ensure. Soon they would arrive from Balmoral.

Pedestrians streaming past him from Haymarket Street and Waterloo Place went to stand quietly along the softly illuminated street which led to Buckingham's glorious gates. Some stopped first to gaze up at the pale splendor of Clarence House; many whispered together, wondering if within its elegant interior their beloved Queen Mum, aged ninety-seven, was sleeping. They were all reeling from the shattering news of the past midnight hour when word of Princess Diana's accident had swept through Piccadilly Circus. In their minds, a connection was being made regarding their love for the young Princess and this commoner turned Royal, the beloved Elizabeth of Glamis, wife of King George VI, mother of the present Queen.

During the dark days of World War II when bombs were Londoners' daily fare, the sweet and courageous little woman would not turn her back on the East Enders of London who suffered great devastation. She chose to stay with the King in the city keeping themselves and their princesses close to the British while Hitler blitzed London and the countryside with bombs.

'Ah, but she isn't here, the King's fearless little Scot,' one theatergoer whispered to his lovely lass whose blonde head rested woefully upon his bomber-jacketed shoulder. Dawn, stealing in on dormouse tracks, cast a soft pink glow over her hair.

'Is she at Balmoral with Her Majesty and the Princes, do you think?' the pretty bird asked.

'I think so, dear. But I don't know for sure. One thing is for certain. I hope that no one wakes her early to tell the shocking news; even though she's a strong one. There is nothing to be done from here. It all came to rest in the hands of the doctors and God at four thirty, the blackest hour of any night, let alone this one!'

The pretty lady turned her face into her lover's leather jacket, and silently shook with sobs upon his comforting chest. Her Princess had died.

By now in the blazing fire of dawn, Old Blue had walked along the southern edge of dew-soaked Green Park, which extended from St. James Palace and grounds to Constitutional Hill Drive on the north-western edge of Buckingham Palace grounds. Surveying another street beyond Victoria Memorial which emptied onto the Mall, he walked over to the television crews who were setting up shop at advantageous spots all around. Press passes fluttered or clinked plastically as they slipped, slid and finally became secured onto harried cameramen and reporters' lapels. Wires were already everywhere underfoot.

Discarding the cold stump of his Havana cigar in a newsman's open video case, the chilly CIA agent plunged both hands deep within his trouser pockets and headed toward Cockspur Street. Before having to bed down in his rooms at St. James Palace, he was taking time to see an old friend. A shower, shave and sleep with no worries until his next shift appealed to the tired man. He had exactly twelve hours in which to do whatever needed doing to fortify his own spirits before he would be needed at all hours, perhaps for weeks. Ducking into the stairs, which took him down to the Underground, Old Blue let the train do the walking for a change.

The morning sun had risen by the time he unlocked a tidy but occult-looking shop door in the heart of Piccadilly not far from Eros Fountain. He looked around before entering. All the excitement of England's answer to Times Square in New York City was gone. The city was at a virtual standstill. Old Blue surveyed the silent urban sprawl of towering buildings; streets laid out like spokes of a wheel around the fountain, entrances to subways on various corners, and shops everywhere. Shaking his head in disbelief at its dormancy, he walked through the storefront door, hung a sign that said, 'OUT TO LUNCH' on its windowed front, and locked it.

Walking past a counter which faced the door, Old Blue parted midnight-blue curtains blazing with silver stars and fake jewels. Smiling deliciously, he observed an orange-headed dame with black roots coming from her scalp, sleeping peacefully on white sheets and pillows. The top sheet was loosely swirled around her lovely hips, one shapely leg was over the edge of the sheet, the other covered beneath as she lay mostly on a flat tummy, tiny top and the left shoulder. Her face was not pretty, but it was attractive... full lips, tan face, black lashes, and eyebrows neatly arched from plucking, oblong face awash in sleep. In her arms was a pillow which served as a comfort against her stomach, and against her neck and cheek as a replacement for her 'sometime sunshine' – Old Blue.

They were old working buddies. She didn't know he was in town, and with the early morning would come joy in the finding out; for she loved him. Of course, she would never let *him* know that. She didn't want him to leave and never come back.

She also didn't know that the Princess had been in an accident a few hours earlier, let alone died.

Chapter Four

America, August 30, 1997, 2400 hours, midnight

Soft black hair, emerald green eyes which sometimes startled people with their clear brilliance, surrounded by impudently straight, bristly black lashes framing almond shaped orbs made Christiana Deerfield, youngest of three daughters, quite fetching. Her frame was tiny, but she was tall, reaching five foot seven inches. Not needing mascara, none ever ran onto the high cheekbones, straight little nose, full mouth and dimpled chin of the compassionate Deerfield of Minnesota. She looked twenty-six years of age, but actually was thirty-six. Divorce, that plague of the twentieth century, had caught her also. Before she realized what was happening, a husband who had obviously adored her, left suddenly, saying that she would always be the woman he loved. It had been a gut-wrenching experience. She simply adored him and worshiped the ground on which he walked. He was her sun, flowers that bloomed in sweet springtime, mysteriously beautiful blizzards of wintertime, bird song of early June in a wintry land, the meadowlark of her heart was he.

One day he was there. The next day, he was not. She and her son had almost lost their minds grieving. To this day she could not help but weep at times for want of him. Cleverly and compassionately, she had taught their little one to love his absent daddy, to be proud that he had a good man as a father; and to understand that just because someone is called 'grown-up' doesn't mean that problems won't overwhelm one and send that person to self-discovery elsewhere. For she firmly believed that loving someone sometimes meant letting go if that loved one needed to save his own peace of mind. That was Christiana. Understanding, self-sacrificing, loving. But she had a latent temper, lying asleep deep in her soul ready to surface if anyone abused those tender characteristics of herself, or her son, or anyone whom she loved.

She was honest to a fault, which oft-times caused her great anguish. To lie was not her way. She wouldn't even consider it, unless someone's life depended upon it and that had not needed proving.

Presently, Christiana was stretched out on her couch, watching live coverage of the sadness in London. She was unashamedly letting the tears flow, the quiet kind, which run down one's face without realizing it. It was seven in the morning in England, and it was obvious that no one had gone home to bed the night before. Seven hours behind them, she was still up listening to commentators' criticism of the Royals. It upset her to hear it and she wondered did the world criticize so harshly because in that family's imperfections were mirrored their own?

America, August 31, 1997, 0100 hours

Society. It was a great mix, but a troubled mix. The times were fast and happily prosperous with waves of sex, gossip and violence blatantly sensationalized on television, in the newspapers, most movies and music. Anything gory or hideous was instantly loved by the young, much to their elders' consternation. Even the clothing of the children and young adults was anathema to many concerned but laughing parents... pants from which the crotch hung below the knee, T-shirts with shoulder seams to the elbow and hems almost to the calf. Sneakers... and on top? Turned around baseball caps out of which tufts of hair poked through a hole in the adjustable band right in the middle of the forehead. Oh yes, and a delicate loop earring – or three or four or five or six in one ear of both girls and boys. Happy-go-lucky, loud, brilliant kids, Americans all, who didn't realize the extent of their brash freedoms because of not having had their liberty denied at any time, any place. One could discuss whatever one wanted, except evilly planning to harm someone, of course. On the whole, American kids were a good sort full of *joie de vivre.*

Midst all this happy, fast living born of prosperity, they had a President who was two thirds loved and one third hated. He ignored media and prosecutor sniping to continue holding an olive branch, not only to his own constituents in the Senate and

House of Representatives, but also to voters and the world at large; for he believed that love overcomes evil. The cynics gleefully waited for the First Family to be caught in a lie; others staunchly believed in their country's constitutional 'innocent until proven guilty' and upheld the leader in daily hopes and prayers.

Christiana sighed and thought of Britain, the Americans' strong ally, unashamedly reaching hands across the sea to strengthen decency's cause along with her unruly stepchild of the eighteenth century who had since become Freedom's favorite leader. For in both countries it seemed that dirty politics was no longer seen as a virtue even by formerly shady but otherwise conscientious politicians. In both countries, post-war baby boomer votees were joining their grass-roots people; and it seemed to Christiana that for a long time the monarchy in England, which she herself dearly loved from afar, and their existing form of government had faithfully accepted the will of the voting public for many years, espousing the compassionate into office and public representation; their bipartisanship briefly set aside in an effort to heal not only their own hurting places, but those of the world at large as well.

Regarding American politics, little did Christiana know that deceitful partisanship was sprouting from seeds of hatred by men who meant well in her own capitol, Washington, D.C.; that before the year 2000 rolled around, scandal would try to rip her beloved country apart, but because of the constitution which governed the land it wouldn't succeed.

Outside Christiana's small, Midwestern town door, America was pulsating with joyful yet excruciating growing pains. The television had been babysitter to one generation of kids now become parents. The children of that generation now were thrilled with the computer age. Most children had a computer of their own, and were drawn to it like bees to perfume. Sometimes when the tongue of the mind was stuck in to extract sweet nectar, something else came out not quite so savory, which would corrupt young minds. Worldwide web brought enlightenment but also clandestine smut into the sanctity of a child's bedroom even though that child may have been taught by cautious parents what could or could not be viewed. It raged on, the battle to have electronic age savvy, competitive children, while mom and dad were away at work, or at home on their own computers, with Junior doing his homework down the hall.

Christiana had wondered aloud at her father's funeral luncheon to a retired movie mogul of the 1950s, 'Do you think that the human race is replacing the touch of a hand, the inflection of a voice, the warmth in the eyes of other humans with the controllable coldness and impersonal robotness of computers in order not to experience the hurt of rejection?'

'Well, maybe,' he answered. 'But I think it goes deeper than that.'

'How so?' she asked.

'I think that a computer is a fascinating toy, which brings instant gratification in business to most people. It's almost like going to the arcade to play pinball machines and the like, only you don't have to pay a quarter every time you want to play.'

'That's true,' Christiana agreed.

'There's more to the reason our society is losing its original values regarding human life, respect for others, and the familiar closeness experienced during the first sixty years of this century,' her friend said.

'For instance?' Christiana queried.

'For instance, when I was making movies, certain theological and Hollywood greats warned that a democratic republic could easily be torn asunder within a generation by subtle films, reading materials, even musical lyrics which constantly chipped away at a nation's moral habits. Especially if such behavior previously seen as unacceptable was suddenly portrayed as absolutely the norm.'

'Ah, I see what you mean! I remember how fascinated my grandmother and sisters were when soap operas on television first showed adultery on a daily basis between perfectly honorable professionals, housewives, what have you. They were shocked, but gradually we all started to think that everyone must be doing it. We weren't offended by it anymore. Years later it no longer was terrible to get a divorce. No one was ostracized for it even in our small towns. Look at me, I'm a prime example. I've victimized myself in a sense, doing something I didn't even believe in – getting a divorce when my husband decided to have his cake and eat it too. It tore my emotions apart to be sharing him with a shadowy someone when he decided to leave home to "find himself".'

'Did he want to come back?'

'Oh yes, several times, although he never wanted to stay because he would then have had to give up whatever and whomever was in his other life. He didn't want a divorce; however I couldn't stand the betrayal of my feelings of true love and my natural instincts of fidelity. I was truly influenced by the movies and television programs of the day. It seemed that love was like holding water in my hands when I would go swimming – it all ran out between my fingers. Glisteningly beautiful, it all seeped away.'

She bowed her head thinking that her father, who now was cold in a fresh grave, had been the only man who never made her cry. Looking up at the family friend, she remarked, 'Was the reasoning behind the moralists of the 40s and 50s that we become what we dwell upon?' Christiana's green eyes were intense as she searched his of brown.

'Yes. But, that wasn't all. You see, in America we have the constitutional Freedom of Speech amendment, which enables all types of expression via print and word of mouth. That freedom is easily abused, I'm afraid. It shouldn't be abused, but it is. It should be carefully used by everyone. One must be responsible, for what one says and does affects others.'

'Therein lies the area in which we've failed as a nation, I suppose,' Christiana acknowledged. Suddenly she chuckled. Zeroing in on her now favorite elderly man's eyes she asked, 'You don't suppose the Hope Diamond has anything to do with the state of the Union, do you?'

Being of quick, sophisticated mind, he joined in the laughter. 'I don't believe in jinxes, and I hardly think so. What are you going to do – go to Washington and entreat the powers that be to sell it back to its original temple in India? The temple lies in ruins you know.'

'Well, with rise in crime, and the confusion amongst some of our children which makes them bring injury and death to others, including their classmates, maybe that wouldn't be such a bad idea. It could be removed from the Smithsonian, fabled curse and all, and become the glorification of an Eastern god or goddess once more where it belongs.' Even white teeth enhanced her smile.

'Just because a few people who bought or owned it came to disaster doesn't mean that the deep blue diamond had anything to do with it. All people suffer tragedies. Our gathering today confirms that we do.' Mr. Mogul took a sip of black coffee from the white porcelain cup belonging to the church in which they sat. 'Does your family own the Hope Diamond?' he teased. 'Part of France's French Blue, Blue Diamond of the Crown? Did it escape from the Smithsonian, or its sister from around Spanish Queen Maria's neck in Goya's painting? Or from destruction on the *Titanic* into your father's safe?'

'I suppose it would take more than 45.52 carats of Hope Diamond splendor to bring a nation to ruin,' the bereaved woman admitted. 'As long as we are careful not to abuse our freedoms, perhaps the ills of the nation will find healing soon. Our freedom of speech and expression certainly was not intended as an excuse for insubordination toward loving but firm parenting, church and state, was it.' Christiana made a statement rather than asked a question.

'You're correct,' she continued, 'a bit of the original 112.3/16th carat Blue Diamond of the Crown from which it came was supposedly on the *Titanic* when it sank – if indeed that necklace "Heart of Hearts" was also part of Louie XIV's purchase. The woman who rejected it on board survived. Perhaps by way of breaking her engagement to be married she eluded the evil omen. Who knows if there truly is a curse on the Indian goddess's eye in its entirety? Certainly people and kingdoms who owned portions of Sita's eye have come to naught. Maybe Heart of Hearts had an effect on some aboard the ship; but it seems that the Hope is another matter. It belongs to the people of the United States of America now and God knows that we are a nation being submerged in violence even amongst our children!'

That had been a month ago at her dad's sudden need of a funeral. Now, Mr. Glamour Mogul (as she fondly called the family friend) had gone back to Carmel, California and she back to the little town where fate had decided to hang her hat. She had chosen her little town in order to be near water; to be away from having to lock one's door all day and night, and to be away from the reminder of that which had wrenched her beloved from their son and herself. She had wanted to live where wedding vows meant exactly what they said, where men and women didn't follow soap opera values regarding marriage. She wanted to be around people who had remained as strong as the soil that they tended on their family ranches and farms. Realizing that almost fifteen years of living in urbana was enough until the wounds to her psyche healed, she admitted being a bit of a dichotomy inasmuch as following rural examples where certain modes of behavior such as going to church every Sunday morning were concerned. Basically, her admiration of everyone else who did was boundless.

What they thought of her, she didn't know, and didn't ask. Her life consisted of working practically seven days a week as a nurse, accepting Sunday shifts in order to earn more money with which to keep her child's days secure with the hope of a college education in the future. To that end she had endeavored. He was in the final years of high school, and the advanced halls of learning were already a part of every night's selective process as they filled out forms for the desired institutions. As to church, her son attended. He missed her presence, but he also knew that without the extra dollars she was earning that day there'd be no future for him in an ever-changing society. So they comforted themselves by dwelling on the goodness of the life they shared even minus a husband and father.

Now, with her son out and about with school activities for a few days, Christiana sadly reflected on a princess she had loved from afar, and how much her heart ached for the three princes who had been the focus of the young life which had been suddenly cut off.

Christiana felt like falling face down on the floor, giving vent to great sobs, kicking and beating the carpet with her feet and fists. But of course that would be out of the question for she had never done such a thing in her life and wasn't about to start now.

Besides that, if she *did* indulge in that behavior she had no doubt that the neighbors would call a paddy wagon and have her sent to an institution in a straightjacket. Opting for the peace of home, she wiped tears.

A knock came at the door. Christiana got up, dabbing her moist cheeks with a tissue as her face broke into a relieved smile. Into her gloomy thoughts of death regarding the father she adored and now the Princess, came her older sister's beautiful face smiling at her through the leaded glass panes of the door. In the moonlight, Christiana could see the trees on the lake shore behind her sibling's red head, branches flailing, ripples on the lake full blown into whitecaps from the stiff wind, which was also tousling Angela's short, curly bob. As usual, the serenity and love emanating from her sister's amber eyes brought instant comfort to the younger who was opening the door.

They threw themselves into an embrace. In spite of herself, Christiana sobbed upon her sister's shoulder. Angela's arms firmly holding felt good, secure, stable, as if they would never be taken away by even more death or desertion of any kind. Angela gently put Chrissy from her, the heavenly night light playing upon them through the open door. With this human being, Christiana could let her hair down in the privacy of home. Same with her middle sister, Pamela Jarvis. They felt comfortable together, as if they were part of each other's very bosom. Soulmates, all; very different in modes and tenants of belief, but soulmates who understood one another's reasoning. In public they did not weep in order to strengthen the weaker amongst them, such as children; or their elderly who had suffered strokes and other mishaps peculiar to old age.

It was heart-wrenching for the older to witness the devastation of the 'baby' sister. 'I thought you might need a friend tonight,' Angela smilingly wiped tears off Chris's cheeks.

'You thought right.' Christiana, suddenly ashamed of herself, choked back the urge to continue weeping. 'It reminds me of losing Daddy so suddenly. I don't like it, and what's more I wish I could act like a complete baby, which I am doing with you admittedly.' She blew her nose into the tissue pulled from a green silk sweater thrown around her shoulders.

Her sister laughed. 'We all need to have someone with whom

we can act infantile at times.' Clad in black, she was gorgeous.

'Thank God!' Christiana closed the door. 'Quite a wind out there. Do you think a storm is blowing in?'

'Possibly. But the forecast didn't call for anything but tranquil weather the next few days.'

'Why are you up and roaming around the countryside at this ungodly hour, Angela?'

'Because I couldn't sleep for worrying over you, so my darling husband Jack told me to get dressed and come see if you were alright,' she smiled. 'Where's the teapot? Would you like a cup?'

'It's on the third shelf in the right-hand cupboard, and yes, I'd love a spot of tea.' She looked forlornly at the television screen. 'Look at all those people. The streets of London, and parks are jammed with tear-stained men, women and children. Look at all the flowers! All have their arms full of bouquets.'

'What kind of tea should I make? The water is almost boiling, sweetie,' Angela answered.

'You choose, unless you're in the mood for mint, which I deplore. How about...'

'How about a little "Grandma" tea?' Angela enticed.

'Green? Oh, I'd love it. And I have a few shortbread biscuits in the cookie tin. There are a few molasses crinkles in the cookie jar too if you'd prefer those over the other.' Suddenly her train of thought changed.

'Come look at that man! He's tossing his cigar stub into a cameraman's empty video case!' She stared at her sister. 'Awful. Just awful! And right in front of the Queen Victoria Memorial, too!'

'He must be an American!' Angela laughed from the kitchen.

'Why do you say that?' Christiana indignantly queried.

'Because only an American would be so bold and brash in such a tidy, structured country, let alone in front of a palace of all places.' She poured boiling water into a warmed teapot, put the lid in place, covered it with a pink cozy and carried it into the living room on a silver tray set with china cups and saucers.

Placing it on the tea table, Angela looked up to see the incorrigible herself. 'Do you mean the fellow with the Harris tweed, and gray slacks?'

'Yes.' Christiana helped herself to a midnight cup of tea.

'Mmmm. He's a handsome devil in an ugly sort of way, isn't he,' Angela decided. She went back for the cookies. 'How many do you want?'

'How about the whole jar? I forgot to eat today.'

'In that case I'll make you a sandwich. Where's the canned tuna?'

'Do I really have to eat a tuna sandwich at nearly one in the morning? That sounds about as attractive as Cowboy up there throwing his old stogie into an unsuspecting person's carry case!' Christiana looked as if the world were about to come to an end.

Laughing, Angela reached into the refrigerator, pulled out an apple and brought it to her 'baby' instead. For a baby Chrissy had always seemed to the delicate elder who practically raised her since birth due to a seriously ill and incapacitated mother.

Handing the apple to a disinterested sister, Angela set a plate of cookies on the tray beside the teapot. Pouring a cup of steaming brew, the pretty lady, amber earrings flashing, settled on the cream-colored couch beside Christiana. Sheer draperies of soft pink lined with white batiste embraced the room.

'There goes your cowboy,' Angela remarked as they watched the impeccably dressed man wearing what they, neighbors of the North and South Dakota prairie, recognized as pointed, highly polished cowboy boots. Being that the tops, stretching to mid-calf, were under his pant legs, no one else noticed.

'He forgot his Stetson,' Christiana dryly remarked.

'Don't be funny,' Angela said. 'He looks so cosmopolitan I dare say that he would not have taken it with him to London.'

'What do you think he is doing, up and about at such an ungodly hour? He really is quite handsome, isn't he!' Christiana watched the man as his back receded up the Mall.

'It is seven thirty in the morning there, not so early.'

'Well, for a tourist it is early, isn't it?'

Christiana selected a shortbread, and took a nibble.

'I suppose it would all depend upon what one was going to do on a particular day, as to whether or not this is an early hour for an American to be up and about.' Angela yawned in spite of herself.

'Do you want to spend the night? The guest room is ready, as usual. You know that I like overnight company.'

'Actually I would like to, but can't. I need to get home.'

'But, you really shouldn't be popping about the countryside alone in the middle of the night. What difference does it make whether you sleep in your bed or this one? Your hubby is fast asleep and won't even miss you until morning,' Christiana persuaded.

'Well, you're right. If I wake up early and go home in time to have breakfast with him, he'll be just as happy.' With that the little woman hugged her sister goodnight and retired to the spare room. Calling back to Christiana, 'Now that you're feeling better, why not turn off the television and go to bed, dear?' she smiled and shut the door. The visit had worked – her sister's tears had ceased. Oh, the power of love's presence, she thought.

Out in the other room, the telephone rang. 'Only one person would call so late at night,' Christiana murmured to herself. 'It must be Pamela.'

And it was.

'Are you coming home tomorrow? I'll pick you up at the airport if you are,' Christiana offered. The airport was one hundred and thirty odd miles distant in Minneapolis, one of Minnesota's large twin cities which were divided by the famous Mississippi River that flowed due south into the Gulf of Mexico at New Orleans.

'I've a mind to come because Rick suddenly had to leave at noon or so,' the middle Deerfield sister replied from Phoenix, one thousand eight hundred miles away in the south-western United States.

'Where did you say he had to go?'

'He didn't say, but I suppose to London. Must have been on a job.'

'Well then, why don't you come up here? The three of us can sorrow together watching the tragic event. I would certainly love having you around. In fact, so would Angela... she's asleep here right now.'

'Really? Where's her husband?'

'Home in bed. He urged her to come to town to see how I was

taking things. She arrived at midnight...' Christiana's voice broke.

'I bet you were happy to see her at your door and quite surprised, too.' Pamela sneezed.

'Do you have a cold?'

'No, I just took a sip of water and swallowed wrong.' She sneezed again.

Christiana laughed, then added, 'Well, I think that you should pack your duds and get your little self on the next plane to Minneapolis, or for that matter Fargo. I'll get up early and fetch you.'

'Don't worry sis, I'll rent a car. You've convinced me, I'll be right up. Tell Angela to wait before she goes home in the morning. There's a flight out of Sky Harbor in an hour. If I hurry, I can make it. You're two hours ahead of us with your daylight "slaving" time, you know.' She laughed.

Christiana was overjoyed and said so before she hung up the receiver.

Bringing the tea tray and cups back into the kitchen, she snapped off the light and went to her own bedroom. 'Oh botheration, I forgot to turn off the television!' she exclaimed aloud. Walking back to the living room, she reached for the controls. Glancing at the screen she couldn't believe her eyes.

A disgruntled camera man was disgustedly extracting an old cigar butt out of his open case. Holding it up to a buddy, he scowlingly mouthed words. They looked around, obviously trying to spot a trash can.

'Dream on!' Christiana giggled. 'You're in front of Buckingham Palace. Do you really think you'll find a garbage can in front of those splendid gates?'

Thinking that 'Cowboy's' mom must have had a tough time teaching him manners, she went to bed. Snuggling between percale sheets trimmed with eyelet, Christiana was unaware of her true heritage. The only one in the family beside her parents who knew, was Angela. Often, Christiana had wondered why she was so enamored of England and the Royal houses, which she studied insatiably. The hunger had been fed by her grandmother before she could even remember clearly, and by her grandmother's aunt who had lived to the age of ninety-eight. Her mother also had taught Chris to love the Crown of England, having set her upon one knee to listen to the wedding and later the coronation of the present Queen Elizabeth II. To listen to the festivities was to be awakened, by her own request, at two in the morning, carried downstairs in her adored father's arms, and warmly tucked into an eiderdown on her mother's lap. Now as Christiana fell asleep she could still remember the radio description of Princess Elizabeth's wedding gown, which had been encrusted with gems. She remembered the apparent handsomeness of the groom, for the radio on the desk from which these glories spilled was a magic box of fairytales come true those two separate occasions. Christiana wouldn't have wanted to trade those memories for anything in the world as into her heart stole the joy of having been born of English descent.

Chapter Five

The truth of Christiana's heritage was that she had a Royal father and mother. They were Stuarts, descendants of King Charles Stuart I and his Queen, Henrietta Maria. Historians and some biographers disagreed as to how many children were born of the King and Queen's union which took place on May 11, 1625, by proxy in France.

Although the marriage started badly, it became extremely happy. After four children, the Queen was soon to be delivered again. It was 1639 and their trusted friend Lord Strafford asked whether or not the fragile personal rule of the House of Stuart could survive not only the malcontents in the English House of Commons, but also the wrath of the Scottish religious communities who were violently opposed to the new Prayer Book which King Charles I had forced upon them in 1638 when endeavoring to bring the Scots into line with the Church of England's religious observances. Because of it, the first one third of the English Civil War broke out when the furious Scots rebelled. Subsequently, there were two wars, the First and Second Bishops' Wars, won by the dissenters. By 1641 a new Parliament had to be called in London. Indignant Parliamentarians who were angry over what they called King Charles' illegal taxation methods, were insisting upon the privileges of Parliament which they felt were being ignored. Red-hot rebellion had been seething beneath the surface, building pressure within the kingdom like lava within a volcano. As a visionary precaution from the King's friend, it was suggested that an attempt be made to save at least one Stuart from possible annihilation if all hell broke loose over their Royal heads. The heartbroken expectant Queen and husband, who unlike most Royal parents truly doted upon and spent time with their children, agreed to a conspiracy. For no guarantees existed regarding their nine-year-old Crown Prince Charles and his younger brother and sisters.

Into this uncertainty, the Queen brought forth a girl, Katherine, who was smuggled by a lady-in-waiting to a sister whose baby had just been stillborn. The living was exchanged in the grieving mother's arms for the dead whom she had been loath to relinquish. To comfort the mother, her own little one was bathed on a bedside table, anointed with rose oil over every inch of soft skin and swaddled in the finest of linen, gift from the Queen. Fragrant herbs were laid carefully around the little dead cherub as she was sewn tenderly into a length of canvas, then concealed in a wicker trunk midst dried lavender. Had the child lived, twins would have been presented to the world. As it was, the Royalist family made for Corfe where, carrying the little cooing Stuart in their arms and their own dead child in the locked trunk, they sailed for the New World. After land was not seen for a fortnight, the King's captain buried the little one at sea. In London, a private funeral was held and to anyone who asked, the Queen's pregnancy had ended in 'disappointment', as indeed it had.

Weeks later, disembarking at what later became Charles Towne, Carolina, the guardians of the Royal baby were settled into an area eventually named The Battery where their surname was recorded as 'Deerfield'. Hence the little Stuart was protected by her new daddy's name in the Lord Captain's opulent home. The Queen secretly bought the mansion from the naval officer who immediately purchased the house next door which had a tunnel extending not only to the nursery at Deerfield's, but to the wharf where he docked his ships. In truth, he was Lord of the Admiralty, a man hard put to pass his time on land in his own castle by the sea in England.

Growing up ignorant of her true identity, Katherine now Christiana, had heard of their faraway King being executed. She was only ten years old at the time, but it made a profound impression upon her. She had heard of his beautiful Queen, Henrietta Maria, after whom Maryland had been named which the King through Calvert had set aside for English Catholics to have as a safe home without the current religious persecution suffered on the Scept'rd Isle. Being in love with his doting wife, he found her repressed attempts to worship in good conscience as a devout Catholic in an Anglican world hard to bear.

Within a year, Christiana heard of the sweet Princess Elizabeth's death of a fever brought on by a broken heart as she grieved her father King Charles I. For some reason Christiana could not explain, her heart stirred almost to the breaking point within her eleven-year-old breast. It was as if her own father and sister had died. She wept and wept and could not be consoled.

Ten years later, as a bride freshly wed to a Royal son of Europe in Le Chapel within her parents' walls, the nuptial couple were taken into the confessional where the truth of her birth and Royal blood were presented. Oaths of secrecy were sworn along with promises to preserve the Royal House of Stuart in like manner when they too would become parents.

Monsignor Roy had said, 'Only one couple in every generation must be given the knowledge of their heritage. The children of such couples must be schooled and granted social access with other Royal progeny who have settled in this hemisphere such as the Caribbean, Canada and Mexico unbeknown to most. Only in this way can Royal marriages take place under the guise of New World names and status.'

'But, honorable sir, how can you guarantee that our children will make the right choice in a marital partner?' Christiana's new husband, Prince Jon, now Deerfield, asked.

'We can't. However, arranged marriages are not new to Royals, and possibly this will never be a matter of choice by the children for some time to come. The concern is that there is already a trend to allow freedom of choice here in the English colonies. Your countrymen stick to the Royal rules more faithfully, Prince Jon; for France has not secured holdings on this continent as of yet although they thrive in the West Indies, namely Guadeloupe and Martinique.' Monsignor smiled.

'Thank God father gave me property in Martinique, or I'd have not met ma cherie.' He looked tenderly at his beautiful bride who was dressed in rich white satins and brocades, a veil of the finest French lace frostily covering the exquisite coronet of diamonds and pearls which his mother, the Queen of France, had sent for the occasion.

The ecclesiastical father continued, 'To be certain, some heirs will marry the young man or girl next door. Royal blood will mingle with common. It cannot be helped and we are prepared for that. Hopefully, one of each family in every generation will be smitten by the proper person at a soirée, cathedral function or university. Once the Royal match is made, you must divulge to them and them alone after the wedding, their true names and ancestry. This you must promise by signing here.'

He indicated the proper place on cloth paper printed in very black ink, handing them quill and inkpot. After the couple had signed the oath, the holy father continued, 'These are perilous times not only in England; but continuing jealousies and unrest between kingdoms does not assure any Royal of safety even on this continent. The anointed of God to rule have the kiss of death regarding jealous siblings, cousins, noblemen and neighboring greedy thrones.' He paused for breath as suddenly, looking pale, he broke into delicate beads of moisture on his forehead and upper lip. An attack of malaria, the disease which raged throughout the lowlands of the South, was resurging through his bloodstream, bursting into tiny malarial parasites which had lain dormant in his liver for a few merciful weeks when salubriousness seemed to have returned. The southern colonies' curse was making a bid for his life. Mopping his sallow skin with a white linen handkerchief, his hand started to tremble. 'Ah, excuse me, my children,' he whispered, his fever suddenly increasing in great intensity. 'God be with you both. Teach your children "noblesse oblige", to serve in humility, integrity, compassion and with grace and style even as you have been taught. Above all, keep your identity hidden. It suffices that your parents and step-parents know who you are, and where you are. In case of need, you will be recalled to sit on either the French or English thrones...'

He gasped as an abdominal pain streaked through and excruciating pain slammed into every bone and muscle in his entire body. The larvae in his blood were making a bid to ruin the young couple's wedding day. The monsignor felt his consciousness seeking an out as his strength deteriorated in the attack.

'Monsignor, let me be of assistance,' the groom helped the ailing man out of the confessional. 'Lie on this chaise. Darling petite,' he said all in one breath, 'please be so kind as to bring a glass of water for His Excellency.'

The bride ran to the altar where she knew there was always a fresh pitcher of liquid placed out of view for the clergy's use. Carefully carrying the pitcher and a silver chalice back to her husband, she poured the water. Offering it to the stricken man she held it to his lips, forgetting that she was in her wedding gown, remembering only that a man could be dying, a man she dearly loved for he had taught her French, Spanish and Latin, besides all the English letters and everything she knew. From him had come the faith instilled into her heart. He had comforted her in the very confessional where she and Jon had signed the oath; where, as a ten-year-old child, she had wept inconsolably over the deaths of whom she now knew were her father and sister.

'Father, *mon dieu*, don't leave us now. We love you. We need you,' she whispered serenely.

Monsignor's eyes opened to take in the vision of virginal exquisiteness kneeling beside him. Like her mother, this child was, except for the hair which was fawn. Her mother's was a delightful brown of mixed golds with deep strands of red here and there midst the brunette, noticeable only in sunshine. He replied, 'The royalists who brought you here kept you in safety at great risk, and guard you still.'

Christiana, who had the creamy skin and beauty of her mother's sloe eyes and oval face, looked earnestly at her friend.

'I thank you Monsignor for the part which you've had in keeping me safe and out of harm's way. My only prayer is that some day I shall be able to hold my real mother in my arms before she too dies... as did Father.'

Tears glistened on her lashes. Her handsome French Prince put his arm lovingly about her tiny waist as he knelt beside her before the failing man.

'Ma petite, I shall take you to her. We will go to Colombes to her palace there. As soon as it is safe, we shall make the journey.' He held his motionless wife in his arms as a Franciscan monk rushed in to administer herbal medications. With him was the parish priest who gave the last rites.

★

It was April 1659, and Christiana had been sampling spousal delights for a month. Carolina in all its natural beauty was aflower. Hot pink azaleas carpeted the forest floors, which were blushing up at the sun. Violet blossoms trailed the boughs of the towering redbud trees while creamy magnolia blooms the size of a silver tray glowed with paraffin sheen in the moonlight of spring. Soft sea breezes had not yet become sticky, for the heat was not murderous and the earth was blessed with the promise of new life. Sitting on the piazza in the cool breeze off the beach, which glistened white before her eyes as it marched into azure waters, the new bride despaired of ever seeing her real mother. She held a little miniature of Queen Henrietta Maria, which was encrusted in diamonds and pearls – a wedding gift from her mother via the aging Lord Captain. As much as she loved the new bliss of marriage, a deep sadness beckoned.

'Almost, I wish that I had not been told,' she passionately whispered to the beautiful visage held within her hand. 'But I now know what it was that tugged at my heart when I heard of Papá's and Elizabeth's deaths. They must have come to kiss me goodbye from beyond the pale.' Suddenly she clasped the painting to her lovely bosom, which was held in a basque of mint green, watered silk. Emeralds glowed upon her skin, the largest settling comfortably in the hollow of her ivory throat.

'Mamá! Mamá!' She felt tears splashing onto her décolleté. Looking to the heavens, which stretched above turquoise Charles Towne harbor and its street of crushed mother-of-pearl shells, a little bird soared in from the sea and perched on the marble balustrade beside a Corinthian pillar. Snow-white, Christiana could not name it. They looked at each other.

A whisper came to Christiana's ears. 'I love you, my sacrificial lamb.'

Christiana turned around to look at the door to her left, which led into the drawing room expecting to see Jon standing there. No one and nothing greeted her questioning gaze, except the Easter lilies stirring demurely in the moving air.

'Come home,' as if softly borne upon the damp sea breeze her senses picked up a broken-hearted mother's deepest desire, 'Oh, to look upon your sweet face, even once.'

The wind sighed in the sycamore and acacia trees.

Christiana turned to look at the albino bird once more. Even though her movements should have frightened it away the bird stayed, unafraid.

And then Christiana heard a cry as of a soul being torn from the intimacy of its mother's innermost body never to be rewarded with the mother's breast, the mother's arms.

She looked at the snowy bird, which calmly surveyed her.

'Mother? Mother?' she whispered.

The bird started to pick at greenery, which hung over the white marble enclosure where red bougainvillea grew, delicately spilling onto the balcony rail. As if by design, a bud was grasped in the little fowl's beak. Breaking it off, the dove took flight over the garden. Circling back, it dived under the roof straight to Christiana in a path that would have made an archer proud. Without slowing, the crimson bud was dropped onto the folds of pale silk, which covered the twenty-year-old's lap. In surprise at being brushed by the rush of air and musty nest smell of the bird's flapping wings, Christiana turned her head away and jerked back so as not to be cut by its sharp feathers. A curl of blondish hair mussed out of place over her forehead. Tucking it out of her eyes, she turned to see what had fallen into her lap. There, glowing like a ruby shot through with sunlight, lay the bud. Picking it up carefully between the manicured nails of index finger and thumb, she looked into the sky to find her celestial friend. All she could see were gathering cumulus clouds, white and puffy on the horizon above the Atlantic where row after row of white froth rolled upon shimmering blue, hissing into nothingness upon the buff-colored sands. Shaken to her very soul, she whispered, 'Mother, I will come!'

In spite of the mysterious little bird's visit, Christiana was terrified of going back to England. In her dreams many a night she would cry out as she saw a splash of red around her father's face tearfully staring at her from inside a basket of straw. She had grown to know that face from a painting by Van Dyck, which her mother had sent along with her own miniature.

'Darling, darling, don't weep,' Christiana's husband would console. 'Don't tremble; it will not happen to you, I promise.'

'But how can you promise? My father was a king, and even he was not safe.' She would shake until the candles were lighted, and a cup of warm milk laced with sweet herbs and sugar was placed into her cold hands.

'My precious wife. We will not go to see your mamá until it can be done in safety. Please do not worry so. We are safe here in Carolina.'

She protested, 'But Jon, sometimes when you've gone to your plantation in Dominique, I fear so. How do we know that we are not hunted like mice by the Cromwellian Cat even as my brothers Charles and James? The full power of the throne has irrevocably changed. Henceforth only Parliament can set laws of taxation, and determine the position of religious dissenters within or without the Anglican Church of England. My mother and Catholic siblings will never be safe... nor I. And, sweetheart, you too are a Catholic. You are not safe because of having married me!'

The cup of milk shook in her hand as she lifted it to her lips. Suddenly she laughed softly, musing into the cup, 'Can't you just see thirteen-year-old Elizabeth, that spirited but gentle sister of mine, surprising James out of captivity by exclaiming, "If I were a boy, they'd not hold me!"'

Her husband chuckled. 'Yes, I can see her saying that. I used to play with her when we were children. Your mamá would let her climb trees with me, fence, and ride the ponies like the wind. Was it long after that, James *did* escape?'

'Not long. And then the Lord Captain said that it was a miracle he was not caught. He was just a fuzzy cheeked boy trying to find his way to his big brother.'

'Ah, mon amie, that fuzzy cheeked boy knew how to thrust home with his sword. He was trying to find Charles to join in the resistance.'

'And proud of him for it I am, too!' his new wife declared, taking another draught of milk. 'Jon, why did they kill my father? Why was it necessary to kill so fine a man? Why could they not have merely exiled him?' She turned somber green eyes toward her remarkable groom of one year. Candlelight played over his noble features. She dearly loved his dark eyes and warm face.

'My precious, that is something I think you must ask your mamá. The Lord Captain said that it had to do with the surrender of his loyal friend and servant, Lord Strafford, whom your father turned over to Cromwell to save the Queen from impeachment. Even though the action went against his promise of safety if Strafford would but come to London, I cannot but believe in my heart that once they met, your mamá's position was explained and Lord Strafford then helped devise the plan; they both believed her life to be endangered.'

'I can't believe that my father would surrender his best friend after promising no harm would come to his person, purse or fortune.'

'Darling, a man will do most anything to save the woman who is the light of his innermost self. Do you remember Antony and Cleopatra? Your own fourteenth-century John of Gaunt and Katherine Swynford – she who suffered terrors untold when his great Savoy Palace burned to the ground after being torched by the mob? Do not underestimate the power of love.'

'Yes, even mamá valiantly raised money and men to help not only Father before he died, but now Charles. She takes terrible risks, the Lord Captain says.'

She placed the teacup and saucer on the nightstand as Jon asked, 'You know what your father told Charles before he died on the scaffold outside the second-story window of Whitehall don't you?'

'What did he say?'

'Regarding Strafford, he admonished the Prince of Wales: "Never to give way to the punishment of any for their faithful service to the crown". It was regarded by your father as the cause of his own subsequent misfortunes. The King's bishop said that on the scaffold, the remembrance of it plagued his last moments.' Jon sighed.

'Did he say anything else to Charles?' Christiana wanted to know.

'Yes, and herein lies the basic flaw which took the life of a fine man whose character will some day be regarded as above reproach when it came to family matters. He said to his son directly, whether by letter or word of mouth when the Crown Prince boldly marched in to see his captive father: "Avoid the duplicity for which I am to pay with my life."'

'Oh,' Christiana bowed her head and crossed herself. 'Mon dieu, Jesu, have mercy,' she whispered, 'on my father's poor soul.' She then slowly pushed her blankets back, slipped out of bed and ran across the floor in bare feet to the pardieu where the Blessed Virgin stood in a white marble shrine overlaid with fourteen carat gold on scalloped edges. Falling on her knees before the Holy Mother, she wept as if her heart would never be healed. She prayed that her father would not have to wander through purgatory for had he not lived in hell on earth because of his dichotomies?

Jon knelt silently beside her and took her tear-splashed hands in his. Gradually, her sobs ceased. He picked her up in his arms and gently carried her to bed.

April 1660, and again the south of Carolina was spreading its fan of springtime as a peacock chanticleer dancing before its lifelong mate.

One day, a servant dressed in turquoise livery presented a folded parchment to the young 'Mr. Deerfield' at the dining table which was glistening with prismoid goblets, silver flatware and plates beneath a massive chandelier of cut crystal which held one hundred white tapers all aglow.

Opening the seal, he noticed the imprint of the Prince of Wales' crown adorned with three feathers imbedded in the wax. Carefully flattening the parchment enough to be able to read, a smile came to his princely face.

'My darling,' he softly intoned without raising his head, 'in my hands I have what we have been waiting for. You will be overjoyed.' Looking up, he raised the information in his right hand, lace cuffs falling onto the lower half of the paper.

'Yes, dearest?' Christiana had gone pale for she, too, had recognized the great seal on the wax and was waiting to hear that another member of her unfortunate family had met death by way of the dreaded Cromwellian Parliament.

'No need to fear this time, my love,' he tenderly said before continuing in order to bring color back into her beautiful face. 'It is from your brother, Prince Charles. He is inviting us to come to London to witness his accession to your father's throne.'

His wife gasped, 'But what has become of Oliver's son, the Lord Protector, Richard Cromwell? How can this be?' She brought a silver fork from halfway to her mouth, resting it on her dessert plate.

'The Lord Protector has stepped down complaining that the Parliament and House of Lords are too unruly. Here, let me read: "He has not the strength of character, as did his father, of handling such a politically boisterous House of free thinkers. You know that Oliver has been dead these eight months."' Young 'Deerfield' looked up wiping his delicate mustache with a fine linen napkin before taking a sip of cream sherry from etched stemware.

'Does that mean... does that mean? No, it cannot mean. Darling, my lord, can it be possible that I may finally pay court to my honorable mother, Queen Henrietta Maria?' Briskly fanning her face with an ivory and lace fan, her stays felt altogether inadequate for allowance to draw breath. The thought of at last feeling the motherly embrace for which she had longed ever since her wedding day almost overwhelmed her. She wanted to laugh, to cry, to faint, to run, skip, and hop like a child all at the same time. But being a twenty-one-year-old princess, she could not.

Her husband rose from the silk and mahogany chair at the other end of the long, damask-covered table. Strolling toward its foot where sat his devastatingly attractive wife, who was the exact image of her mother, he laid the letter before her. Extending both hands to his lovely princess, she placed her small hands in his and rose into his arms. 'Do you wish to go to the coronation?' he whispered into her lovely honey-colored hair.

'No,' she shuddered.

'Cherie!' He put her from him and searched her green eyes. 'What is this?'

'No. I shall *never* wish to set foot upon the soil where my gentle father's blood was spilled; and my sister was held prisoner until she died of fever at so tender an age...' she quietly bristled, 'and from which my mother had to flee for her life;' she shook with wrath, 'and where Charles and James were chased like vermin to the very death had they been caught!' Her breath failed as tears welled into the emerald eyes her husband loved so well. 'And where it was necessary for a newborn babe to be torn from her mother's arms for fear the whole family be annihilated. No. I *despise* those who did that to us. I cannot be sweet about it like Elizabeth, my thirteen-year-old sister who lies moldering in her grave these many years. Furthermore,' she turned her eyes away, 'for what reason have the wretches invited my brother back to London? To behead him as well?' Turning back to search her husband's brown eyes, excitement caused a lack of oxygen to her head and she half fell against his shoulder.

'Mon amie. Shh shh,' he patted her little shoulders holding her firmly. 'No, darling, no. Not that at all. Come, sit down and I will explain.' He gently eased her into the chair she had previously occupied and pulling another close, sat down. Fanning her with the lace, which she had dropped, he waited for Christiana to recover. 'Here sweet one, drink a little cognac. It will bring a bit of refreshment to your mind.' He held an aperitif glass to her lips. The aromatic strength of the liquid helped clear her head and she was able to take a sip. Choking, she rapidly waved one little hand back and forth in front of her open mouth as tears popped into her startled eyes.

Jon could not help but laugh. Patting her on the back until the coughing stopped, he continued, 'Dodging death and capture while defending the Crown has taught the Prince of Wales how to compromise and rule within the limits of the Parliament.'

Christiana looked at him doubtfully.

'Your brother has offered a manifesto, which is very moderate regarding religious and political matters. That has sealed a certain group's determination to engineer a Restoration. You see, if Charles is willing to rule minus the absolute power of kings...' Jon laughed deliciously. 'Clever man your brother. The powers that be cannot deny that he is a brilliant soldier as well as politician. Of course, with Richard gone from the office of Lord Protector, and no one qualified to fill that throne-like position, what better person to lead your country than the Prince of Wales?'

He smiled as if enjoying a manifestly wonderful joke.

'But, I still don't believe the Parliament is sincere! I am afraid for him. I won't go. If it is a trap, we need to be elsewhere where we can help James mount another resistance... or at least send money to aid in securing his heritage.'

'What do you propose to do, darling?'

Christiana dejectedly said, 'I so wanted to see Mother, and Mary, Henrietta, Henry and James – my siblings from whom I was spirited at Corfe.'

'And so you shall!' Her husband jumped up, pulling her into his arms, twirling them about the room. He stopped suddenly and kissed her. 'I shall order my ship to prepare for our first trip to France. We shall set sail two days hence – that is, if you agree?'

With trepidation mingled in a cauldron of sheer joy at the thought of actually beholding her birth mother's living body; of being seen by her mother's exquisite eyes; of knowing that warmth the Queen showered upon her children which was legendary even as she lived... Yes, she would most certainly go to France! Hopefully, the lull in hostilities would last long enough to safely usher the longings of this far-flung daughter into peace.

Christiana 'Deerfield' Stuart, Princess of England, entered an immensely vaulted room of white marble. The nave ceiling was frescoed with golden panels from which cherubims and lovers were caught in God the Father's eternally benevolent eye. Rich baroque colors dominated every inch of the ceiling, which was otherwise given to ethereal blues and whites of the artist's dream heaven.

Across the splendid room, a golden throne held her mother. Over the middle-aged beauty was a canopy of gold holding crimson velvet draperies edged in sparkling fringe, which framed the shimmering, red-cushioned chair upon which sat the exiled Queen of England. The Queen's tiny feet, barely peeping from the hem of her opulent skirts, were dressed in white embroidered silk stockings and pointed slippers with ornate French heels, which rested upon a tasseled pillow of crimson velvet. Over a gown of heavy white satin, ornately embroidered organdy of the same color billowed on each side of the flat panel, which extended from the center of her tiny waist to the floor. A train of sky-blue velvet, lined with cloth of silver, subtly cast a glow from the precious gems caught in its fabric by threads of silver metal embroidered into intricate designs. The heavy wrap was attached to the square-necked gown at the shoulders with blue diamonds, pinkish amethysts, and yellow canary diamonds fashioned into flowers of May entwined by emerald leaves of various sizes, all of which trellised around the shoulder clasps, and décolleté of the heavy white satin dress. Her matching necklace glowed, dipping into the hollow of her throat where was displayed that creamy skin for which she was famed throughout the known world. On her head was the golden Stuart coronet.

The scent of gardenias perfumed the air as the daughter approached her mother. Christiana's head bowed low as she sank deeply into a curtsy where she remained motionless; her pale green silks trimmed in flesh pink velvet graced the twenty-one-year-old replica of the still beautiful, mature flower of womanhood who sat upon the throne tearfully beholding the grown babe who had been taken from her by impending doom.

'My child,' Christiana heard the soft, full voice of her mother for the very first time, its warmth enveloping her like an infant's receiving blanket. 'My darling Katherine, come to me.'

Her heart bursting with longing for the touch of her mother's hand, her face, her bosom, Christiana raised green eyes to the windows of her mother's soul.

'I love you, my sacrificial lamb,' her mother whispered in broken majesty.

Christiana's mind flew to the bird on the balcony in Carolina. Her head felt awash... Those words! That whisper! Exactly the same, she had heard them before. Overwhelmed, Christiana could not move, and dropped her head, fawn hair shining in a ray of sunlight streaming through the French windows of leaded glass. She felt tears welling behind her closed lids.

'I have never heard your voice,' the Queen's murmur was choking with emotion, sweet and low.

'Mon dieu! How I have prayed to the Blessed Virgin and her Son for this day! Always, El Capitain would bring me something from my tender babe whom I had cast into the sea of life for fear we would all be killed... a lock of hair, a baby tooth, a swaddling cloth from your crib which had the sweetness of my baby in its folds. I padded my bosom with it for then your lingering scent was with me all day, and far into the lonely nights.'

Dignity complemented the Queen's rush of words. Still, Christiana could not move. She had not the strength. The Queen saw dark spots developing on the swirls of silk beneath her daughter's bowed head as she remained in the attitude of obeisance.

'Ah, my darling babe, come to your mother?'

Christiana would have if she could have. Her breath was cut off by tight stays, her legs trembled, and she felt she would faint if she tried to rise. That voice. How she loved her mother's voice! She could not stop the silent tears although she did not want her mother to see her cry; she kept her face down. The pearls in her tiara glowed up to her mother as if with secrets from the deep sea out of which they had come.

The Queen wished to sob from her daughter's hesitance, but controlled herself from years of practiced dignity. Drawing a lace-edged linen square from under one edge of her skirt, she put it to her upper lip and the corner of one eye briefly before tucking it away under the red cushion discreetly.

All was silent in the great room. Jon stood a solitary figure against the far wall; for it had been deemed unwise to inform anyone of their coming, save the Queen. He was worried lest his wife faint. Now he saw her stir in response to that which made the princess believe in God for the rest of her days as the Queen started to speak once more.

'It was April a year ago, my lamb. My heart was breaking for want of you; for what we had done to you thinking all the while that we were doing the right thing.' The mother's voice was soft, tragic. 'It was Evensong. With a heavy heart, I knelt on the pardieu in my sleeping chamber before the Blessed Mother. "Mother of God," I prayed, "once more the sun has risen upon my lost child in Carolina. She is now a married woman, and still, I have not heard her voice, I have not felt the warmth of her hand in mine, I have not looked into the emerald eyes I see in my dreams."'

The Queen's voice choked. '"Forgive me for not being content never to see her although she is out of danger," I beseeched the Virgin. "Sweet Mother, thou who lost thine own child, surely thou canst see my torn soul."'

The sovereign sighed and continued, '"Mother of God and Jesu, God's son, I am asking that you take my words upon the wind to my fair-haired daughter across the sea."'

A pregnant silence ensued. The lady on the throne continued: 'Into the breeze which passed from the eastern window through the room to escape out the opposite casement, I whispered: "Come home. Oh! To look upon your sweet face, even once!"'

'Suddenly, something brushed against my bowed head and fell into my lap. I opened my eyes to follow the whirring movement of what sounded like a bird's wings, which had come and gone from the western window. There on the marble casement sat a tiny, white bird looking at me. He stayed until I remembered to look at my lap. Caught upon my skirt in the setting sun's rays was a red blossom, glowing translucently like a ruby. It was a flower called "bougainvillea"; Lord Capitain once brought me one from your garden to plant in mine for he said that you sat amongst them on your verandah to feel the cool sea breezes. I planted the bush, but it died many years ago – on the day your father was executed.'

The Queen could not continue. She could not see her daughter for the tears, which were blinding her own eyes.

With tremendous effort, self-control from a lifetime of regal behavior during adversity took over, and reaching toward the submissive girl on the floor before her, said, 'I picked up the tiny blossom and looked at the sill to see if the feathered messenger was still there. Gone, he was. Then I heard the cry as of a babe for its mother! I know not whence it came. I remember no more, for when I awakened I was in my bed. My lady had found me fainted away.'

Christiana could not stop the silently falling tears as her heart thrilled to the bird's message of love yet again, this time coming from a voice which seemed so familiar, for she had heard that voice while still in the womb.

Jon, her husband, stood by the massive fireplace along the wall. Protocol held him in its iron grip even though he wanted to rush to his wife for he feared that she would faint.

Until the Queen moved? No one moved... not even God Himself.

'That's why you're stuck on the ceiling, mon dieu,' he murmured, casting a quick glance overhead. Suddenly, he crossed himself. He didn't want to incur the wrath of the Almighty, especially not now when they were so close to England's shores; and his own jealous cousin, Philippe le Duc d'Orleans, in the very country where Jon now stood!

'Pardón.' He quickly looked up over his head, hope and fear becoming inseparable.

Again, he became entranced by what was happening. The drama before him had not lost its focus. To the mother and daughter, no one else existed. Christiana was still overcome and bowing low before Queen Henrietta Maria. The Queen, tears upon her alabaster cheeks, rose, and with hands outstretched to her daughter, stepped regally off the dais, her skirts rustling like the wings of an angel.

'My darling, I am your mother; can you not forgive me? Oh, my precious lamb, what was I to do?' Placing her hand gently beneath Katherine's chin, she raised the sad face. The Queen gazed into the green eyes, which she had heard likened unto emeralds from Lord Capitain. For that very reason, she had chosen jewelry abundant in the green leaves and floral decoration of her person. They were to be recognized by Christiana as a token of her mother's lack of neglect the past twenty-one years; of her mother's ever-present thoughts and prayers regarding the child who had been taken from her.

Gently taking her daughter's face between both hands, she bent to kiss her forehead. The Queen's tears dropped upon the upturned face, mingling with those already there. Slowly, the young woman rose into her mother's arms. For the first time, Henrietta Maria heard her fifth child's voice.

'I love you Mamá, there is nothing to forgive.' Sweetly and sincerely it came; and to the Queen, it was as if her soul was condemned no more for having given away her darling babe twenty-one years earlier in order to save a dynasty. In each other's arms they wept themselves into joy.

During the years to come, neither mother nor daughter could ever remember just how they embraced, all they could remember was the scent of 'her'... the feel of 'her'... the aura of 'her'... the exclusive world only a mother and the child who was wrenched from deep within the womb to breathe the air of life, can know.

Returning to the colonies with Jon, Christiana always felt that God had rewarded her mother for being a supportive, loving wife to her husband as well as for being so devoted to her children. The sacrificial lamb living in what later became part of the United States of America, rejoiced that her matriarch lived to see the eldest son placed upon the throne after the death of her slain husband's Achilles heel. The short 'reign' of the office of Lord Protector brought no tears to Christiana's eyes nor to the eyes of her exquisite but strong mother. For as far as they were concerned, the rightful heir was now where he belonged, where he had been anointed of God in heaven to be – upon the English throne[1].

Henrietta Maria Stuart, Queen of England, Princess of France as daughter of French King Henry IV (Henry the Great) died August 31, 1669 in Colombes, near Paris, France. Centuries later would follow another ravishingly beautiful mother of a future English king: Diana, Princess of Wales, who died August 31, 1997 in Queen Henrietta's country of birth in Paris, France.

Acclaimed as Royal beauties of their day, both women were exceptionally warm, devoted mothers of British Crown princes and their siblings.

---

[1] From 1660 through 1669, the Queen divided her time between Somerset, England and Colombes, France. She received from Parliament a grant of thirty thousand pounds a year in compensation for the loss of her dower lands. Her son, King Charles II, added a similar sum. Finding she had no place in the Restoration, the Queen Mother returned to live at Colombes, France.

Chapter Six

Alexandria, Minnesota.

It was August 31, 1997, and twentieth-century Christiana
Deerfield lay fast asleep in her Minnesota home. She knew
nothing of her history, yet her father Mr. Deerfield who was
actually a Stuart had often spoken of Cromwell and King
Charles I. It seemed that her dad was fascinated by history,
especially English history. Of course, she had eaten it up. Telling
her anything about England was like feeding candy to a baby.

In her sleep, she was dreaming that her father was wondering
if Queen Henrietta Maria had thought, upon her deathbed in
Colombes, France, that the chief murderer of her husband had
since met his Royal victim in heaven where understanding
between them finally had an opportunity to flower.

'I certainly hope so,' Mr. Deerfield was telling his daughter in
her dream state. 'After all, they were both fighting for the right to
worship according to their conscience; as well as for that which
divided them most. One believed in the Rights of Kings as being
anointed of God to rule absolutely, and the other did not.'

Christiana asked her father, 'What did the Civil War in
England accomplish?'

'Division of power from purse; and the freedom to worship
according to conscience.'

Christiana awakened. She got out of bed and went to Angela's
room, tapping on the door.

'Come in.' Angela sat bolt upright in bed, turning on the
bedside lamp. 'What is it? Are you well, Chrissy?' she asked
sympathetically.

'Yes, quite well, but I had the strangest dream.'

'What was it?' Angela motioned for her sister to sit down on
the edge of the bed.

'It didn't make any sense. It was Daddy. He wondered if
Queen Henrietta Maria Stuart mused on her husband and Oliver

Cromwell settling their differences amicably in heaven.'

Angela laughed. 'Well,' she said, 'I wouldn't be surprised if they have.'

'Meaning?'

'Both men did ask forgiveness of their Creator as they bowed to the death angel,' Angela replied.

'How do you know that?' Christiana wanted to know.

'History, darling. It's all there. I believe that they were two good men fighting for the same thing in one instance, but quite divided when it came to the Rights of Kings.'

'That's what Dad said in the dream.'

Angela asked, 'Did you know that Queen Henrietta and Diana shared many things in common?'

'Such as?'

Christiana smoothed her black hair.

'Well, both were unusually beautiful to look upon; both were unusually exceptional mothers who doted upon their children; both became members of English Royalty by way of marriage; both died in the same country of France; and both entered heaven's gates on the same day, only centuries apart.'

'When did Henrietta die?'

'The 31st of August, 1669,' Angela replied. Looking at Christiana who knew nothing of her own heritage, the older sister remembered their father and mother baring the truth two days before his demise. At that time they had presented a tiny miniature of a beautiful Queen for safekeeping. The parents had decided to tell Angela because Mr. Deerfield had not been able to rid his body of pain. He felt that his time was drawing nigh. Someone had to know, because so far, in the younger generation none of the girls had married royalty as befitted their blood. They had been thrown together with others whose ancestors had come to New Orleans, Canada, Mexico and various places hundreds of years ago, as had the Deerfield/Stuarts. However, neither Pamela, Angela nor Christiana had fallen in love with any of the eligible fellows, hence Mr. and Mrs. Deerfield had to honor the code of silence. Only upon a marriage with the right beau could that silence be broken by the priest through whom the wedding would be solemnized.

'Help guide Christiana into a second marriage, which will protect the purity of our line,' their father had instructed Angela. 'I don't think that it is by chance that she was left by her first husband, nor Pamela. Pamela found what she was looking for in Rick. That was fine. We've never forced anyone, nor have we ourselves been forced to select beyond love for no one knew until the vows were actually sealed with the proper person that there even was a plan.' He had smiled. 'I certainly fell in love with the right lady, and I love her still. I would have been perfectly content to love her as we were, just Mr. and Mrs. Deerfield.' His eyes had twinkled, 'Do you know what, daughter? I take pride in being a Stuart! It's a real kicker for the self-esteem and the noblesse oblige I've always felt within my heart all my life. Until I married, I never knew why I wanted to help others. After Father Roy informed us, great peace flooded my heart for I then knew why I liked to help mankind in my humble way as conservator of the soil for chemically free crops and naturally raised beef for human consumption. To develop methods of farming minus insecticides, and to raise animals minus steroids that chemically produced maturity was my contribution to that great pledge to serve.'

That conversation had been five weeks ago. Watching Christiana who sat on the bed beside her, she said, 'Well, are you ready to go back to bed?'

'Yes. All except for one thing. Did you know that the present Prince Charles loves natural methods of farming, and is as keen on preserving ecology as Dad was?'

'Yes, I do know. I believe that those endeavors are his first love.'

Christiana smiled, got up and went out, shutting the door behind her.

The next morning the sisters received a call from Pamela saying that she would be half a day late. A shopping spree at the Mall of America had suddenly appealed to her as she skirted Minneapolis on Highway 494.

The other two siblings spent an hour together having breakfast. Of course, the television had been turned on immediately so they could catch up on the night's news in London and see things as they happened during the new day.

'Do you want tea or coffee, Christiana?' Angela asked.

'This morning I prefer a stiff cup of coffee. I think I need it,' she smiled as place settings were laid on the pink tablecloth, which covered the round table in the dining area. Going to the counter and fishing out two slices of bread, she popped them into the toaster, ladled jam from the jar into a condiment dish, pulled out the drawer to get a little preserve spoon, set both on a proper small plate, and came back to the table to join her sister.

'Please pass the jam,' Christiana asked as she stirred the boiling hot brew her sister had poured into salmon-colored china cups.

Angela handed it to her. Christiana took a sip of coffee, and set the cup down onto its saucer, the sound of fine china slightly stirring the quietness with the magical music of dining.

The woeful but beautiful strains of Bach were heard quietly coming from the television in the other room along with, 'It seems the whole world loved her'.

Not feeling very hungry, they made an attempt to eat without telling the other how unhappy grief made them.

The white cathedral ceiling over the sisters' heads made the tiny apartment, Christiana's home, appear brightly spacious. All the walls except one were of glass, bringing nature inside as it were. Sliding glass patio doors to the north-east, through which one could see a deck outlined by pine trees of balsam and blue spruce plus the profuse green umbrellas created by cottonwood and oak trees sporting handles made of huge, taupe trunks which thirstily drank of surrounding bodies of fresh water, made the optical banquet of nature complete. A lake to the south-east connected with a pond to the west. Cumulus clouds, mirrored in the rippling waters below, formed individual cotton-ball proportions in blue skies. The sun seemed to dab its eyes every now and then with one of the clouds as it hid briefly, only to blaze white glory over the earth when the puffs of condensation sailed away, one by one, in the wind. Shade and sunshine played cat and mouse over the green corn fields and adjacent, honey-colored plots of wheat, which rose beyond the lake shore. Shimmering and shaking in the breeze like a woman's lush head of long, taffy-brown hair, the tall shafts of grain promised to fill America's bread baskets. Minnesota was full of life while human hearts everywhere were full of death.

The two lakes were connected to yet another larger fresh body of water curving in natural depressions below the fields situated on the hillsides rising all around. Streams flowing in and out two sides of the crescent-shaped lakes wound through the thickly wooded neighborhood. Brown cattails, slender, cigar-like, suede blooms of nature, grew thickly at the tops of tall, green reeds midst the bulrushes at the edge of what the sorrowing, youngest sister called her own Thoreau's Pond behind the apartment.

'Listen to the mud ducks, Angela,' Christiana said as the nesting sounds came through the open window beside the table.

Indeed they could hear the small, blackish-brown birds, still hatching young in nests concealed beneath the waving blades of wild marsh grass as they chortled in their sleep, heads under their wings. Bits of fluff, which had already thrust off incubators of shell, wriggled beneath the warm breasts of their mothers.

'I wonder what it is like to be embraced by eggs on each side as those newly hatched ducklings are,' Christiana sighed. 'It must be a hard experience.'

'Not so hard,' Angela quietly suggested, 'for they are softly surrounded by duck down and soft grasses over and under... just like the little princes. This family of fowl is a typology, don't you think?'

Her sister smiled. 'Yes, it is. What appears to be hard and unyielding to the world in general, that being the Royal household, is not necessarily so in the minds of the Royal children for they are still surrounded by the private, emotional softness of their paternal matriarchy, and a very tender father. No mother, commoner or queen, who has felt the quickening of desired life beneath her heart during the sixteenth to eighteenth week of pregnancy, could ever truly forget the tenderness, wonder and joy one feels at that semblance of butterfly wings fluttering in so intimate a first bid for life... at least I've not been able,' Christiana smiled wistfully.

'Nor a father,' Angela continued the thought, 'forget the pride of intimate manhood when his bride shyly takes his hand and places it on her expanding tummy in order to share the first, delicate movements within.' Angela's amber eyes filled with the wonder a woman feels when remembering the moment of conception between herself and the choice of her passionate heart, the young, handsome bridegroom of twenty-five years earlier.

'Why, you're blushing, Angela!' Christiana said in amazement. 'After all these years, you are blushing over the sweet memories!'

'Ah, yes. I can't help it. How I loved him, my dashing Royal Air Force captain from England! How I love him still. When I felt our first baby quicken in my very depths, how breathless and excited I became.' Her eyes became a deeper color. 'It was a deeply private feeling, one I had never felt before... almost holy in its innocence. Known only to me in total exclusion of the rest of my surroundings, was that little call to life. I had to share it with my better half after excitement set in, the sooner the better.' Angela laughed lightly – a sound as unto tiny bells pleased the ear. 'I sure can become angry with him sometimes but for the most part he is still the man I love.'

'You are lucky to have him yet,' Christiana observed with a sad little smile. 'Fifty per cent of American marriages end in divorce now, as mine did. If a rocky marriage lasts, it is fashionable to agree with psychological findings that it lasts only because each of the spouses has a codependency problem. Well, I guess I am impolitic and incorrect because I don't always agree with that reasoning. I think it depends upon the two persons involved. I don't know what other religions teach, but Judaism and Christianity teach from Genesis that God saw man's loneliness and created a female to make things jolly. What's so wrong with that idea? I can't think of anything more fun than to have a man I truly love around. It's great!'

Christiana was silent for a minute, munching toast. 'I've often wondered why fate suffered my man to go quote, unquote "find himself" without his son and me.' Her dry wit took over, 'He was so big and tall, how could he have *lost* himself?' Her eyes flipped toward heaven and mouth took a dive toward Texas.

They laughed.

'How about a little more orange juice?' Christiana offered.

'No thank you, I've quite enough.' Angela stirred a little cream into her coffee. 'Have you been single eight years already?' she asked her sister.

'Mmm,' Christiana nodded assent, her mouth full of succulent South Dakota muskmelon, the sweetest cantaloupe this side of heaven.

The TV mourned on in the background.

'The television reminds me of losing Dad... He and Prince Charles had similar interests which they doggedly pursued for the common good in spite of a great deal of criticism.' Christiana had swallowed the coral sweetness to express her thoughts.

'Yes they did, didn't they?' Angela agreed. She accepted a crystal fruit compote from Christiana's hand. Helping herself to a dish of mixed fruit, and setting it back onto the table, she continued, 'Prince Charles chose ecology and preservation of the earth as his forte... organic farming as well. Everyone poked fun at him in ignorance twenty years ago; even as our poor papa in the fifties when he rejected using chemical fertilizers and sprays and steroids in feed in order to mature his registered Angus.'

'Yes. Didn't Dad say that by using steroids in feed the new calves could be matured and ready for market within six months time?' Christiana wiped her mouth with a pink napkin.

'You're right, he did say that. He rejected such methods because not enough time had elapsed from the start of such fast food production and they were still in the experimental stage. Dad said that such things, if used, would be passed on to humans when they consumed the meat; let alone insecticides from the grains, which were ground into flour.'

'Not enough time had elapsed for science to truly determine the full impact on the human body from those synthetic methods before the market was flooded with such foodstuffs. He always felt that was one reason cancer was on the rise in our country. "We are what we eat," he'd always say while cramming bone meal disguised in honey down our throats in his ever so gentle, persuasive way.'

Both girls laughed, remembering the chalky sweetness, which used to ruin Christiana's idea of a good meal.

'I didn't mind it,' Angela said, laughing at the memories of her little sister gagging the stuff down.

'Well, I did,' choked Christiana. 'It came from dead cow bones, after all.'

'But the bones had been sterilized before being ground into bone meal, Chrissy!' her sister cajoled.

'Well. All I could think of was the smell of the rendering truck which used to come pick up the carcasses from the pasture after a cow or steer was struck by lightning!' Her face turned red.

At that, Angela really laughed in her quiet dignified manner. 'Oh, Chris... is that where you thought bone meal animals came from? No wonder you couldn't stand to eat your daily dose!'

'Yes, and for a kid who hated milk that was a serious offense in our family of organic nutritionists. Poor Daddy, what a time he had with me. I must have caused him a great deal of frustration although he never showed it. After all, he had to foot all the dental bills for my soft teeth... which, by the way, bone meal or no, I still have in my little head,' and she showed her pearly whites which were exceptionally even and pretty.

'I suppose now you will conclude by feeling superior!' Angela dryly surmised as she took a bit of apple from her fruit dish. Smiling up at her kid sister, she winked. 'Well, go ahead. I took the bone meal, drank milk and already have a bridge in my mouth.'

'Of course, that's because you belong to the older generation!' Christiana teased.

'Okay, spring chicken, I'm not that much older than the rest of you. You have to look up to me as an elder if I'm over the hill already.'

Laughingly rising from their chairs, each cleared her place from the table, and then strolled arm in arm to the living room.

'Dad, Charles and the Duke of Edinburgh were all ahead of their time, weren't they?' Christiana observed quietly.

'Yes, they were... and I've always admired Prince Charles for sticking to his guns in spite of ridicule years ago. It's not easy to have an unpopular cause when one is young and wishing to impress people.'

Angela looked at the television to see an even larger ocean of flowers developing before Kensington Palace. Everyone gathered in weeping silence before its pretty gates and park, looking as if nothing else mattered... and it didn't.

The women in the Minnesota living room sat down to watch

and finish their conversation.

'People always ridicule, and joke about the things which they don't understand, don't you agree Angela?' Christiana continued. 'For instance, some say there shouldn't be a monarchy any more because they don't pay taxes, amongst other laments, but Prince Charles has always paid them voluntarily. He seems so reasonable and fair-minded; as was Father.'

'You're correct,' Angela said. 'In spite of it all, both Dad and the Prince seemed to feel compassion toward their detractors, rather than antagonism. When one is right about something, it really doesn't matter what others say even if one's opinion and knowledge isn't the popular consensus at the time.' Angela touched her sister's arm, 'Look at that man by the gate, Chris... the one smoking. Isn't that Pamela's husband standing beside him?'

Christiana looked. 'You're right, Angela! That *has* to be Rick – golden head of hair, cowboy boots and all! Wait until we tell Pamela!'

'Well, he sure looks smart in his business suit. No one would ever guess that he has boots halfway up to his knees under his slacks, would they!'

'You're right. I wouldn't know the difference if I hadn't been around cowboys most of my life.'

'There they go, walking through the gardens. Whatever do you think Rick is doing with Peck's Bad Boy who threw his stogie into someone's empty case right in front of God and everyone yesterday?' She looked incredibly at Angela. 'Do you know what else? Before I went to bed last night, I took one last peek at the London scene. There was that loathsome fellow's cigar in the hand of the unlucky chap who wanted to put his filled videos away. He looked quite disgusted.'

They looked at one another not knowing whether to laugh, cry or make a face.

'How'd you like to be married to *him*?' Angela asked.

'Who? The walking smoke stack? No thanks!' Their attention became riveted on the television again. Suddenly Christiana said softly, 'We had a fine and unusual father, none better, didn't we?' Her voice broke. 'Now his stewarding of the little corner of earth

God gave him is over.' A tear trickled down the side of her fine nose.

'Darling,' Angela comforted, 'when the elderly die, the young such as Prince Charles seem to have already grasped the torch of good causes, holding it high to light the way for the rest of the world,' she stood up and crossed the room, 'fulfilling the legacy of the soul.'

Chapter Seven

August 31, 1997, The Adriatic Sea, 0145 hours, 1:45 A.M.

On a British ship in the Adriatic Sea, scarred hands and wrists sporting lines of discreet proud flesh where a scalpel had restored a certain man's usefulness, packed Navy skivvies and a little ancient miniature into a duffel bag.

Her Majesty's government had called Scar-P home, effective immediately.

'Report at St. James Palace at 1800 hours,' his commanding officer told him. 'The tornado is waiting on deck.' They saluted. Scar-P bent under the whirling blades of the helicopter jet fighter and climbed in.

The tall, gaunt man with blond hair and gray eyes with a grim face to match, was not surprised for he had just arrived from the Mediterranean after a week at Langley, Virginia. He'd been on duty aboard a private yacht as a 'sailor'. Now two beloved friends were gone.

London, Piccadilly Circus, August 31, 1997, 1515 hours, 3:15 P.M.

Old Blue's occasional sweetie, Orange, stepped through her store-front apartment door, decked out in her usual black leather and shades, hoop earrings and golden bangle bracelets which jangled as she locked the front door. Cramming the keys into her large black patent purse, which matched her boots, she walked to a Mercedes Benz pulled alongside the curb directly in front of her abode. Climbing in, she patted the sinewy hands of the driver.

'Ready?' he breathed dispassionately.

'Ready,' she responded, pulling a cigarette from its half-empty pack as the car moved right along.

'Have a light,' her partner said as he held a Bic lighter toward her. Flicking the corrugated wheel with his thumb to ignite the wick, the tongue of flame caught the orange-lipsticked mouth, aquiline nose and glasses in its glow.

'Thank you,' she said, inhaled and resumed sitting back against the passenger seat.

The car turned onto the Strand. 'Let's go past St. Paul's this time,' the lady said. 'Makes me wish that the Duke's effigy was still inside. One of these days I want to go into the basement to see if we can find at least a few pieces of it.'

'As you wish,' her gaunt, blond-headed friend said as scarred wrists became slightly exposed while turning the wheel.

He pulled his shirtsleeves down.

The Middle East, August 31, 1997, 0900 hours, 9 A.M.

The President asked his diplomat to the United Nations, 'So. What have you told the Americans? What have you done about it! They must not come to the palace!'

'Yes, yes… I agree and have told them that very thing,' the emissary coolly rubbed behind one ear, displaying a scarred wrist where discreet white lines belied skin grafts covering burns acquired during the *coup d'etat* in the sixties. 'The United Nations Council is adamant regarding the inspection of all our buildings since we moved the operation from the textile plant.' He drummed manicured fingernails on the armrest of the green upholstered chair in which he was comfortably held. His Mediterranean blue suit iridescently whispered shades of peacock blue; a Lorengini silk shirt languidly reached perfection in the exquisite ensemble by framing a paisley tie of rainbow colors, which graced the elegant, olive-skinned man. Soft ostrich leather shoes completed the exotic look. He uncrossed his legs sitting forward to leaf through papers that were spread before him on a silver table inlaid with Mexican turquoise. Picking up a crystal tea glass by its silver and gold base the hot liquid was relished minus the sting of burning fingertips.

'Geez Louise, this tastes good!' he suddenly smiled after taking a sip.

The men looked at each other, and laughed. They had been in

New York as inhabitants many times over the last decade and a half, and the phrase from the Italian quarter was a nice, cozy bit of togetherness in an otherwise nerve-wracking, isolationist type of debriefing day.

Finding the pictures he was looking for, the visitor from New York handed them to his interrogator.

'As you can see, they had reason to be upset. I am sure that Your Excellency realizes that a factory sporting telltale signs of hurriedly spilled powders and other residue mingled into scrapes on floors is not the best way to convince NATO inspectors that we are complying.'

'Yes! Yes! The fools! Can't they ever do anything correctly?' his white-hot anger was quietly expressed. Scowling and pulling at his tie, which irritated him even more, he ordered, 'Have them arrested!'

'Who, sir?' his compatriot nervously asked.

'The men who emptied our cache and hid the evidence in different places, of course!'

'Sir?' Raised eyebrows, stunned silence.

'Yes! They and I are the only people who know the new location... or if indeed there even is one... or if there was even anything to hide! We must make certain that only I know where the factories and arsenal are. In spite of our international agreements, we must secure our defenses.'

'Cannot the armed forces handle the matter, sir? May I not call the General?'

'No. He will not approve of needless waste of some of his best troops – needless to him that is. Furthermore, I do not care to explain my reasons at this point. You shall do it!'

'Sir, that may be well and good, and I see your logic. Precautionary measures are indeed required. But I am merely a Chief of Staff's assistant and the country's ambassador in certain instances and ways. I do not have authority to enforce the law – as you yourself have often most graciously pointed out.'

His superior rose pushing back the yellow leather chair in which he had been reclining, pulled a drawer open from the desk beside him, and withdrew an insignia of valor. Walking over to his friend, who had stood simultaneously, he said, 'Now you are commissioned as a general!' Fastening the pin onto his friend's lapel, he saluted. 'Go to it.'

The sometimes ambassador, sometimes governor, sometimes deputy, sometimes man about town in New York, felt his heart trembling clear into his expensive soft shoes, happy that a pistol hadn't been pulled from the hidden compartment instead. Not that it would have been used on him, but even seeing one was enough to make his knees turn to water, hence his diplomatic assignment. He was an excellent statesman, not a murderer.

'Consider it done, sir!' He saluted back, his heart sinking within him.

'Allah, send a reprieve before I must do this ignoble deed...' he prayed silently then steadied his eyes and courageously controlled his face, showing no signs of temerity.

Halfway across the palatial room of pink marble, gold etched pillars of alabaster with turquoise tiles underfoot, the commander turned about, searched the other's visage and asked, 'What about the United Kingdom? Are they still aligned with the U.S.?'

Without waiting for an answer, he resumed his exit toward the massive doors of inlaid precious metals, gems and wood which created stunning peacocks with tails fanned into radiant glory. As the door opened for him, he spoke over his shoulder, 'After you finish this little matter, leave immediately for London. They are in mourning. Your job should be easily dispatched, as everyone is distracted.' Glancing back he added, 'We need the money desperately now that our exports are largely halted.'

The middle-aged man who was left standing in the cold imposing silence of the regal room felt a sudden urge to mop the perspiration which had unceremoniously popped onto his brow and neck. Wary of hidden eyes, he chose to let the overhead fan do it instead, selecting safety at all costs... it would never do to allow those eyes to see his nervous reaction regarding an order of execution. Picking up his briefcase, the man left the room, wondering why his nation had to be the pernicious teaser of the world regarding illegal biological and chemical weaponry.

Thinking insubordinately, he noticed the beautiful golden crescent at the end of the spacious hall, which lay before him as the doormen started to open the grand portals.

Mohammed, Buddha, the Dalai Lama, Christ, on and on – all taught peace and, initially, doing unto others as one would have them do unto one's self, the uncomfortable man thought. Walking briskly toward the outer doors, he asked himself, 'Why can't the world live and let live without exploiting one another in order to live well... to have power? If West, East, North and South must meet, why cannot it be in peace?' He smoothed his hair. 'Furthermore, why do Harvard and Oxford graduates or any graduates of higher learning, who were buddies while pursuing doctorates, have to kill one another once they come home to their respective countries to serve humanity? What is the point? Will man never become civilized? Will he never cherish the gift of life? Will greed rule the world forever? Will intolerance of other faiths forever create holy wars?' The ever tender-hearted diplomat shook his head.

Walking behind the disappearing back of his friend who preceded him down a red carpeted hall, he remembered that since childhood, they had been closer than brothers. He wondered, Are we still? An Oxford man himself, he suddenly thought of someone else who had been. 'I wonder whatever has become of Old Blue that crazy American cowboy!'

Mumbling aloud over OB made him chuckle in spite of himself. The laughter did him some good. Instantly he believed that the indiscreet workers who had bungled hiding the secret operation would not have to perish. He himself would talk the commander out of it or die trying... and he felt that he could appeal to their childhood in common which had seen them raised by the same woman's hands as she ground, mixed, and fried the victuals which had kept them from starving so very long ago.

'Not only Old Blue has a soft spot. So does another good friend. They are alike in so many ways, Old Blue and my childhood companion,' the harried man concluded.

Relieved, the ambassador-turned-general was waved into a black limousine and whisked to the airport where his bags were already waiting for the flight to London. He picked up the telephone and called his chief for the stay of execution, which he knew, would be given.

London, the Mansion House, August 31, 1997, 1500 hours, 3 P.M. The Ambassador

A well-dressed man with naturally tanned skin and jet black, wavy hair, exited the front door carrying an oblong case which matched his outfit of expensive mohair. The ambassador had made good time. His toes wiggled against the soft ostrich leather of his expensive shoes in satisfaction after he climbed into the chauffeur-driven limousine. The car's paint glinted in the sunshine, bouncing corresponding color into the man's brown eyes.

'To the Tower please, Raffael,' he said as he took his seat.

'Of course, sir.' The chauffeur shut the glass window between them as he pulled carefully into the line of traffic.

The passenger in the back seat pressed a button on his cell phone, and started speaking. 'Yes, all is going as anticipated.' He smiled.

London, England, August 31, 1997, 1500 hours, 3 P.M. Raoul Juan Pedro DeSilva

Raoul DeSilva walked briskly through a tunnel eight thousand miles distant from the Deerfield girls as they strolled the lake shore in Minnesota, U.S.A.

Under the streets of the city, which had virtually come to a grieving standstill except for the silent mourners who thronged towards the palaces, the tunnel led to the Tower of London.

Raoul was hoping not to be late. He slithered along on the slippery legs of his mind. No one noticed the black-headed man whose straight, thick locks were neatly trimmed and shining from ointments. His black eyes, under a glowering forehead sporting fine brows of the same color, furtively encompassed peripheral scenes to the height of his naturally tanned self-awareness. For being such a little fellow, his five foot, eight inch frame fairly flew along on Armani-clothed legs. Trim waist, slender hips and shoulders were revealed when his open coat caught the wind blowing in from the River Thames.

He shivered under his white Brioni shirt, thankful for the solemn gray cashmere muffler around his elegant neck. Being macho, he didn't button his black wool coat.

Across town Rick and his captain, Old Blue, were just emerging from the Orangery on Kensington Palace grounds where they had gone for a look-see to make sure all was secure. Not realizing that Rick's sisters-in-law had spotted him on television a bit earlier halfway around the world, it was in his mind that soon he must call his wife Pamela to tell her that he was in fine feather, and not to worry. She, in turn, already knew his whereabouts having not only guessed as much, but having seen the same picture on television as her sisters. At the mall while having a cup of coffee and pancakes, she almost choked in surprise when there before her eyes, stood her gorgeous husband, on worldwide live television.

'I wonder where Sam is,' she mused softly to herself.

The fellow in the neighboring booth of the coffee shop looked at her and asked, 'What say?' hoping to strike up a conversation with the pretty, auburn-haired lady who was obviously alone.

'Nothing,' she smiled, looking down at her plate, avoiding eye contact to get him off her back.

Chapter Eight

Ned DeSilva, London, August 31, 1997, 0900 to 1600
hours, 9 A.M. to 4 P.M.

The River Restaurant was quiet this particular morning, everyone
hushed over the sadness which gripped all of the world regarding
the Royal family. Even Ned felt devastated.

Ned wiped his meticulously shaped black mustache with a
napkin, which matched the table linen. His brown eyes
sometimes seemed black, complimenting wavy hair of the same
color, a strong Roman nose, thunderous black brows and
muscular cheeks set admirably into handsomeness by aristocratic
features and a charming smile of even white teeth which made
him quite irresistible, even at the age of fifty-six. His hair had not
lost its color; workouts at the gym on a daily basis insured the
strapping legs and body of an athlete who loved boxing. As a
matter of fact, he had won the gold in his class at the Olympics
years earlier.

Looking at him when he smiled, one could understand how
he had won his fair-haired wife Jill, née Farthing. Although
twenty years had passed since their wedding day in Phoenix, they
were still madly in love. True, he had started to wander once
upon a time, but when the lady under siege by his attentions
learned he was married, her hot Spanish temper matched his with
a resounding slap; and he decided on the spot that it was not
dignified to be slapped in public. (If he could have choked her on
the spot, he would have, but since murder at Mimi's wasn't
acceptable in Scottsdale, Arizona, nor anywhere else for that
matter, he simply glowered and watched her flounce out of the
crowded restaurant.)

After that, he decided that Jill was worth ten of anyone else
and dived into his marriage with new fervor. Like any old horse,
he now looked but didn't get excited for his wife kept his ardor

well satiated, and his mind constantly piqued with all the interests he could handle.

He truly adored Jill, thus the annual trips to their favorite spot on earth – London. Sadly, this week's trip had been shattered by the untimely death of their favorite public figure, the Princess of Wales. Yet, they were grateful that they could be with the island people to mourn her as befitted such a lovely, transcendentally compassionate woman.

Now Ned waited once more for his younger brother who was to meet him for a substantial late breakfast although they both had met for coffee earlier. Jill had wanted to sleep until noon, so Ned felt no pressure as he luxuriated at his usual table. Actually, he came to London alone frequently, so the particular dining room in which he was sitting was his favorite, barring none.

The Savoy Hotel, that opulent establishment built upon the foundations and grounds in London of what had once been the most splendid palace ever built in all of England and Europe, suited his ego and sense of history as none other. This place stirred his inner self as royally as did cathedrals such as Westminster Abbey begun by Edward the Confessor before the Norman conquest, not to mention the Great Hall started by William Rufus in 1097.

Beautiful as a snow-white dove, The Savoy Palace had been built by Henry, the first Duke of Lancaster in the dawn of the fourteenth century. It had graced the banks of London's great flowing Highway of the Kings, the River Thames. Behind it stood Westminster Abbey and its grounds. The two properties were separated by the Strand, a medieval road. A little brook had run through the Abbey's pasture lands there, where contented cows grazed in their efforts to produce milk, butter and cheese for the holy fathers of then, Catholic England.

The street outside the present day Savoy Hotel was still called the Strand after its medieval past, only now one couldn't see the river for the tall buildings and crowded conditions of this prosperous business section in London. Even so, it was an exciting place to go when one wished to enjoy entertainment at the famous Savoy Theatre, the home of the Gilbert and Sullivan operettas years ago. Ned liked joining the elite in that rebuilt deco classic. He always wished that the fire of 1990 had not razed the original theatre, but no matter, it was great to be able to attend functions there now.

Ned nodded pleasantly at an acquaintance whose ruddy cheeks suggested that he had just arrived from out of doors. Ned's thoughts were gripped by history unfolding quietly in his fermenting mind as the man was seated behind him.

He could almost see his golden-haired great ancestor as he slept, ate, lived upon the very ground where Ned now sat. Wishing for a blueprint of that which used to be, he watched the River Thames grayly passing by, still as glass upon the surface.

As Ned DeSilva reflected over history, the optical banquet of The Savoy River Restaurant thrilled him. Lofty ceilings made him feel grand. Regal, deep salmon-colored draperies gracing huge glass windows afforded views of the River Thames directly beyond his table. In fact, with a little stretch of the imagination, he sometimes felt as if he were sitting midst the greenery on its banks. Looking straight ahead and opposite the windows, were massive pink marble pillars, or at least to Ned they were marble. To an architect they may have been a perfect simulation. Whatever the case, Ned was satisfied totally to sit in chairs, which were dressed in matching colors at a table sporting the softer shades of barely pink. Toying with the handle of a white china cup rimmed in four lines of pink around the circumference, he wondered who had designed the avant-garde 'S' where his lips met the steaming black coffee. Taking a sip of the richly flavored brew, he set the cup back into its matching saucer. Yes, Ned was one American who thought nothing equaled the elegance of Auguste Escollier's haute cuisine, The River Restaurant's distinct culinary heritage.

Ned's mind didn't dwell long on the comfort of his surroundings. His mind went through an entire litany that early morning of August 31, 1997. He wished that Raoul, his little brother, would hurry and come back – they both were from Phoenix and not used to waiting. Hotter than a pepper was that desert city and the inhabitants seemed to walk on red-hot coals, they moved so fast.

This particular morning, history was needling Ned's impatient soul with little pinpricks of ancient animosities harbored within the DeSilva generations. He wanted to vent on someone who would not cajole him out of his hatred, as did his wife Jill every time he started to lament angrily over his heritage and having not received an inheritance nor the recognition he felt was his due.

His surly thoughts dwelt on The Savoy Palace and its inhabitants in medieval times for the great second Duke of Lancaster and his second wife had been Ned's direct ancestors.

The Savoy Palace had been utterly beautiful in 1355, as were Henry, First Duke of Lancaster's two children, both female. One girl died which left Blanche as sole heiress. Her blonde exquisiteness, ethereal frame of mind and promised wealth caught the eye of the King, Edward III. For equally gorgeous blond John of Gaunt, King Edward III's fourth son, needed a wife, titles and lands worthy of his chivalrous character and valor. The King arranged the betrothal with Blanche's father. John and Blanche were married in 1359.

After her father Henry died, lovely Blanche, Duchess of Lancaster, endowed her husband to become Second Duke of Lancaster in 1362. Love in a Royal arranged marriage was unusual, and this marriage was just that, for they loved truly and had eyes only for each other. The wealthiest duchy in all of England and Europe could not have belonged to anyone more angelic nor chivalrous, both being kind and good and physically beautiful. They as a couple were very popular with the people.

The Duke married three times. Early deaths snatched the first two wives away. After Lady Blanche's sudden demise from the Black Plague in 1369, he fell totally, blindly in love with her younger friend, Lady Katherine de Roet Swynford, the woman who was to become his third wife many years later. But now a previously unknown, unfathomable love was awakened in the Duke merely by observing Katherine; and after he took her for his own, he was never to shake the oneness which they found together. The highest tribute he was ever to give anyone was etched onto his stately sarcophagus. It was a touching expression of a man's undying love for the woman who understood all of his body, mind and soul, words of praise for her unsurpassed spiritual understanding and physical beauty. For even though tragedy had repeatedly befallen Katherine, her spirit of softness, compassion and quiet strength did not lessen privately nor in public; nor did her devotion to God. Not born of high station, she was persuaded that to be the Duke's Lady of The Savoy was fine in God's eyes. Many heartbreaking years later after the terror of being burned out of The Savoy Palace when the Duke was away on campaign in Scotland, she and their four children were raised to legitimacy by young King Richard II upon her marriage to the Duke in their twilight years.

However, great suffering and chastening of the spirit had been endured by these, the Duke's adored, previously illegitimate family.

Wife number two?

Ned's attention was caught by his younger brother Raoul entering the eatery where he paused to shed his coat, check it and enter into a little banter with the clerk. Ned's mind reverted to spitting out history that was locked away in every cell of his brain.

Costanza, the deposed Queen of Castile, had been John of Gaunt the Second Duke of Lancaster's second wife. Her father, King Pedro the Cruel (another DeSilva patriarch), had been killed by his bastard half-brother, Trastamara, in the latter's successful bid for the Castilian throne. Trastamara cared for his nieces kindly enough, but of course took Costanza's rightful place as ruler of Castile.

Costanza lived with bitter and deeply religious feelings stemming from the death of her beloved father coupled with losing the throne to his illegitimate, eventual murderer. She hated her exile in England, but loved her glorious husband who was the toast of England until after he married her. Although granted all the regal honors of a reigning queen's court in life with John, her bitterness of soul and self-flagellation which included not washing in certain areas, drove away the Duke's feelings of amour like a nail into a coffin.

Ned tapped his bejeweled pinkie on the pale mauve tablecloth wishing that Raoul would get himself over to the table. Ned was ravenous and wanted to eat. Besides, he had to get upstairs to suite 713 for Jill was expecting him shortly. They had plans to execute on this sad day and he had no doubt that his tender wife would want to pay her respects to the fallen Princess in some way, shape or form. Jill had been crying over the telephone with her friend in Arizona, Pamela Jarvis, and hadn't accompanied him to breakfast. She was too grief-stricken to eat.

Watching Raoul poking along, Ned's mind did summersaults from fact to fact regarding the history he was spitefully savoring... he loved to hate when the mood possessed him. Feeding his hatred of the Duke and Katherine, Ned continued down the path of his own legacy from them.

In 1371, Ned's great, great, et cetera grandfather, the blond Plantagenet, John of Gaunt, had married Queen Costanza of Castile in order to gain the titular kingship of her country. Costanza was seventeen. In those days, princes were expected to use marriage as a tool to procure lands, titles, countries for the expansion of kingdoms and power; oft times to secure peace. Caught in a cruel vice of being totally in love with the available, twenty-one-year-old widow, he married another, forfeiting the bride he truly wanted – the sweetly regal Lady Katherine Swynford who had unwittingly captured his heart and mind.

As word of mouth had it in the DeSilva line down through the centuries, John's dutiful marriage to haughty Costanza was to become a king in his own right despite being the fourth son of the English monarch. Making a vow, the Duke pledged his love to Lady Katherine Swynford who was conscientiously resisting but yearning to love him. Explaining to Katherine that only his troth would be given to Queen Costanza at the wedding, he sealed his word to love only Katherine from his heart. Taking the great sapphire seal off his own finger, he placed it on hers. Katherine reportedly wept as his hands caressed the ring into place. The fire in her heart and body for this man, which had capitulated into the ice of her devout beliefs regarding the sixth commandment, quickly resurfaced.

Ned remembered his own mother spitefully saying, 'They say that Katherine wept in confusion and hurt. I can understand why! Those tears were born in her devout young heart, for she was an innocent, having been brought up in a convent after the death of her parents in Flanders. They died from the first Black Plague that swept through England and Europe in 1355 or so.'

Fifteen-year-old Ned had asked, 'If she was so conscientious, how then did she become the Duke's leman?'

His mother, detecting a note of sympathy in her budding young man's voice had said, 'Don't go soft on me, young man! She stole your rightful place in the world. Your inheritance was given to the Duke's and her four children and their heirs, as I see it.'

His mother's coal black hair had shaken with indignation, upswept though it was into a beautiful arrangement which was held in place by a fanned comb of yellow gold thickly set with rubies.

'What happened, Mother?' the teenager had asked, ready to love the sweet Katherine anyway.

'Well. She lost her ferocious knight of a husband with whom she was loath to live but did without betraying her natural sentiments...' his mother's ruby earrings danced from deep-seated feelings as she sat on the verandah, fanning herself with the latest Catholic daily devotional.

'Why did she not love him?' Ned inquired.

'Well son, she meant to love him, but there was antipathy from the first. In his ardor, he quite lost his head and frightened her when she was but fifteen. She had arrived at court from the convent in Shippey, you see. Within days he, Sir Hugh Swynford had pursued her. Alerted by screams coming from The Savoy Palace gardens, Hugh's liege lord came running and pulled the enamored knight from the sobbing girl. That liege lord was John of Gaunt, Second Duke of Lancaster. He was twenty-five and married to lovely Blanche at the time.'

'From that time Katherine was repulsed by the knight I suppose,' Ned concluded.

'Yes. But the Duke and his mother, Queen Philippa, felt sorry for poor Hugh, and gave Katherine in marriage to him a few days later. I must say this for Katherine; she tried to love him in spite of the repulsion that had been created in her soul. She had been stalked and assaulted, but it was with the intent of asking her to marry him that her admirer had done so.' His mother stood to walk into the house. 'He had not counted on being overcome by his passions, she was quite the little nun, you know. Had not seen men since she was five years old except for the saintly priest who tutored her in Latin, French, and so forth.' His mother's black Castilian eyes had snapped. 'Go read about it yourself! Then you'll understand what I mean!'

The Arizona breeze, hot and dry, had stirred the magenta bougainvillea on the white walls surrounding them. Verdant leaves and the delicate little golden spires in the heart of each blossom seemed to whisper to her bitterness, 'Misplaced Princess of Castile, you are.' It stirred her blood with the ancient genes rising to be noticed, always rearing up just when she had managed to still her discontent. 'Por Dios!' her heart cried out, 'I belong in a palace on the lands of my ancient ones!'

Softening, she turned to Ned. After all, it had not been her gorgeous son's fault. Seeing the intense but hurt look in his sable brown eyes she said, 'It's a long story. Go to England, darling, and look for the answers in the archives of her lord's manor, Kettlethorpe near Lincoln. The churches there should have something recorded from the fourteenth century. You know the English – they save everything.'

'Mother,' he had said, 'I don't want to wait until I am out of high school and college to hear the rest of the story.'

His mother returned to her chair and sat gracefully into the white wicker, settling onto the soft chintz cushions of flaming yellow.

'Okay, son. In a nutshell, the two years Katherine had withstood the Duke's wooing after the demise of his beloved Blanche saw Katherine still a wedded wife to Hugh and mother of his two children. John was generous to his impoverished knight and family – perhaps Hugh wasn't a good businessman. But suddenly Katherine found herself widowed by war. She was without the protection and responsibility of a living husband to sustain her fine conscience regarding the attraction she felt for the widowed Duke.'

'You have to hand her that, Mother,' Ned had murmured.

'I don't have to hand her memory anything except my stinging hatred for depriving me and mine of their rightful honor!' She glared at Ned. 'Her heirs owe me! Some day you'll know what I mean.' She got up and walked toward the house entrance.

Ned, knowing the ways of men with women thanks to the excellent tutoring of an uncle, murmured, 'I think I already know what you mean, Mother,' and smiled darkly beneath the black fuzz above his sensuous mouth.

His mother looked at him askance. Already? she asked herself silently. That brother of mine! It's of his doing, no doubt. Why must men rush little boys into being grown-ups? But aloud she said, 'This much I'll concede: the death of a woman's husband leaves a chink in the armor which she needs against Cupid's arrows; and so it was regarding Katherine. John of Gaunt was after all quite irresistible, the toast of the kingdom and her ducal lord. That he was the chivalrous Second Duke of Lancaster didn't escape her notice.'

'You can almost forgive him of Katherine's bastards-turned-legitimate, can't you Mother,' Ned had then stated softly while observing her face as she recited John's qualities. For an instant, he had seen a soft side to his mother regarding her lost title of Princess of the Blood Royal through the washing away by the heavy seas of time.

'Yes,' she murmured. Suddenly her head had snapped up imperiously, causing her jeweled earrings to dance. 'No!' She about-faced. 'I cannot! I will not! I may be rich! I may have Royal blood! But because of him and that infernal mistress-turned-Duchess, who knows? Who cares? Where is my title? Where are my legitimate lands? Where is my big house on England's green and lovely hills?' Her eyes narrowed. 'I shall hate him, Katherine and the Beauforts until the day I die!'

'Is this a private wake, or may I join?' A quiet, teasing voice interrupted Ned's reverie. Raoul's chair was being situated for his seating opposite the table from Ned. The maître d'hôtel bowed slightly and left.

The thinker smiled at his kid brother. Still dwelling on his mother's pain, Ned's heart acidly remembered the divided allegiance by the Duke between Katherine and the DeSilvas' haughty Castilian ancestor, Costanza. He looked at his younger brother now seated across from him, knowing that his hatred of the history was shared, and that each of them loathed not being on equal social status with their Royal cousins who now ruled and possessed the lands and titles of the Duke of Lancaster. Even to be acknowledged or accepted by them would be gratifying. It would be the balm, which would heal their ancient wounds but irritatingly, that was impossible.

No matter that nearly six hundred years had rolled by for within the DeSilvas burned a living hatred. A passionate despising it was – the kind that Esau felt for Jacob after selling his birthright over an empty stomach, for only one child had been born between John and Costanza as a result of, as they saw it, the Duke's interest in Katherine. That Princess significantly, but accidentally named Catherine by her mother who knew nothing of her husband's mistress, later inherited the throne of Castile by way of marrying King John of Castile, who was chosen in 1385 to rule. So it was that Castile's warring brothers, Kings Pedro and Trastamara, eventually ruled together, as it were; for their blood coursed through the veins of the newly-weds who were Royal grandchildren each had sired indirectly.

'What a roundabout, hard way to acquire the patience and fairness of temper true majesty requires!' Ned darkly mused. 'Thank God I am also partly Plantagenet due to the Duke. I want to be regarded and honored as such.' Jealously reigned supreme within the DeSilva heart.

Looking up from searching for answers in his coffee cup, Ned challenged Raoul, 'How do you think the War of Roses would have ended had there been more males born of our ancestoress, the Queen of Castile?'

'Costanza?' a flabbergasted Raoul asked.

'Of course!' Ned softly, but emphatically responded. 'English wealth and titles would have then been shared! All would not have been relegated only to Castile.'

'What does that have to do with me in 1997? Absolutely nothing! I'm hungry, let's eat something,' Raoul suggested.

The waiter stood by to take their orders. After he had gone, Ned continued, 'What that has to do with you, little brother, is simple. Had the Duke not been so in love with Lady Katherine and gone home to Costanza's exiled court at Hertford instead of to these very grounds to enjoy sweet amour, we might now be part of English Royalty. We have English Plantagenet and

Castilian Royal blood coursing hotly through our veins!' Ned leaned forward over the table, zeroing in with an eye-hold on his brother. 'Think of it! We could even now be joining our Royal cousins to mourn this morning's tragedy!'

Raoul returned a soft stare to defuse the volatile look in his older brother's angry, black orbs. Softly he said, 'Yes, and had my aunt been born a man, she would have been my uncle.' His apathy on the subject seemed to emphasize itself as he smiled at the waiter who placed a steaming plate of hot scrambled eggs mixed with Italian sausage, Hungarian pepper, onion, green pepper and cheeses before him. Sprinkling the concoction with ample doses of Tabasco sauce, he delicately availed his fork of the victuals as he said, 'Really, Ned. Aren't you a bit over the top about this?'

'Get real, Raoul!' Ned darkly growled as he devoured a piece of sweet roll off the tines of an elegant silver fork on which the underside of the handle bore a discreet 'Rogers Sterling'.

In spite of themselves, they could not help bursting into quiet laughter over the mouthful of tongue-twister Ned had inadvertently spoken. Their expensively clothed shoulders shook as they tried to suppress themselves. Ned wiped his mustache with a napkin and took a sip of strong coffee. Setting the china cup back onto its saucer, he smiled darkly at his younger brother.

'I think that I am the one who is being real,' Raoul finally said.

'You wouldn't like to be sitting at Balmoral or Sandringham, or Lancaster House? How about shaving at one of the palaces lining the Mall every morning? I wouldn't mind it,' Ned teased his brother with a wicked little gleam in his eyes and a toothy grin.

'I could live with it!' his brother answered, suddenly out of sorts. 'But forget it why don't you! It's over. Done. Six hundred years cold in the pan. What's eating you, anyway?'

'What eats me every time I come to stay here is that the illustrious Duke, our grandfather of long ago, left little Costanza living in splendor, but minus his company when he was home from campaign. He'd come here to these very grounds, not the building but the grounds where we sit eating our breakfast, to live with the Swynford Lady. No matter *how* lovely and undemanding she was reputed to be, no matter her shy grace and regal mien, I resent it!' His voice continued in its low, savage tone, 'She bore him three sons plus a daughter during that time.' Ned fidgeted on the green and salmon-colored chair. 'Doesn't it strike you that if he had been with his legal wife where he belonged, that wife may have borne three sons and a daughter instead of the one child they managed to produce?' Ned took an exasperated breath, continuing, 'Good gracious man! She was an only child, that offspring of Costanza, our grandmother!' Ned's black brows sullenly thundered as kinetic energy streaked through murderous eyes. 'He should have gone home to his wife!'

Raoul chased a Spanish olive into the egg ensemble before him, wiping his tidy mouth with the damask napkin.

'That's a pretty hard thing to ask of a man when that wife smelled unsavory from lack of washing due to her vows to God to love only the King of Heaven! And! She wore chaffing, hair undergarments to remind her of the suffering of her murdered father. Queen or no Queen, relative or no relative, I'm with the Duke on this one. He's our ancestor also, you know,' Raoul kept his eyes bent on his plate, studiously selecting a hot piece of Italian sausage from the scrambled egg dish.

'How can you say that about our ancient grandmother?' Ned wanted to know, in a savagely quiet voice.

'Because, whether we like it or not, according to history it is true. Look Ned, here we have the memory of two women, both roughly the same age. Times were not easy for women, Royal or common. They were possessions... chattels of their lord and masters... first of their fathers and then of their husbands.' Raoul choked elegantly on a piece of hot pepper. Tears started in his eyes. Fishing for a handkerchief, he came up empty-handed. 'Where the deuce?' he muttered.

'Okay, smart one, what next?' Ned handed him his handkerchief. The brothers hands simultaneously touched the monogrammed DS above which rested a Castilian crown of gold thread.

Dabbing the moisture from his sooty lashes, Raoul continued, 'Well, if you look at the character of both these young women, you will find that their loyalty, integrity and sense of loving God were basically the same.'

'And?' Ned urged him on.

'But... and here is a *big* but...'

Now Ned couldn't help but laugh, causing Raoul to grin in spite of the burning sensation in his eyes, nose and throat caused by choking on the pepper.

'Which Lady fits that last sentence?' Ned asked.

'Don't be a donkey!' quietly demanded the younger brother. 'Come on. Get serious, you hot-blooded Castilian!' Raoul glowered. 'Do you want to hear me out, or not?'

'Yes, yes, of course I do,' Ned sipped more coffee, chuckling to himself. His dark eyes mirrored indulgence.

'As I was about to point out,' he looked squarely into Ned's eyes, 'our little ancestoress was not pretty; neither outwardly nor most of the time in her inner regard for others. She was considered to be very harsh-minded, arrogant, unforgiving, spiteful, proud and conceited. To top it off, she was judgmental to a fault. Now I ask you, big brother, would you be inclined to rush home to someone such as her, no matter how many thrones she endowed you?' Raoul settled back in his chair waiting for a response. Suddenly leaning forward he added with a rush, 'Let's not forget, she wasn't the only one of the two women in question who lost her father and all she possessed by the sword. Yet, little Katherine de Roet Swynford grew in grace from her adversity. So, what do you have to say to that, Ned? In my opinion she, Lady Katherine, deserved the Duke's protection, love and care by way of that alone; especially after her husband died when she was only twenty years old and the mother of his two babies.' He snorted quietly. 'I wouldn't want an unbathed woman in my arms! I don't care how pious she might be. And this other little lass was the opposite of our unfortunate Queen ancestor. God doesn't require... oh well, what does it matter now?'

'A little squeamish are you?' Ned wanted to know.

'No. Maybe a little realistic, as you should be.' Raoul smiled at his hot-headed, pretentious brother. 'We're lucky that he didn't swear off women altogether on his wedding night! We'd never have been born!'

'Nonetheless, I cannot forgive that our line was relegated to only the Castilian side of things,' Ned pouted, 'and that there were no children except one princess born between the Duke and Costanza. He should have done his duty in bed and sprinkled Lancasterian-Castilian Englishmen throughout the shires and palaces. We'd now be at least hobnobbing with our cousins at Ascot and Buckingham instead of being rich Americans with no social standing in our rightful country of England.' Ned was obviously still not happy.

'By the way, did you ever find the miniature of Costanza which disappeared from the mantel at home?' Raoul wanted to know.

'Do you think I would not have told you immediately had it been recovered?' Ned grumped.

Raoul pushed his chair back and stood. 'I hate to leave you in such a vile mood, Bro, but I have to get a move on. Thank you for the great breakfast and cheer up – you're so rich, King Midas was poor in comparison. Why do you brood so? Lighten up... smell the roses instead of our Castilian grandmum's unsavory history. With a wife like yours who is the epitome of another Katherine Swynford, you are one lucky man,' and walking over to his brother's chair, he patted him on the back. 'I'll see you later.'

Hurriedly, he donned his coat at checkout and headed out the door onto the Strand.

Thinking over everything his brother had observed, Ned DeSilva decided that even though Raoul had a point, it didn't ease the stinging rebuke of the ages that they were not recognized as Royals and on equal standing with the present female Duke of Lancaster and all of England's upper crust. He so wanted that for his family.

'We belong with them. They are our very cousins!' he muttered aloud, looking into the brilliant reflections of clear water in his prismoid Waterford.

'Why did our branch of the family have to give it all up and head for the New World so long ago? What an unfortunate choice, in my estimation.' He tinkered, elbows tucked neatly at his sides, with his fork, pushing bits of food here and there on the plate. A feeling of displacement filled his mind. He was like his mother and all the DeSilva ancestors in stubbornly insisting that they had been sinned against. Forgiveness came hard to any

Castilian in Ned's line. As a result, murderous thoughts were harbored, discussed and hidden for centuries. Sitting as a lord might where The Savoy Palace used to be, placated Ned's stinging feelings. Staying in the best suite of apartments in The Savoy Hotel gave a sense of equality regarding the royal blood to the brooding DeSilva. The real estate had once been that of his medieval grandfather, after all, a man without taint of disloyalty to his favorite brother's son, King Richard II.

'Another coffee, sir?' the waiter asked Ned.

'I thank you, no, but I will have a bit of light wine since it is after noon.' He smiled through his reverie.

'Of course, sir.' The formally attired waiter offered the wine menu as Ned graciously waved it away.

'Moselle, Bernkasteller Doktor is fine.' Ned made a mental note to go upstairs to fetch Jill in half an hour's time. They were going to go to the Tower of London to see the Crown Jewels, a favorite dalliance every time they were in town. In the meantime, he could brood longer. He was obsessed.

'Sir, your Moselle.' The elegant goblet was set before the equally elegant Ned.

'Thank you.' Ned tapped manicured nails on the damask table top, the slightly ostentatious diamonds in his yellow gold ring sparkled from the depths of its uneven, nugget perfection. The waiter couldn't tell which was more brilliantly reflected from the crystal chandeliers overhead, the Waterford stemware or the gentleman's fabulous jewelry.

Later, Ned walked along the corridor to the elevator which would take him to his lovely, blonde beauty of a wife. As he knocked lightly upon the door of suite 713 in their secret code before entering, he thought, it doesn't matter that some Royal biographers wish to deny the connection between the sweet commoner Katherine and the present line of monarchy, she is grandmother to seven monarchs in the past.

Facts were facts to the DeSilvas and had been for centuries. He was not happy that through John and Katherine, heirs sat openly upon the greatest, richest, most tenaciously durable throne on earth – that of the present United Kingdom.

'Jill?' he called softly as he walked into the lovely suite. Then he spoke another thought, 'Darling, did Raoul find that little sister of ours at her hocus-pocus shop in Piccadilly?' Mumbling under his breath, 'What a girl who graduated from Vassar is doing in a place like that, I will never know and with a Ph.D. from Harvard, too!'

Jill came sailing around the corner from the bedroom, a vision of blonde loveliness in lavender wool organdy. She hugged him. 'I don't know, darling,' she smiled into his eyes after holding him at arm's length to see how good he looked. She loved his dark, brooding handsomeness.

'Where's your coat, dear? It will be chilly on the way to the Tower,' Ned admonished.

'Here, sweet,' she gathered the rest of the St. John ensemble. He helped her put it on, and they went happily out the door.

'You know, dear, lavender is one of your best colors,' Ned observed, giving his wife a kiss as they entered the elevator.

On the way to the Tower of London, they noticed the street filled with mourners bearing flowers in their arms. There were queues in front of every florist shop.

Somberly Jill asked, 'Sweetheart, would you mind so very much if we buy a bouquet to take to Kensington Palace?' Tears glistened on her golden eyelashes, as aquamarine-colored eyes thoughtfully implored.

'Of course I don't mind. Which kind would you prefer?' he kindly responded.

'I would like to take white roses. She was so lovely, so beautiful; and both she and Prince Charles seemed such good people. I wish we could take some for him and their children as well.'

'Would you like to send a bouquet to St. James Palace also?'

'May we, darling? Oh, that would be so splendid if we could... addressed to Prince Charles in particular. He must be feeling terribly low right now.'

Jill reminded Ned of an angel. Who but she would know the pain in a man's heart at a time like this when formerly dormant, even forgotten love in all its first-time sweetness would come rushing back on impact of swift tragedy. Ned thought his wife the most intuitive of creatures. Surely DeSilva himself would become nostalgic if he was in Charles' shoes. Even to have loved someone enough to marry and make love was memory enough to be agonizing when she died, Ned thought to himself.

Ned suddenly noticed the sound of hundreds of feet treading the pavement. 'Darling,' he said to Jill, 'listen to the sound of people walking. Shoes are made of good leather, which are worn even on their days off here. I'm so used to sneakers used by the masses in our malls and on the streets, I'd forgotten how agreeable leather sounds.'

'Yes, dear,' Jill smiled. Suddenly she asked, 'Aren't you happy that you're not a Royal who has to be held up in the public eye? Your past history doesn't hold you up to ridicule or approval now. We are the fortunate ones living in America where everyone's dreams can come true and if tragedy falls, we don't have to be in the spotlight and condemned or approved over our personal manner of handling grief. Yes, we do live in a land where dreams come true!'

'Do we? Whose dreams?' Ned darkly whispered.

'Darling?' Jill looked at him worriedly. Ned was *not* happy!

Chapter Nine

August 31, 1997, 1600 hours, 4 P.M.

At the Tower of London, security guard Joe Bly looked at the Crown Jewel display, which was shining dazzlingly within its thick walls of glass. The automatic walkway, which encircled the jewels, had been turned off while exterior cleaning of the case was in progress, for word had just come down from Buckingham Palace and the Prime Minister that the Tower was to be closed indefinitely until a suitable time of mourning had passed.

Today, the crowds of sightseers in the castle had been subdued and polite. There hadn't been too many patrons due to the tragic events of the past night. Usually patrons always made the security force feel quite jovial by four o'clock of an afternoon; and later after closing time, it called for a pull of bitters at the local pub en route home.

Contemplating the Imperial State Crown, Joe reflected as to how the Queen reigned but did not rule his beloved England. He had always been a staunch supporter of Britain's government which, he explained to foreigners, was as the mists rolling in from the sea... it had undefined edges which allowed for changes as needed to provide protection of their ancient freedoms as well as those of the present, plus suggested freedoms yet to be tried for the good of all. He'd tell how any number of things and appointments could not take place without the Queen's signature and how the British considered that very thing a safeguard to freedom.

'Why, if we're confronted by treason or insanity in a Prime Minister, the Sovereign can force a general election for she has the sole power as Queen to do so. Be it King or Queen, that authority was given to the Crown. Our royalty is more than ornamental,' he proudly would point out.

Joe loved his Monarch, his Parliament, his country, his town, his house, his wife, his children, his grandchildren and last but by no means least, his God. He was as tidy in his mind as his five foot eight inch, squarish body looked. From under his black hat, one could see a few sprinkles of gray at the temples adorning little black tufts of hair ending at the ear lobes. The twinkle in his green English eyes made one think of all the sea wonders an emerald must have beheld during its eons of creation.

'Joe Bly was a peach of a guy,' his wife always shyly told her matron friends when stating why she had married him; and indeed, still in love, their tidy bungalow in the East End was as charming as the couple themselves. Loving every paid-for nook and cranny of the little house and garden just as heartily as their carefully stored retirement fund in the local bank, life was free of care for the Blys. Surviving nappy changes by courageous mothers in dark tunnels under London while it was being blitzed during World War II, to safely growing up, marrying and working toward their present secure comforts in a safe society had been their experience. That safety and society seemed a wonderful blessing indeed.

They had always looked up to their beautiful, kind Queen, who, born on Wednesday, April 21, 1926, at 12:40 A.M., was considered almost an older sister during wartime and reconstruction. Always in her soft voice, she had insisted to her father King that she be allowed involvement in the war effort. Finally, he made his Lilibet a member of the Grenadier Guards, creating her Colonel-in-Chief on her sixteenth birthday. The country was overjoyed. When she became eighteen her father went one step further, sanctioning her enlistment in the women's service of the British Army. It was there, in the ATS where she learned mechanics and how to drive large vehicles, ambulances amongst them. She, the beautiful darling of the island realm, gave courageous, dependable service, asking for no favors in joining Joe's parents and millions like them in repulsing the Nazi tentacles reaching over England from across the channel and surrounding seas.

The Princess's pluck had captivated little Joe's heart. He remembered that by the time he was old enough to sit on his mummy's knee, he used to hear the heiress's voice floating pleasantly into the living room, encouraging the children and young people to help the war effort by being brave and helpful to their parents during blackouts and the Blitz. To Joe, comfort came knowing that even the Royal children were living as were they. Their kitchen was even blasted by a bomb; that was one badge of courage chalked up for Princess Elizabeth, Princess Margaret and the lovely Queen Mum in his sight!

Little Joe would huddle in his mother's arms under the streets, his little ears being blasted to near deafness hearing the whirring-kaboom noises above his head.

'If they can do it, I can do it,' he would think. Imagining Princess Margaret, not much older than himself, cradled in her mother's arms, heart thumping like his own but bravely enduring without crying, as was he.

Somehow, he imagined that her older sister was out in the palace gardens putting fires out with the garden hose, she and her dad the King squirting water everywhere. He wondered if they wore firemen's hats or their crowns. He preferred seeing the crowns in his mind's eye. It seemed more safe somehow, more omniscient, more powerful. The King would save them... he and Lilibet. As long as their crowns didn't get knocked off by a blockbuster, they would save little Joe and his mummy. All would be saved by the magic wand in the King's hand. Joey had seen it once... that great, powerful flash, the scepter!

Yes sir! Joe Bly heartily loved their gracious Queen; and sorrowed every time the House of Windsor shuddered from the growing pains of its children, the natural growing pains of its roots reaching into the uncharted seas of becoming twenty-first-century vintage with the royal offspring being largely forced into selecting mates from the only source left to Royals since World War II – their own country's landed nobles. But then Joe and his wife reasoned, Royals had always been Royals, sometimes to a lesser, sometimes to a more sterling degree, depending upon who was available for marriage and/or into whose heart Cupid had flung his wild arrows down through the centuries. So, the Blys didn't think it was so out of the ordinary when their beloved Prince of Wales fell in love with the lovely English rose from Althorp whose shy sweetness and mischievous eyes bespoke fun and loyalty to her chosen role in life. The demure little Lady's understanding of youth's pains and joys made every baby and child she ever met love her instinctively.

The Blys felt as did their neighbors, for anyone with an ounce of sense knew that there'd be problems caused by mismatched basics from Royal-common marriages. Royalty was Royalty. Nobility was nobility. The twain often did meet in marriage, and nobility rose to the occasion, sometimes happily, sometimes bitterly, sometimes in between. They hoped for the best. Maybe not every historical account provided details, nor did every such marriage have problems, but most seemed to have had. Therefore, the weathered veterans of solid marriages just took for granted that their beloved kids of Windsor would fare well enough.

'When you're young, you're pliable,' old Joe had winked at his wife the days of three separate Royal weddings. 'But it won't be easy. The bride and groom have come from two different worlds, we'll just have to try to be supportive of each partner when they stub their young toes, now won't we mother!' He relished being a proper subject and countryman in so doing.

Now the air seemed a bit stuffy in the Tower, and he heard an unusual noise.

A sudden thump with a simultaneous, 'I say, old chap,' from a man approaching Joe in the corridor broke his 4:45 P.M. reverie. Joe quickly glanced into the open vault toward the jewel case, peering in the direction of the loud but muffled noise, and started walking toward the case to see if the person who had been bending over the container of cleaning implements was okay. Turning to resume the hall, he noticed a blonde woman walking toward the exit, so attractive, a second look invited. 'My star gazing days are over; and anyway, where's Old Tom?' Joe couldn't see him anymore. Maybe he'd had a dizzy spell. God knew that the engineer was no spring chicken anymore. A traveler at his elbow detained Joe briefly before he could return to the vault entrance.

'How do I get to Mansion House from this point?' the man with a permanent tan, dark hair, eyes and coat inquired, unfurling a map of the Underground before Joe's nose.

'Excuse me sir, if you'll wait right here I think a friend needs me. Be back directly.' Joe rushed behind the display, finding Old Tom who sat dazed on the rubber, automated sidewalk, his back propped against the base of the Crown Jewel case.

'No wonder my star gazing days are over! It appears you are seeing them!' Joe exclaimed, reaching down to assist the sixty-nine-year-old janitor.

'What? What? Where am I?' Old Tom's rheumy eyes looking up from under his red, white-frosted eyebrows looked like two blue hedgehogs peeping out from the bushes.

Joe pushed wisps of coarse, faded, strawberry hair from the dazed man's eyes. Tom's sudden fall had propelled his head against the glass as he went spinning in a half-turn, and now with his back against the case on the walkway, he sat propped up as pretty as you please. A knot rose on his forehead like yeast dough in a bowl atop a warm appliance.

'Matey! You'd better go to the medical office or the hospital. Can you get up?' Joe took hold of Tom's elbow.

'Oh. I'm a bit dizzy yet. Mind if I sit a spell? The room is goin' round and round and round faster than the Queen's horses at Ascot!' Old Tom put a trembling hand to his head.

Joe squatted down to take his pulse and look into the eyes.

'The funniest thing happened,' Old Tom continued with a moan, 'the walkway started a-movin' again, and then she stopped, d'rectly.'

Joe whipped out his cellular, made a quick call for help, popped the telephone back into his shirt pocket and said, 'Just rest easy, Tom,' as he patted his pal's blue chambray shirt back. Thinking to lay him flat on the floor lest he was having a stroke, he wadded up the towels Tom had been using, made a pillow for the elderly man's head, and improvised as much comfort as possible. 'I'll be right back, old boy,' and Joe rose to help the waiting businessman who must have stepped away from the door into the adjacent corridor.

The man was nowhere to be found.

Paramedics arrived, administered first aid and left with Tom on a gurney. Old Joe went to pick up Tom's oblong cleaning box in order to put it away for him.

The box was nowhere to be found.

It was about that time that Joe caught an odd sparkle coming from the glass case itself on the side facing the door where the harried visitor had flourished the map. Walking around to inspect the odd, dull prism of light, Joe came to a dead standstill.

'*Glory be!*' Lifting his hat with the left hand, and scratching a well-endowed head of hair with three fingers, he let out a low whistle. 'Why didn't the alarm go off? Why isn't every bobby and MI5 agent in the country here this very moment?' he wondered aloud.

Hearing Joe talking to himself, another security guard came to join him.

Before their very eyes was a neatly cut hole near the upper edge of the thick, oblong case. The circular piece had been quietly, efficiently extracted, and then reinserted so perfectly that not even a glass shard scored the edges, nor lay on the floor of the case or walkway.

'Oh, my poor soul!' Joe exhaled in disbelief, for the golden, bejeweled Royal scepter in all its majesty, in all its radiant beauty was gone! In its place stood a small, ancient miniature of a medieval, royal woman. The famous 530 carat Star of Africa diamond midst all its constellation, which had glorified the Kingdom since the reign of King Charles Stuart II, was simply gone.

'The Mona Lisa she ain't,' whispered Joe's buddy.

'You're right there... look at those haughty, condescending eyes.' Joe's heart was beating one hundred miles an hour.

'Yah, but look at that luscious hair and those sweet lips, and I don't think her peepers look as you say!'

'You're right, pal. She looks like a kid all dressed up to go see her papa, the King. Look at the way she carries those little shoulders.'

'There's majesty in her bearing, isn't there!' the other security guard conceded.

Within moments, the Tower of London was the scene of the best Scotland Yard and England's MI5 and MI6 had to offer. The combined elite forces were swarming around the Jewel House and entire grounds.

Joe noticed scarred wrists and hands carefully operating a camera in and around the crime scene. The camera seemed the size of a pea, or a sweet grape used in the sauces, which smothered red-hot, succulent Dover sole at his wife's favorite hideaway, Channelside. A glow shot up through a crack in the walk.

Much later, Joe and his wife sat in disbelief at the kitchen table over a cup of tea. Gone in Joe's mind was the material reminder of Shakespeare's 'Royal throne of kings, this scept'red isle, this earth of majesty, this realm...'

'My England!' Joe mourned. 'Wife! Our sceptred isle has been insulted mightily this day. Our dear Queen, God bless her. I've failed my Queen!' He hung his head low, a tear threatening to make fun of his stoic heart.

'Joe. You mustn't be talking like that now. No matter who was on duty, it would have happened. You've been on the force for nearly forty years, and never an untoward thing has happened. Now come, let's hear no more of that talk.' She poured a shot of her gin into his cup, stirring it briskly as she comforted him.

'Thank you, darlin', but I mustn't have a drink until the investigation is finished. I need my clearest head for the next hours and days. I may need to help in more important matters. We've all been told that we will be needed on the streets of London for the funeral cortège. I will not fail my bonny Prince and his sons in this, nor his lovely mother!'

His wife stood, went to him, and put her arms gently around his muscular shoulders, which sagged beneath their clothing of black.

'Come to bed, dear,' and she helped him up.

'But, darlin', you don't understand,' he complained. 'Someone stole our radiant, enduring symbol of sovereignty! Oh, our realm! That scepter has always been used as an instrument of merciful temperance and understanding and unity! Now it is gone, and it's my fault. Somehow, it is my fault!'

'Come, dear. Come along. I see what you are saying.'

Joe picked up the ringing telephone, 'True majesty is the... huh? Oh excuse me, Jane. I'm having a conversation here with the wife. Is the Captain in? No? Well, would you leave him a note, and tell him that Old Joe will come in early if he needs, in the morning. What's that? No! I don't think so. Goodnight, lass.'

'I'm ready. Let's go to bed,' and he put an arm around his wife's little shoulders.

Sitting on the edge of the bed, he spluttered, 'I love my Queen, I love my bonnie Prince Charlie and I loved our darling, little Diana... oh, I don't know what I want to say! But wife! Who would do a terrible thing like this at such a time? Who?'

'I don't know, dear, but he has the hands of a surgeon, the heart of a jackal and the morals of a libertine.'

She turned off the light.

Back at the Ranch near Phoenix, August 31, 1997, 0700 hours, 7 A.M., CIA Sam

Rick's sidekick, was still asleep after returning from Sky Harbor International Airport where he had seen Rick off on the private Lear the day before. The telephone was ringing off the hook. It was 7 A.M.

'Yes?' he softly said into the mouthpiece. 'What's that?' He started to laugh. 'Jeez... what next! Someone is working overtime, don't you think?' He roughed up his black hair.

He listened awhile, blue eyes trying to stay open. 'Okay. I'll be out of here in fifteen minutes. See you at Dulles Airport.'

Never one to get excited, he lay still for a moment, then jumped out of bed and hit the shower, dousing long legs, narrow body and shoulders, neck and all in the fastest wash that side of the Pecos. Dashing out the door still combing his wet black hair, it was off to Washington, D.C. and London.

Chapter Ten

U.S.A. and England, the night of September 1, 1997, the Dream Prince

The full moon, peeping from behind silver rimmed clouds spread white light over Christiana as she slept in her little bed, gloriously enveloping her slenderness in an ethereal blanket. As if a coverlet of heavenly consolation, it lent comfort to her subconscience. The overwhelming sorrow of her father's sudden death from a coronary, and the equally abrupt death of her family's beloved Princess from afar, prompted a dream. Given over to forces of nature which some say rule destiny, her mind took a trip into enough healing to help face the days which lay ahead.

Half a globe away in England, Old Blue was sleeping through a thirty-minute nap after being briefed at headquarters regarding a caper, which shocked his boots off – almost. Someone had taken on the 31st of August from the Smithsonian in Washington D.C... the fabled Hope Diamond. Has the whole world gone mad? OB had wondered, as he fell asleep and started dreaming of the Prince whom he had been called to town to protect. Mixing in with the best of British MI5 and MI6 – some of the greatest minds and daring-do fellows in the world, Old Blue felt privileged to be working amongst the British law enforcement specialists.

The Prince, in the dream, had suddenly appeared as St. George, England's patron saint. He was protecting the populace's right to grieve. By so doing, as dreams go, his leadership in that emotional arena was magically healing an ancient tapestry, which was hanging at the entrance to the throne room.

Old Blue turned over on the cot, getting tangled in his necktie. Disentangling by rolling over the other way, his dream continued.

As the tapestry wove itself together through the magic of love, no one in the kingdom was tolerating but rather enjoying one another. The three Princes and their Sovereign were being embraced by the people and embracing back. Affectionately, the people and their governmental representatives of every level were enjoying the attributes of all concerned. Then the Royal scepter, that symbol of sovereignty as enduring, as radiant as the country's history itself, was suddenly snatched by a hand and arm bolting from cirrus clouds. Old Blue couldn't discern whether the marks on the thieving limb were cirrus or scars. It seemed that he had seen that arm and hand someplace before and it startled him so violently, that he woke up in a cold sweat.

Sitting up and rubbing his head while eyeing the clock, he said, 'Geez Louise, I've got to get outta here. I'll be late meeting Rick who is waiting to hear from Sam.' Jumping up, he stripped, took a quick shower, jumped into new duds, smoothed his hair, mustache and beard while hopping on one leg, pulling on the last cowboy boot and smoothing his perfectly creased dress pants over its top. Bolting out the door, one piece of the dream came back which had been so subtle it was almost forgotten.

'Who in the world has green eyes with thick, bristly lashes? Durned if I know,' and with that he bolted out the door and headed for Trafalgar Square.

At that very moment in time halfway around the world, cosmic forces were unveiling beautiful sights to the Minnesota dreamer with the green, ebony-lashed eyes. While busy London street sounds were engulfing Old Blue and Pamela's husband, the sleeper in America was enticed by the sound of loons calling to one another as they swam the lake twenty yards from her front door. The moon not only bathed Christiana through the night light in her ceiling, but also frosted the serene surface of the water outside her flat in silver. A magnificent tree on the shore by the dock stood absolutely still. Not a leaf stirred in the heavy, windless air of late summertime. The Minnesota state birds relished the night vapors rising from the fresh water; the smell of vegetating reeds and grasses which the lake had enticed into life and death; the sight of the beautiful old cottonwood, leaves dipped as if in precious metal.

The girl who did not know she was a Royal started dreaming

of another one, the one whom she had always admired since aged eleven.

She saw him with Shakespeare of old. The present Crown Prince and the English bard were sharing one of the latter's popular works while standing beneath the shelter of slender white birch trees in one of England's loveliest places, the setting which stole King Henry VI's heart inspiring His Majesty to build a great university, King's College, across from what became Queen's Green facing the town of Cambridge.

The Dream Prince loved his alma mater with its River Cam winding quietly a few yards from the walls through stands of flowering chestnut trees and wild flowers. It flowed under the streets of Cambridge Towne as punters stood in flatboats upon its gleaming surface to carry passengers, propelling their small crafts along with slender poles with which they pushed against the river bottom.

Before the Dream Prince and Shakespeare, across an ancient gray footbridge made of native stone, rose the majestic wonder called King's College Chapel, one of the pure white, man-made splendors of England. The lacey corner towers and lesser spires rising every few feet from the filigreed stone, which was the roof's edge, kissed the blue heavens. Religious symbols atop this breathtaking beauty made the idea of God in His heaven seem utterly plausible.

Across the way lay more of the beautiful college town of Kings emptying into lovely, green wooded places such as the water meadows of Coe Fen where cattle peacefully grazed midst the beauty of medieval architecture. Again, the River Cam peacefully made its presence known, now a silver ribbon of light and shadow.

Shakespeare, looking sorrowfully at the Royal Prince and the beauty surrounding them recited from his own works:

'...this blessed plot,
　this earth,
　　this realm,
　　　this England...'

The greatest poet of all time since King David of old, placed a loving hand on the future King, and as dreams go, dissolved into thin air.

The Dream Prince was surprised at tears which started to well into his own blue optics. He suddenly was looking back at a golden time. Christiana, the dreamer, followed his sorrowful gaze. The dream continued.

She saw a sunny, beautiful day in London. At St. Paul's Cathedral, she saw the Dream Prince standing at the altar, looking the happy, splendid bridegroom dressed in dashing black and white with splashes of color marking Royal orders on his uniform. In Christiana's dream, she saw him remembering with fondness, even yearning, his own breathlessness when that beautiful vision of white elegance, his little bride walked shyly toward him on the arm of her stately, happy father in shimmering clouds of white silk and laces.

Her family's diamond tiara of interwoven hearts held the yards and yards of delicate illusion and lace which enveloped her untouched beauty... its sparkling purity seemed to hold special promise from her hopelessly in love heart to the Prince and to him alone. The circlet seemed to bespeak the love, compassion, respect and loyalty in which they sincerely wished to hold one another, that symbol of purity crowning her golden tresses emphasized the shy but proud love she bore the man of her choice. As she and her father came abreast of the Dream Prince, he joyfully held his arm out to her and together they entered a moment which no one else in the cathedral, nor indeed the world, could truly share; for they and they alone were the bride and groom. All others were on the outside of this particular romance and commitment.

Suddenly, as dreams go, the dream man was at Balmoral. Now, the handsome blue-eyed Prince to whom that bride had once been escorted, stood alone in the darkest night of his life. The love which they had once known, even now, was raising its brutally submerged head for recognition, as the pain of a shocking telephone call surged through him. Memories, reaching out to him with longing arms, compelled his naturally sensitive, compassionate nature to protect and comfort their young.

Remembering the first shy, hopeful glance through thick lashes, which had fluttered to him and him alone from their mother long before the children were born, the Dream Prince walked through the antiquated, majestic castle in the Scottish highlands to the boys' room.

In the dream, he stood solemn, heartbroken, wishing to spare them from the anguish, which would be theirs upon waking. Gazing lovingly upon the cherubic faces of the two whom he loved more than anyone on this earth, he saw the best of her and the best of himself lying peacefully in the untroubled sleep of youth.

Yes, he had loved her, he thought to himself. She had loved him. Now he would not have had it any other way. Their love was differently defined by one another, perhaps, but nonetheless it had been their moment in the sun at one time, before everything had gone awry.

Suddenly, his heart wrenched within him. From Shakespeare's *Hamlet*, the passage 'To Sweet Ophelia' came to mind, and the Dream Prince, in anguish of soul, whispered to her as if, between life and death, she now hovered near her sons.

'Oh, rose of May…
  Nature is fine in love,
   and where tis fine
    It sends some precious
     instance of itself
      After the thing it loves.'

Two tangible instances of that to which they had thrilled in the first finesse of love's private domain, lived and breathed before his very eyes, asleep in innocence. With tears slipping quietly down the grooves of his middle-aged, handsome face, he prayed quietly:

'God, please hear me… please tell her that I didn't intend to crush my fair rose of May… that budding blossom of youth from whom these precious slips of green didst spring; for she gave to me those whom I love more than even my own self. Please, dear God, tell her thank you for our precious instances of nature… and if you would be so kind, please tell her that I appreciate every pain, every sacrifice of love which birthing them represented. Please God, I am not insensitive... youth and confusion went hand in hand for both of us. Please thank her for her gifts to me... to the boys... to the world. Neither of us intended hurting one another as we fell in love so long ago.'

The moon shone through the rustling leaves of late summer as fragrant hill and dale greenery spent itself on high, craggy peaks of indescribable Highland beauty, and rushing mountain brooks tumbled head over heels in anticipation of the sea. Even nature seemed to celebrate 'some precious instance of itself', in time with the rhythm of procreation.

To the north-west, over an eventual sliver of sea to the Isle of Skye, the ruggedly beautiful and windswept Hebridean island was bathed in silver light and mysterious shadow. Shaggy Highland cattle, looking docile in spite of their massive horns, didn't realize that yet another Bonnie Prince Charlie within Scotland's borders was facing perhaps the greatest challenge of his turbulent life. For how, when death strikes one of an estranged couple, does the remaining person find license from harsh contemporaries and the public to grieve from the very heart which had been half of the bonding when love was new? He had more to consider than just himself during this dark, beyond anything he had ever known, moment. He had his tender instances of nature; and his soon to be stunned, grieving countrymen. Regardless of what anyone would conjecture, he dearly loved them all; including certain aspects of his lost love.

The moon, coolly glowing in the darkness, was surrounded by pinpoints of light in the vast heavens. That moon, hoped upon by all lovers since the beginning of time, had also looked down upon the demise of couple after couple through the millennia... the moon and stars enduring, the couples on earth dying.

In the dream, the Dream Prince again sadly thought of the pain his boys would face upon waking next morning, and quietly returned to his own bedroom.

As Christiana tossed and turned in her sleep not only from the dream, but also from an impending storm, which was being signaled by distant lightning and rumblings of thunder, she saw her Dream Prince being escorted into a car. The driver headed for an airstrip en route to a larger airport. The dream was shadowy. She observed the passenger with great sympathy and she even wept into her pillow unknowingly.

In the continuing dream, all the shattered Dream Prince could think of in the time warp of Christiana's historical musings was his dead Princess, the girl he had loved enough to marry, for he also remembered rejecting several ladies during his long bachelorhood.

The chauffeur was driving the car skillfully toward the plane. From the Aston Martin, the darkly outlined trees and hills passing by the moving car window seemed to take a different shape.

'Forgiveness,' something whispered into the shadows. 'Forgiveness.' Were those sky-blue eyes and a wisp of a smile he could see? Was that rekindled love abiding there? Was such a vision's gaze into his heart of hearts saying, 'I forgave you as you stood by our sons' beds, and then God gathered me into his arms. There is no more pain, except in my heart. I need *your* forgiveness.'

He bowed his head into his right hand. Salty wetness met the palm.

The vision continued, 'Please forgive me?'

'I hear you,' he whispered, 'and yes, I do forgive even as in death you have forgiven me, for we were mere mortals struggling to survive.'

'Take care of our children,' the apparition continued.

'How can I without you, excellent mother that you were? They need both of us.'

'I know,' she soothed, 'but, it will come to you,' he seemed to hear her voice softly murmuring in the slight sounds of the quietly humming motor of the car in which he was riding.

Goosebumps made the hair on his arms under the sleeves of his suit of clothes stand and be noticed. It felt as if a shy little kiss brushed his cheek.

The dream car stopped. He was ushered out. Walking across the tarmac, the wind whipped at his somber suit of gray. Climbing into the aircraft, he was suddenly surprised at a little touch of hope,which started crowning the grief in his breast as he thought of their boys.

'Yes, our children it will be. I hear you. I will endeavor to provide the real world, which for them must be a combination of Royal and common principles, which will enable them to appreciate and love those who have set them in high places – the people of our great realm. Thank you, sweet and loving spirit. I hear you.'

Knowing somehow that every soul becomes perfected when it rejoins its Maker, he felt that all was well between them once more.

The plane started circling from its short flight over the larger airport and the aircraft which was needed to bring the body of the precious one home. As it settled into a landing pattern, the Dream Prince thought, hope does spring eternal. Somehow, our boys, the kingdom and I will get through this with her mothering and intense caring as our inspiration.

The dream dissolved. Christiana was awakened by a crash of thunder. She lay watching the branches of the trees outside her windows writhing in agony from the tempestuous wind, thinking that only two tactile relationships had ever touched her Dream Prince's heart before marriage, and the shy whispers of understanding from behind the heartbreaking pale, belonged to the one whose love had brought his life full circle as a man, father and husband. For this, in spite of the pain, he would always cherish her no matter everyone's criticism.

Christiana also thought, as she watched the rising winds, no wonder Hamlet said: 'The dram of eale doth all the noble substance of doubt to his own scandal.' Does all the noble good become spoiled by one drop – one mistake made by each party in a marriage? Christiana wondered aloud. 'Well, if it does, that is one father who is going to set things onto the right course! As individuals, all their noble good will not be lost. Too many of us love them both for that to happen!'

She drifted off to sleep despite the strengthening storm raging outside her walls.

Chapter Eleven

The English news was globally bringing to mind how alike human beings the world over react when death takes a loved one; because of it, Angela was again at Chris's. Suddenly a bulletin flashed across the screen of the television and the announcer said: 'We interrupt this broadcast to give you the following bulletin, which is coming in even as we speak.'

Both women were riveted in silence as they looked at the picture. Apprehensively sitting down again, Angela sighed.

'Great excitement is erupting at the Smithsonian Institute in Washington, D.C., as personnel have just discovered that the fabled Hope Diamond, which many believe as having been cursed, is missing. Since its disappearance from the original setting as an eye of the Hindu goddess Sita, wife of Rama, who sat on the altar of a ruined temple in India in 1668 or so, it has been owned by various parties. Its original one hundred and twelve carat splendor was brought to France by a Mr. Tavernier who sold it to King Louis XIV. Tavernier reportedly was killed by wild dogs on his next trip to India. In the meantime, King Louis had the diamond cut into a sixty-seven carat heart-shaped stone and called it the Emblem of the Golden Fleece and Blue Diamond of the Crown. Louis XVI and his Queen, Marie Antoinette, inherited the "French Blue" as it was popularly called at the time. In 1792, at the time of their executions, the diamond was stolen along with all the French Crown Jewels. The amazing gem was never recovered by France, but oddly, one similar to the Hope is worn by Queen Maria Louisa of Spain in a portrait painted by Goya in 1800. Many believe it could be a portion of Sita's blue eye called "Heart of Hearts".'

'Do you think there *was* bad luck connected with the Hope Diamond?' Angela asked Christiana as they looked across the room at one another.

As if he heard, the anchorman answered the question:

'Reportedly, a Dutch diamond cutter by the name of Wilheim Fels, cut the original stone to its present size of 45.52 carats. Fels is said to have died of grief after his son Hendrick stole the gem and then ended his own life. In 1830 the recut, now oval gem appeared in London where a man by the name of Henry Hope purchased it. The diamond moved on, seemingly bringing havoc in its wake... an Eastern prince gave it to an actress and later shot her; a Greek owner and his family were killed in a car mishap; Abdul-Hamid II had owned the gem only a short while when an army revolt toppled him from the throne. An American by the name of McLean bought the gem in 1911 and oddly, the three closest to her seemed marked for disaster although she consistently scoffed at the superstition until she died of natural causes in 1947. Notwithstanding that her son was killed by an automobile, her husband died in a mental hospital and her daughter of an overdose of sleeping pills, the lady loved seeing the diamond pendant on a diamond chain worn by her dog. After her demise, Harry Winston, an American jeweler purchased her jewels including this fabled beauty. He gave the stone to the Smithsonian Institute in Washington, D.C., in 1958, where those who own it, the taxpayers of the United States, can go see it on display in the Janet Annenberg Hooker Hall of Geology, Gems and Minerals.'

'That sounds like convincing evidence to me,' Christiana said. 'Spooky... and I also hear that under certain light, red sparks seem to emanate from its depths.' She shuddered.

Her sister laughed. 'Oh, you are superstitious!'

'Well, if I were the goddess Sita I'd want my eye back,' Christiana laughed nervously. 'What's given to God should probably be left with heavenly notables.'

Scenes of London instantly came back onto the television.

'Let's turn the boob tube off for a while,' Angela suggested. 'It looks so pretty outdoors, a few minutes' stroll before I go home sounds ideal, it's already near nine o'clock.'

'Okay. I don't want to miss anything, so I'll start the VCR and tape it while we're gone.' Christiana popped a cassette into the machine and turned to look at her sister after turning it on, saying, 'It's about time someone got rid of the Hope Diamond from the display case at the Smithsonian in Washington, D.C.!'

'Why on earth would you ever say a thing like that?' Angela asked in surprise.

Christiana launched into the two subjects which were overwhelming her – the two deceased and those left behind.

'Well, if it really did bring bad luck to its owners, maybe it's affecting our country internally. I even intimated as much to Mr. Mogul at Dad's funeral. He was going to make a round robin through the Smithsonian en route to Carmel on the way home. "Research" he said.'

'Speaking of Dad, which makes me think of the Crown Prince, Mogul said that not only is Prince Charles an architect of God's cathedral by way of restoring the out of doors into eco-balance in Britain, but he is also a bright architect/designer of actual buildings as well; and that Dad had pointed out how Charles carefully tries to weave England's glorious architectural past into the future with his work. He preserves rather than destroys. I wonder if his countrymen appreciate that about him,' tears had started to roll down her soft cheeks once more. 'Some of the television commentators don't sound very kind right now. Listen.' The girls listened.

'If all the things our wise father told us about him are true, which I believe they are, the world will see evidence of those graces starting right this minute.' As she bent to hug her sister, Angela continued, 'Look at the television dear. As the days, months and years go by, I am certain that we will see the fine metal of which this future King is made. Both he and his wife were good people in their own way. It is unfortunate when two personalities don't mix well. For the joy each brought to those about them as individuals and to their children, we all loved them.'

Somberly, they watched a news rerun, forgetting the proposed walk. The wind whipped the Prince's hair as he emerged from a plane. He waited while a casket was taken from cargo then soberly he walked beside the country's service men as they carried the precious burden upon their shoulders, the Princess's sisters following.

Christiana, not realizing that tears were running down her

cheeks, said, 'I despise the Royals detractors who are criticizing them over this television channel right now! This is not the moment, nor the time to be casting stones or speculating! Have they no respect? We're Americans. What do we know of a kingdom? We threw them overboard two hundred years ago. The British elected to stay with their constitutional monarchy. How dare anyone here criticize any person within that lovely island? America I love; but some of our countrymen think they are God's gift to humanity on every subject this side of eternity! Who are we to say what is right, wrong or indifferent regarding those lovely people who make up the British Isles?' She was so disgusted, her body trembled. 'Or a form of government which embraces their former blood sacrifices into civilized ways of being, even as does our own!'

Angela softly answered, 'People who criticize an ex-husband for going to escort his children's mother home probably don't understand that love wears many coats. Just because love seems over, doesn't mean that it is not remembered.'

Christiana looked into her wise sister's amber eyes, which were framed by feathery lashes of reddish gold.

'Why is everyone criticizing the Queen so fiercely right now? She has always tried to prepare her children for the twenty-first century. For instance, she approved of sending Charles to Eaton and Cambridge University at King's College, where anyone can go if they've a mind. He was even sent to austerely masculine Gordonstoun in Scotland to round out his duty to the people of Britain and the Commonwealth. I doubt if any of our nation's young men would choose to go there in this day and age. I hear that it is considered by some to be almost brutal. So why do people say that she is unfeeling right now?' She fidgeted.

'And while I am at it, no one can see her with X-ray vision. How do other cultures know an English woman's mode of grieving; or caring for her grandchildren? Our grandmother cried only to me when Grandfather died. She waited until her children had left for the day saying that it was because one had to be strong for their sakes; but once they had gone home to sleep I heard, "Now I can cry in front of you. You are my twin in spirit and it is alright for me to shed tears for Henry for he told you how he loved me when we first met.'"

'Yes, dear. The English have stiff upper lips for the sake of others, but behind closed doors they cry just like everyone else in the world,' Angela comforted.

'When will the world in general realize that every nationality, every culture, has its own way of expressing joy and sorrow?' Christiana wanted to know.

'Probably never.' Angela stroked her sister's hair.

'Well, that is indeed a pity!' Chrissy retorted. 'In that case, everyone will continue condemning everyone else as being heartless and cruel, unfeeling and selfish for ever.'

'Wouldn't it be a wonderful planet on which to live if tolerance of others in kindness and love was the order of everyone's day?' Angela smiled into her sister's reddened, green eyes, 'and if everyone had a sister such as mine whose eyes resemble a Christmas tree in color, at least when she cries?' Her finely boned face looked like a cameo as she tucked her mouth upward.

In spite of their pain, laughter eased hurt and anger. They had come from a non-judgmental family, and had never been allowed to cast derogatory remarks about others within their parents' home. For Christiana at least, to stand by and hear or see someone pummeled by those who knew nothing of a person was a pill too big to swallow without coming to the defense.

They went outside and started walking along the lake shore.

'Tell me about the Hope Diamond, Chrissy,' Angela requested. 'I know a bit about it, but probably not the things you know.'

'Hmm, what you and I know is the same I suppose. It was given to the United States government by the last American who owned it; and the jewel has been on display at the National Jewels Gallery in Washington, D.C. for some years, but of course you know all those things.' She looked at her sister, 'You know how violent our society seems to be getting — at least we all keep grumping over the merciless dissection of everybody and everything; irresponsible sex in television programming all hours of the day and night without regard for the young children's impressionable minds, not to mention suggestive song lyrics, books, movies – and the vulgar vernacular someone in power thinks we as a people love lately.'

Suddenly laughing, she exclaimed, 'The blue diamond strikes again! Maybe it's the Hope Diamond curse which is raining havoc on our nation's sense of values!'

'Don't laugh little sis, that particular diamond was once a holy jewel of India. Maybe as you mentioned, it wasn't meant to be taken from its temple,' Angela admonished. 'What was dedicated to God possibly should have stayed in His house, even if its former home is in ruins. Surely another temple would accept it. You know that the Father of us all has more than one mode of communication with the children of the world who are His creatures.'

'You do share my apprehensions! What's this heresy? I thought you were a Christian.' Christiana looked at her sister in surprise. 'You sound as if you believe God speaks in different ways to humanity. Do you mean that you think He can communicate with people who believe in Mohammed, Buddha and such?'

'Of course I do. Even though I love the message of the Prince of Peace, it seems that most of the Christian world forgets the first principle of loving one's neighbor as oneself in order to maintain peace and goodwill. I reject that kind of so-called Christianity which brings suffering upon others. Furthermore, I don't think that God our Father is as small-minded as most humans make Him out to be. I can imagine that His understanding surpasses that of those He made in His own image whether He is called Yahweh, Allah or The Great White Spirit. Those names are just ethnic names. In Spanish, the name John is pronounced and written Juan, in French, it is pronounced and written softly – Jon. Most don't realize that Allah is the Arabic for God. "God" is merely the English.'

'This coming from the lips of the church organist!' Christiana looked at her older sister in amazement. 'You'd better not tell the rest of the congregation. You'll be ostracized.'

'Oh I doubt that, Chrissy. I still believe in the power of the Gospels. One cannot deny that if they are followed in the spirit in which they were written, great peace ensues. I've seen miracles too, you know. However, what I would like to see most of all, is the miracle of love becoming the creed of every human across the globe who uses the name of Christ in the title of one's religious belief, i.e. "Christian". In the meantime, I like Native American lore about the most. It appeals to me, scandalous at church or not.'

'Then you are quite serious when you say that to have desecrated a temple by taking the Blue Diamond of the Crown from one of its gods could bring unhappiness to those who, shall I say, borrowed it?'

'Perhaps,' Angela replied. 'All I know is that in studying history down through the ages, various cultures have not respected one another's methods of worship. If those methods did not include human sacrifice, I see no reason for anyone else's interference.'

'I don't think I can agree with you on that score,' Christiana said, 'but I respect your right to believe and say whatever you wish.'

'Yes,' Angela smiled, 'you love Christ's message and gift of Himself devoutly, don't you?'

'He is my teacher, the friend of my inner heart,' Christiana affirmed. 'I don't cast stones at other faiths either. Who am I to say? If someone asked to know in all sincerity the wellspring of my joy and strength, I think I'd share how I feel, but only if I felt they'd respect my beliefs. I don't like taking them out like a bag of marbles and casting them indiscriminately around.' She smiled, 'I wish that other faiths embraced total forgiveness but that would require "doing good unto those who despitefully use you"; and that is impossible to do if one's leaders embrace "eye for an eye, and tooth for a tooth".' She brushed a tear away. 'If only the world knew Jesus and the love He taught... the selflessness.'

By that time, they had walked halfway around the lake. 'Maybe we should turn back, now,' Angela suggested. 'Jack will be waiting at home for brunch.'

'Okay,' Christiana turned about and they started walking in the other direction.

'It's nice to be sisters who can respect one another's deepest religious persuasions, isn't it?' Angela said quietly. 'With Pamela's New Age philosophies, it's especially important because it gives us an opportunity to consider one another's thought process.' Angela hugged her little sis.

They walked past the reeds where redwing blackbirds were trilling joyously to one another and feeding from nearby trees laden with late summer fruit. Cottonwood leaves were softly parachuting through the air, thickly gathering in the dried ruts and edges of the graveled, clay road.

'More than a hint of fall is in the air this morning,' Angela observed. 'This sweater feels good.'

'So it is,' agreed the other.

'I really need to leave now, Chrissy. Jack will be waiting. Thanks for everything,' and with that Angela turned to her Buick Regal, climbed in and drove off.

Savoring the white and mauve petunias and impatiens lining the walk, Christiana slowly strolled to her door and went inside to watch more of the proceedings from London.

Chapter Twelve

At Number 10 Downing Street

The Prime Minister's boyish, good-looking face had wisps of brown hair hanging on the brow. Tired blue eyes swimming in pools of blood-shot whites studied the hand-delivered statement from Scotland Yard. Already red box number two had been dispatched to Balmoral Castle the evening before with news of the theft. Then, at one minute past midnight, red box number one for September 1, 1997 had flown overhead by helicopter to Her Majesty.

Now he was studying the Queen's responses plus additional information from Scotland Yard wherein the Queen's questions were already partially answered. Both, plus the Security Council, had already conferred and agreed with the indefatigable Prime Minister. The communiqué stated:

> We call upon the MI5 and M16 forces of our country in conjunction with covert CIA field operatives of the United States. Specifically:
>   1. Scar-P, Captain, and his group. U.K.
>   2. Old Blue, Captain-Adjutant, and his group. U.S.A.
> Regarding the following assignment which requires their services, maintain absolute secrecy:
> Obtain paste scepter from Bahamas immediately. Replace stolen item with same.

'No problem,' the Prime Minister said to himself as he stretched back into his high-backed chair. Putting his hands behind a weary head, he gazed up at the chandelier, which was centered in an ornate ceiling.

'Old Blue is already here due to the events of Saturday night, so is Scar-P. The others are on the way. Together they represent the most brilliant, trustworthy handful in the entire world.'

Reaching for the telephone, he pressed a blue button.

'Thank you.' He smiled after listening for a moment. 'Yes, the very ones. Have Old Blue, Rick and Sam pop by at the usual time, but save our boys until later. Better yet, tell Scar-P and his pals that their togs are here, pressed and waiting. Feed them sumptuously as if we truly appreciate them, for we do, and then take them to their rooms at St. James for they'll need all the sleep they can get during the next few hours... I beg your pardon?'

He laughed remembering the incongruity of orange hair with black roots in the service of Her Majesty, the Queen. 'She's good, though.' He again listened. 'Of course, that was precisely correct. Well, let Orange continue on duty until Old Blue chooses otherwise. However, as soon as OB's cowboys get here, send the three men over to me.'

The person on the other end of the line continued talking. Sadness descended.

'Thousands lining the streets you say?' A lump came into the PM's throat, 'a steady stream of flowers for our crushed blossom.' His head dropped into his left hand, elbow on the leather top of his desk. 'Goodbye, and thank you.'

Slowly he hung up the receiver, and wondered why the good must always die young.

He stood to go to a much deserved rest thinking that Her Majesty was right in requesting that the Tower of London be closed not only in respect because of the tragedy which had befallen the Royal family during the past forty-eight hours; but also in lieu of the political affront that had blatantly followed upon its heels by the scepter being stolen. Once the paste mock-up of the Royal scepter was in place at the ancient palace, and the sad funeral over, the building could be reopened for the multitudes who would want to pass through to feel the comfort and reassurance that goodness would survive; and that their tried and true ways of justice would prevail as would the sweetness of a young mother who had birthed a future King to follow in the footsteps of his daddy.

Wondering if the theft of a sizeable piece of France's former Emblem of the Golden Fleece, the Hope Diamond in Washington, D.C., had any connection to the heist of England's

Royal scepter, the tired Prime Minister exited the room.

Everyone had congregated in London by now, that is everyone except the Deerfield sisters.

Rick and Sam were busily hopping the Piccadilly Line on the Underground to go find Old Blue. Old Blue was standing once more outside St. James Palace contemplating the insulting threat to Her Majesty and Prince Charles which had been told him by the Prime Minister over a quick sandwich in the latter's kitchen barely half an hour after the jangling telephone had awakened him in an empty-of-Orange bed. The whole city was eerily quiet although packed with thousands of people on every curb, in the Mall, Kensington Gardens – wherever they could mourn silently with flowers, sentiments and tears near the homes of their cherished Sovereign, Princess and immediate family.

Pulling a Marlboro from his lips between pointer finger and thumb he threw it to the sidewalk, grinding it out with his heel not noticing the disgusted looks a few people gave him.

Old Blue studied St. James Palace, looking for signs of Scar-P whom he knew was around someplace. Good man, Scar-P, he thought.

Old Blue's loyalties to the British Prince of Wales were well known. It made OB steam to think of the brazenly executed theft of the scepter. It seemed such a thumb on nose gesture toward a man whom he admired, and who, some sweet day Old Blue wanted to see inherit the throne.

'He's a patient, obedient son and liege. Forty-nine and counting can't be easy, no matter how much one may love one's mother.'

The tall man, dressed in ye olde gray slacks and Harris tweed, started walking back toward town. A dressy cowboy shirt of white glossy stripes alternated with dull; sedate buttons, and open neck added a touch of intrigue to his appearance. He didn't give a damn if no one in England wore expensive cowboy boots with pointed toes, tops hidden by creased dress pants. He did, and he liked it. They were comfortable. Of course, if he had to go to court he dressed appropriately; but for casual hours, comfort was the name of the game for him. He was so charming, he knew that he could get by with it.

As he walked, admiration and respect for the Royal Family stirred in his heart. Yes, he would protect them and their place within England's heart and land. All they had to do was ask – and they had asked.

Part of his task was to take the political pulse of the assembled masses at this sad time by being a part of the crowds. For inadvertently, certain American anchorpersons had innocently played into the hands of what the CIA called 'rabble-rousers'. Worldwide, millions had heard that the Queen was in the doghouse over the demise of the Princess – not only the Queen, but the whole Royal House!

It never pays to accentuate the grumbling of a few in mass media coverage, Old Blue thought, shaking his curly head. 'It only opens the door for true revolutionaries to enter, or true enemies to make trouble not only for the Royals but for Parliament as well.

Yes, Old Blue could and would ferret out troublemakers, foreign or otherwise. Happy he had been a few minutes ago when the PM had told him that even as they spoke, Rick and Sam were landing at Heathrow. 'And I wonder if they have news of the Hope,' he mused to no one in particular.

Something flew into the beautiful curly black lashes of his right eye. Squinting and trying to get the fleck of annoyance out, he was reminded of how he hated his lashes, in his mind they were the province of females, durn it! Short, stubby ones would have been just fine... and straight, thank you very much!

Now his eyes searched the crowds of passers-by quietly, calmly, shadowed by those startlingly pretty lashes creating a dichotomy on the hardened features.

He had passed under the gates and could see Trafalgar Square ahead. Lord Admiral Nelson's figure shining in the sun high above London seemed a benediction on all men such as Old Blue... seasoned, brave defenders of country, hearth and home.

After waiting for the light to turn green, he left the base of the street lamp, walking into pedestrian traffic of scurrying bodies in front of the corner shops. Suddenly, his chocolate eyes smiled along with his mouth, and flashing an irresistible grin of even teeth sporting one slightly chipped front tooth, he exclaimed,

'Rick! You old goat, you!' and clapped his buddy on the shoulder. 'Geez, but it's good to see you. That blond hair of yours sent a signal straight out of the blue with the sun hitting it full force.'

Rick laughed and hugged his old compadre.

'Where've you been, you old Bozo you?' Old Blue enthusiastically asked. 'I thought you'd never get here. Where's Sam?'

'Want a cuppa?' Rick laughed, taking Old Blue by the elbow. 'Let's duck in here. I need a cup of coffee.'

They walked into Dalton's, went up to the second floor of the bookstore, found a table by the glass wall, and sat down. Fishing in pockets, the men produced a pound or two.

'Sad and dirty business, isn't it?' Old Blue said.

'Yes, it even tears at *my* heart. Thank God Pamela has sisters. She jumped at the chance to fly up to Minnesota to be with them while I'm off and running,' Rick replied.

'Want cream or sugar, pal?' Old Blue asked as he stood up moving toward the refreshment counter. 'Need something to eat, a roll, a biscuit?'

'Black will do fine. Not hungry yet though, but thanks.' Rick's amethystine eyes flashed brightly.

Over coffee, Old Blue offered his pal a cigar. Laughingly, the tip was bitten off, and a light started. Suddenly they both noticed the no smoking sign and blushed in embarrassment.

'Well, that's that,' stuffing the stogies into breast pockets, the two men settled down to coffee.

'What's that on your finger, man?' Old Blue probed.

Rick's lavender eyes smiled with pride under his shock of curly hair.

'You mean my wedding band?'

'Yes. When, where, and to whom, pal?'

'Three months ago I finally gave in after years of marriage and said that I would wear a wedding band. I haven't worn one before this time because felt it unsafe,' Rick explained.

Old Blue was amazed that Rick had never let on he was a married man.

'I just thought you were religious or of a different persuasion when you'd not party with us after assignments all these years!'

Old Blue exclaimed. 'Who's the lucky lady?'

'Pamela Jarvis nee Deerfield,' Rick answered.

'She and her sisters are quite something,' Old Blue whistled under his breath. He wondered if Rick knew who Deerfields really were.

'How do you know them?' Rick wanted to know.

'I know everybody, pal,' Old Blue laughed, 'everybody!'

They smiled over the rims of their coffee cups as the last drops were emptied.

'Where the devil is Sam?' Old Blue wanted to know. 'We've got to boogie.'

'I'll take you to him. He's with Tony.' Rick rose on lanky legs, a stunning three-piece suit of pinstripe blue making him look debonair.

Old Blue looked into his coffee cup.

'Brrr! I have a chill. Wish this black stuff had been golden with a blue ribbon. But being with you that's a no-go. I'd not do it for any other buddy, sit in a bookstore coffee shop,' he laughed at himself.

They walked out onto the crowded sidewalk of silent mourners.

'Speaking of your buddy,' Old Blue said under his breath as he lit the prized cigar, 'did he come by way of Langley?'

'Right on. We came in separate planes,' Rick accepted the proffered light.

Walking across the street into the large square, an out of the way bench was found. No one was nearby, affording an opportunity to confer.

'What do you think of all of this?' Old Blue squinted at him against the glare of daylight.

Rick thought carefully for a moment, drawing on the cigar which was a treat as he usually didn't indulge unless it was with his old, hard-nosed captain.

'Well, first of all I don't think that the two tragedies here are related, but I'm not so sure about the two thefts.'

'Yeah?' Old Blue gave him a penetrating look. 'Why not?'

'One clearly was accidental, and the others appear to have been planned around the accident. They happened the next afternoon.'

'That's what I think, too,' Old Blue concurred. 'The heist had been in the works for quite some time, I bet. The accident in Paris merely gave the golden opportunity to add insult to injury, not only to the throne, but also to the English, but where does the theft of the Hope Diamond fit into all this?'

'Let's not forget that Butler is a part of the Commonwealth, through Australia. I believe that the thumb on nose was to the entire British Empire, and the U.S.A... they both head NATO as Big Bro, you see? Inspector Butler always staunchly backs both; angering many.' Rick leaned forward, elbows on impeccably creased knees. His black dress loafers sporting soft fringe on the tops glinted in the sun. 'The combo seems to be a certain country's nemesis, let alone others in the world whom no one openly worries about yet,' he concluded.

'Butler seems to be their nemesis who causes them emesis,' Old Blue chuckled, suddenly thinking fondly of his long-lost pal in the Middle East. Wondering what his Oxford hall fellow was up to these days, he heard Rick ask, 'Are we both thinking the same?'

'The only thing,' Old Blue puffed on his stogie and blew smoke rings which wafted toward the much scandalized, but beloved Lord Nelson above his head. 'To think that my pal's country did it, is just too pat an answer.'

'Too obvious,' Rick murmured. 'The picture doesn't fit.'

'Well, look at what's coming our way! A storm cloud, complete with lightning. We'd better catch a taxi and get over to Number Ten because we've only twenty minutes to make an appearance. I wonder if Scar-P will be there?' Old Blue stood, wondering aloud.

The two agents smiled over memories. Scar-P was an old buddy.

A bolt of lightning suddenly flicked toward the ground.

'I'm gettin' old,' OB growled at Rick. 'This wet cold goes right through my old femurs, and even makes the top of my head cold from the steel plate. Good Lord! The way that metal conducts energy, it's a wonder I've not been struck by lightning during thunderstorms! I'd make a perfect lightning rod.'

They both laughed over the possibility.

'After all we've been through, it'd be downright comical to be wiped out by a bolt of lightning while getting out of a black taxi at Victoria Station or on my horse galloping across the South Dakota hills!' Old Blue's sense of humor, which was considerable, got the best of him and he had to wipe tears of mirth out of his eyes with one big strong hand.

As Rick hailed a taxi, he laughed in agreement. 'I don't know which would be worse – being drowned by a black snake one thought was a hanging vine at the edge of an African river, or being a living, breathing, lightning rod.' Rick laughed. 'Think I'd rather take my chances with the snake! There's a possibility for control there, but not with the elements.'

The taxi pulled up, and one of the world's elite cab force greeted them.

'You know, you guys are the most polite, courteous group of cabbies in the entire world!' Old Blue congratulated the driver as he climbed into the back seat behind Rick.

'Thank you. Where would you like to go?' The driver turned around to look at the men.

They found themselves staring into the face of Scar-P.

'Well I'll be a monkey's uncle!' Old Blue laughed, hopped back out of the cab, reached through the window and hugged the skinny blond man's scrawny neck.

'Hop in, mate. We've got work to do,' the driver smiled.

'Gotcha... let's peel rubber.' Old Blue jumped back in beside Rick and they were off toward Downing Street.

Finely scarred wrists and hands guided the wheel as lightning, wind and rain set upon the city with a fury.

The downpour made traffic snarl. Suddenly the deluge stopped.

'I have to pop by Piccadilly first,' Scar-P said.

Old Blue's eyes lit up in appreciation, for he had a fun and vice-loving heart which turned directly upwards at the thought.

'Boy, howdy! Do I love razzmatazz, and weirdos! Look at that blue and green spiked hair headed this way. What is it – a boy or a girl?' Old Blue's eyes glistened with desire as he suddenly saw a sign in a pub. 'Is that a Pabst I see advertised there?'

'Yes it is,' Rick affirmed, 'but we've business to do. You know the old saying business before pleasure? Come on, pal, let's get on with it. Get serious, will you? We're on assignment and I'm going nowhere with you if you have even one drink!'

'Sure. It's just that the old thirst starts rising in this type of setting,' Old Blue laughed.

'Which thirst?' Rick countered, good-naturedly.

'Oh, maybe one or two thirsts.' Old Blue caught Scar-P's eyes watching them in the mirror.

'I wonder if Orange is still shopping at Harrod's,' Old Blue sighed. 'Now, she is worth her weight in gold when soothing a broken conscience at work's end. Some day I'd like to make an honest woman of her and take her to the straight winds as they flow over the South Dakota prairie.'

They all burst into laughter when the same thought exploded into their minds: Agent Orange!

'What would she do with her orange and black hair, miniskirt, belts and bangles atop your buckskin horse?' Rick grinned.

'Lordy! Well I'd teach her to ride, you nitwit,' Old Blue confessed. 'I'd also take her to town and buy jeans and boots for the girl. She'd look great in them!'

'Better buy her a wig too while you're at it. Better yet, shave her head,' Rick said.

'Actually, a bottle of black dye would do the trick. She could then keep her own hair so the wind wouldn't snatch her bald-headed!'

The cab stopped in front of the little shop where the Dakotan had slept many times. A tall, slender woman with orange and black spiked hair, sunglasses, golden bangles on her left wrist, matching hoop earrings through which one could play basketball, and a leather miniskirt and vest with no blouse stood in front of the shop. Pulling the cigarette holder from her bronzed lips, she sauntered to the cab and asked for a light from the driver. Cole black sandals with chunk soles and heels pointed seductively.

'Sure, honey,' Scar-P said, digging in his breast pocket for a lighter.

Faint scent of Cobra perfume pleasantly skipped through the cab, making the guys wonder if they had actually smelled it while she unscrewed the very tip of the mouthpiece, dropping it into the cabby's outstretched hand which was lighting her cancer stick. Deft movements, unimpressive because of not being seen due to clever expertise was the name of their game.

Old Blue didn't miss a trick. Nor did amethyst eyes.

'Hi, girl. How ya doin?' Old Blue asked huskily.

She turned her disguised eyes toward him, lips curled in a sardonic smile, corners down to hold the ebony apparatus in place. Smoke curled lazily upward from the gray cigarette tip.

Why did the sight of her always make him want to lay his head on her shoulder and cry? Vietnam was so long ago!

The steel plate, which formed part of the top of his skull, started to pinch, causing pain to crash through the top of his head. Too much electricity and humidity could make life miserable; thunder rumbled, heralding the next rain shower.

Rick saw the wince of pain as it shot across Old Blue's brow. He patted the bony knees propped next to his own as the cab turned into the street and threaded its way through the hushed crowds slowly, carefully, to private lanes of a very private garden.

At Number Ten Downing Street the Prime Minister and Sam were waiting.

'What do you think of that plan?' the youthful statesman asked, looking sincerely into Sam's blue eyes.

A moment of silence followed as Sam studied the papers in his hands, which the sandy-haired politician had just handed him.

'It seems a bit risky, but taking chances seems to be our forte. With Old Blue as our leader, I see no problems. He's a master at such things.' His black head was lowered, skinny shoulders hunched forward, long legs spread wide even in the pants of a three-piece suit. Sam pulled on the knot of his red tie, which added flare to the charcoal ensemble sporting a pale gray shirt with white collar and cuffs. He hated business suits and ties with a passion.

'Three of America's finest to join our ace in Kuwait, if we go. Don't worry... when Old Blue is on duty, he stays away from alcohol... at least he always has in the past. Was he briefed at Langley on the way here?' the government official asked.

'No. They contacted him in Spain. Too risky, too many eyes and ears in Washington. Better to keep a low profile regarding him. It's only been six years since Desert Storm, you know.'

'Is that why you were sent to headquarters?'

'Yes, I'm the greenhorn as it were. I'm not flashy, and am never taken seriously anywhere I go – which is on purpose, of course. My persona is to allow the powers that be to think that I'm rather stupid, sort of a good-natured, illiterate, but rich playboy.'

'I see,' the Prime Minister smiled. 'Harvard man?'

'Yes.'

'Ph.D.?'

'Yes.'

'What was your major?'

'Girls.'

The PM did not laugh.

Sam sat up straight and said, 'I beg your pardon. Serious I should be. Actually, I majored in political science... helps in my line of service. Keeps me from putting my foot into my mouth most of the time, present not included.'

The British man smiled. After all, work could be hell and it was refreshing to find an irreverent guy every now and then when no harm was intended.

Suddenly Sam became serious and changed the subject to matters at hand.

'I beg your pardon, perhaps I should wait for you to inform me without my asking, but does Her Majesty know of the heist?'

'Yes. Her Majesty must know such things immediately, and is always informed.' A pen was carefully adjusted along the edge of the desk blotter. Looking down at the brief spread before him atop his desk, elbows and forearms resting on each side, he continued, 'You realize of course that she is the most able, knowledgeable, political figure in the nation; and willing to flow with the times to preserve this constitutional monarchy.' He shifted in the swivel chair, aiming his body squarely toward Sam who was sitting slightly to his left, and continued, 'The Queen loves the people and has spent a lifetime trying to honor their needs and wishes in a courtly way.'

'Magnificent woman,' Sam agreed. 'Truly magnificent and magnanimous to a fault. I'm sorry for the things which must surely be causing her pain the last couple of days in the media and press. I also feel it's a pity that her own family has been so assaulted by the changes in society during the past fifteen years. She has borne it well. Now for the scepter to be stolen hours after the death of her grandsons' mother... I hope we catch the S.O.B. who has attacked not only the Royal Family, but all of the British Isles as well.'

The phone rang. 'Show them in,' the Prime Minister said, pressing a button instead of picking up the receiver.

The doors opened and in walked Old Blue and Rick. The other two men stood, there were handshakes all around, seats offered and taken.

'Now back to the business at hand.' The PM cleared his throat. 'Have you discovered anything, Old Blue?'

'As a matter of fact, I have.' Old Blue pulled a picture out of his breast pocket. Stretching across the desk from his chair to hand it to his host, he continued, 'This bird flew in from the Middle East the morning of the heist.'

'I know him,' said the Englishman. 'Weren't you together at Oxford?' he asked as he looked at Old Blue.

'Yes, as a matter of fact we were. He was a great guy, very tender hearted. The principles of Christianity and Islam were very dear to his heart for he believed in peace and I believe those characteristics formed this diplomat. However, I don't see how a soft touch like him can survive in the political climate in which he must serve.' He leaned back in the gray wing chair, which supported his tall frame. 'His country is cash poor.'

'Why would he have left a picture of an ancient lady in the scepter's place?'

'Who knows? There could be many possibilities, but your archivists would have to run a check on his bloodlines. Maybe there is a connection. Maybe not. May I?' Old Blue pulled out a pack of cigarettes, offering them to everyone. All declined.

'Surely, go ahead,' their gracious host nodded.

Pulling a tiny, gold lighter from his pocket, he flipped the top to an instant flame, and ignited the strong smoke.

'If I may say so,' Rick excused himself, 'his country would be the first anyone suspects due to the problems their defense department poses. That is precisely why I doubt they are involved.'

Sam looked sideways at him from the depths of a burgundy chair.

'True,' Sam said. 'However, it is a deed typical of a chihuahua nipping at the heels of a bull. No great damage, just a durn nuisance which is terribly embarrassing to a super power and their strongest allies.' He sat up.

'It could be them, alright,' their host looked at the three men. 'Any more suspects?' he asked.

'What about the Irish factor?' Rick quietly asked.

'And the Korean?' Sam echoed. 'North Korea isn't too happy with any democratic country.'

They all talked on for half an hour, agreeing that somehow this deed tied into the world's focus on a former husband of a beautiful, estranged wife for it was being used to thwart accession to the throne for not only the Prince, but their son.

'I for one,' said Old Blue, 'even though I'm an American, am determined that the man who loved her but could not find a way to live with her, shall eventually have that ancient throne to sit upon. Some day he will pass it along to their child.'

Pulling on the cigarette, he blew smoke toward the ceiling.

'I almost had a wife; but how to live together was another story. Just because two people can't get along doesn't mean they never liked one another. I'm sick and tired of their imperfections being magnified. It's time we put forth both of their good points... never too late to do that.' Old Blue ground the cigarette out in a Waterford ashtray on a table beside his chair.

'I'm concerned about the rumblings over the telly,' the Prime Minister spoke. 'Someone used the word "revolution", I understand. It must not be encouraged. Other kingdoms besides ours have fallen due to insidious speculation. We have a constitutional monarchy and I believe that the majority of our people love it. I, too, shall do everything in my power to save it. I think we all loved our Royal couple, who at one time were headed together for the throne and today we are indeed drowned in sorrow. For someone to come along purposely thumbing a nose at the heart and soul of our country, was the wrong thing to do.

They do not understand what puts the backbone into an Englishman, a Scot, the Welsh and Irish. The Prince is our future Sovereign, and he is a good man and because of all those factors we shall all rise to this double tragedy and surmount it, securing the throne for him and his heirs, so help me God.' He looked down at the floor, and then raising his head to view the three Americans, said, 'We'll conceal the theft from the nation and the world by replacing the genuine article with the paste scepter, which is on display in Freeport.'

'The Bahamas?' Rick asked.

'Yes,' the PM answered. 'It's already on its way to Jerusalem where you three will retrieve it.'

He stood to his feet with moist eyes and a tired, bitter smile.

'When you get there, you'll find that everything enclosed herein will occur. God bless you all.' He shook hands all around, placing the brief into Old Blue's grasp. 'Be back in two days. We need all three of you at the palaces when the family is in residence; furthermore, our MI5 and MI6 enjoy your company on such assignments. You'll have rooms assigned for sleeping at the appropriate residence. Would the Palace of St. James suit all three of you? We love our Prince Charles and wish you to be there as soon as possible for added protection, of course.'

'Who will fend for the Queen?' Old Blue was concerned.

'Probably you, per her request.' Brit and American clasped hands. 'But we need you at St. James first.'

The PM's gaze swept all the men. 'You'll be gone thirty-two hours at most. Bring back the scepter from the paste Crown Jewel display.' He started to leave the room, stopped, turned around and said, 'Old Blue. One other thing, if this whole situation proves nothing more than a tragic accident and mere theft with no political overtones, we are sending you to Minneapolis to escort a certain Royal and her sister back to London.'

'Me?' Old Blue was dumfounded.

'Yes, you,' his host smiled.

Strolling toward the taxi, which would take the three Americans to their digs, Old Blue spoke quietly.

'I need to check out of headquarters downtown, need to pack up. After that's done, I'll be ready to go at 1700 hours. Does that satisfy you guys?'

'Sam?' Rick looked at his second mate.

'Okay with me, big boss… and boss,' he winked at Rick.

'Fine. We'll all take our duds over to St. James, and then can take separate routes to the Tornado,' Rick answered.

'Our contact from the Bahamas is in the Holy City. Not a word to anyone, not even those we are supposed to trust.' Old Blue lit another cigarette and then smiled at Scar-P, their favorite MI6 agent who graciously opened the door of the taxi.

Wondering why their driver had been out of the taxi instead of in it, Old Blue climbed in.

'Sam,' Old Blue inquired, 'is there any way that Rick could throw a few of your rags into a bag so's you could come to my room with me? I've something on my mind.'

'It's fine with me. Is it okay with you, Rick?'

'Sure. What should I pack for you?'

'Just the usual.'

'Consider it done, pal,' Rick smiled.

The taxi stopped at the Hyde Park Hotel for Sam and Old Blue to get out. Rick remained inside and the cab drove on.

An impressively turned out doorman opened the heavy glass, brass and wooden doors. The men passed through into a marble-floored foyer. Walking up the steps, Old Blue checked for messages at the desk, then took the key from the clerk as he and Sam caught an elevator upstairs.

Once inside the privacy of the comfortable accommodations, which the U.S. government leased out by the year for operatives who were needed in joint clandestine operations, Old Blue lit a cigarette, threw the matches on the bedside table and walked toward the closet to retrieve a blue duffel bag. Tossing it across the room as if playing basketball, the soft luggage landed squarely on the bed.

'Neat shot,' Sam laughed. Going to a wing chair next to the fireplace, he sat down. 'What's on your mind, Captain?' he asked of Old Blue.

Pulling a couple of shirts out of the highboy near the closet, followed by jockeys and T-shirts, sport socks, a complete suit of dress attire and tie, OB walked briskly to the bed and started arranging his clothes inside the tote.

'In an aside, the PM asked me to get the rest of my briefing from you. Time is of an essence, so I agreed to quiz you, better yet, just lay it on me, pal.' Old Blue put his cigarette from his lips and carefully pressed it into the groove of a green ashtray under a red lamp, bedside. Ducking into the bathroom to retrieve his shaving kit, the clinking and tinkling of metal against plastic, plastic against glass, was followed by the quick zip of a hurried hand closing the small bag. Old Blue came striding out, tossing the bag ahead of him into the little space on the left of the duffel, which he had reserved for it.

Again Sam laughed. 'You still love basketball, I see. So far you have four points racked up these past three minutes.' Leaning forward, elbows on his knees, he asked, 'Where do you want me to begin?'

'Well, how about everything said previously to my entrance into the office at Number Ten?'

'Alright.' Sam spoke quickly, telling all the things burned into his mind.

'We started out with our host explaining that we live in a black and white world with many diverse shades of gray thrown about to confuse the issues of morality. The objectivity to cling to integrity and compassion in all of our individual and political endeavors is a great challenge,' he said.

'Hmm,' Old Blue acknowledged that he had heard.

'Secondly, he said in answer to my question that it will not be announced that the scepter was stolen until the paste from the Bahamas is replaced at the Tower of London with the real thing.'

'In other words,' Old Blue grinned, 'no one will ever be the wiser.' He chuckled and did a high-five with his buddy. 'The culprits won't even get an ounce of so-called glory out of their thieving. Ha! I love it! No media coverage, no long, drawn-out court activity – at least none that is exposed to the world.' He laughed again, wiping tears from his eyes as he contemplated the deflated ego of some suave thief who thought that the cheeky act would get worldwide attention.

'If it's who I think it is,' his brown eyes mocking the person in his mind, 'he'll get nailed in his own country and hijacked out, compliments of three guys dressed in Bedouin robes. Oh, I love it!'

'Cap, your adrenaline flows when planning action. Sure glad I'm on your side. You even like the idea of getting our second skins put on in Jerusalem. I hate the stuff,' Sam grimaced.

'Maybe I aspired to the stage once upon a time,' Old Blue twinkled. 'I've always thought it neat to fill the shoes of another mortal... be someone else for a little while and see if I can outsmart myself, let alone some poor sap who thinks he's God's gift to the world of espionage, crime or injustice. Yes, I do! I do like being put into another skin, another role. It's a great perk of this job, but, I think I'm getting a trifle old to go jaunting around the world like this and after this tap-dance I'd really love to retire.'

'No lie!' Sam exclaimed. 'Wouldn't you go bonkers with nothing to do? Course, you could always play basketball in the major leagues.' He chuckled.

'Don't be funny, pal. I could!' Old Blue zipped his duffel bag shut. 'Frankly, I'd rather ride the rodeo circuit again but my ribs won't take it anymore, nor my poor head.' He scowled.

'One last thing, boss.' Sam's eyes became serious, all fun and games over. 'The Square Mile City will not rest easy until the scepter and all it represents is returned and the crook caught. If the thief can do this so easily, it makes me shudder to think what else he and his cohorts could do to bring the British system down.' Sam shook his head.

'I agree, sport. I hope that internal grumblings of a few can't be fanned into negative attitudes throughout the country. I believe the British are a loyal people to their Crown and Parliament. This symbolic taunt was aimed at their very way of life and I don't like it one bit!' Checking his armpit holster, Old Blue finished speaking, picked the duffel bag from the bed and said, 'Come on. Let's get the hell out of here. We've got a great lady to protect and a great people!' and headed toward the door.

'Well Churchill and other greats before him like Walpole, Disraeli, Gladstone and Pitt, saw England's strength in that symbol of sovereignty; and of the scepter they said its radiance was as enduring as their cherished monarchy which fits into a constitutional form of government along with the House of Lords and the House of Commons.'

Sam noticed a red light blinking on the telephone.

'Yes,' said Old Blue. 'They also said that the Imperial State Crown was the symbol of stability, and the Orb, held in the Sovereign's right hand as the ermine cape graced the shoulders signified the monarch who reigns but does not rule. She sits before the House of Lords to address them once a year. She addresses her Lords Temporal, her Lords Spiritual, and Commons; and she speaks words which were written by those voted to rule by the British people who are legislators all.'

Old Blue saw the flashing red light also. Walking away from the door and to the side of the room while Sam ducked well away and to the side in the other direction, Old Blue finished his train of thought while hurriedly pulling a pen of pepper spray from his Harris tweed pocket.

'But the Monarch speaks those words, for she or he is England's voice,' he finished, while hopping deftly over the bed to find shelter.

'Yes, boss!' Sam whispered, 'and the *people* made the Crown Head just that so let's help them keep it that way! Who do you suppose is out in the hall?'

'Hell if I know, but I don't aim to go out there to see. Get down. I like playing pin the tail on the donkey, but not if I'm the donkey who gets poked full of holes.'

He fell on his stomach between the beds, facing the hall door. Sam chose to duck into the open closet panel and silently pulled it shut, getting a truncheon out from under his blue suit jacket.

'Makes a good surprise on the back of the head for unwanted guests in a nice, quiet hotel,' he grinned.

A rap came at the door.

'What's the password?'

'Go roast a turkey,' a Marlene Dietrich voice chuckled in reply followed by eight taps on the door which were syncopated exactly as the first notes of the song, 'Deck the Halls with Boughs of Holly'.

Old Blue picked up the phone and asked, 'Orange?'

'Yes sir,' the desk clerk answered.

'Let her in,' Old Blue ordered.

The lock on the door opened and the sardonic lady walked in.

'What the deuce are you doing here?' Old Blue asked, rising from the floor and straightening his jacket. 'I don't mean to be a rude son of a gun, but we have to boogie out of here.'

'I'm glad you said "we",' she replied. 'I'm ready to go.'

'Go where?'

'To find the thief.'

'What thief?' Old Blue bored holes into her shaded eyes.

'Don't tell me you don't know about the scepter?' she asked.

'I don't know that I do. What are you talking about?' Old Blue craftily asked.

'For a man about town, you certainly must know more than you're letting on.' She fished a tube of lipstick out of her huge black purse, opened it and ran orange color over a petulant bottom lip.

'Look, sweetheart,' Old Blue came alongside, encircling her little waist with one strong but tender arm, 'I have to leave. Please excuse me and as soon as I get back we'll pick up where we left off this morning. You know how my job is.' He kissed her on the temple.

'I want to go along,' she pouted. 'You know that I am the best partner you have. I can do things which you can't.'

'Please, Orange. Let's not argue the point. Yes, you are an ace, but this time I can't have a lady along and I can offer no explanations, so let's part on good terms. I won't be mad at you for inviting yourself, and don't you be crazy and riled because I'm not accepting your offer to accompany me.' He grinned and patted her derrière.

'Don't patronize me!' She swatted the hand that had caressed.

'I do have something for you from the powers that be, my willful pet,' he said pulling an envelope from his left breast pocket. 'I think that someone is waiting for you at the remains of the Roman Temple of Mithras nestled under London wall, at least hypothetically speaking.' He handed her a blue envelope sprinkled with stars.

She opened it. A slow grin spread across her face, making a tempting orange slash, good-looking enough to sample with a kiss, so Old Blue did.

'Okay, you win.' She smiled and sauntered without a backward glance from the room, closing the door softly behind her.

'What a weird duck... but then I like weird ducks,' Old Blue said to Sam as the latter came out of the closet, tucking the billy club back into his belt under the vest and jacket of his suit.

'Guess we need to go out the back way, Captain,' Sam suggested.

'You're right, let's "gick outa hyea" as my kid bro used to say. We're late.' Old Blue looked one last time around the room, pulled his travelling bag from under the bed, and left the room with Sam hot on his heels.

'What was that all about?' Sam wanted to know, 'and where in the h-e-double-toothpicks did you send her?'

'I sent her to no one at a destination she will need to look up, and will not find in our guide reference. So she'll get ticked off, call her Wise One and be told that she will just have to go to the library tomorrow to find out for herself. We planned it. We all knew that she would come asking, and this is one time I don't want a woman along.'

How did she know that we were leaving... and about the scepter? he silently wondered.

The men slipped into Knightsbridge Underground and caught the Piccadilly Line to Heathrow, quite aware that representatives of opposing forces probably were slinking about in the night, looking for the three Americans who were greatly feared by their own elite, and by leaders themselves; for three hostile heads of state had met Old Blue and his hard brown eyes had reflected the absolute savagery in their own. Of Rick, there had been speculation. His amethystine-eyed good nature belied any malice within. They couldn't figure him out. And Sam? Well, everyone knew he was the reincarnation of Walt Disney's Goofy. Why anyone would want him on their team, no one in the hot beds of espionage ever knew and that misconception tickled Old Blue no end!

No one knew what to think about Orange, other than to wonder whether the strange being was male or female. A few knew the difference.

Meanwhile, across town, Raoul DeSilva was tucking a golden silk shirt into the waistband of deep brown slacks. Slipping into a matching taupe vest and jacket, he stuffed his pockets with keys, a worry stone, and into the hip pocket went a fine cotton handkerchief monogrammed in gold and brown silk thread.

The telephone sounded.

'Hello.' A statement, rather than a question of the word, emitted from a habitually low-toned voice as Raoul scowled at being detained.

Eventually Raoul said, 'But sir. The quality of the stones must be ascertained. I already have an estimate as to their value.'

He listened for a space of time.

'I don't care that much about the metal. Do with it what you will... just make sure that I get its fair value.'

He listened more.

'Hang in a museum? It's far too insignificant! No one will even notice!' He laughed with derision.

'The devil you say!' His temper boiled, causing black eyes to flash from deep within.

'Well, I don't give a damn. I'll see you in a few hours.' He ran impatient fingers through his hair. 'And take your pills!'

Dropping the receiver into the cradle, a slim case was pulled from under the bed, which matched the fabric, color and elegance of his brown suit. It even had golden silk piping on either side of the elongated zipper with matching shoulder straps and handle.

'Quite a dandy, ain't he,' one of the hall cleaners remarked as they observed Raoul departing his room.

'Quite,' the other custodian smirked. 'Wonder what he keeps for trinkets in them thar rooms, o' 'is!'

'Let's have a look-see when Lolly goes in to change 'is bed linen.'

'Aye.'

Two tooth-gapped grins helped make light work of it as carpet sweepers hummed hotel monograms into blurs of activity.

'Damn fools. Always leavin' val'ables aroun... that's yer men fer ya.' The shorter man scratched an itch behind one knee.

'Yeah. And, the lieedees think tha'r so durn clever, and hides 'em in the first place a fun-lovin' man would look!' He laughed raucously.

'In between their lovely undies in de drawers!' both men chorused, smacking each other on the back in gleeful anticipation.

Rubbing his uniformed elbow, the taller man asked, 'I wonder w'oo thet birdy is w'oo let's 'erself inter 'is room now 'n agin?' Shaking his head, he kept on sweeping the carpet. 'She's got the ugliest hair I ever seed!'

Ned was busily arguing with his old uncle over the telephone. Jill was brushing her hair, getting ready for a nap. The River Thames outside their ornate window was flowing along as ever she had done for centuries untold.

Ned was obviously irritated. Jill was obviously full of peace. The River Thames was obviously full of energy and intriguing secrets, age-old and otherwise, and one of the latter, a small boat, was slipping along as if on greased lightning in and out of shadows caused by tall buildings, street lamps, bridge lights. Not many ships were there for the night.

It's not like it used to be when I was a teenager, thought Jill as she looked out at the river which she loved. It used to be a Mecca of activity. I hate to see it so quiet of trade. She glanced at the skimming boat, shook her head to shake her hair and put the silver-backed brush onto the dressing table. Rising, she walked over to Ned and put her hands lovingly on his shoulders. She couldn't help a little smile. His volcanic nature always was a source of amusement to her. He was all steam and no push when it came to his temper, she thought.

'Where is she, Uncle?' Ned did a slow burn, sputtering into the black phone. He gave Jill an exasperated look.

'You don't know... how should you know? She only adores the ground you walk on... should I say grounds in that medieval castle of yours! You're everything she aspires to be... well-heeled, stable, living in 1482 splendor.'

A shout which even Jill could hear came through the phone, 'It isn't mine!'

Ned chuckled in spite of his anger. 'I'll believe it when I see it on paper. You know that you don't need my advice regarding your finances, your investments, nor your pool of trade. And what do you mean you're not related to the heirs of the Hall?'

Taking Jill's fingers from his right shoulder, he drew the rest of her around the edge of his chair and seated the beautiful lady on his silk-pajamaed knee.

'Let's just say that I'm here to earn a bundle and leave it at that,' he continued to his uncle.

He grinned at Jill.

'No, honored great-uncle. No and if you see that scamp Raoul, tell him to keep a low profile but not so low he can't come up for air now and again.'

Both Jill and Ned heard a shout of laughter that almost blew the latter's eardrum into the Thames. Hurriedly pulling the receiver from his battered ear, Ned gently massaged it. The insane laughter continued pouring like venom out of the telephone.

'Uncle! Uncle! Get a grip!' Ned called loudly into the instrument, holding it away from himself directly in line with his mouth.

'Eh? Eh?' Ned and Jill heard coming faintly through the ebony piece.

'That's right, Sir Gork. Let Anton hang up the telephone now and go have a nightcap. Sweet dreams!'

Ned cradled the phone, and again rubbed his newly tenderized left ear.

'Poor old fusty piece of near insanity. Thank God he has staff who adore him. I couldn't live with the man, nor would I subject you to visiting for more than an hour at a time with me in his actual presence.'

'I wonder what will happen to the old dear,' Jill said. 'He certainly is eccentric, is he not?'

'That's hardly the word,' Ned retorted. 'He seems more and more like what we've heard of Trastamara. You don't think the gene pool has been that strong, do you?'

'I hope not,' Jill wrinkled her brow, 'or one of these days one of us will be murdered in our beds during an overnight stay!'

'How you do run on, dear,' Ned rumpled her shiny hair. 'He'd never do a thing like that.'

'I'm not so sure,' Jill the psychologist quietly concluded.

'Well, I'm sorry that you feel that way, because we're going up there the day after tomorrow to pay a courtesy call. I promised him we would spend at least a fortnight with him.'

'Oh, Ned! How could you?' Jill rose off his knee, trembling at the mere thought. 'Have a little mercy.'

She was obviously upset and Ned tried to calm her with a kiss.

She spoke with her lips touching his, volunteering, 'This is supposed to be a second honeymoon, and men do not conduct business during such.'

'This man does, I'm afraid.' He brushed his lips over the top of her nose. 'You ought to know that by now, Jill. When opportunity knocks, one needs to grab it.' Ned put his hands on her waist.

She pulled away. 'Well, I'd just as soon fly home and visit Pamela and her sisters in Minnesota while you're tending to the needs of your uncle.' She sauntered into the walk-in closet and started selecting an evening dress.

'I thought we were going to take a nap,' Ned said, smiling deliciously.

'We were. But who in their right mind could possibly sleep now? I'm going to the theater for the second curtain and you're welcome to come along.' She pulled a blue velvet from the closet rack, bringing it into the bedroom.

'Okay, dear. We'll go to the theater; but I don't see why you take the old man so seriously. He's crazy as a bedbug and just as harmless. The only area in which he is perfectly logical is when it comes to money and that's what I am going to see him about.' He started unbuttoning his black silk top. 'Someone needs our money and will pay a great deal of interest for the privilege of using it; and we'll settle an old score.'

There were storm clouds in his eyes... and dollar signs.

'Maybe you could twist my arm to go to Lincoln Cathedral while we're in the neighborhood, if you smiled for me,' he added seductively.

She smiled.

Chapter Thirteen

Minnesota, September 1, 1997, 0300 hours, 3 A.M.

A shout of thunder awakened Christiana, making her jump seemingly ten feet. Throwing back the covers and scrambling out of bed, she ran to the French doors, throwing them open to see the carnage outside – a foolish thing to do with lightning striking all around but she didn't care. Driven by grief, still half in her dreams, she was as in a trance. Walking in the windswept rain across the deck, she grasped the oaken railing with both hands to strengthen her stance against the air which was whipping her batiste nightdress into soaked billows behind her body, wrapping the hem around her wet ankles and bare feet. Black tresses flowing and snapping in the wind, the rain pelted her face, neck, arms and body unmercifully. It seemed that all hell and heaven had broken loose in a battle over the injustice of the death of two great humans – Christiana's father and the Princess.

Above the dark, turbulently broiling waters of the lake at the edge of the garden, a huge cottonwood tree growing along the bank gave a shudder. A full half of it was projected over the normally serene lake. It was a massive, full-leafed branch almost the size of the trunk itself. Several boughs grew from it in summertime elegance. The only problem of such unusual beauty was that it seemed supported merely by the magnificent trunk which actually had roots and a tap root penetrating deeply within the earth below, anchors which extended ever farther and farther as the days, months, years rolled by. Guardian of its little realm, the cottonwood had always been.

Christiana, pelted in the face by bullets of wildly driven rain, felt her body being snatched backwards. She grasped the railing more firmly, fascinated by the life and death struggle before her as the massive tree writhed in agony, for the glorious branch suddenly shook violently, ripping downward as if the hand of God tore it from top to bottom. The massive trunk groaned as if alive, straining against the wind and weight of its other half to remain upright, its wildly flailing top resisting being broken so as not to shred into the ground on which it stood.

Christiana watched the tree tremble for another instant as it struggled not to be entirely uprooted. Huge waves, riled by the sudden storm, bit into the soil at the cottonwood's roots, aiding and abetting the gusts of devil wind in trying to tear it to pieces.

She couldn't believe it. Just hours ago the night had been calm, sparkling with moonlight and star formations. Awestricken, she watched the half of the tree toward the lake wrench itself totally free in an ear-splitting shattering of bark and fresh, golden wood as it crashed into the choppy waters below. Christiana watched, expecting the other half of the tree to fall over on top of the rest in the next gust of wind. But the wind suddenly died. In spite of the torrential rains continuing to soak her body, she couldn't stop looking at the poor, noble tree. Half of it was in the calmed waters, branches reached up beautifully from its watery grave, its tangled roots exposed toward its other half still firmly attached deep in the soil where fusion had taken place years earlier as life-giving force had joined the tap root. With a great slash of white inner timber exposed to its very heart, the separated lay mutilated, clinging by the two roots to its upright partner. Battered, the part of the tree which had survived seemed to be sheltering the two exposed roots joined to the fallen half, for some of its foliage had encircled them; the tree suddenly reminiscent of the tragic family in England.

The storm clouds passed, dawn was tentatively peeping over the freshly washed eastern horizon, pale, as if it too had been scared half out of its wits. Christiana suddenly felt tired, turned and splish-splashed over the puddled deck floor back into the house. Dashing into the bathroom, she took a hot shower to kill a chill. Fragrantly clean from soaps, shampoos and oils, she shimmied into a dry nightie, and hopped back into bed to wait for the seven o'clock morning news.

Dozing off, the dream from which she had been awakened stealthily returned as if on cat's paws, holding her spellbound and grieving in its grasp once more. Deeper and deeper she fell asleep.

A cool breeze stirred the sheers, gently bringing the scent of fresh land-water and sweet, wet petunias across her face. Freshly mown hay was embodied in the fragrance; and she loved it fiercely. It made her feel as if she was at the home of her formative years where those leaders of whom she had been dreaming were loved, revered and held up to her as God's gift. She loved her wonderful country of birth, but she also loved the stories her grandmother told of that distant land of her dreams, England. For it was there that the first Christiana had been born centuries ago. Somehow, the spirit of that faraway past, that first transplanted love and longing for home, had come to the fore in this progeny's genes. It was coursing through her being, causing a lifelong restlessness to find the green island of kings and queens, vassals and serfs, lands and seas, religions and ideals that finally were forged through blood and blade, conscience and heart, greed and beneficence, justice and tyranny into its present judicious, gracious civilization.

Deep sleep overtook the American, exhausted as she was from the storm.

Suddenly, Christiana's princely vision was once more at her side, and she was saying in tears, 'To a child, the death of a loving parent is grievous indeed. Little Elizabeth Stuart was hugged goodbye in her father's arms, probably knowing that perhaps history would forever dub him as evil, this man whom she had known only as kind, honest and gentle. He was her father! They were very close in heart and now your young suffer!'

Loving one's father welled within the sleeper's heart.

Struggling to talk to the Dream Prince, Christiana couldn't make sounds, but as if by magic he caught the story of young Princess Elizabeth Stuart, born December 28, 1635, in the very palace in which he now lived; and whom Queen Victoria lovingly honored in 1856 by erecting a fitting monument to replace a mere stone simply inscribed, 'E.S.'. Inadequate, that field rock, because the thirteen-year-old's spirit had automatically grasped the meaning of the word 'majesty' long before she was laid to rest on the Isle of Wight in St. Thomas Church at Newport.

Separation. Children from parent, parents from each other, a branch from the tree, had probably been on Queen Victoria's mind.

Love of her own father welled within the sleeper's heart, bringing his words to mind: 'You talk so frequently of the Prince, maybe you'll meet him someday.'

Suddenly, the Dream Prince wasn't with Christiana, but surrounded by thoughtful, caring masses who first had always loved him ever since he was born; and then a bride appeared by his side, who by association with him had been elevated into prominence where the same masses could and did partake of her sweet caring and goodness; and last, but by no means least, Christiana saw the populace lovingly embrace the Royal couple's offspring.

Then, as dreams go, the word 'Gotterdammerung' dusk of the gods, sprinkled itself in sparkling gold over the Royal's heads.

The populace groaned, 'No!' They turned anxiously toward the Royal children's father, watching and listening intently.

First they saw him dare to be himself as a truly grieving, former husband of his young ones' deceased mother, whom he was properly laying to rest midst splendid proceedings.

Secondly was seen the sensitive, deep love he bore their issue.

Thirdly, although the masses were a bit dubious, but politely contemplative while willing to listen, Christiana saw the Dream Prince ask his people to help bring the regal past, 'this realm', into the complicated present by the continuation of actively interchanging ideas with the Crown through their elected representatives in Parliament and the House of Lords. Parliamentarian representation for all gladdened his heart, and the masses caught the Prince's vision of a blending of two worlds – the ancient with the modern – whilst the Crown continued to act as guardian over the freedoms the country enjoyed as ever it had via centuries of evolvement with that august body.

In the Prince's heart was the dream to be a servant of the people whom he had been born to serve, by God's grace. He wanted to see an ever-expanding field of opportunity for them coupled with solid futures where every person could fulfill their dreams of success; kindness to one another, love for God, sovereign, country and government, family and neighbor.

Christiana felt better in her sleep. She could see the land

musing over how truly nice and refreshing, how unique it was to be British! Everyone was proud deep inside of having retained their British individuality, which had kept them from being swallowed into a melting pot of Europeans where loss of their beautiful, polite culture would be imminent. Diverse? Yes but British to the core which meant, amongst other things, being doggedly chivalrous and thoughtful of others even in the worst of times and honest not to mention being unwaveringly brave.

As dreams go, Christiana could see a pleasant wind of new ideas fanning over the monarchy, government and people, heavy with seeds labeled 'change'.

Striding on these winds came not only the Prince, but an older man, glowing with health and happiness, as pink of cheek and kind of hazel eye as ever he had been before his demise. The sun shining on his golden, wavy hair and his tall, mild self bespoke the joy which had filled every day of his presence upon God's green earth as steward; protecting it from certain chemicals which adulterated grains and vegetables, burned the soil, ran off into streams, lakes and aquifers below, polluting humanity's drinking source.

He and the blue-eyed Dream Prince walked onto center stage of the dream – a wheat field over which they were rejoicing. The Prince was listening to every silent word the elder was saying. They understood one another's passion.

'Why, Daddy!' Christiana exclaimed… but he did not hear her. 'They are of one mind. What is Daddy explaining to him?'

The field in which they were was ripened unto harvest. It was surrounded by ponds, lakes, and wild verdure growing in neat profusion around the fields and rolling meadows, sheltering little creatures in the forests through which clear, clean streams and rivers meandered to the sea.

The elder was explaining the majesty of the earth to one who understood.

Suddenly, with gentle grace and enthusiasm, her father broke his stride, leaned forward and gently took a few heads of the grain into his squarish, capable hands. Breaking off the stems, he rolled the golden heads between his palms; then he blew gently into the arrangement. The chaff flew away, leaving the clean, honey-colored harvest. Her father briefly clasped the younger man warmly on the shoulder, and then took the youth's right hand, palm up, and poured the bountiful fully developed seeds from his own grasp into that of the other.

'Wisdom shared,' Christiana whispered aloud in her sleep; for her father had been ahead of his time, having pursued successfully the preservation of the earth through natural methods of farming and protecting the eco-balance of the land surrounding his thousands of acres. At first he had good-naturedly absorbed only laughter from his world at large; but by the time he died, he had been given accolades by universities, major newspapers and magazines, and the worlds of agriculture and earth preservation.

Grinning at the Dream Prince, her father said, 'The earth blesses those who carefully tend her.' As if both understood a secret between them he continued, 'Soil is a living thing and must be treated that way.' Somehow the Prince knew that the elder had invented new methods of tillage which included discarding invasive deep plowing of the lovely soil, contour plowing and planting, and had incorporated Torah Old Testament methods of rotating crops and resting the fields every seven years by returning them to pasture lands or alfalfa and clover meadows. Even by allowing thistles and ragweed to remain if they happened to suddenly infest a plot of ground, porosity was restored to the soil via the weedy root systems. Once the refiberization and natural chemical balance was regained, the thistles would disappear entirely, proving that God wasn't as dumb as some farmers thought when He decided to create the common lavender-burred thistle to live together with grass.

'Grass can maintain meadows as long as its roots don't become compacted by soil. When the grass becomes compacted, along come the thistles and ragweed, their strong root systems aerating the soil, freeing the grass roots until a natural balance is restored. The thistles and weeds then die because they've done their job for their compatriot grass,' her dad explained to his young, dream companion.

Smiling, her father said to the young English Crown Prince, 'An inborn love for natural methods of tending the earth, and wisdom to seek those methods in order to apply them, is quintessential majesty from the greatest King of all – the God of heaven and earth.'

Together they said, 'The earth is the Lord's and the fullness thereof.'

They clasped hands in joy, the elder then complimenting that Prince Charles had one interest in particular which had been reported in the United States for years. Sophisticates of the world had laughed for years over such wisdom as being quite ridiculous, but the mild Mr. Deerfield had prayed daily for the Prince that God would strengthen resolve in the face of adversity regarding that all important endeavor of cleaning up the green island's environment with natural methods and means to restore its eco-balance.

Christiana awakened and lay in bed remembering. Summertime orioles were singing their silvery notes from deep within orange and black plumage. The rustling green of their tree outside an open window perfumed the warm, soft air as it gently flowed over her drowsy face. Noticing the little nest hanging like a purse near the birds, she could again hear her father say, 'In time, the Prince's example of restoring Britain's ecology in relation to farming will make other world leaders sit up and take notice, for the day may come when each country will have to produce enough food for themselves. Through this wise example, God is making sure that foods containing adequate nutrition, without depletion of their farmlands while growing it, will enrich every household's table.'

Her father had then pointed out the deadly Dust Bowl experience of mid-America in the 1920s, which he felt had been brought on by the overzealous use of chemical fertilizers during years of favorable precipitation in the area. When drought came along, as it sometimes will, the winds were able to completely erode the topsoil because the native root system of the region's natural vegetation had not only been plowed out by deep-digging, but also burned out unknowingly by the new chemical fertilizers which had been producing such bumper crops.

'My father bought a bag of the stuff,' Mr. Deerfield had laughed, 'and as he was pouring it into the duster, a bit got onto his denim coveralls. By suppertime, there were holes replacing the dust. He declared that if chemical "nutrients" could do that to his pants, what in the world would it do to the soil, and to the people who ate the food the soil produced. He never touched it again because he felt that God held us responsible for the quality of our products in relation to humanity's health.'

Christiana had felt pride in her unknown grandfather, who had died before she was born.

'I wish every food producer was as conscientious as he was and now as you are. I'm proud of you, Daddy. In spite of having sworn off man-made inducements, your crops yield more bushels per acre than most in the state!' She had laughed, for it was a fine joke on those who used to poke fun at her father's methods. Christiana was keenly interested in her dad's work.

'Now, Chrissy,' her father had rejoined, 'stay humble. God it is who has blessed us with common sense. It isn't our own attribute and you must always remember that.'

'From whence comes the grace and strength to chuckle when neighbors ridicule?' She had looked admiringly at her handsome father. 'I'm afraid that I'd rather box their noses than be as gracious as you've been.'

'I'm afraid you would, my little firebird. But,' he had laughed, 'you mustn't get your dander up, darling. Every time a person loses temper, a day's quota of vitamin C is expended, you know.' He had patted her on the back good-naturedly.

They had been walking the fence, checking it to make certain that slough grasses or broken limbs from surrounding Dutch elms, red oaks, tamarack, poplar, and towering evergreen trees had not been tossed upon the electric wire during a brief storm that had blown up hurriedly that afternoon.

A quick storm, followed by sunshine which dazzled the eyes as it peeped through droplets of rain left on green grass, purple violets with yellow centers and green leaves shining translucently, had made the fence-walking a treat; even though swimming gear would have made more sensible attire than the jeans they worked in.

'Look at the sky, Daddy. So majestic, the towering clouds to the south-west, they remind me of cathedral domes, and the clear blue skies above are like naves soaring above an altar.'

He jerked a grass encumbered wire up and away from a broken tree limb that straddled the fence; his leather gloves turning dark where moisture started to soak through. 'I can appreciate your love of the great outdoors. You must take after your father!' he had laughed, flashing a big grin.

Christiana loved her father's even, white teeth, square jaw, and ruddy cheeks. He was all muscle in a subtle way, his lean frame not given to bulges.

'Daddy, did you know that Prince Charles is an architect?'

'Is that right!' her dad exclaimed. 'How fitting. He is inspired by two ennobled interests. Lucky England. Some day he will be their wise King. Lucky Commonwealth too, including our Canadian neighbors two hundred miles to the north. You talk so frequently of the Prince, maybe you'll meet him some day.'

Christiana blushed and said, 'Fat chance.'

Her father merely smiled knowingly.

That day had transpired long ago. Later, just before her dad died, they had discussed findings of the Royal Botanic Gardens in Kew and Edinburgh, patronized by the Duke of Edinburgh and his eldest son; the Smithsonian and other environmental groups. Of prime interest was the discovery that one out of every eight known plant species on earth was threatened with extinction meaning that there were fewer than ten thousand individual plants of each threatened species left, less than one hundred locations of the same remaining upon the entire globe.

Christiana had fallen asleep again. Seeds of change, which had not yet been seen, started sprouting one by one in the fields of her dream as she surveyed the Sceptred Isle's antiquities dotting the landscape wherever one chose to look. Strange as it seemed for such a tiny mass of land, another 'seed of change' evolved with the British becoming scientific leaders of mass food production in space. Shortage of acreage notwithstanding, they were finding an alternative to feed their expanding populace and that of the world.

Another seed flowered. Seeds of psycho-politics for the forces of justice, and goodness round the world, were springing from the great universities such as Oxford and Cambridge. Why shouldn't they? she thought in her dream state. For many years Marxism and Bolshevism incorporated negative psycho-politics elsewhere in order to settle a yoke of disrespect for all freedom's heroes around democracy's neck.

'Now let's give the world a dose of positive conditioning,' someone whispered in her ear.

The Dream Prince reappeared. In him were embodied the sleeper's admiration of the courage of the Scots, the endurance of the Welsh, the pride of the Irish, the remarkable forbearance, civility and tenacity of the English and their extended British society. The superior education of the small island's people down through the centuries of this last millennium at such prestigious colleges as were to be found in Oxford and Cambridge, was proclaimed by a golden banner high over his head.

As if a video were unfolding pictures before her, she saw herself overcome the revulsion she had initially felt regarding the country's appallingly fierce beginnings which the Crown Prince represented; for from such beginnings one and all had been hewn, including herself and her own.

In Christiana's sleep, she realized that had George Washington, the first President of the United States of America, said 'yes' to the victorious, colonial troops who insisted that he be crowned King of the new world, she too would be living under a monarchy, a constitutional version similar to what was now embraced in her yearned-for England and the British Isles. Knowing the good, common sense of the American majority, she knew it would be as exemplary as the current arrangement in the land of her dreams. Maybe common sense would rule and there would be no more wars.

In her dream, she realized all these things and turning to the Dream Prince who was at her side asked, 'Why must men fight, breaking the hearts of the women and children who love them?'

Somber green eyes turned to the blue. 'Our own history makes one realize that American forefathers indulged in the same vicious cycle when need and ambition blew its clarion call.'

'It would be preferable if men didn't relish fighting, wouldn't it? Unfortunately, except in extremely civilized families, it seems that they still do.'

The vision said, 'Such behavior in our two countries and the world seems unenlightened and archaic.'

Looking up at the apparition she continued, 'Those who participate with violence in the UVF, IRA, UDA, even Sinn Fein in Ireland and the people in our United States who think that the words "freedom, liberty and justice for all" mean free license in all things, even to the disregarding of their fellow man's right to life, frighten me. In one's pursuit of happiness, others' civil liberties shouldn't be violently nor diplomatically squelched. Our prisons and jails are overflowing, and I often wonder if it is because of a misunderstanding of the word "freedom". An unwillingness to work for what one wants doesn't justify stealing, for instance.' She sighed.

As dreams go, they both thought of the founding fathers of the world's great religions... all were men of peace.

'Has everyone forgotten one teacher's mother who forgave the murderers of her son? Have all forgotten that His name was Prince of Peace?' Christiana asked the Prince. 'And as far as anyone knows, neither His Father nor He has ever changed it.' She shook her head. 'Even if one isn't "Christian" but embraces Islam, Buddhism, or one of the other great religions of the world, were not the founding fathers of those religions, prophets of peace as well? So, why is everyone fighting in their names?' Tears spilled. 'Christ said to turn the other cheek.'

'Love without forgiveness, and forgiveness without love are incomplete emotions... worthless,' the Dream Prince smiled. 'Governments without the discipline of love, justice and mercy are the same. Their days are numbered.'

'Is that why you care for your nation's underprivileged youth by providing resources to start businesses of their own and is that the reason you support the free educational system for anyone who wants to go to college – providing they study diligently?' Christiana asked.

The Dream Prince smiled, vanishing to do more good upon the winds of change.

Chapter Fourteen

London, September 2, 1997

A limousine pulled up outside the Mansion House in London. The door was opened by the chauffeur and a dark-headed man emerged, pulling a long black case from the seat behind him. Adjusting a briefcase in his other hand, he walked into the building. The limo drove off.

Joe Bly was on the beat, having joined the rest of the force in doing double shifts because of the press of people come to be near the comfort of their government figureheads. Noticing the visitor arriving at the Lord Mayor's, he took mental note of the car tags, the oblong, skinny case and attaché case the sophisticated man was carrying above ostrich shoes.

True, the paste and gold scepter from the Bahamian Crown Jewel display was safely ensconced in a new glass case at the Tower of London, but he could not get the theft off his mind. Even when he saw a tennis racket being carried by someone, he double-checked the long, narrow handle. He mourned the dazzling symbol's loss no end.

The three American cavaliers had zoomed to the Middle East and back in time for the duties which had been assigned them in London for the first days of September. Scar-P had been one of the team in and around St. James Palace and on the Mall. As always, they all got on superbly together. It was as if each anticipated one another's thoughts before they were fully formed. The only one who seemed to notice anything odd about Scar-P was a very jealous Old Blue. Old Blue wasn't jealous over the quality of work Scar-P was performing, excellent as it was, but over the attentions the tall, skinny blond was receiving from Orange. OB couldn't exactly put his finger on what was irritating him about them, but his instincts were telling tales, which he felt were better left unthought. It just seemed that after seeing Scar-P light Orange's cigarette cabside, neither one of them were ever where they were needed when an emergency arose.

'It's just my imagination, I suppose. I'm just too edgy since getting back from Israel. I could have gone alone and saved wear and tear on Sam and Rick.' He lit his everlasting cigarette. 'Course, if everything hadn't gone according to Hoyle, they would have gotten my skinny backside out of a jam.' He blew smoke through his nose like an old bull.

The agent was sitting on the train en route to Hampton Court Palace to chase a lead, minus his golden-haired buddy from Arizona as a call had come in for Rick to pop down to Rye late the afternoon before, something to do with the Hope Diamond theft in Washington. What the two could possibly have in common was a matter of concern to everyone, but Old Blue thought it would be discovered that both incidents were unrelated. Being a little superstitious, he thought it might be good if the Hope Diamond was returned and then given back to India where the spooky thing belonged, since bad luck seemed to have plagued most who had owned it.

Reflecting on the orders, which he had tucked into the metal cabinet of his mind, Old Blue had continued the business of the next morning, which was to hightail it to Hampton Court before leaving for Minneapolis. Another lead had come in regarding the miniature, but Old Blue had dismissed it as being unimportant – it being that Old Joe, the policeman, had seen a suspicious piece of elongated, narrow luggage being withdrawn from a black limo in front of Mansion House in the city. Listening to the description of the person carrying it, Old Blue felt that the guy in the ostrich leather shoes could be none other than his own dear buddy from Oxford days, doing business of a legitimate nature or visiting the Lord Mayor of London. 'After all, he is a representative to the United Nations from a Middle Eastern country. Just because jewels were stolen doesn't mean that the fellow was running around being a thief. The long bag probably held nothing more sinister than the guy's favorite golf chipper. He was always landing balls in sand traps and tall weeds, good at hitting the ball into very unlikely spots, but then so was I!' OB thought aloud.

He should stick to basketball. He's even better than I at that game, Old Blue fondly remembered. Besides, he would then escape being thought of as a hit man around town or a thief by not having to carry his precious club. OB laughed at his next thought; We don't need chippers when visiting the UK. We need swim suits and scuba gear. Our shots are so wild and far-flung, the balls sail clear into the English Channel! Laughing aloud caused the other train passengers to look at him as if they wanted to call attendants bearing straightjackets.

'Pardon me,' Old Blue said, 'a thought tickled me. Oh. Here we are at Hampton Court. I beg your pardon.' So saying, he rose and stepped over the legs of the man who was sitting next to him. The man nodded and scrunched his legs back and to the side to help Old Blue's long limbs and raincoat become disentangled.

The covert agent got off the train adjacent to the ancient stone bridge which connected that side of the Thames to Hampton Court Palace. He didn't cross the bridge, choosing to walk down the undeveloped side of the river first midst the greenest grass he had ever seen and trees sporting full-blown leaves of late summer.

'My, but Old Henry VIII and his second queen Anne Bollun turned Boleyn, had a beautiful setting in which to dally… not to mention King William III and Queen Mary a couple of hundred years later. The Thames forms a wishbone right here. Mighty pretty, if I must say so myself.' He looked appreciatively across the broad river, which had not retained its blueness but was a leaden gray. 'Can't wait to see Christopher Wren's additions to Wolsey's original part of the palace.'

Looking across the river at the beautiful grounds he muttered, 'A guy could still fall in love with a young lovely who happened to be taking the sun alone in one of its gardens. I hear Anne Boleyn was quite fetching in yellow the day Henry spotted her there while visiting the Wolseys.'

Getting a move on, Old Blue started to walk, searching the ground and river bank. Suddenly he leaned over and fished a square of white, fine linen from the Thames with a twig. Examining it, 'RdS' announced itself, embroidered beautifully in a corner. Poking the soggy handkerchief into a little plastic bag, which he had kept in his pocket for just such surprises, he retraced his steps back to Hampton Court train station where a cup of black coffee took the chill out of his bones. As he sipped, thoughts of Rick in Rye went through his mind, and he wondered if he was coming up as empty-handed regarding clues as to the infamous thief as he himself had done so far that day.

'Well, I need to get across the bridge to the Palace and see the gallery of paintings. If my hunch is correct, I should find the identity of our little mystery lady from the miniature. She should be hanging, painted in regal splendor, in the Renaissance Picture Gallery in the Wolsey Rooms.' He smiled at the clerk who thought OB had addressed him.

Off OB went at a brisk pace across the bridge to Hampton Court Palace, which sat beckoningly on the opposite bank of the river as ever it had in 1525, growing even more splendid under Christopher Wren's brilliant architectural and design genius in 1702. Splendid, ancient, proud, the palace warmed itself in the afternoon sunshine like a russet and tan lion sleeping midst manicured gardens, splendid bow and arrow-yielding yews of days gone by, with flowers of every description. An unusual gift of Wolsey to King Henry VIII, a bronze astronomical clock worked its magic beneath the heavens yet another day.

'What a magnificent present that clock was,' Old Blue said to one of the liveried gatekeepers with a tilt of his curly head toward the huge bronze contraption in Clock Court. Seeing the uniformed gentleman, Old Blue wondered how Sam and Scar-P were getting along at St. James Palace, and where Orange had gone. He had called her that morning to see if she'd like to go on the little outing to the Palace, but she had been gone virtually all day.

That woman! he laughed. What a trip!

Oh well. He could get along without her. He prided himself on being able to squelch sentimental longings.

Applying himself to a different type of pleasure which never ceased to satisfy him, he paid for a ticket and went inside the Palace to visit the exquisitely crafted and embellished Chapel Royal where King Henry VIII had worshipped through the years, and which still looked as splendid as it had the day he, Henry, had stood by Jane Seymour's side as an ardent bridegroom. Beneath its blue, star-spangled ceiling and golden ribs which gracefully ended in pendant-like epis, Tudor works of craftsmanship enriched with golden figurines depicting Henry's symbolic heraldry, Old Blue's breath was literally taken away to see its gold-leafed elegance. Painstakingly painted, the shining golden stars twinkled midst the jewel colors wrought by patient men who had 'embroidered' the baroque ribs. Beneath such concave splendor, the present Queen's own Bishop, dressed in crimson robes, was gently addressing a group of eight to ten year olds from a public school. The children dressed in impeccable uniforms of plaid skirts or slacks with matching trim on their solid, deep-blue jackets were heartily enjoying his humor and gentle wisdom mingled with the history lesson which was being given. Old Blue smiled, for it was as if he were partaking of a bit of history in the making.

Walking up the steps to the balcony at the back of the tiny chapel, his appreciation of excellent finish work was underscored in his mind, for he himself did such things with floors, ceilings, cabinets as a form of relaxation. He was always inspired by the craftsmanship in such places as this, which had been made centuries ago. Spying Old Henry's massive chair hidden behind thick, heavy red tapestries where the King had worshipped unseen after exhausting nights of partying, legislating, studying and what-have-you, the agent chuckled.

'The old boy tended to two things at once. Deeply religious having been groomed for the priesthood during his young life, he also was adamant regarding keeping his head on his shoulders; signing documents and such by being accessible for any slight wind of governmental intrigue and change, was he not?' he asked another visitor standing by his side.

'Yes,' the tourist answered thoughtfully.

'And,' Old Blue continued, 'maybe if he had partied too hard the night before, he could catch a nap back here on his way to bed. His private hall to the bedrooms is right through the door opposite.'

'Makes me shudder,' replied the tourist's wife, 'to think of Catherine Howard's dash down that very hall six feet away, to pound on the door of his bedchamber the night before she was beheaded. How did she escape her guards? And to think he even heard her, and thought it was a bad dream! I think it eventually drove him mad. He was crazy about her you know and the discovery of her bigamy and betrayal was too great for a middle-aged man, apparently. He would have killed her on the spot had not the Privy Council held him and taken the sword he grabbed.'

'Was she there... in the same room with the Privy Council when they reported her treasonable actions to King Henry?' Old Blue asked.

'No,' the visitor replied. 'But he was going to chase out into the hall to her private apartments to slay her with the sword in hand, you know, he exploded into such a jealous rage. His love for her, combined with the charges the Privy Council laid at her door with accompanying proof, proved to be too much for him.'

'So he had her beheaded instead.' Old Blue rubbed his neck without thinking.

'Those were perilous times.' The couple turned to go.

'Yes... equal to the Bolshevik Revolution my grandfather and family escaped. They were eventually hidden in an attic in Minneapolis in the States.' He stopped short of giving his lineage. He didn't like it to be known. He valued his own neck for it was kept on, so to speak, by being secretive about such matters.

'They say that Catherine's ghost calls to Henry in this hall to this very day... terrified, sobbing loudly. Glad I don't work here,' the woman smiled back at Old Blue as she and her husband bid him adieu.

Old Blue advanced to the Wolsey Rooms and Renaissance Picture Gallery, bent on his mission. The small Tudor rooms were handsomely preserved, and he could imagine Wolsey living quietly in them with his family. The linen fold panels of the oak doors caught his attention as well as the life-sized original oils of such greats as the Princess of Castile who later became Queen through the wise and fierce protection of that heritage by her father, John of Gaunt, Second Duke of Lancaster, the Titular King of Castile, toward the end of the fourteenth century.

'There she is! The lady in the miniature!' Old Blue exclaimed. 'It's none other than Costanza and John's daughter, Catherine!'

OB jotted particulars in his mind regarding the history of the painting, and scurried down the narrow, circular staircase which led out to the exit. Deciding to leave by the East Front of

Hampton Court Palace, he first stopped by the men's room to spruce up a bit and wash his hands which felt grubby after the last few hours work. Rubbing soap into the grooves of his sinewy hands and fingers, he said to the gentleman next to him, 'The splendid ceiling and stained glass windows in the Great Hall have King Henry and Jane Seymour's entwined monograms in them. It must be an indication of his respect and love for that quietly loving and pious wife who replaced the decapitated Catherine Howard to whom she had been appointed Lady in Waiting from 1540–1542, the duration of the union.'

'Yes, I suppose so,' the dignified man replied, 'reportedly, Jane's calm and thoughtful way was soothing to the violently disappointed king. His princesses loved her as well. Too bad she had to die from childbirth complications five months into the marriage on the day of their son Edward's baptism and proclamation as Prince of Wales, heir apparent.'

As the men turned to leave, Old Blue observed, 'That sly creature Catherine Howard, who had been beheaded for adultery, was something else! Can you imagine having the nerve to cuckold the King? Knowing that she was to be wed to the King, the Lady secretly married another prior to the Royal ceremony; and then had the audacity to sweet-talk His unknowing Majesty into appointing her existing husband as Lord of the Royal Bedchamber. The guy even slept at Henry's feet, bathed and dressed him, and knew his most intimate secrets! Then, he'd sneak out after old Henry was snoring and go to Catherine's bed down the hall, spend the night and high-tail it back to crawl into his own bed which was located at the foot of Henry's ornate tester.' Old Blue shook his head in his habitual manner when digesting incredulity.

'No wonder the Royal crib was so soon filled by the sweet offering of yet another wife who was mild in manner and circumspect,' the other man declared as they bid one another farewell.

'Couldn't help but overhear your conversation, mate,' a cockney chap addressed Old Blue.

Old Blue eyed him with his characteristic charm and genuine interest, 'What's that mate?' he mimicked.

'Oh, I was just thinking that the molten, colored glass was as hot and lustily colored as the aging monarch's passion for Jane when it was poured into the forms used for those magnificent windows we see before us here,' the slender East Ender answered. 'All those rich reds, purples, greens and blues were an indication of a king's passion for his new young miss who hopefully would produce a male heir; which he felt (by the way) was his duty to give the country.'

The fellow dug his hands into hip pockets of the Levi's he wore. Grinning at Old Blue, he said, 'You're not too dumb for being a Yank and all. Where you from?' He looked at the American through pale gray eyes, the pupils rimmed with charcoal rings set in clear whites midst almond shaped lids sporting dark brown lashes. The clear look emanated from his good nature and intelligence.

'Oh, I'm from here, there and everywhere, I'm afraid. How about you?' Old Blue asked. 'I really like that jean jacket. Where did you get it, in a shop around here? I left mine at home.'

'And you want to buy one, right, mate? You Americans are made of money, me thinks,' the guy said jokingly.

'Dream on,' Old Blue laughed. 'I wish I were!'

'Actually, my brother sent it to me from Cleveland.'

'Your bro? What's he doing in Cleveland?'

'Ah, he went to America to get rich. He thought the streets were paved with gold, he did. But he found out different.' The guy scratched his fuzzy cheek sporting golden down as fine as on a peach. 'And, about the Great Hall windows – they say it was Wolsey's idea.'

'I see,' Old Blue twinkled. 'Hey buddy, I gotta go. See ya around sometime.' He patted the kid on the shoulder and drew a hasty retreat.

He headed south to walk through the gamekeeper's domain – the deer park and forest. Boggy lowlands rising into fair meadows were full of buff-colored deer. They appeared regally delicate as had the Queens, whose exquisite bone structure and refined features adorned the great Wolsey's home after he presented it to King Henry VIII. Little blue tit birds sang lustily from the grove of youngish trees along the path Old Blue walked. Lush, green grass moistened by a fine mist which had rolled in on low clouds enveloped the keeper's home in a soft, pearly sheen which touched everything near and far, moistening the toes of OB's soft cowboy boots. The herd of small deer lazily watched him move along. Some were lying down, many standing fat and full, fit for a medieval king's crossbow or the first Queen Elizabeth's bow and arrows. He could understand Henry's daughter, Elizabeth's passion for riding in this particular forest every day, whether she hunted or not. It was a beautiful, refreshing place.

'Why, when one sees the sky and boundless natural landscape, is one's mind so uplifted?' Old Blue asked aloud of a couple of blackbirds eyeing him distrustfully from a lone oak near the west end of the park. 'When I'm outdoors in a natural setting, every ounce of depression and negativity flies away. Geez! I'd love to go home to my own spread... a ride over the endless hills would be welcome about now. Things are too sad around here for me. I'm getting sick of idiots who want to ruin everyone's happiness. Durn the man who stole the scepter! Of course he will get caught. He must want to be caught!'

He thought over the clues, which had been left behind at the Tower. Nothing, absolutely nothing, except that little miniature. Now, since observing the paintings in Hampton Court Palace, he knew exactly who the lovely little lady was.

'I knew it! I knew it!' he said aloud with a chuckle. Blowing smoke rings into the crisp English air as he gained the road in an adjacent park which led to Hampton Station at the other end of town, he gleefully looked at the clouds scattered like puffs of white fleece here and there. Suddenly he laughed boisterously right out loud. He always enjoyed a good joke. He wondered how Rick was coming along in Rye, and what further reason for such a heist he would find. His thoughts rambled from point to point aloud:

'Someone is fighting mad that they aren't sporting the name, title and lands of the Duke of Lancaster. I wonder if my friend in the Middle East is playing upon that anger; or if indeed, someone's progeny is cashing in on a little of what they think is rightfully theirs. Course, there is a third possibility. Maybe actual Royal houses have nothing to do with it, defunct or otherwise.

Maybe some revolutionary who wants to turn this into another little United States minus nobility and monarchy is using ancient history to fan the flames of a very small minority into a virtual bonfire while the populace is angered and bereaved over the tragic loss of their favorite Royal. Let's face it. In the people's hearts, the lady was Royalty, mother of two princes; one to be crowned King after his papa.' He blew more smoke into the country air. 'The populace's anger and hurt at losing their Princess can be played upon by a clever anarchist and directed against the very ones whom they want to see as their future kings. Whether the British know it today or not, they love their Queen, upset though they may be.'

Suddenly, he grinned again. 'I bet if the chips were down tonight, and bombers flew over London, there wouldn't be a professional, a noble, a farmer, an architect, a clothier, a warehouse foreman, a laborer who wouldn't answer the Queen's summons if she went over the airwaves to back up the Parliament's call to arms.' He punched the air in glee. 'This island is a family. Family members get mad at each other. But when a bully comes along, they all rally around Mom and Dad!'

Finally gaining Hampton station, he happily climbed on board and found a seat in the coach. A hankering to see those good old boys and gals who would not hesitate to answer their Sovereign's call to protect the princes' future filled his breast. He looked around at the white-collar workers; the blue-collar, tiredly sitting with evening papers in hand. Ladies were dabbing at their eyes, reading of the sadness which gripped their country. Suddenly Old Blue felt so proud and in love with the whole car full of people, he wanted to stand up and hug them all whether they thought him crazy or not.

'You'll see her little one ascend the throne... oh, yes you will. That will be your legacy to her, even as he is her legacy to you. She lives in him and in his little brother... and even in Prince Charles' heart as the good mother she was.' He patted the hand of the startled little English matron sitting beside him, her nose suddenly needing delicate dabbings from a handkerchief as Old Blue nodded toward the picture of the people's Princess in the paper which was clutched in one tidy hand. 'You will all do it as a country. There's nothing and no one as fiercely independent and hearty as the British. We all know it, too!'

The lady smiled up at his otherwise ugly face, the beauty of compassion and pride pouring from his brown eyes into hers of reddish hazel.

'Oh, you Americans!' she softly said. 'You're such a mess… sometimes we wish you'd stay in the colonies and quit pestering our pretty countryside with your uninhibited manners and modes of dress. But we're cousins… and we love you. We never forget a favor. We've never forgotten World War II.' She sighed.

'Awe, shucks, ma'am. Look how you helped us during that time! We're grateful to you too, you know,' Old Blue smiled. 'Besides, we count on your open friendship during these present times. Couldn't have a better buddy than a Brit in battle.'

'Really, young man?' she asked.

'Really,' he smiled.

'Thank you,' she quietly replied. 'It makes the loss of my James easier to bear.'

'Oh, I'm sorry ma'am.'

'He died chasing the Desert Fox… Rommel, you know.'

'I beg your pardon, but you can't be that old,' Old Blue expostulated. 'You look so young! As young as my own mother!'

In spite of herself, the little lady laughed. Merrily she forbade him to guess her age and to thank God that she could still get around, continuing, 'He was my brother, you see.'

A little woman's heavy heart was lifted for the evening. As they parted in town, things in Rye, England, and Minnesota, U.S.A. started heating up.

Chapter Fifteen

September 2, 1997, U.S.A.

That morning and following days found all three sisters together at Christiana's home to join worldwide mourners. Certain anchorpersons droned on about the Queen's supposed unfeeling way of mourning. It made Christiana's emotions boil as hot as the water she was pouring onto the loose-leaf, black tea in the warmed teapot. She demanded, 'How can they forget her goodness? How can they so crassly overlook the duties she performs on a daily basis with the Prime Minister and Parliament? Such effrontery! Where do foreigners find the gall to criticize a lovely woman who gave so much of herself during the World War II effort when bombers were zeroing in on London, let alone the rest of the country? Have they forgotten how her father begrudgingly allowed her to become Colonel-in-Chief of the Grenadier Guards after two years of speaking to other young people her age via radio to encourage their morale? You know, she and her sister lived in and near London during those dark days when Hitler was invading Europe. Along with their courageous mother, they stayed with the King and worked hard. She even drove a truck and learned how to fix the crazy thing if it broke down, and joined the Women's Royal Naval Service. My friend from Cornwall was in the service as well, and admired the Princesses and their courageous mother. Have these anchorpersons been ambulance drivers while bombs were flying? They shouldn't be so critical of someone and a system they do not know, it seems to me!' She handed Angela and Pam tea in cups with saucers, her face pale from lack of sleep and anger.

'Thank you, sis,' Angela said. 'That war was worse than terrible. Britain and France combined, suffered one hundred and sixty-nine thousand civilian deaths at home from buzz bombs and such.'

'Appalling! Where did you read those figures?' Pamela's cup stopped in mid-air.

'The Minneapolis paper quoted the figures the other day.' Angela sipped her tea. Putting the cup into the saucer, she said, 'Every person participating in war represents a husband, a wife, a lover, a child, a brother or father.'

'Look, Angela. Listen to what this anchorperson is saying! He makes me so angry! He has just used the word "revolution"! He is a guest in England. How dare he use such a term? As far as I am concerned, people like him need to go back to school to learn that newscasters and media are supposed to report the news, not give their own interpretation upon everything. Those who jump to conclusions not based on facts are disgusting. No wonder Mama always maintained that if it hadn't been for reporters inflaming and sensationalizing the news we wouldn't have had any world wars... Well, I'm generalizing. Sorry.'

'Tell me the duties of the Queen,' Angela injected to cool the younger down.

'They may have changed by now, but not long ago Mama said that most everyone thinks the Queen is just a ceremonial part of English government. But that wasn't the case when Mom told me that every day dispatchers go back and forth from the House of Commons to Buckingham Palace, for instance, carrying locked boxes full of current secret, sensitive state documents for her perusal, approval and signature. They are sent to her from the Prime Minister for her information and wise counsel; and regardless of the Prime Minister's party affiliation, they work closely together on these matters. The Monarch's opinion, consent and signature are needed in order to make numerous appointments and certain matters legal. The people of Britain regard this safeguard as double insurance against corruption and as a great precautionary measure against being subjected to the possible mental deterioration of an elected Prime Minister. It is a double-check system which safeguards the freedoms the British people enjoy.'

'What would happen if a Prime Minister suddenly showed signs of madness or Alzheimer's, dementia, whatever?' Angela asked as she poured herself another cup of tea, offering refills all around.

'The Queen would call for another general election.'

'Couldn't the House of Commons do that, dear?'

'When Mom told me of this, only the Queen could do so. Whether or not it has changed by now, I cannot say,' Christiana replied. 'One trip to the library coming up,' she smiled.

'What if the House of Commons doesn't want to call a general election, can the Queen force it?'

'Before I get into that, I really must go to the library to discover the answer. At any rate, the moral to the story is that a Sovereign who has served in such capacity for many years is probably the most well-informed person regarding state affairs in the entire country. At the time Mom told me these things, incoming Prime Ministers were not privy to the sealed personal records of the outgoing PM. Therefore, only the ruling crowned head was and is knowledgeable of all state secrets from the past to the present.'

Pamela added, 'That would make the Queen perhaps the greatest public asset the country possesses. No wonder you become so upset when she is misunderstood.'

'Yes, she stands ready to influence the greatest good for her people considering the wealth and scope of the knowledge she has acquired through the years.' Christiana's determined little chin squared itself with conviction. 'How dare our American news media criticize something as being archaic and worthless when they don't dig into the reasons behind the survival of the monarchy in Britain? Let them criticize everything here; that is their right. However, when it comes to another country's way of mourning, or a person's accepted position within this type of monarchy, I think they have taken undue license in order to acquire a lead story!'

Christiana walked to the television and turned up the sound. 'You know girls, when a monarch is loved, respected and wanted by the people in Britain, someone like that little lady we've just been discussing, holds a fertile basket of seed for the fields of opportunity regarding her own subjects' prosperity, education and security as we enter the new millennium. She is undoubtedly passing it along to her son. If anyone will give him a chance, I think he will cast that seed to the four winds of progress for the British Isles and her Commonwealth.'

Pamela stood, popping a dainty cookie into her mouth, walked over to her ever so 'English' sister and gave her a hug. 'I'm glad Rick had to jet off suddenly, I need to be here with you, little sis. We can all fume and cry together, and it's no one's business except our own.'

'Christiana, come look at the television, dear. You won't want to miss this,' she said.

Christiana looked at the screen. 'Oh, it's a rerun of the morning after the accident. The Prince is emerging from the chapel with the coffin, along with the two sisters! Oh, how heartbreaking! Look, the Queen's own standard has been draped over her!' Christiana's eyes filled with sudden tears. 'If anyone in the media misses that symbol of love and respect and warmth from the Sovereign they have to be ignorant or cynical indeed – if not both!' Tears were pouring down Christiana's cheeks. 'Above all, look who went to retrieve his lost love. I don't care what anyone says! He did love her once upon a time. Is the world so foolish as to think that he is not remembering what brought them together in the first place... that from which their children were born?' Tears spotted her blouse. Looking at her sisters with imploring green eyes, Christiana continued, 'Now, what more do the American and British people want to see to prove that the Queen and her family do love the boys and their poor mother's memory? This should be a time of mourning, not of casting stones by people who live in glass houses.'

'Yes, I agree, Christiana,' Angela soothed. 'I remember when Jackie Kennedy, our stoic First Lady, was applauded for refraining from tears in public after the shocking death of her husband. Such behavior was approved at that time, and now the same behavior of courage and remarkable self-possession for the sake of two children who must handle their grief in public is being perceived as inappropriate.'

'I might be a dumb American, but even I know how to recognize love, sympathy and grief when I see it from the Royal family! Why, even we didn't cry in public at Daddy's funeral. We were taught not to, in order to be a source of strength for Mother and for our young children. That is just the English way!'

Reflecting sorrowfully, she remembered stumbling in the darkness over her father's land the night following the funeral. Everyone else had gone to bed; and with a breaking heart she had gone a mile from the quiet house to walk in his footsteps which had long since been dissolved into the sands of time. Footsteps in the snow... footsteps through the tall grass... footsteps through slough and meadow, field and farm road... footsteps in which she had followed as a child when by example he had taught her *joie de vivre*. Had anyone heard her sobs of anguish? Or had the clouds, scudding low over the earth, enveloped them up and away over the troubles of mankind below, protecting her from the cruelty of misunderstanding?

She tossed her head, reliving the rending of her own soul... the criticism of those who had self-righteously said that unless a person cried in public, they had not truly loved the deceased. She looked up and said, 'I dreamed that the Prince came near, stretching a kind hand toward me regarding Dad's death, for he and his house understood my pain.' She looked up at his image being beamed over the TV and smiled tremulously, wondering why the world always judged according to their lack of one another's exact experience. Did not the world know by now that every culture taught various behaviors when it came to joy, grief and life itself?

'First of all, you are not dumb, Chrissy,' her eldest sister said. 'Secondly, because of your particular ancestry, and the pride with which it was embraced by the family for generations, you probably know more of English history than the average American – including the anchorperson whose statements are causing you such grief presently.' She handed Christiana Elizabeth Stuart a box of facial tissues. 'Here, darling. Wipe your eyes and chin, and blow your little upturned nose which we all envy until it turns beet red from crying or from the cold.' Smiling, she walked over to her sister, put one arm around her shaking shoulders, cuddled her oval face and glossy black tresses against her maternal breast. 'Please don't cry, little one,' she comforted. 'You know that the dear persons for whom you sorrow are happy now. All the troubles which plagued them on earth are over, and they are in a place where God promises there will be no sorrow, only comfort, joy and rest.'

'Oh, but I can't help it. Those poor, poor boys. Poor Prince Charles. Look at him!' She glanced up at the telly, 'He knew that if he went to bring his one and only bride home, he would be damned if he did and damned if he didn't. I don't care – the world is cynical, cruel and unfeeling regarding that which drove them apart. If he hadn't been such a sensitive person in the first place, he would not have turned to someone else for understanding and comfort when their problems kept erupting. When an individual is caught in a relationship which is not working, and that one strives to overlook or ignore the odious part of their loved one's problems, it is natural to at first be forbearing and act as if it must be one's imagination. I did that; for what if one is mistaken and because of one's own flagging self-esteem, sees something in the other's behavior which does not really exist? Does no one think that he had self-doubt as a first-time husband? Why won't everyone give the man a break? Just listen to the sensationalists! Let's turn the channel and see if anyone has the sense God gave a goose and can interpret the significance of the Queen's own standard draping that coffin – and the deceased's obviously more than sympathetic former groom walking beside her!'

Angela turned the dial, but no one sounded well-versed in Royal, British heraldry nor the sensitivities of separated, former lovers.

'Well, let's turn it back to the clearest channel,' Christiana Elizabeth mourned. 'I give up hoping that anyone will recognize the significance of the Crown Prince accompanying the sisters and bearing the Royal Standard to one whom they all loved in their own way, and for their own reasons.'

As the forty-eight channels were perused, a clear picture came in. The Prince and the fallen's sisters were sadly walking beside the draped coffin after deplaning in England. The wind was whipping the ladies' hair but they didn't notice, nor did the Prince mind being whipped by the gusts, so great was their loss. The gold, burgundy, white and blue colors of the standard were held firmly in place as the beloved burden was borne on the stalwart shoulders of members of the Royal military. Watching their faces through tears of their own, Angela, Pamela, and Christiana could see their individual grief mirrored on the faces of the men who were carrying the remarkable beauty back to her people.

'Any man who loves his children as does the Prince, would still bear a bit of loving memory for the moments during which they were conceived,' Christiana murmured. 'I know. I've been there.'

'Yes,' Pamela answered. 'In my estimation, the world is willfully misunderstanding him. Or are they reading into his every action only the evil everyone has become used to? Most movies and television stories are no longer filled with familial love and innocent romance such as the Brontës and Jane Austen... or even Tolstoy wrote.'

Angela replied, 'Even in *Anna Karenina*, the heroine had an innocence about her. She was not promiscuous in nature. Yes. I think you are perceptive.'

All were silent for a moment, the strains of Mozart's *Requiem* filling the quiet hush which had fallen even on the anchorperson as the live pictures from London beamed into the living room.

'You know, Angela,' Christiana softly mentioned, 'the charm of a man is in the respectful warmth and attention he pays a lady... at least in great part, wouldn't you agree?' She turned to look at her red-headed sister becoming gladdened by the impression her exquisite beauty made.

'Do you remember the works of the poet, William Drummond?' She paused. 'Now there was a Scotsman who wrote the most tender, sheerly exquisite poetry regarding his fiancée. To read his works is to know the heart and soul of a man who coupled passion with integrity of purpose and lack of deceit. He was much like our father regarding the undying affection and esteem in which he held Mother, and because of Daddy's example I've noticed down through the years that I reverence, admire and wish to emulate those women whom Daddy held in high esteem such as his own mother who died before I was even born.' She pressed a tissue to her left eye briefly.

Pamela said, 'Daddy was very charming when speaking of her and of our maternal grandmother, who thank the Lord was still alive and well and so full of goodness, in her quiet, undemonstrative, dignified way. Her affection was shown by invitations to tea, the everlastingly open cookie jar, the absolute approval sparkling in the depths of those sea-green eyes, the constant sense of acceptance and importance which emanated from the abundance of her heart.'

Angela answered, 'Yes. She would have probably been bewildered by this present generation's insistence of "letting it all hang out" emotionally. Between you, me and the gatepost, I never suffered from being bred to act like a lady. Did you, girls?'

'No, as long as you don't mind my hysteria when we are alone at home,' Christiana said.

They all laughed.

'I don't think that natural grieving and shedding of tears over someone you really cared about is hysteria within one's own four walls, dear.'

Angela's brown eyes were as pink as those of her sisters. Christiana looked up, observing Angela's red-rimmed peepers. She laughed again. 'We all look like St. Bernards with colds.' Suddenly, looking up at the skylight above her head, she said to the clear, blue sky, 'Dear God, why must humanity suffer?'

To which her sisters gently asked, 'Are we above our Lord?'

They all rose to their feet, walked toward each other and embraced in their sorrow as scenes from a grieving city, whose inhabitants were laying an ever growing sea of flowers at the fallen heroine's gates, cast colored shadows over the white walls.

Joining the bereaved thousands of miles away across the Atlantic, Angela, Christiana and Pamela said a prayer. Then the three, holding one another in a circle of love, smiled through their tears, so grateful that God had seen fit to prolong Pamela's life twenty years earlier. Loving looks passed between them while new sadness from across the sea bonded them even closer.

Chapter Sixteen

Rye, England, September 2, 1997, 0800 hours, 8 A.M.

Rick entered a red telephone booth on Mermaid Street in Rye, East Sussex. He had spent a few hours resting up the street at The Mermaid Inn, a charming hotel where Queen Elizabeth I had occasionally laid her regal head when meeting with her maritime lords as matters of security required visits to that ancient seaport town. Paintings of her on the hall walls, which had flattered that person's regal eyes into pleasure, still graced the amazing half-timbered structure. Leaded glass windows, which she herself had once opened and closed in her suite, allowed sunshine to spill onto the tester and high bed on which she had slept. Rick had been fascinated when he entered the room after treading up narrow stairways, which circled through a labyrinth of tiny hallways and short doors. It was as if the walls palpitated with her presence, the fiery, brilliant daughter of Henry VIII who realized that by staying single she had a greater chance of keeping her head on her neck with which to balance the crown. Shrewd and brilliant, she brought her country into riches and respect, as if taking the best from both her parents' gene pool... that of the shocking Anne Bollun and Henry.

'I am married to England,' she said, and so she proved to be.

Notwithstanding the awe, which filled him upon entering her room, Rick was happy to discover that a new mattress or two had been put on the frame of the high bed since Her Royal Highness's last visit.

Rick could imagine her preparing the sea captains Howard, Drake, Hawkins and Frobisher to attack the Spanish Armada which had sailed to invade England, circa 1588 in vindication of Catholic Mary Queen of Scots' death.

'Against her advisor Walsingham, and her Privy Council, the Royal redhead prepared and did attack King Philip of Spain's fleet,' Rick told the fellow who helped him to his room. 'I sure would have liked to witness the briefing between the dashing English captains and herself when she met them in the Royal dining room downstairs. I wonder which man was in favor at the time. Do you know?' Rick smilingly dropped a tip in the chap's hand as he gave him a Pentecostal handshake, pressing a bill into the palm from his own without being obvious.

'No, sir, I'm afraid I don't, but I know that all of them met her here at one time or another. She reportedly visited the inn frequently.'

'That I believe. Thank you.'

'She wouldn't have seen victory had not a storm aided our brave captains,' the interesting fellow said as he closed the door going out.

Going to the leaded glass windows across the slanting timber floor, which was amazingly straight for being five hundred years old, Rick opened the pane to look out across the parking lot, imagining the rowdies who used to pull wine at the pub across the tiny cobblestone street.

'If I lean out holding a broom in my hand, I could open the leaded glass window above the pub,' he smiled. If only Pam were along. She'd have loved it, he thought to himself as he shimmied out of his clothes and hopped into bed.

Suddenly, he burst into laughter.

'Well, how do you do?' he said to the tester high above his head which glowed warmly. 'I never dreamed I'd have a man in my bed! Just make sure you stay up there, Henry!' Four feet above his head carved into the tester of heavy, burnished oak, was the Virgin Queen's father himself... eternally stuck where he could give any visiting lady nightmares wondering if her head would still be on her neck in the morning.

'Don't mean to be hard on you, pal, you just startled me. Actually, you had quite a tender heart as a young Prince studying for the priesthood. I don't envy your struggles one bit during those early years; but, in all respect, I have to part company with your ideas after a certain point in history even though you did an immense amount of good.' Rick turned off the bedside light and rolled over. 'Now for a quick morning nap to make up for last night. Excuse me Your Royal Highness,' and before the final 's' sounded, he was fast asleep.

Halfway around the world in Minnesota, a nervous Pamela answered the telephone.

'Rick, darling! Where are you? I've been worried sick. I can't wait until next year when you retire!' she sighed with concern.

'I'm sorry, darling, truly I am. I'm fine and I'll be home soon.' He was in the red phone booth on the corner near his hotel.

'But where are you? I saw you on television in front of Buckingham Palace the other morning. What in the world are you doing there, and why have you been gone so long without a by your leave?'

'Sweetheart, you know that I can't satisfy you with answers to those questions. But will it suffice to know that I love you and should be home around the middle of September, or so?'

'Yes,' she answered, 'if you promise you'll be safe in the meantime.'

Rick laughed softly. The last seventeen years of marriage had been good.

'That's a tough order to fill, sweetie.' As he spoke, Rick noticed a blonde woman across the street who seemed to be lost for she kept disappearing and reappearing to check a certain shop window. 'Did your boss mind that you wanted to go to Minnesota to be with your sisters?' he asked.

'You know that he didn't,' she smiled. 'He is seventy years old now, but still a dear... works just for the fun of it and told me to go home and share the world's sorrows with my two lovely sisters.'

Again the blonde, who seemed a little thick of waist, caught Rick's attention. He noticed that her face and jaw were quite large-boned in comparison to most of the diminutive sized female population of England. She surely is ungainly, he thought while listening to his wife's narrative.

Suddenly the fine hairs on the back of his neck started to rise, for as the woman started crossing the street toward him, he found himself staring into steely brown eyes, and a formerly broken nose with unmistakable midnight shadow on the upper lip and jaw which the thin net of her hat covering the face no longer concealed.

'Baby – I've got to go. Kiss kiss!' his calm voice didn't betray the sudden adrenaline flow to limbs and organs. With both hands he put the receiver back into the cradle of the telephone, never taking his eyes off the odd woman, simultaneously releasing a tiny sharp object from the stem of his watch, burying it between the middle and ring fingers next to the palm of his left hand. Instinctively, he burst out the door in a dive at the he-she's feet, hearing the silenced 'pop pop' of a tiny gun which was concealed in his assailant's kid-gloved hand.

He-she was down with Rick on top, the aggressor's legs and ankles tangled between the American's strong thigh and calf muscles. Rick's fingers dug into the impersonator's neck all around long enough to inject a dose of liquid brucella from the tiny syringe held between his tightly held fingers.

'That'll really make you dotty, you loser you! This serum isn't designed to kill, just to incapacitate until you are behind bars,' Rick said as he rose kicking the gun out of the already 'looped' lady's right hand. Standing 'her' upright, Rick used the tail of her red silk scarf to make a gag by stuffing it into the mouth, winding it through the fake glasses and over the brim of her fedora where he laid it over the crown, bringing it back down to the person's top button, and tying it into a decorative bow after passing it through the eye of the coat. The scarf in the mouth looked like a bit too much of a good thing – lipstick – when Rick rearranged the black veil all around. The blond CIA agent couldn't help but laugh at the comical sight.

'My! But aren't we pretty today!' he exclaimed.

The he-she rolled brown eyes.

'Get up!' Rick softly, insistently ordered as he jerked the hapless foe to full stature. 'Here, you lost something, honey,' and Rick swooped something off the pavement; then slapped a black, wide-handled purse onto the blonde's arm. Adjusting the five foot eleven inch man's sexy black coat sleeves around the straps of the purse, Rick laughed.

'Now, sweetheart, take my left hand with your right as I carry you along in the right arm. Act as if you're in love with me; and come along like a good little girl!' His unlikely companion wobbled back and forth with a goofy expression on his face. Rick swiftly bent to retrieve the assailant's weapon, stuffed it into his belt above the right pocket, and reclaimed the 'lady's' hand. 'Oops, your wig is slightly askew,' Rick chuckled again while twisting the crown of the black fedora a bit, making it cock-eyed in order to straighten the 'woman's' pageboy underneath.

'Now that's better! You look very smart!' Rick's amethystine eyes sparkled with glee. 'Come along then, darling!' He guffawed with laughter, pulling his assailant a little closer. The blonde snuggled closer in response to unbearable pressure from the fingers of Rick's left hand.

'The pox on these stupid rings which I wore to be convincing!' the now unladylike and obviously unfemale captive mumbled incoherently while trying to bring the solitaire to the top of his ring finger from the tender flesh in between.

They made quite a pair as, arm in arm, the 'lovers' strolled down the quaint street toward the train station, the 'lady' reeling from weakened knees and head thanks to the injection, which scrambled his brain and weakened his muscle reflex.

Rick preferred an injection of it for his enemies when in the field and carried a potent dose in the stem of his watch, rather than using lethal bullets. He always liked to ascertain his foe before deciding what should be done with them. He figured that the authorities should be judges of such matters, unless of course circumstances would not and could not allow. Common sense had to reign in his opinion, simply because of the tender heart within him, and the Oath of Hypocrites, which he had taken upon becoming a licensed doctor. His interest was in saving lives, not wasting them.

He and his 'lady-fair' slowly walked along.

'Look dear,' a little wife said to her hubby as they walked toward Rick and his companion. 'A new couple is in town. She's had a little too much at the pub, now hasn't she!' The couple tittered together quietly and looked knowingly at one another.

'Hello,' they said to Rick and his loving mate.

Rick politely nodded his head in a reciprocal greeting to the amused woman's husband who tipped his hat toward Rick with a merry wink of one eye. The return smile on the Yankee's face was that of an angel as he nodded graciously back. He gently kissed the top of his little, loopy assailant's demure, crazily angled hat.

The people passed, and once again Rick and company were in the clear strolling down the hill toward the station.

'Take me to the thug who sent you,' Rick said with a face of concealing benevolence.

'Me no speak da Englese!' drunkenly the smallish man muttered.

'Me know you speaka da English, sir!' Rick countered, still smiling lovingly upon the head of the shorter man. He casually let the little 'lady' support herself more on her own two feet.

'Oh! Oh! Please, I'll fall. The world is spinning,' he grabbed at the arms and hands of his supporter. 'Yes! I speak English, you jerk!' suddenly angry, the would-be murderer demanded, 'Take me to the train. I'll tell you everything!'

Rick thought, perfect English spoken here. No accent; but he said, 'Well, darling, I'd rather take you home in my marvelous toy. While my buddy operates it, you and I can have a little chat on the way to London.' Once again, Rick supported the 'little woman'. 'Besides, sweetie,' Rick nodded at another passer-by, 'since you are anxious to catch the next train, I suppose your buddies will be waiting on board. I prefer my own mode of transportation, thank you very much just the same.' Rick said hello to another couple who were looking at them oddly.

Arriving at the train station of red brick which had neatly painted doors and trim, he peeked inside at the little waiting room, noticing that one window was open for tickets. A black cab pulled in front of the station, and Rick escorted his little 'lovely' to it, hiring the familiar cabbie on the spot.

After pouring his assailant into the back seat, Rick slid in beside him, still clutching firmly even though the brucella had done its amazing work.

'Okay Sam, let's go find the magic bird.'

The black-headed driver smiled at his partner in the rear-view mirror, and Rick added, 'We need to leave immediately, the train is due in forty-five seconds. This fellow has buddies waiting on board, and if he doesn't get on, they'll spill out of those cars like squirrels out of an open barrel full of black walnuts in the middle of a cold Minnesota winter!'

Sam took off slowly enough not to arouse suspicion and headed out of town toward backwater canals which had been dug in defense against Napoleon's promised invasion ages ago. Finally reaching an area which was well hidden by man-made ditches big enough for the Jolly Green Giant to lie down and take a snooze without being seen, the car was brought to a halt. As the two able-bodied men exited bringing their antagonizer with them, a fourth party emerged from behind a clump of sand and tall grass, got into the car and drove away. Rick, Sam and their new acquaintance scrambled to the bottom of a canal, which was bone dry, where the flying machine was waiting, already revving to go. They jumped in, pulling the groggy visitor with them as his hat fell forward, totally covering nose and eyes. The plane soared straight up like a hummingbird and then took off toward the north.

Rick and Sam secured the passenger with handcuffs on his wrists and ankles before attaching both to the door latch and automatic control. Moving either arm would manually open the door. Once the door started opening, there was no way to reverse the motion.

Rick observed the prisoner, who drunkenly asked, 'Did the sun go down already? I can't see a thing... I just got up a couple of hours ago. Tildy! Hey, girl. Come to bed!'

Rick and Sam laughed, pushing the fedora back in place.

'Where's Tildy? Who the deuce are you?' the guy looked up sideways at Rick and Sam.

'It doesn't matter who we are, pal. Here, put this between your knees and your head. No need for you to break your neck during the next few minutes before we land.' Rick stuffed a wadded up cammie between and in the appropriate places.

'Got a cigarette, doc?' the captive drawled.

'No, sport. Never touch 'em,' Rick laughed. Drawing his medical bag round, he opened it and looked for the stethoscope. Taking it out, he examined the man's heartbeat, then putting the apparatus back into the bag, withdrew an antidote for the brucella. Carefully drawing a little into the syringe, and making sure there was no air in the tip of the needle, he had Sam hiked up one of the captives sleeves, and gave the injection.

'Ouch, you brute! What'd ya do that for?' the goofy man complained. 'Here I am, going for a nice ride with you on a sunny afternoon, and you poke me! Durn American!' His eyelids closed suddenly in sleep.

Rick observed his charge for a moment, then reached overhead to pull something out of a compartment.

'Oh, heck! If he moves… well… he needs a parachute.' So saying, Rick attached the object in question to the zonked out man, taping the rip cord into his confined hands, then secured a radio band around the fellow's neck… already, the cuffs which had been slipped onto the door handle were loose enough to slide right off if the door opened.

Rick had a real thing about hearing the other person's side of the story.

'Here is your fella, Captain,' Rick and Sam motioned to the unconscious assailant as MI6's Scar-P came aboard in London when the helicopter had landed.

'The dumb (expletive,)' Scar-P mumbled.

'What did you say?' Rick turned friendly eyes on their British buddy.

'Oh, I said what a screw-up he is!' Scar-P smiled laconically, gray eyes cold as the sea. 'They're waiting for him down at headquarters. Want to come along of course, don't you, to file a report and check the black bag?' He picked up the purse and handed it to Sam.

'Hell's bells! Don't make me carry that thing across the tarmac to the limo,' Sam scowled.

'Carry it in your arm like a book or something,' Scar-P laughed. 'I didn't ask you to wear his high-heeled shoes!'

'Here, give it to me,' Rick said, grabbing it from Sam, 'I'll carry it with my bag. No one will even notice it.' He put it in the same hand with his med-kit. 'You did check the contents while we were airborne, didn't you Sam? I'd hate to be walking around with a time bomb ready to go off.'

'Yea, boss. Negative. Wait till you get a load of what's in it. Washington will rejoice for evermore,' he grinned.

'No kidding?' Rick asked.

Scar-P just looked up briefly while strapping the unconscious man to a British trolley. His American partner was securing the other side as he asked, 'Why do you Brits call gurneys, trolleys?'

Scar-P laughed, 'Dunno,' and got back to the subject at hand.

'So, the little man has the Hope Diamond,' the MI6 ascertained. 'I told you he was a screw-up. Apparently he was in Rye to meet an estimator from Paris.' He chuckled. 'Who in their right mind would actually carry the booty while going after the detective who is looking for it?' Rising, he said, 'Come on, let's go.'

Lifting the trolley, the men jockeyed it out the door and down the steps to a waiting medivan. Opening the doors, they shoved the guy in, hopped into seats beside him and were off before Rick and Sam could get their long legs all the way in to shut the door.

'Criminee! What's the hurry?' Sam asked.

'See that blue car coming across the tarmac?' Rick asked.

As they looked, a car full of men dressed in business suits drove like a frantic beetle toward the van.

'Get down,' Scar-P ordered, 'and stay down!'

'Someone wants the black bag, I take it,' drawled Sam.

'How'd you guess?' Rick breathed. 'That cursed diamond should be taken back to India the first chance someone gets! I don't want to get popped over it.'

Scar-P laughed. 'That's precisely what the fellows in the car think. Only, I don't think they want to return it to the temple.'

The van hit a bump, sending them all a foot into the air. Grabbing the secured gurney to steady themselves, everyone burst into laughter.

'Hot dog! This is like going over Seven Hills outside Hastings, Nebraska, when I was a kid!' Sam laughed. 'We used to take Dad's old V8 Hudson and go flying over the hills and dips to make our cousins lose their stomachs on the way to the swimming hole!'

The blue car behind them was suddenly cut off by four police cars, their sirens wailing.

Soon the van reached 64 Vauxhall Cross on the South Bank of the Thames, where an interrogation team was waiting to debrief all four and grill the prisoner.

Scar-P suddenly asked Rick, 'Where's Old Blue?'

Chapter Seventeen

After dropping off the linen handkerchief retrieved at Hampton Court and debriefing his findings regarding the Plantagenet Princess of Castile, Old Blue left Vauxhall Cross, his British buddies' headquarters, and headed for a hotel room at the Hyde Park in Knightsbridge. Old Blue had to give up his luxurious room at The Savoy once the other two arrived. That place was a treat from the powers that be only as a perk when having to be alone in the city.

I sure could use a nap, he thought to himself, but there's no time… got to call Wise Acres and ask where the H is the money for this trip? He scratched his head.

Getting off the Underground at Knightsbridge Station, he came up into daylight and walked the short distance to his hotel. Once in the room, Old Blue sighed, picked up the telephone and called his contact person who was eight thousand miles away to the west.

'Where the h-e-double-toothpicks are you, sport?' his 'lifeline' asked.

'You'll never guess,' Old Blue said. 'I'm in London, busier than a worker ant in an anthill. Now I have only two hours to catch a flight to Minneapolis. Unless you tell which flight to take, they'll be leaving without me.'

'Okay. Here's the skinny. Ready?'

'Shoot!' Old Blue lit a cigarette, sitting down on the edge of the red bedspread to listen.

'First of all, when you meet the objective, mum's the word. No explanations why a trip's necessary. Second of all, and this is a direct order, hands off the merchandise. Not for you, understand? Capisce?'

'Capisce. But why?'

'Don't ask. Just do what you're told, it says here. 'Okay. Take Northwest Flight 540 leaving Heathrow 12 noon, arriving

Minneapolis 5:30 P.M. Pick up a car at Alamo Car Rental – and not the most luxurious you can find.' They both laughed.

'Thank God I wasn't ordered to hire a mule.' Old Blue deftly mashed his cigarette into a gray smudge between his fingertips.

'Ready for the rest, sport?'

'Yah… go ahead,' OB agreed, tossing the butt into an ashtray beside the telephone.

'Hotel Hilton downtown, room 206. Voucher will be waiting in the safety deposit at the desk. By the way, got your international license in your pocket?'

'Roger.'

'That'll be good enough… Robbie, dear.'

'Oh, cut it out, smart acres! I forgot I had a name.' The fellow in Minneapolis laughed as OB asked, 'Well… where's the rest of it, dumb cluck?'

'You mean the green stuff?'

'Yes. I have exactly two pounds and six pence to my name.'

'Don't worry, it will suddenly appear in your smoke-searching hands when you expect it the least. Use the Piccadilly Line to get out to the airport – you already have your travelcard. Once you're on the plane, they'll wine and dine you first class this time.'

'Hot dog! I must have done something right for a change.'

'One thing.'

'What's that?' Old Blue became cautious.

'No Pabst, no wine, no scotch, no nothin', it says here… not until this assignment is finished, and you are in Mexico having a blast at the retreat. Do I make myself perfectly clear?'

'Shucks, geez and four thousand cuss words! Yes, I hear you. Do you think I hadn't figured that out already? What do they take me for – a fool?'

'Of course they don't, they say this to all the guys and gals. Speaking of gals, how's Orange?'

'How should I know? The dumb chick is making eyes at some skinny Brit lately. I haven't seen her for almost a week. There's something strange about the dame lately. Have you heard from her?'

'No. All I know is that she is near you regarding location. On my notes, it says for you to watch your back when Orange is the color of the day. Got that?'

'Oh, you're all frickin' crazy. She's harmless as a pet flea.'

'She may be your pet flea, but don't you remember? Fleas bite.'

'Hey pal. She's been the closest thing to a loyal wife I've had all my life.'

'Now you're a poet. Don't get so steamed, I'm just reading your assignment here. Got it?'

'Got it. But you can tell them from me, they can go stuff it. I like that color! Most beautiful sunset there is!'

'Just make sure it doesn't become your most beautiful sunrise. "Red-orange in the morning, sailors take warning".'

'I don't believe it, but if you insist, I'll watch my skinny behinder.'

'That's better. By the way, if you get a chance, I'll see you in the lounge at the Hilton. Here's the rest of what you need to know. You get an hour for dinner at 8 P.M. Business. A bath. The works. The goods will be delivered to the table.'

'Okay. See you sport. Got to go or I won't make the plane. One last thing, when do I get to sleep? And by the way, in all due respect, I'm glad to miss the funeral. This whole mess tears me up!'

Silence. 'Sleep on the plane. Cheerio.' More thoughtful silence and then a compassionate, 'Are we having fun yet?'

Old Blue laughed miserably and said, 'Go take a flying leap at a doughnut hole.'

They both hung up.

Old Blue started packing, brown eyes scrutinizing the clothes laid out on his bed. His tall frame was shirtless, again his jeans were still open from just having crawled into them from toweling dry after a shower. Renegade that he was, he had no underwear on as usual. Barefoot, his slender feet still moist from the water were impeccably pedicured.

'Going home,' he grinned. 'Maybe I'll get to see Mom and Dad this time around! No matter how old a guy gets, he needs his mom and pop!' Suddenly the tap dance didn't seem so bad after all as South Dakota loomed largely on his horizons. A familiar rap sounded on his Hyde Park Hotel room door.

'What's the password?' he demanded.

'Go roast a turkey,' a voice identical to that of his London officer answered.

Laughing, Old Blue cautiously looked through the security glass and jumped sideways and backwards as bullets pinged almost noiselessly through the door.

'Jesu, Mary and Joseph!' the Black-Catholic cussed as he scrambled across the room on his belly to retrieve his shoulder holster off the bed where it was lying by the open suitcase. Gun in hand, he waited between the beds flatter than a fritter. By this time, his sagging jeans had been pulled back where they belonged after having been unceremoniously brought to his ankles by rapid shimmying across the carpet. A shirt, which he had grabbed in a simultaneous swoop with the gun, covered his naked chest. Stealthily zipping his jeans ever so carefully while again swearing not ever to be caught in unzipped pants without underwear again, he lay still as a mouse. With a sigh of relief at not entangling himself in his zipper, he pressed a call button, which was on his white Gant shirt pocket disguised as a pearl snap. 'Code 14,' OB breathed into the mother-of-pearl device.

'That'll take care of him, the poor sap,' Old Blue grinned wickedly – sheer pleasure beaming from his black pupils. 'Now to finish packing and get the F out of here!' He jumped to his feet, threw on a gray dress jacket, and stuffing the ever-present Harris tweed into his duffel bag exited the room through the wall panels after depressing one of four red roses in the carpet next to the fireplace with his cowboy boot. Hidden as it was by a copper wood basket, the rose provided safety for the boys whenever the need arose to exit by unorthodox methods between walls.

'Just a tap of the toe and out I go,' he laughed to himself as he hastened through the faux wall and shimmied down a narrow staircase of marble. Descending between the walls into a private drawing room which was festooned with red draperies shining like a woman's lips, the mocking man grinned at the bellhop.

'They got him,' the youth whispered with a knowing wink.

'Good!' Old Blue gave the kid a friendly slap on the back. 'Thanks. I'm fond of staying alive,' he whispered.

They laughed.

'Your taxi, sir,' the hop handed him into a waiting black vehicle. 'The underground is stalled,' he winked at Old Blue again. 'You'll be delivered to the very door of the plane.'

'Thanks, pal.' Old Blue settled back into the deep seat of the cab, not noticing an orange-haired woman observing them from a third-story window of the hotel. The vehicle pulled away from the curb and raced down the street as fast as a cockroach on a hot skillet.

Chapter Eighteen

It was still the sixth of September in Minnesota, and the seventh of September in England. It was the saddest birthday Christiana could ever remember having. She and her sisters stayed up all night to watch the funeral beaming in from London. All of them wept when they caught sight of the nosegay of white roses on the foot of the majestically draped coffin. It said 'Mummy' and fresh tears started upon seeing the bouquet of pure white tulips at the other end of the casket.

Those two arrangements said it all for any mother on the entire earth, and the world wept.

'The boys, within their paternal family, feel comfortable in so honoring their mother,' Angela said.

So it was with great feelings of justification that Christiana and her sisters quietly observed and felt every bit of the funeral.

The early morning afterward, September seventh, the girls had tea and toast with honey. No one was hungry, but the two eldest needed a bit of nourishment for the drive to Angela's house where Pam was going for dinner. Christiana had decided to stay home from her job as a nurse in Minneapolis.

'Do you think that the present Prince could not have married the love of his life as a young man even if he had wanted to? She's a Catholic, you know,' queried Christiana.

'I don't know,' Angela said, looking at the sad sister whose hair was still as luxuriously curly as the day she had been born. The rising sun was casting its rays through the eastern window upon the raven-headed Christiana, causing blue highlights to shine from the rich blackness, which crowned her head.

Angela could imagine a tiara on Christiana Elizabeth's ebony locks, for she was so unselfconsciously regal... so refined. Angela was brought from the brief daydream by the other sister's voice.

'Laws have not changed regarding the protection of the Anglican Church which was established through terrible bloodshed from Catholic and dissenter alike during King Henry VIII's time, and later during the Civil War of 1642–51. A Catholic cannot sit upon the throne.'

Christiana set her teacup down. Her thoughts were related to Pamela's statement, but at a slight variance.

'Here a virtual book of questions could be asked. For instance, do you think that every married person who found themselves ensnared in a *ménage à trois* purposely broke their vows? I can't believe that myself.' She glanced at her sisters. 'Furthermore, I don't believe that all-consuming love happens every day… you know, the kind where one feels part of another's very soul, mind and body.' She nibbled on a soldier of toast.

'In fact, it probably happens only once in a lifetime,' Angela concurred, smiling at her younger sisters.

'Yes, I tend to think that as well,' Pamela quietly said. 'Consider… I think that the present tragedy which we have been weeping over today would never have ended as such for that beautiful fairy Princess and her darling Prince had he been encouraged to seek others to help him, rather than having to be accepted by his former confidante who happened to be his first sacrifice to love's sometimes cruel fate.'

'I truly don't believe that he set out to deceive his young wife. I really don't!' Christiana's tendency to trust had taken over, for she truly was all heart.

'Oh?' Angela raised her fine eyebrows over her sibling's consensus. 'I can see where, once true love is thwarted, one would become confused when it visits the senses again.' She accepted a fresh quarter slice of toast, which had been spread with raspberry preserves, the sun glinting off flowered Haviland.

'Right!' Chrissy continued. 'What's more, maybe the former lovers were saddened but determined to end their physical relationship once a wife had been found, especially when the soon to be wife was such a shy, innocent candidate. Any man feels extremely flattered and protective of a beautiful lamb full of sparkle and mischievous fun. He is not about to let her naive love of new delights in their particular pasture of life, cause her to be caught in the brambles. Furthermore, to deny and conquer the tremendous feelings one experiences in an active relationship, right or wrong, takes immense effort when it's time to put it onto the back burner and turn the stove off. I know for it has happened to me.' Christiana dabbed a fleck of dust from her eyelashes.

'Perhaps that was the premise upon which the new leaf of marriage was turned,' sighed Pamela.

Looking out the window at the lake which was beginning to stir with the mid-morning's first breeze, Christiana said, 'Nothing, absolutely nothing, hurts and scorches the mind and heart as does the discovery that the one you adore has betrayed you. The one whom you believed, and by their own admission, loved only you, would never touch another person, nor even desire another...' she sighed again. 'Nothing hurts as terribly as when you discover unfaithfulness and deceit in your first, bedded true love's life... or you can't marry because of religion.'

She was quiet for a while. All the ladies were stilled, plunged deeply into thought, while the orioles outside the window fed their young, then suddenly started scolding and chasing red-winged blackbirds who were darting up from their nests in the bulrushes twelve feet away to attack the hanging purse high in the poplar tree which held the tempting morsels of barely feathered babies within.

As if in a trance, Christiana continued, 'As you already know, when I discovered my husband's lover I wanted to die. I truly did.' She caught her breath as an eight-year-old-hurt grabbed at her throat. 'I thought I would die of agony. But I didn't.' She stirred in her chair.

Neither sister wanted to break the breathlessness of the confession, for it was the first time that Christiana had spoken of her pain.

'I was never bitter, you know, just excruciatingly wounded and the hurt stung like a thousand bees attacking my mind, my heart, my depths physically.' For eight years pent-up emotions had been waiting to be shared with someone who wouldn't accuse her, wouldn't condemn nor blame.

'No, I wouldn't allow bitterness, for you see,' she cleared her throat, 'I understood that contrary to my narrow perception of the world not all were raised as I, nor even if they had been did they necessarily share my opinions. I guess everyone is entitled to the pursuit of happiness.'

Twisting the napkin in her lap, she suddenly looked up again… from deep within her green eyes… a steady, warm, kindly flame. 'No one truly knows what happens except the couple. *They* interact. That is why I will never join the world in harsh criticism against the Prince, nor Princess. Most of us do whatever we must in order to face the challenges of our psychological hurts and joys. No one but the participants can truly know what happened deep within their minds and hearts. No one but *they* can even know when it began. One cannot say of another, "I know that this is how you perceived," for that is an impossible thing for one human being to ascertain of another.'

'How do you feel about the triangle we've been aware of especially these past few days?' Pamela asked her younger sister.

'I empathize with the estranged, but find it almost beyond my mettle to think kindly of the one who offered solace to the Prince. However, because I don't know what pain she may have endured when youthful passions were tormenting as they do the very young, I refrain from harshly criticizing. They *could* not marry.'

She looked at her sisters and continued, 'Only God can see the heart and He is the only One who is qualified to be the judge of those whom He made in His own image, as far as I can comprehend. Don't you agree?'

She looked anxiously at them, bringing the faraway gaze in her warm eyes back to that of her sisters, noticing how very pretty they were even though life was already half lived in its entirety by them. Hopefully, accidents would not befall to snatch the living soul from their earthly temples for many years to come.

'Many of us have sacrificed our true loves, and yet we accept duty and go on with our lives,' Christiana murmured, looking down at her napkin to rearrange it upon her lap. 'After all, life is what we make it, in large part, is it not?'

'Yes, dear.' Angela put a kind hand over that of her youngest sister.

'And now,' Pamela enjoined, 'on this graduation day into the heavenlies, one whom we loved from afar is being rewarded for having tried her best along with her ex this past year to dissolve any bitter actions between them. Both of them joined together and did an admirable job as parents, no one can deny that, and it won't stop now.'

Chapter Nineteen

Old Blue arrived safely in Minneapolis, picked up his car, got to the Hilton, showered, shaved, trimmed his curly hair, mustache and beard, then sat on the bed deep in thought. Looking sideways into the hotel room's dressing table mirror, Old Blue sighed. Suddenly, he had been yanked out of Knightsbridge and sent to Minnesota, of all the boring places.

'Sometimes it's enough to make a man nuts!' he grumbled out loud. He always talked to himself, literally sotto voce, when alone. He liked the company.

'Well, tomorrow's another day promising a real treat!' He made a wry face in distaste. 'Now, I have to pick up an old broad thirty-six years of age and haul her back to London. Hell's bells! How'd I ever land this job in the first place!' He plopped onto his back on the wide bed and pulled a pillow over his face. Soon he was snoring.

Pamela's sister! Old Blue thought while hiding his amazement.

Attila the Hun! Christiana's mind was stunned as she silently looked up, hand outstretched to Old Blue. They were being introduced by Monsignor Ralph for the first time. In that split second, when green eyes met brown, it seemed as if centuries rolled away, as if no longer was she sitting at table eleven in the Hilton dining room of a twentieth-century city. From the ancient steppes of Russia, the tragically mismatched compassion, cruelty and brilliance of the Mongol ruler seemed to beckon from Old Blue's eyes as they snapped with intelligence while gazing upon her. An involuntary shudder shook her one hundred and twenty-five-pound frame, causing her curls to dance a bit around the five foot seven inch girl's shoulders. Her little squarish but soft hand was totally engulfed in Atilla's big clasp of long, lean fingers. She looked down from the brown X-raying eyes framed by the most luxuriant black lashes she had ever seen on a man. Black curls subtly streaked with white fell charmingly on his forehead, disarmingly masking the violence beneath the little boy look. In spite of the apprehensive touch in her innermost soul, she felt a complete sense of protection emanating from his wide grin, which exposed a most handsome set of teeth. The chipped front tooth added to his charm in her mind's eye. 'What a rascal!' she said aloud. 'The stogie rogue from London!'

'Pardon me?' Old Blue bent his head nearer to hear what she had said.

'Oh, nothing worth repeating. How do you do will suffice.'

'What did you say my name was?' Old Blue asked the Monsignor. They all laughed.

'Rob,' answered Monsignor Ralph.

Rob grinned amiably, noticing in a split second everything about Christiana to confirm his assignment. Persona intact, his inner soul squirmed over the absolute trust, honesty and naivete he saw mirrored in the warm eyes of her disarmingly youthful face.

'Oh, no! A bunny rabbit. A G.D. bunny rabbit!' he said. He swept his hand through his hair. 'Jesu, Mary and Joseph, forgive this Black Catholic long enough to help me take care of her! Amen.' The man who was called black of heart for not having attended mass in twenty years crossed himself involuntarily, still smiling into her wide eyes. Her smile was as brilliantly deceptive as sunshine on innocent-looking snow when the temperature tapped fifty below zero. In her heart of hearts she felt a chill, yet a warm breeze was fanning her barometric romantic pressure.

Seeing the dichotomy in her facial expression reminded Old Blue of the opposite poles within his own nature. Suddenly while gazing into her incredible green eyes, he saw recognition in her spirit regarding himself as well. He noticed that it didn't change the sweet expression of her mouth and face. She already understood. The difference between them was that he was tortured by a life of legal vice; and she was at peace having never had to do anything more deceptive than hide a warning shudder. His power reached out to her and wrapped a mantle of security around the vulnerable inexperience of the sheltered.

As if a shout from heaven, the voice of his superior was

suddenly recalled: 'Remember! This is not for you!'

In his heart, he decided there on the spot that she would be for him if he had anything to do with it! Remembering the friendly slap on the back from his boss which had sent him to Heathrow... (by way of a taxi of course... his boss wasn't THAT strong)... he decided to do all in his power to abort someone's designs for the fetching creature standing before him. Not having been told why she was being taken to England at such a time, he developed a strong suspicion; for he knew her heritage.

This girl is an American, and I'm going to try to make sure she never forgets it. Let them find some other candidate! His square chin jutted out defensively with the thought.

The eye of Father Ralph caught his, and instantly the jaw receded and spread in a wide grin, merriment replaced the grim determination and lust in his black eyes.

'Touché, Father,' he laughed softly.

'Thank you,' responded Father Ralph. 'Shall we all order dinner?'

'But of course,' 'Rob' said as he held the chair for Christiana and scooted her gently to the table. 'Pardon me, I couldn't resist doing your job,' Old Blue murmured to the maître de who stood helplessly aside.

The next day, Old Blue drove Christiana home one hundred and thirty miles up Interstate ninety-four to Alexandria, her hometown.

'Would you mind stopping by Herberger's department store once we arrive?' Chrissy asked her unlikely chauffeur. 'I need to pick up a lightweight wool coat. I understand that it is somewhat chilly in London at this time of year. Of course, I've never been there. Have you?'

Old Blue looked at her as if she had lost her mind. Didn't the dame know anything about him and if she didn't, why was she placing herself into his hands for a trip halfway around the world? Father Ralph had certainly done his job in inspiring trust for the journey that lay ahead of them. He couldn't believe that anyone in the world could be so trusting of a complete stranger.

'Yes, I came from there, little lady. It's a great town.' Old Blue turned on the blinkers, for Christiana had also asked that they stop by St. John's Catholic college in order that he see the majestic east wall of the monk's chapel which was a symphony of purple, red, yellow, green, pink and lavender stained glass encased in steel frames without the interference of brick or other materials supporting its splendor. The morning sunshine would give her rough-looking companion a visual treat, which she hoped would touch what she felt was a sensitive nature. She had noticed his plea to Jesus, Mary and Joseph. Who else but a Catholic would address the heavenlies in such a manner? Maybe he would like the soaring nave of the austerely masculine building and his rough, old soul would be tempered by the jeweled wall.

Pulling the car into the parking lot, Old Blue turned off the engine, hopped out and went around the other side to open the passenger's door. Happily surprised, Christiana allowed the man to be a gentleman, appreciating the gesture which her father had always provided for her mother and his girls.

'Thank you,' Christiana smiled up at him as she stepped out. He grinned back, took her elbow and guided her onto the sidewalk, leading the way to the church.

'Have you been here before?' she asked in surprise.

'Once or twice,' he answered. His curly hair blowing in the wind, he opened the door for her. The strains of Handel's *Messiah* soared to the chapel ceiling from the able fingers of a young monk who was practicing for morning mass. Shivers of something Old Blue couldn't explain traveled down his spine and pierced his heart and very gut. It was his fifty-sixth birthday, and he hadn't been in a church for thirty years, let alone ever felt quite like he had since meeting the gentle creature at his side the night before.

He glanced around looking for Father Ralph. The pipe organ lent a surreal feeling to the bath of multicolored sunshine which fell upon Christiana and himself, as they stood awe-stricken, gazing up at the eastern wall.

'Maybe there is a God!' he said aloud. 'This gives me goosebumps!'

It was only eight o'clock on a chilly September morning in Minnesota. October was breathing hard upon the season's heels, and time was racing madly for those who wished to recover the scepter and those who wished to provide a gentle solution to ease the pain of a nation. In the chapel of St. John's College stood the hardened master teacher of deceit for the CIA, upon whose shoulders rested a large part of responsibility in producing those two things. Smitten into awareness that there could be more to life than lurking through the shadows of a subterranean existence, the shining sword of Christiana's spiritual purity and innocence created an aura about them. True, she was no untouched teenager. She was a full-blown, formerly savored by the love of her life, middle-aged woman. But as 'Rob' looked at her lack of facial and neck wrinkles, the high bosom and little waist peeping demurely from behind her stone-washed denim jacket and matching jeans, he wanted desperately to kiss the somewhat stubborn chin of his travelling companion.

Oh, that mouth! Old Blue thought; it's too sweet to lend truth to stubbornness in the chin. What a dichotomy – and those eyes! Again he hastily prayed to his sometimes on again, sometimes off again saints (depending on how much trouble he was in determined how often he contacted them). He was now in *big* trouble. For it was the first time in fifty-six years that his heart was totally, irrevocably swept away.

Glory be! I'm in love! he thought exuberantly. The organ peeled forth shouts of 'Hallelujah! Hallelujah! Hallelujah!' The fifty-six-year-old grinned.

His partner, totally unaware of what was happening in the lanky frame and mind of her escort, stood mesmerized by the music and glories of the eastern wall, her heart swelling in rapture. Old Blue was the farthest thing from her mind. In fact, she had forgotten he even existed.

Old Blue stood staring at Christiana who was totally immersed in the vibes flowing abundantly around them.

I'm an old fool already, and now I choose to fall in love head over heels. I'm sick! A sick, senile, old man for doing this! he thought. Then, looking up at the ceiling he called aloud, 'Help!'

That brought Christiana out of her reverie with a start.

'What's wrong?' she inquired. The organist stopped in mid-hallelujah and turned around on the organ bench to stare at the bearded fool who had interrupted his recital.

Looking helplessly down at Christiana, Old Blue saw the sea in her eyes... the restless strength of each breaker, the stillness of each lagoon lying deeply within their depths. Green upon white with starburst black lashes too bristly to be called truly beautiful... the dream eyes with unruly lashes that refused to be shaped by a curler no matter how hard she tried. He thought to himself, It's her! And in those eyes lies the key to her character if a man is wise enough to read the hints lying there.

Old Blue sheepishly scratched his chin with one, lean finger. He laughed, for in the windows of her soul was a challenge: 'Lead, and I will follow; but if you screw up, get out of the way; I'll do things myself.'

Aloud he said, 'Am I supposed to lead, follow or get out of the way?'

'Something like that,' she reproved, sending a consoling smile toward the upset organist. Waving demurely at the little musician with the fingers of her right hand, she worked her way back toward the outer door of the chapel in no uncertain terms, reaching out to take hold of the door handle. Old Blue had embarrassed her and she was irritated at his lack of reverence in what was to her a holy place.

'Well, what did you expect out of a rough-looking character like me?' Old Blue asked as he beat her to the punch, opening the door while covering her hand on the brass and wood inset.

'If you don't know by this age in your life, I certainly am not going to tell you!' She walked out ahead of him with great poise, smiling as if nothing had upset her.

'Geez Louise! Dames!' Without any warning, he suddenly remembered why he had never married. He was struggling with his own temper. How dare she walk along, her little nose stuck in the air. He was no small potato! Who did she think she was, anyway! Scowling at her, he mouthed, Up yours! Again, as if by some courier of doom, he heard Wise Acres say, 'Behave yourself.'

'I hear you!' he angrily said aloud.

Thinking Old Blue was answering her smart remark, Christiana opened her own door, and got into the car, fastened the seat belt and proceeded to observe her odd companion as he set the car in motion. Being that her tempers were like tempests in a teapot, good feelings overtook her sentiments almost immediately, sending a bit of laughter into the car.

Old Blue looked over at her. Relieved that she was once again in good spirits, he dared point out the lovely flora and fauna outside the car windows. Golden rod and red sumac which had deepened in certain areas into burgundy with its fern-like leaves and deep purple berry clusters lay in the road ditches where they crested onto hills of tall, dark spruce near golden and orange-leafed maples. Purple thistle blossoms in starbursts of beauty reached toward the heavens at the end of spiky four-foot stems. Heralding the coming winter, orioles, blackbirds, and barn swallows instinctively congregated on defoliating branches to plan migration with others of their own kind. At the first bite of Jack Frost's teeth, they had shivered in their skinny little boots, and with toes sticking out to clutch the boughs on which they were assembled, decided to head out of the north country as soon as chicks were able to withstand the thousands of miles as high-flyers. It was September… time to get aloft, even as it was the September of Old Blue's tormented life and time to get aloft into true love, his spirit nudged as he sat at Christiana's side guiding the blue Escort over the spacious interstate highway toward Alexandria. He looked down at her. Seeing his look, she smiled without understanding that more than the glory of surrounding hills and fields was in his mind.

Gosh, he's ugly from the neck up, she sympathetically thought. The rest of him is sure a beaut, though.

After a couple of hours of riding through wide open spaces dotted with prettily situated, tidily kept farms sporting red barns, white clapboard farmhouses, and neat gardens that had been cleaned of vegetable plants (the yield which now graced the pantry shelves in Kerr and Ball glass jars or plastic bags in freezers) the Alexandria exit appeared.

'Would you mind stopping at Herberger's at the Viking Mall?' Chrissy mentioned again.

'No problem. Where is it?' the man Christiana knew as Rob inquired. 'It doesn't irritate me that you've asked twice,' he growled.

'Follow Highway twenty-nine for approximately three

quarters of a mile and turn in at the sign to Viking Plaza.' She started gathering her purse in anticipation of getting out of the car. 'While we are there, we could eat lunch at the little restaurant inside. They have cowboy fare... are you familiar with hot roast beef sandwiches, mashed potatoes and gravy?' She tempted the cowboy with basic grub, ignoring his rude remark.

'I sure am and it sounds good to me,' he responded as the car approached the signals at the entrance to the mall.

'Good. Afterward we'll go to my place and I'll pack. We can still make it home in time for the evening newscast. I'd like to see if there is anything more regarding London or the Hope Diamond. Oddly, I'm very tired from my one day of work. I've been glued to the TV ever since the Princess died except for that one day.'

Rob parked the car; they got out and went inside.

As Christiana packed, Old Blue was sitting on the couch admiring its comfort. Looking at the skylight overhead in the cathedral ceiling and at the pine trees, pond and lake through the glass all around, he fell in love with the place.

'What do you do for a living?' he asked.

'I nurse,' she said, folding a pink sweater into a shoulder bag.

'You do what?'

'I do private duty nursing – mostly with Alzheimer's patients.' She carefully folded a white turtleneck sweater.

'How do you stand that disease?' He scratched his head. 'Isn't it maddening to attend an afflicted patient twenty-four hours a day?'

Christiana contemplated a while as she secured the straps of a matching bag over skirts, velvet slacks and silk organza tops peeping from the depths of coordinated jackets, wondering how he knew of her live-in shifts.

'I'd describe Alzheimer's as getting lost in the shuffle of one's mind. When it is mild, I am not daunted by it. If it has progressed to the point of unintentional meanness, an eight-hour shift is all I can do. If the person is much taller than I am, I must refuse the case in its latter stages.'

'I see.' Old Blue understood that her strength would be

inadequate to protect herself if her tongue failed to persuade an irate person into compliance with gentle suggestions.

Thinking that it was a very servile profession for someone who was being sent for by the Queen, he moaned aloud, 'The servants shall become the greatest among you, and the great shall become servants of all.'

'You certainly have a way of screwing up scripture quotations,' Christiana mildly frowned, 'and you said that you had studied law at Oxford? Surely when reading the Bible's judicious portions, you with the retentive mind, should have remembered better than that. They always use it in law school, do they not?'

'Yes... at least where I attended. It's just that it rattles my soul sometimes, therefore I ignore it for the most part. It really irritates me... don't start preaching at me, kid.' He grinned at her, the smile at variance with his warning. 'Who told you that I had such a mind?'

'I did. You act as if you are God Almighty sometimes,' a sweet smile took the sting from her words as her great orbs burrowed little sweet holes into his of blazing brown.

Suddenly, as their eyes locked in a smouldering battle of the souls, he burst out laughing. 'You're absolutely right, you know that? Absolutely correct. I do act like Cock of the Walk every now and then, although I am a dumb donkey at times. I apologize if my boorish behavior incensed you in the Monks' Chapel.' His eyes were no longer angry, but were sincerely apologetic and kind.

'I accept your apology, Rob,' she softly zipped the bag and set it on the floor by the door, turning to ask, 'In the future, would you try to remember that you are with a lady who takes things like churches, cathedrals, temples and memorials very seriously? When someone shows disrespect for them, my temper flares. I'm far from perfect, you know. You seem to be an incorrigible specimen of humanity who also possesses a heart of gold.' She walked to the refrigerator to get two Coca-Cola drinks.

'I'm a reprobate alright; but you like me.'

'Don't be too sure,' she handed him a welcome refreshment. He wished it was a Pabst, but while on assignment he could only be tormented by such pleasurable memory. Sometimes it was hard, especially when confronted by a fetching female in nice circumstances – and a saucy one at that. Her honesty floored him, frankly. He didn't know whether to be mad or pleased with her. All he knew was that he already hoped she would be in his life until no life was left in his scarred, tight body.

This time she read his thoughts and blushed, looking away.

'Maybe you'd appreciate putting these things into the trunk and going to your motel room about now? It's past midnight and I suppose you're quite tired,' Christiana held her hand out to shake his. 'Peace between us, I hope?' she inquired as their hands met for the third time since Monsignor had introduced them.

Sparks flashed in the depths of Rob's eyes, which he was quick to conceal with blandness. He knew his gaze had betrayed him. Her hand had stiffened in his, and she pulled away hesitantly.

She's too gentle, silently Old Blue decided. The world will eat her for dinner if we're not careful. Out loud he said, 'Good idea, I'm beat.' He opened the door, stepped out and with a look over his shoulder said, 'Don't ever lose the fire in your soul.' Once out of the door and down the steps, he turned around to look up at her as she stood framed against the interior of her apartment. 'See you at eight in the morning, capisce?'

Wondering what 'capisce' meant, she said, 'Fine. Goodnight.'

Locking the door behind him, Christiana turned around to go to the bedroom to get ready for bed. She noticed that he had forgotten the packed luggage.

'Lordy! Now what am I getting into?' she asked aloud of her sisters who came in from the den where they had politely waited for the half-known guest to leave.

Angela being the half who knew said, 'probably nothing that you won't like,' while setting two large suitcases beside Christiana's in the hall.

'Where are you going?' an astonished little sister asked.

'The same place as I,' answered Pamela who also set two bags beside her sisters'.

'What is going on around here?' Christiana asked with surprise spread across her face.

'You don't think we'd let you go off with a strange man all the way to London, do you?' Angela laughed.

'And alone?' Pamela teased.

They all laughed together as Chrissy embraced both at once. 'Oh, good! I was so uneasy about the sudden change in my boring little life and so apprehensive even though Father told me that I could trust Rob and go without fear. I don't mean to be suspicious, but how was I to know if he was on the level?' She glowed from relief.

'He's okay; and we were asked to go along in order to bolster your confidence,' Angela replied.

'Now we will see the sights and maybe we can pay our respects to our Princess, even though we will be so late,' Chrissy hoped aloud.

'Last one to bed is a goose!' Pamela sang out as she hurried down the hall toward the bedrooms.

'Right on,' and her two sisters followed close behind.

'What did you say?' Old Blue sat on the edge of his motel bed, flabbergasted. 'But, I thought this was such a damn secret! Now I am expected to escort *three* women to London?' He groaned.

His caller droned on.

'Ya, ya, I know. Sure. Easy as keeping three frogs from jumping out of a box in different directions. Sure. I'm absolutely aglow with anticipation! I can't even cuss around them. Do you know how hard it is not to say a swear word for twenty-four hours straight when you are *me*?' He sent forth a volley of unsavory vernacular that would have singed the mustache and goatee off Hitler.

'Slow down, pal,' Wise Acres said. 'Angela knows the reason for this trip. She has been appointed guardian and lady-in-waiting to Christiana. Pamela knows nothing, and it is to stay that way. Savvy?'

'This is the biggest bunch of nonsense I've heard in all of my life, and it makes me mad!' Old Blue stormed.

'Calm down, cowboy. Get a grip. The big boss said that if you need it, you can go get a beer... two at most.'

'Yah! And if I have a third they'll fire my skinny behinder and send me to the Langley Hilton, I suppose. Why don't you tell those fricken freaks to come to this godforsaken hole and escort this bunny and her sisters themselves if they think it is so much fun?'

Old Blue was just plain angry that he had to deliver something he loved for the first time in his life to the powers that be instead of seeing her safe and happy in the little town where he thought she belonged... and amongst people who didn't give a fig whether she wore red shoes with pink dresses, or jeans with pearl necklaces, or ostrich feathers sticking out of her back pocket instead of her hat. He wanted to protect her from the media, who would dissect her as soon as they laid eyes upon such a beautiful and tasty little morsel. They'd want to find something wrong with her!

'The world is going to have a holiday with her propensity to speak up when someone insults her principls,' he confided in a tamed voice to his patient contact.

'She'll learn not to voice them to just anyone. Don't worry, she'll be fine. Besides, methinks that nobody falls in love when told to. It doesn't work that way, and if she is as independent as you make me believe, she may say adios and walk out of the PM's office before this little project even gets off to first base. Cheer up. When a knock comes at your door in approximately five minutes the guy's name will be Jack, and he will be delivering a pepperoni pizza and two Pabst in bottles, no less.'

'If the beer is not chilled, I'll *really* see red,' the irate agent threatened.

'Then run for a bucket of ice and bury the bottles for ten minutes in the sink. Don't be such a sorebones. What else can I do to cheer you up?'

'Shoot me.' Old Blue buried his face in one hand.

'Awe, come on, man. You know I don't own a gun.'

'Otherwise you'd be happy to oblige, right?'

'Wrong,' his friend answered. 'Seems to me that something is stuck in your mind other than delivering three lovely women to Court. You haven't gone and fallen in love with Rick's wife have you?'

'I haven't even seen the lady – don't start putting ideas into the bosses' heads. I get into enough trouble as it.'

A knock came at the door.

'Hang on a minute. The pizza is here,' he set the telephone down and went to peek through the door. There stood a kid with a big flat box and a brown paper bag.

'Thanks kid,' Old Blue called out to him. 'Lay it down in front of the door. I'll pick it up when I get some clothes on. I'll stop by tomorrow morning to leave your tip... what's your name?'

'Go fly a kite,' the young man grinned.

'Okay. I'll write that on the envelope.' The tired man couldn't help but smile.

'Some day I hope to meet you again,' the young fellow responded. He set the stuff on the floor and took off jauntily down the hall.

Old Blue lifted the telephone from off the bed and said, 'Thanks. The kid was skinny, blond and smiling, but he didn't say that his name was Jack.'

'But he said go fly a kite, right?' the fellow on the other end of the line asked.

'Yes, he did.'

'It's our new man. He's been following you around for quite some time. Sort of protecting your back.'

'Gee. Thanks for telling me so soon. With friends like you... what do they say... who needs enemies?' he laughed.

'I must go now. You have all the information you need to arrive safely; and go to The Savoy this time. Rick will meet you there to take Mrs. Jarvis off your hands. We've put them into the bridal suite for the night as a perk.'

'Where've you stuck me?' Old Blue asked.

'In the twin bed in the walk-in dressing room closet of Christiana's bedroom... it has no door,' Wise Acres informed dryly.

'Jesu, Mary and Joseph,' OB groaned. A night of torment was yet to come. He'd never been in love before and now he had to act like a eunuch in a harem while lying only six feet from the sleeping delight which had captured his heart. He would writhe all night.

'You guys sure know how to make a man suffer,' he said. 'Now goodnight, sweet dreams and may your armpits become infested with a million fleas before dawn.'

Wise Acres answered, 'Go get your pizza before it gets cold and the Pabst before it becomes lukewarm. Good luck.'

The telephone went dead in Old Blue's hand.

Chapter Twenty

En route to London it was thought expedient for certain purposes to bring the ladies by train from St. Paul, Minnesota, to Chicago, where they would then board a flight to London. Amtrak seemed just the ticket for a few hours of relaxation, where Angela and Pamela found the club car to be much fun and Old Blue had an opportunity to study his travelling companion's character and personality.

Choosing to eat dinner before the other two who had found a group of interesting people with whom to wile away the hours, Old Blue and Christiana had a leisurely meal.

'This plastic service and styrofoam china is rather different from the trains in England, isn't it? The Britrail is fabulous, using commercial china teacups and saucers, which are set on the tables in every morning train taking people to and from London. It is a real treat... complimentary shortbread cookies, tea, coffee and cream are served in first-class, along with a daily London newspaper. The seats are cushy velour and carpeting is underfoot. I hope you will have the opportunity to avail yourself of the service while you are in England,' Old Blue told his very interested partner.

'It sounds wonderful. I hope Amtrak will perk up and follow suit some day. Plastic cups and plates just aren't very romantic. In my estimation, nothing is as marvelous as a train on which to enjoy trips. I just love them!'

The diner car swayed along past the bluffs and waterways of Wisconsin where green hills suddenly become naked sides of shale. Abruptly changing the subject she remarked, 'I understand that there are rattlesnakes in those mini mountains and rocky inclines.'

'That's correct,' Old Blue affirmed.

'I had a friend in Arizona who died of rattler venom after being bitten by his pet snake,' she somberly announced.

'Oh?' Old Blue shifted his weight in the booth of their dining car table.

'Yes, and he was only in his late twenties. To be bitten by his pal of five years really surprised him. The snake would want to leave the house to nest in the desert come spring; every fall, he would show up at the door wanting to come in to his glass cage where he would enjoy the winters with Larry and his family.'

'Did your friend's family enjoy the snake?' Old Blue's expression showed his predisposed judgement against such a pet.

'Let's say that the ladies of the house were understanding, not enthusiastic... especially if the viper escaped his glass house in order to explore. Frankly, I would have died with a loose snake slithering around... and without being bitten first!' She involuntarily shuddered.

'Was the fellow married?'

'Yes, and to a wife who had been an airline stewardess for Pan Am. She was totally devastated by the tragedy. The antidote didn't even help, as it turned out, he was allergic to it and death was hastened after the inoculation.'

'Dying is so tragic when it happens to the young,' her compassionate partner remarked.

'Yes, look at the Princess recently. She was such an angel of light for the misunderstood in the world, and now certain detractors of Royalty are trying to use that against a man and a family whom my father and I greatly admired and still do I might add. I hope common sense will stem the tide amongst the Parliament and our own leaders, in favor of the Royals. They've done so much good for others... they just weren't as photogenic and glamorous in my opinion. Therefore, they were not sought after by the media so frequently.'

Old Blue thought a moment. 'I defend the Prince. I know that he is a good man, and very conscientiously wants to be of service to the country – hence his unusual pursuits. The first passion he embraced seemed to be ecological balance being restored and maintained in the Isles; architecture and design followed shortly thereafter in an effort to bring their anciently beautiful nation to blend with the new buildings which are being erected. That takes great wisdom, talent and skill.' Old Blue's eyes squinted, as he looked at the lady across the table through the blue haze of cigarette smoke which was escaping his lips.

'So far, he has done a great job – so my father said before he died. Ecology and inventing methods of tillage, cultivation and devising production of crops in an environmentally safe method was Daddy's forte as well. Dad received honors for the brilliance of his ideas which truly worked.' She brushed her eyelash with a tissue and coughed.

She truly loved her old man, OB thought quietly as he lit another cigarette.

'Aren't you afraid that you'll die of lung cancer some day or cause the death of someone else who has to breathe your second-hand nicotine?' Christiana abruptly asked with a cough. Her eyes were stinging, reddened and watering from the constant cloud of cigarette haze.

'Pardon me. How thoughtless of me. I'll get along without it and go to the smoking car later.' He ground the offending cancer stick out in an aluminum ashtray.

'Sorry to be so late, are you ready to order?' a friendly waiter asked as he poured water into clear plastic glasses and set them on the white paper tablecloth.

'I'll have the vegetable lasagna,' Chrissy replied.

'I'll have your fresh salmon steak straight from Seattle's mountain streams. I've had it before and it is downright delicious,' Old Blue grinned.

The waiter hurried away.

'Speaking of detractors of the Royal family,' OB continued, 'there is always room for majesty in the order of things – that ennobling service proceeding from the heart which seeks to envelop all mankind in kindness, justice and civility. There is a need for such monarchs, presidents, prime ministers and other government leaders who keep order and true justice prevailing.'

Christiana agreed with a nod. 'Quite right, in my opinion,' she agreed as the waiter set two succulent dishes of steaming temptation before them.

'Would you like a little wine with your dinner?' the waiter asked, smiling in anticipation.

'Yes, well. No. Pardon me,' Old Blue had forgotten orders

momentarily. 'But would you like to have a little Chianti, Christiana?' His gentlemanly elegance was coming forth naturally, warm eyes aglow as he looked at his new, one-sided love.

'No thank you,' she declined with a smile.

The waiter went away and Old Blue continued the conversation where they had left off when interrupted.

'Without such world leaders, I'm afraid people would snarl and devour one another in glee like old Madam Defarges. Remember *A Tale of Two Cities?*' His brown eyes studied her face keenly through the smoke of his ever-churning thoughts.

'I do. Oh, if only the world would remember the Queen's gracious, self-sacrificing and kind ways from the very beginning of her youth to the present. She even insisted upon the Prince of Wales attending school with boys from all walks of life in order that he understand what the men and women on the street think and do. Her children went to school outside the palace; no one had done that before in Royal families – she was a visionary. How can anyone call her less? She is greatly respected by men and women of intelligence and goodwill the world over for her temperance and wisdom in many other areas as well.'

'Yes, you are right in my estimation and her son will be just like her,' Old Blue agreed. 'They are very close in heart and mind in many ways, I think.' That's why we must hurry the scepter back to London, he thought after finishing his spoken ideas.

'I think that the Prince will continue to be a person of the people as he always has been but in an appreciated sense as was his wife before him. Actually, extreme shyness in public has been his affliction except when playing polo – but that will fall away... also, he's modest and polite to a fault, you know.' A tiny bite of salmon found its way to his mouth.

'Did you ever hear of Alexis de Tocqueville who prophesied from France in the nineteenth century: "If Americans ever let go of their republicanism, she'll probably slide right into despotism rapidly"?'

Christiana looked across the table at Old Blue, who said, 'Yes, I remember him in history. Well, I suppose no nation is safe from vultures, is it – England, America, Canada.'

'Dad used to tell us to take heed to his words because times were rapidly changing, and we kids might live to see such things taking place.'

'He did?' Old Blue's eyes got bigger than saucers. 'He was a man ahead of his time! I suppose that you are next going to tell me that your father asked you to read Kenneth Goff's book on subversion of a country's democracy and government from the inside out via peaceful methods as opposed to conventional warfare.' Old Blue finished the last bite of salmon and pushed his Styrofoam plate away.

'Since you wonder, yes, I will tell you that very thing. In fact, he and Mama presented each of us with that little handbook when I was fifteen years old during a discussion regarding the Bolshevik revolution in Russia. How do you know about that booklet?' she looked at him curiously, wiping her mouth daintily with the corner of her paper napkin. Now Christiana's eyes were as big as saucers.

'Well, I've had to instruct classes using it as part of the curriculum.' Without remembering his resolve not to do so, he lit another cigarette to enjoy with the coffee which the waiter was pouring into Styrofoam cups. 'Cream?' he asked.

'Yes, thank you,' Christiana smiled, 'and sweetener.'

A little dish of half and half in tiny plastic containers sealed with foil, and another of blue packets were taken from the waiter's tray and deposited on the table with a flourish.

'I find you very unusual,' Old Blue murmured.

'And you are a little unusual yourself,' Christiana answered. 'So amazing you are, that I might dare tell another of my secret views regarding our present day society.'

'Which is?' Old Blue took a neat bite of a fresh stick of gum.

'You will think me nothing but an old sorebones if I express my feelings. I love my country with a passion, and I sorrow over her weakening moral fiber. Observing you impresses me with the idea that you like to go to parties – the kind I do not enjoy. Therefore you may find my opinions quite tedious and old-fashioned... antiquated, if you will.'

'So what if I do. You aren't so thin-skinned that you can't stand a little contempt, are you?' He smiled mischievously, took another sip of coffee and deftly wiped his trim mustache with a napkin, leaning back in the cushioned seat.

'Yes, I am thin-skinned as you call it. I have never minded constructive criticism, but I deplore cattiness, negative criticism and the lack of appreciation for an intelligent idea or valid emotion.' She looked apprehensively at him.

'I suppose you're afraid I will mock your ideas. On the contrary, I won't do such a thing because I find your views quite interestingly refreshing. I perceive that we both are impassioned concerning world affairs and its leaders. Not so?'

'Yes,' she looked at him searchingly. 'You seem like an abominable specimen of humanity, meaning no offense,' she said straightforwardly.

'You have all the charm of a rattlesnake sometimes,' he laughed. 'If your observation wasn't true, I'd be hopping mad at you right now.'

'But I wasn't finished. You seem to have a heart of gold in spite of it.' Now she searched his eyes frankly. 'That heart of gold shines through regarding those things which are right.'

'Platitudes. Platitudes. Don't credit me falsely. I am an evil man.' His eyes suddenly filled with tears.

'Oh, no!' Christiana, instantly chastised by this sudden peep into his miserably contrite soul, exclaimed. She reached across the table and placed her smooth hand over his knotty, broken, rehealed knuckles. 'I didn't mean...'

'It's okay,' he casually moved his hand from under hers which stirred deep longings he had been ordered not to feel.

They heard the whistle blow three long blasts as the speeding Amtrak train soared over the tracks searching for Chicago and Union Station.

'Why did you throw your old stogie in the newsman's case?' Christiana suddenly asked with a twinkle in her now devilish eyes.

Old Blue did a double take, but it didn't dispel his heavy, contrite frame of mind. This was too much. He reached into his Harris tweed and got a pack of cigarettes with a lighter stuck between the cellophane and soft pack from the inside breast pocket. Knocking a poison stick out against the back of his hand, he raised the pack to his hard-looking mouth, catching the white filter tip. Putting the package back next to his heart, he flicked the lighter and lit up.

'It seems that only the good die young,' he reflected, 'the wicked survive.' He stood. 'Let's go to the club car where there is more leg room.'

He ushered her along. As he waved her into a seat in the glass domed car and sat down beside her, he rotated his chair to look squarely at her and asked, 'So, are you going to tell me your eccentric views, which are supposed to bore me to tears?'

'Oh, do you really want to hear them?' she blushed.

'Why not?' he affirmed.

'No one else seems to like such conversation.'

'Awe, go ahead. It's about time I listen to something serious.' Old Blue hitched his long arms by the elbows on the very back of the armrest as if settling down for a nap. He was studying the gradually changing bunny-to-lioness image in front of him.

'It's regarding the masses, the proverbial, teeming masses in my own beloved country's cities. Maybe my type of work has isolated me too much these past few years, but I think not. For I have a sixteen-year-old son who will be attending college, and I have tried to pay attention to the social climate into which he must be submerged. I don't want his sense of patriotism and appreciation for what our founding fathers established for all Americans to be adulterated.' She looked worriedly across the three feet of space between them. 'I believe in truth, but not in pots calling kettles black when it comes to our leaders, nor our heroes past and present. No one is perfect, nor has been in my humble opinion. I deplore the dressing down of Thomas Jefferson who crafted the Declaration of Independence, the...'

She faltered, suddenly embarrassed at her passion. 'No one is without fault during a lifetime.' Christiana crossed her shapely legs.

'In the noise and glare of today's irreverent and sacrilegious society which seems bent on pleasure, sex, and graphic violence pummeling the senses of our youth, I'd say that is a legitimate concern for a young mother, be she single or married. Proceed. I'm listening.' He blew a smoke ring toward the door of the car, rocking with the motion of rails and steel wheels.

Christiana continued, 'I guess what bothers me the most about the shouting masses of late is that they emphasize freedom of speech, yet they are the very ones who deny anyone with an opposite view of that very principle by shouting them down at public forums, or at debates.' She relinquished the floor.

'Yes. When both sides are not given equal respect and silence in which to debate their convictions, those who are shouting commit an act of tyranny against the others, and against the Constitution, which they flaunt and espouse so violently. It seems that rudeness has become the fashion, the platform on which intelligent, well-bred, educated men and women of reason must stand.' He looked at Christiana whose eyes were blazing like Roman candles during Fourth of July nights. 'Since Adam and Eve's sons fell victim to the conviction that one gift was as good as another, I suppose men like to prove it by shouting one another down and killing each other – even as did Cain and Abel,' Old Blue added dispassionately.

'Don't you mean... since jealousy set in, hurt set in, rage set in, when one didn't feel his gift was as good or as accepted as the other?' her irritated feelings were spoken in absolute calm, as she was one never to raise her voice in anger.

'Same thing, Miss Green Eyes. We're saying the same thing with different words.' He smiled and went to get them a Coke.

Enjoying a brief respite from having a constant companion who sometimes made her comfortable, and sometimes absolutely indignant felt good. 'I wish he'd go take a nap someplace for a while,' she said aloud to no one in particular. 'His intensity wears me out.'

'Here, I took the liberty of getting a glass of ice for you in case you aren't partial to drinking out of cans,' her amiable companion said as he sat before her carrying two cans and a glass in one massive hand.

Christiana's irritation flew out the window. Just when one hated him, he turned into a charmer!

The train flew through the country like an avenging angel bent on assailing the ills of the world for Christiana, the Queen, the Princes, the suddenly deceased icons of God's empathy for the downtrodden of the earth not only in England, but in India and her own home as well.

'Two angels have been recalled to heaven – Mother Teresa and her protégé of a few days' teaching, who put what she had learned in so short a time to such astonishingly good use. Our heroines,' Christiana murmured.

'So,' Old Blue said, 'how would you go about implementing the golden rule… that of doing unto others as you'd have them do unto you?' He blew another smoke ring. Christiana smoked only from her ears because he seemed so insolent all of a sudden. She choked on the smoke, which by this time had turned the compartment blue.

'Pardon me, sir,' she said kindly but firmly, 'being you are such a gentleman, would you mind extinguishing your cigarette? As you probably have observed, I am experiencing difficulty, not only in seeing you through the haze but in finding available oxygen to breathe!' She privately wondered how anyone could be so selfish, or at least so unobservant when he prided himself in being the opposite.

'Your fangs are showing… claws too,' he coolly said as he mashed the tip into an ashtray. 'Actually, I should have remembered that non-smokers usually don't enjoy having extra nicotine and carcinogens permeating the air. They like neat, sterile rooms full of boredom as in a hospital ward!'

The tension of the past forty-eight hours was obviously getting to them both, as well as the sexual attraction which was not recognized by Christiana but very much so by her companion.

He remembered arriving in Minnesota where he had been dunned up one side and down the other regarding the fact that she was entirely off limits to him. Finally, when he exploded at his superiors in typical fashion, demanding why, they could have knocked him over with a feather after the explanation. 'I don't believe it!' was all he could mutter.

'Well, you'd better believe it, Jack, and get her to the Palace with nary a hair touched on that sweet, little head of hers.'

'If she's so dang precious, where the deuce is her calf?' he had shouted in sudden rage. 'Are you such incompetents that you have left him alone with danger all about?' Old Blue snarled, looking exactly like a vicious, cornered wolf.

'Calm down. He's safe. He will be joining her soon. We didn't want to disturb his life any more than it already has been. He and she will decide what is best for them both, not you, not me, not anyone but the powers that be, and two unsuspecting hearts. It's worth a try.'

'Oh, quit messing with my brain – the Stuart-Deerfields are not the finds of the century. Their whereabouts have been known all along, as were their father and their grandmother and great-grandmothers before them. Who do you think you are addressing? A dumb cluck? Kiss off.'

'Look, pal,' his CO said, 'your nerves are jangled because you can't have booze on duty...'

Old Blue cut him off. 'I ought to smack you for that.'

'You're being insolent, sir!' his superior advisor said.

'So when has that become such a surprise to you?' Old Blue snarled back. 'I've always been a pain in the neck, but that hasn't stopped you from rejecting my pleas for retirement the past ten years, I've noticed. Who gets all the sucking crybabies who screw up, home again for you? This snarling old dog, that's who.' His anger was spent, and he had dropped his skinny behind onto the plush, white leather couch in the briefing room of the Hilton pent house. Suddenly he had realized what was wrong with him. He loved his charge so much that worrying about her son had become natural, and already feeling responsible for the kid's safety and happiness consumed him. And I haven't even seen him! he thought.

'Jesu, Mary and Joseph,' he groaned in a subdued manner, 'Just promise me one thing. Once I have delivered her to fame and fortune, please let me slink off to my lair out in the rolling flatlands of South Dakota.'

'We can't do that old boy,' was the respectful reply and, with compassion, 'We need to have you find the man who snatched the scepter and deliver both to MI6, of course. We're worried and don't want any anarchy in the streets of London. Only you, Rick, and Sam can find the rest of the gang who disgraced and threatened our ally, if indeed there was anarchy suggested by this insult to the throne, not to mention a slap at England's particular form of government. We need to move quickly if there is more than one person involved. But we need you heading up the team to find that out for us and all three Americans to be the cowboys on this one. Round them up, and bring them in. Think you can handle it? Anyone left in the streets devious enough to steal the scepter out from under everyone's noses makes a nation nervous.'

'Yah. Sure. Since when can't I?' A tear slipped off Blue's aquiline nose. 'You don't care about my skinny arse, so why should I? Some day you'll find Old Blue face down with a knife stuck in his back. Do you think you'll give a damn? Naw! We're just numbers to you. You pick the cream of the crop from Harvard and Oxford and turn us into murderers for justice, and won't let us retire without a lobotomy or something worse if we can't handle our liquor because of a guilty conscience. Oh, what the deuce!'

'Hey, man. Don't be so hard on yourself nor us. It isn't quite like that, and you know it. Without you and guys like you, the Wall would still be up. You know that,' his superior said. 'You're not out there killing the innocent and suffering. You're out there knocking down the things and ideologies which suppress, murder and starve them. Come on, "Joshua". You're the best. Nations have always had warriors who defended good and cast down evil. Sad but true that it is needed in the modern world, but it is and you are the best.'

The train gave a jolt, bringing Old Blue back to the present. Looking at his little soft-eyed companion, he realized that not for all the tea in China would he have lost this opportunity to be with someone so full of majesty, and the thing he loved about her the most was that she didn't even recognize it within herself.

'Are you going to proceed with your discourse, or did I anger you too greatly?' he softly inquired. 'If you'll overlook my somewhat boorish behavior at times, I'd be pleased to hear the rest of what you wanted to say. Sometimes I'm a bad actor, and I apologize.'

Geez! he thought to himself, I've got it bad. I've never apologized to anyone in my whole, miserable life!

'How about taking a walk to another club car where I'll be able to indulge while you expound?' He smiled softly in compassion at her.

'You're on!' She suddenly grinned widely, showing perfect teeth.

With that, OB pressed the Maverick on his tie clasp as if to straighten the ensemble.

The whole club car to which they were advancing was instantly cleared of passengers.

'We have nice accommodations,' Christina observed as they entered the adjacent car. 'Business must be slow. We have it all to ourselves!'

Seated comfortably they looked at the fall sky overhead through the glass dome. She ventured, 'I think... it's wild... are you ready? You'll think I am truly a dolt.'

'It's okay. Shoot.' His left foot was propped against the rocking aluminum sash of the window frame; his cowboy boot reflected the glowing tip of a cigarette as one hand hung loosely off his knee.

'Well,' she continued, 'I think that when a people are not firmly grounded in a religious faith that brings joy, peace and hope into minds and hearts, I believe that such a nation is doomed to failure. There, I've said it.'

'Do you want to share that faith?' Old Blue asked quietly.

'I wish I could. For I see in your eyes a torture at times which I have never seen in anyone's before, and it makes me know that my Teacher could heal your pain, even as He healed mine these past seven years.' She smiled timidly. 'As a matter of fact, you remind me of something in Goethe's *Faust*.'

'And, what is that? I'm afraid to ask.' He looked exaggeratedly heavenward.

'Well, Mephistopheles and God were discussing Faust and Mephistopheles was pointing out how disturbed Faust was deep inside. God said, "Although he serves me now confusedly, I soon will lead him where the light is clear."'

Old Blue continued for her, 'But then, Mephistopheles asked, "What do you bet? The man you're bound to lose, *if* with your permission I may lead him lightly into my path... and as I choose!"'

'Yes!' cried Christiana. 'But God laid rules which Mephistopheles had to follow, he couldn't take him off home base, which was the earth. God was sure that the devil would have to eventually admit that man in essence is *good*… that the "darkly driven" would know the way to that which is right eventually.'

'You are a dreamer, my dear.' Old Blue shook his head as he rested his elbows on his knees in contemplation. 'Men like me are too mean to die when we should. Just the good die young… like the Princess.' He sat there, head hanging down as if sorry for all the sins of the world.

'Maybe, maybe not,' Christiana replied. 'Maybe we don't die until our spirits are truly at their best in order to be presented to God.'

'Too deep for me. I'd rather think on something else and have a beer!' Suddenly sitting upright, he flashed an irresistible smile her way, merry eyes dancing.

'So much for Johann Wolfgang von Goethe's *Faust*, Act I,' she mourned. 'Let's change the subject. I've had enough too.'

'Not so fast,' Old Blue surprised her. 'That classic is just a repeat of the book of Job, in my estimation… same story… different names. All men have a yearning for evil, or at least a taste of it; and the rare one who doesn't, gets the dogs sicced on him which in turn creates havoc. Look at poor old Job. If that is one's reward for being perfect, let me escape his teachings!'

Old Blue couldn't wait to be free of her to go cuss a blue streak somewhere just to relieve his tension. Yet the other half of him didn't want to move. His partner was saying something:

'… of His love on the tablets of our hearts, and it becomes natural to always act kind, good, forgiving… just like Him. We don't have to try to change our natures… it just happens. The greatest thing that happened to me was that I was able to truly forgive my husband, forgetting the shocking thing which took him so suddenly from our son and me,' her head dropped.

Old Blue looked at her like a cat watching a mouse hole.

She continued, 'I loved him greatly, and was totally surprised and hurt by his need to leave; but now there is not a bit of bitterness, nor anger, nor sorrow left within my heart.' She looked up.

'How's that?' Old Blue asked.

'My Teacher, my Comforter did that for me.' She looked over

at Old Blue, her eyes so full of peace and the purity of a love he had never seen before gripped his heart... and he felt a sensation, a Presence which he had never experienced. It gave him pleasant goosebumps clear to his core, which was not a sexual excitement. It felt refreshingly clean, good, like a river of cool, clear water washing over the smouldering coals of his abused soul.

'So,' she softly continued, 'I am ambitious to have wise teachers in our country who will interpret religious texts properly and within context to all; for if the true original teachings of good men, and of the One whom I believe was and is the Son of God, were purely acted upon, wars would cease; greed and disrespect for others of different class would not take food out of our children's mouths; vice and violence would not pollute the minds of our youth via television, magazines, recordings, movies. We'd have a different world, one of peace, hope, love, generosity... majesty!'

She smiled quietly and said, as if to herself, 'I wonder when mankind will ever learn "if your neighbor asks for your coat, give him your cloak, also."'

Looking up at Old Blue she was surprised to see him wiping a tear from the deeply etched lines beneath his tired, suddenly vulnerable eyes.

'"And yet I show you a more excellent way,"' he muttered, for once upon a very long time ago, Old Blue had been an altar boy, '"and, if someone smite thee on the cheek, turn the other one."'

'When are you going to learn to quote correctly?' gently chided a smiling Christiana.

He shrugged his shoulders and smiled in spite of his inner pain, 'When you do.'

Their eyes locked in utter honesty of spirit.

Deboarding at Union Station, Old Blue raced to a payphone while the three sisters settled into a high-backed bench in the main lobby. A porter rolled their luggage ahead of them on a cart as people surged everywhere in the beautiful nineteenth-century structure full of shops and eateries. The marble pillars and walls carried echoes into the high ceiling and back, creating a pleasant din of excitement.

As the girls talked, OB walked across from the ticket counters to check a locker. Unlocking the door, he discovered nothing more than hot air inside.

'This locker wasn't big enough to hold a scepter anyway, unless the rod had a Royal hinge in the center and could be folded like a cue stick for Minnesota Fats,' he expostulated aloud. 'Brains! All I ask is that someone have brains to figure such things out before they send me chasing on a stupid train. At this rate, we'll get to London next year. Next thing you know, I'll be told to bring the ladies by banana boat express across the Atlantic!'

Grumbling he rounded up the women, caught a taxi, discharged the luggage into yet another, and headed out to O'Hare International Airport.

Boarding Northwest flight 409, all were seated in the bulkhead. Christiana was seated in the second seat from the aisle; OB in the aisle seat next to the door. The other two ladies sat across the way in the center section directly next to their guide.

As the plane hushed with anticipation for take-off, Christiana noticed a woman with orange hair peeping out of a black silk hat, eyeing Old Blue with eyes full of malice. As the unusual woman checked her appearance in a huge compact, golden bangles on her wrists softly jangled. She then looked up at a skinny blond kid who said something Christiana couldn't hear before he left the plane's mid-section and went to the seat behind Old Blue.

Christiana felt uneasy. She wished Old Blue had seen them.

He had.

Chapter Twenty-One

Christiana rose from the chair at Number 10 Downing Street in which she had been sitting, to gaze out the window. The draperies had been pulled aside to offer a view of Horseguards' Parade. The midday honey-sun cast a golden glow over the buildings within her view, their white marble facades and steps warmly alight. Part of St. James Park was visible across the way. Tourists were sadly walking, looking about or just standing en masse.

'I will never understand violence and malicious greed in the heart of mankind if I live to be one hundred years of age,' she thought aloud thinking of the recent street chase which had ended in a world of grief; and of the news concerning greed for power by what seemed to be the pernicious teaser of the world in the Middle East. She turned to look at he who was called Rob, with worried eyes. 'The men in my family were strong, sensitive and quietly civil in the home and out. So how do such inhumane persons who spend millions on factories of biological and chemical agents, which can wipe man from the face of the earth, become that way? What causes their selfishness to become depraved? Why do they become filled with lust for power and even more riches? Why don't they want to share with the poor? Have they lost all compassion? Have they forgotten what it feels like when one's own flesh is pinched, punctured, wounded? Have they forgotten the sensations deep within the mind and heart when one's own loved ones suffer, when one's own child, born of our own bodies, is hungry and cannot eat because there is no bread in the cupboard?' Rage and hurt over the suffering of others caused by humans of no conscience seethed beneath the calm exterior, causing her complexion to become totally ashen. Standing there in emerald wool blazer, black gored skirt over soft kid walking boots, she looked smart and chic. The green of her eyes blazed from the depths of color which black spiraled curls created as they framed her face.

'The news is appalling from the Middle East lately, let alone the English tragedy. In my mind, if people respected one another's right to happiness none of these things would be taking place.'

Old Blue looked at her. They were alone in the PM's office. He had not yet arrived, busy Prime Minister that he was.

'Maybe that is why savage behavior became savage in the first place,' he softly countered. 'There is a thin line between hatred and love. If a baby or young child witnesses or feels hunger, barbarity; sees the murder of their own parents, siblings and neighbors, would it not be natural to hate? Would it not be natural to want to do unto others what they've done to you?'

She contemplated his point with understanding and slowly answered, 'I think it would depend upon one's upbringing – those teachings in deed and word which have been a part of that particular familial environment for generations. Anger over injustice, frustration and grief itself can fall under the powerful healing balm of love, returning good for evil,' Christiana conjectured.

'Possibly. But who can or ever did react in that way?' Old Blue wondered aloud.

'How about those who braved modern hell to save the Jewish population in Europe when Hitler reigned almost supreme? Also, the One who brought Christianity in its purest form, and those who embraced the forgiving nature of the commandment to love one's neighbor as one's self?' Christiana hopefully offered in answer to his question. 'Those thrown to the lions in Rome loved their tormentors even as death came.'

'Could you be so brave... so selfless?' His brown eyes keenly watched her without malice.

Christiana bowed her glossy black head. Shuddering visibly as if suddenly chilled, she murmured, 'I truly don't know. I know that I could eventually forgive because I am like that. But to be brave enough to face death or torture? I don't think so.' Self-effaced, she couldn't look up.

'You've already saved a drowning child by diving into a sandpit full of water. You had courage without forethought to do that when you saw the need.' He gently brought up an incident in her life as a thirteen-year-old camp girl.

'How do you know of that?' she raised her head abruptly.

'Oh, excuse me, but here comes one of the proverbial powers that be.'

A door opened behind Christiana who had walked past the window to stand near the council room door. She turned, finding herself staring unexpectedly into a pair of smiling, blue eyes.

'Christiana Stuart, I believe?' The Prime Minister held his hand out to her in greeting.

She clasped it with her own firm handshake. 'Yes, I am she,' smiling in spite of her surprise, maintaining poise and interest, a blush ensued.

'And Old Blue!' The PM turned about, striding toward Christiana's companion who had stood to his feet, looking elegantly tall and lanky in his sharply pressed Armani suit. The men shook hands.

Christiana simply stared with ill-concealed surprise at the name which the dignitary had called her companion. They act as if they are old buddies, she thought.

Turning back to the lady, their host ushered Old Blue and himself toward her.

'Please, come into my inner office,' he opened the door from whence he had come, allowing an MI5 officer to then take the entrance panel in hand. The Prime Minister escorted Christiana into his holy of holies; Old Blue followed, but stopped with arms folded in front of the door, which closed softly behind him. The MI5 officer quietly stood directly opposite, unseen, on the other side of the door, arms folded likewise as he faced outwardly toward the freshly abandoned room.

'Well OB, do you think this young lady would make a good queen?' The British dignitary flashed a smile at the now somber CIA agent.

'I do,' Old Blue answered gravely.

Christiana again showed surprise, and some embarrassment. If this was a joke, she thought it ill-advised but did not lose her composure.

The lady was led to a Queen Anne chair and encouraged to be seated, which her trembling knees welcomed. Suddenly she felt very cold in spite of the cheerful blaze beside which she had warmed herself in the other room.

A servant brought in a silver tea service sporting Royal Doulton cups and saucers, and of all things one large man-sized mug that said 'OLD BLUE' in navy printed around its periphery of white. Seeing the latter made Christiana smile, and suddenly her adrenaline stopped kicking up its heels. She recognized camaraderie between two men, both obviously powerful but in different ways.

Had the US President, Kurt Kousins of country and western song fame, Rob, and the British PM all been students of the same college, possibly meeting as alumni every now and again?

'Impossible!' Christiana said aloud.

'Pardon me?' the Prime Minister smiled as he seated himself opposite her in a burgundy leather wing chair.

'Oh, pardon me; I was just fancying that perhaps your "Old Blue", as you call him, and possibly two other unlikely fellows went to Oxford's Queen's College. The mug inspired my inspiration.'

'Actually you are correct, at least in part.'

Not wanting to pursue it further for fear of being regarded as nosy, Christiana smilingly accepted the tea offered. The butler then poured steaming black coffee into the mug, took it to Old Blue but was waved smilingly away with, 'Thanks but no thank you. I'll catch you later.' His hands needed to be free.

'Oh, take it!' the Prime Minister piped up. 'The others are outside the door at attention. Do come and sit with us.'

'Thank you just the same, but if you don't mind, old buddy, I really would feel more comfortable right here.'

'As you wish, however, may I convince you to accept the coffee? The cook will have a moan if it isn't appreciated after all the fussing that went on in the kitchen to prepare it. Egg was added to the grounds and it was boiled as you do over campfires in your part of the U.S.A.' The PM laughed. 'You'd best drink it all if staying in good graces with Cookie means anything to you.'

The two men laughed together.

'How is that old mutton-cooker, anyway? Convey my thanks, please. It's been a long time since I've eaten any of his fabulous grub.'

'I'll pass it along; and he is fine, just fine.'

Settling back into his burgundy leather, the Prime Minister kindly smiled at the unselfconscious beauty who sat demurely across from him. She was totally unaware of her good looks.

'I can imagine that you're wondering why you've been brought here,' he kindly addressed Christiana.

'Yes I am, sir,' she quietly answered. 'It has all been quite sudden... and very mysterious, to say the least.'

'To answer your curiosity, may I first inquire whether or not you are aware of your particular ancestry?' He continued looking at her in a kindly fashion.

'I am aware of having English roots which date back to the violent seventeenth century. Supposedly, we came from the little town of Corfe. Am I right in assuming that you know my history as well if not better than I?' She smiled.

'Undoubtedly,' he smiled and offered more tea.

'No thank you,' she declined and set the cup and saucer down on the table beside her chair.

'Perhaps; and your sister, Angela. Are you close to her?'

'Oh, yes! As a matter of fact, she is my only confidante regarding certain matters. My other sister Pamela and I are very close to her.' She dropped her gaze, remembering the painful disclosure the day of the funeral a fortnight ago.

'Yes?' The PM observed the integrity of an unusually pure spirit unfolding before him. 'Was not speculation cruel regarding our bereaved notables recently?'

Christiana, recognizing wisdom preceded by perception, which enabled the Prime Minister to project his sensitivities into the mindset of others, raised her bowed head. Searching the kind eyes of her interrogator, she instantly decided that the respect mirrored there deserved a totally unguarded answer.

'Yes, it was. I felt compassion and sorrow not only for the children, but for their father; and grandmothers as well. I felt and still feel that during the days immediately following the Princess's death, all of them were being greatly misunderstood, and consequently misjudged by the majority. Frustration comes from anger and hurt which has no meaningful way of being expressed, I suppose.'

Old Blue sauntered over to the tea tray to pour himself another cup of coffee. The Prime Minister smiled up at him. The men are unusually comfortable and free in one another's company, Christiana thought.

One of the telephones rang. Reaching over to pick up the receiver, the PM said, 'Yes?' Listening awhile, he said, 'Perfect. Now is a good time. Bring her in.' Cradling the receiver back into its resting place on the table beside his chair, he then put the teacup and saucer onto the table before him.

The door opened once more. The men stood up. Christiana's mind did a double take, for into the room came a tired but gracious Queen.

Christiana was at a loss of what to do at first. Then she rose and humbly bowed her head. Being an American, she did not know if it was proper to curtsy, but she did know that humility was always in good taste when before those whose station in life was higher than her own.

The lovely Royal offered her hand to Christiana, and spoke in her little voice, which was warm and inviting. Chrissy raised her head feeling as if she were in a dream... had been here before... a Royal presence... a Queen... a motherly Queen. What was it? Where had it been? She looked sweetly into the clear blue eyes of the diminutive lady who smiled and then was escorted into a chair of pale blue silk. She indicated that the others might do the same, and Old Blue held the chair for his startled charge to sink into.

The telephone rang again. After a brief, 'Yes, show her in,' the door opened and in stepped Angela. Relieved to see her elder sister, Christiana smiled.

Her sister curtsied before the Queen; Christiana wondered as to the reason, which was forthcoming from the Prime Minister.

'Let's get to the core of this little matter,' the man in charge said. 'First of all, it's a pleasure for our gracious Sovereign and me to meet you both at last.' Opening a black leather folder, he pulled documents from its interior.

Handing them to Angela and Christiana, he said, 'As you can see, we are in the presence of three Royal persons, not only one.'

Angela did not seem to be surprised, Christiana thought.

'Please speak, and feel free to explain to your sister,' the PM urged while Old Blue sat grinning.

An hour passed during which the entire story of the Deerfields was explained.

'So we have brought you here in the hope that you will some day fit into our country in a meaningful way. Perhaps you can cheer the heart of a Prince,' the PM said at the end.

Christiana was dumfounded by the last sentence. Old Blue couldn't understand himself, for suddenly he felt angry.

When Old Blue got to his temporary quarters at St. James Palace, he placed a call to the sweet torturer of his toughened soul.

'Hello?' the light, young, and innocent voice floated intimately into his ear from the telephone.

'Hi, Christiana? Old Blue here.'

'Oh, hi! How are you? I thought I'd never hear from you again.'

'No such luck. Anyway, how are you?' his deep, resonant voice sounded delicious over the telephone. If one never saw the man and heard only his voice over the phone, one could fall in love, she thought to herself.

'I am comfortable, happy, a little bewildered, and very sleepy. It's far past midnight, you know.'

'Did I wake you?'

'No. I was lying awake, trying to sort the events of the day into a semblance of sanity.'

'Where's Angela?'

'Right here in the next bed. Without her, I'd feel quite... oh I don't know... quite shaken is the word I suppose.'

'I understand,' he pulled on a cigarette, the tip glowing in the darkness of his room. He'd been too depressed to turn the lights on upon entering – the night light was enough with which to maneuver. He coughed; his heart squeezed with longing for her.

'Well, I just wanted to make sure you were safely tucked into The Savoy's finest sheets before I doze off.' He was silent a moment.

'That was very kind of you; and I wish to thank you for escorting me to these shores and this astonishing surprise.'

'You're quite welcome. I wish the trip could have lasted longer. I found your mindset refreshing and unusual. Your philosophy of life sounds much like that of Rick's and he's a peach of a guy.'

'Yes. He's a wonderful brother-in-law.'

'Well, I must run along and sleep fast. Tomorrow will be quite busy, and will start at 0500 hours for this old dog. Goodnight.'

'Thank you, and goodnight.'

They hung up the receivers. Both laid back, and in the darkness of individual rooms wished to know one another better.

'Thank God I didn't have to set up camp in her room as Wise Acres indicated. I would have died of desire before dawn!' Old Blue moaned.

Chapter Twenty-Two

Eleven hours later, Old Blue sauntered down the sidewalk which lined the Mall. Orange, of all people, had been assigned to stand watch over Christiana and her sisters at The Savoy; however, before either agent had to report on duty they managed to have a break together.

Now his heart was in a bind. He should have been happy for having been with an old friend. It was a bitterly cold night but the chill he felt had nothing to do with the weather, for he had just come from the bangled dame's house in Piccadilly. It was midnight; the moon was full and high on this frosty, cheerless evening of his soul.

He had made two disturbing discoveries while clasped in the arms of his lover. As pillow talk goes between two old confidantes in clandestine operations, Orange had been contemptuously railing against the very Majesty he was in England to protect. True to form and the deep respect and admiration he himself felt toward the Crown, Old Blue had said nothing but lit a stogie and settled back on the pillows to hear the callous derision which verbally poured from her mouth. Blue's cigar smoke had filled the darkened room, while street lights cast shadows over Orange's countenance as she waved naked arms in emphasis, bare except for the ever-present bangles. Never before had the jewelry sounded distasteful to him. They reminded him that those arms could meet wickedness with karate force, the legs could fly faster than most for she had a black belt, not to mention a steady arm and eye as the force's crack shot next to Old Blue with firearm or bow; and she could hold her own when deciphering a flow of lies from truth as it poured from a terrorist's lips.

Not for vain glory had she and OB stolen samples and sacked the biological/chemical lab in Siberia. Barely escaping with their lives as they shot their way back to the Phantom jet which stood in the mists of night, they'd taken off beneath radar capabilities out of the country back to London. Their cargo of samples, film and their own selves being still intact was a coup in itself. Orange fiercely believed in liberty to the point of going overboard. For her, freedom meant no rules period.

That last conviction of hers was what was troubling Old Blue not to mention the personal drawing away from her physically. 'For the first time in my sorry life, I needed Viagra!' He literally writhed inside with embarrassment and sudden anger toward the person whose image had made a mockery of his prowess as she had danced before his mind's eye during the night with those green eyes surrounded by straight lashes!

I'll be a monkey's uncle if I don't love her! Drat, I'm not allowed to love that girl! She's for the Prince. He'll be a fool if he doesn't grab her! he thought. His big old heart mocked and tortured him. With an effort, he turned his thoughts back to the orange flame who had suddenly become a cold lump of coal.

'That woman no longer sees the forest. She only sees the trees!' he later concluded in his mutterings as slowly the Victorian lamp posts slid by, one by one overhead. He plunged both hands deep within his trench coat. The fog was dense and needling to be felt at bone level.

'With Orange's acrimonious attitude, she's showing symptoms of burnout if she's not already there! God-all-Friday! If that's the case, I don't want her as a partner anymore! Soft-hearted as I am toward an old friend whose doctorate from Harvard I admire, I don't want my skinny behinder on the line in such a duo! No way! Too many of our buddies have bit the dirt under partners whose woes overwhelmed good judgment. I need to request a trip to Langley for dismissal on an extended R and R for her. Sorry, old girl!'

A sense of relief swiftly followed by guilt surged through his torn chest. He pulled his hands out of the London Fog coat to fish for a smoke with which to rekindle his soul; his mutterings ceased as he lit up, cupping the flame and cigarette tip against the gusts of wind which ruffled his soft curls as if they were the short, rounded feathers on an ostrich breast.

His thoughts then turned to wondering why there was such a vacant feeling deep within his being after an hour and a half with his favorite old flame, their love affair having ticked off almost three decades. Again, an instant sight of emerald green eyes bathed in innocence mirroring complete lack of guile plagued him... the curve of an intelligent brow. Poignantly, memories of soft black curls spilling onto that smooth forehead assailed. The piquant face with a slightly stubborn-looking square chin and upturned nose with delicate bridge and nostrils, which sometimes suddenly flared as a doe's when caught in a thicket, plagued him. He was a hunter approaching the resting place of her soul, and she sensed it even though no words had been spoken to that effect. Remembering how ashen Christiana's high cheekbones had become when she learned of her true identity, Old Blue's heart ached for the little Royal even as he mournfully lusted upon her.

'Of all the times to be told! Just when the foreign press boldly cries revolution and one gets chased to death, she learns of her heritage. I wish I'd never brought Christiana here. I hate to see her life change – except for the inheritance, which will catapult her into being able to help her son.'

He wondered where it would all end for her. 'I wonder if the Prince will be as taken with her as I... my Romanov blood and all!'

Bingo! At last he named the source of his primary torment – his own identity still fresh from the love he had borne his grandfather and father. The latter's remembrance was still fresh – that of escaping Russia to Paris. From there they had been smuggled to South Dakota in the USA. Their last name had then been changed to Lavernson. When Old Blue had been born, his name was legally recorded as Robert Alexander Lavernson in the United States as it was now with the CIA and Interpol.

Chapter Twenty-Three

Another meeting was called with the powers that be at Number 10 Downing Street.

'Well, boys. Who have you gathered as suspects?' The Prime Minister looked around the half circle of Americans sitting before his inner office desk. Scar-P, the faithful 'taxi driver' stood on guard outside the door, which made them all feel relaxed. No one, apart from Old Blue, was as proficient.

'We don't have conclusive evidence regarding Raoul DeSilva, nor his brother Ned; nor the hapless fellow caught in Rye. The last person mentioned seemingly knows nothing regarding the scepter, even though he comes from the country with the most recently clear motive. I think he is a Kurd so a plot to injure this country doesn't fit. Even the Hope Diamond in his bag was paste. What he was doing stalking Rick seems unrelated to the matter in England regarding the scepter; but it may have to do with the USA's loss,' Old Blue, as captain of his team explained.

'What about the government in the Kurd's country?' the PM inquired.

'Well, we've noticed that the ambassador showed up August 31st, and has since been seen about town carrying an elongated case of slender proportions into the Mansion House.'

'Who observed that visit?' the blue-eyed British man wanted to know. He turned to Sam for an answer.

'As I understood it, Joe Bly saw it while walking his beat,' Sam replied and sat up in his chair.

'Bless old Bly,' the PM smiled. 'We could use a hundred more of the dear soul. He loves his Queen, country, wife and children – in that order. He's been mourning the scepter and the Royals' loss for weeks now. After taking it so hard, I hope he is the one to recover the brilliant symbol. It seems a personal loss in an absolute way, which no one can talk him out of.' A sigh was heard. 'Rick, what are your thoughts on these matters?'

'I think that the Mideastern faction has probable cause for acting out against the UK simply because Butler and his team of inspectors have been a sore irritant for quite some time as politics go. Therefore, to disgrace the United Kingdom at the same time as causing an affront to the United States is quite conceivable. My gut instinct is not with my intellectual reasoning on this one. Of course, I've been wrong before.' He ran a finger over his tie, smoothing it more neatly into the clasp. 'To disgrace the US's arch ally would be a strong incentive to humble both nations' leaders, that is for certain.' Rick looked up at the PM. 'But why bother to take the scepter? Their objective could have been gained without taking it.'

Old Blue stirred, placing one ankle over the knee of his other leg.

'Maybe they needed the money which selling the item to a private party would bring. Blockades have been strong for a very long time, you know. Their coffers must be quite dry by now.'

'But if they took the scepter, why would a golden bangle bracelet be left by accident and a miniature of some ancient princess?' Sam asked.

Rick lifted his golden mane to answer as he sought the eyes of his buddy: 'The bracelet could have fallen off the arm of any tourist prior to the theft; or it also could be a pointed message to the British government, the Parliament, the Throne, the House of Lords and the entire Commonwealth. Reason? Because the scepter along with the crown emblematizes their unity of purpose and the scepter indicates majesty with justice and mercy – or so it seems to me.' He tapped his fingers on the arm of his wing chair.

The Prime Minister thanked the men and then said, 'Old Blue, you've been selected to rendezvous with Scotland Yard when they interrogate all the suspects whom you've listed. We are especially interested in all the DeSilvas. We are wishing to examine as many as we can who visited the Tower the day of the scepter's disappearance. Of course, there will be a few we won't be able to recognize by comparing video camera images with passports, and so forth. Interpol will be able to match many, as well as the International Identification Bureau. All have been busily searching and conducting depositions already.'

'Depositions from everyone?' Sam asked incredulously.

'Not everyone – just those who for some reason give us cause enough to be suspect.'

'That's a relief. DeSilva's wife not only looks like an angel, she is one! I'd hate to see her even hear that the DeSilvas are suspect!' Rick exclaimed, picking his white Stetson from the table beside his chair. His amethystine eyes were clearly troubled.

'And as you know, she accompanied Ned to the Tower, August 31st.'

'She is your wife's dearest friend, is she not?' the Prime Minister inquired.

'Yes she is and a wonderful girl – gentle, kind and compassionate. She thinks the whole world's population is basically good and could be persuaded to let the good side of their natures come through if only encouraged. She doesn't understand violence and evil any more than Pamela's little sister understands it.'

'You mean Christiana Elizabeth Stuart?' the dignitary smiled. 'We hope that someday she will be a very important woman in the land of her birth as well as here, and that those very characteristics will shine softly as a beacon for our kingdom.'

Old Blue squirmed in his seat, sorrow and latent anger rousing at the thought which had just projected from the PM's mouth. 'I might be loyal to my friends, but I don't approve of that plan,' he said.

The telephone rang.

'Yes?' their host asked. He listened a minute. 'You're absolutely certain?' Silence. 'Now that it's there again, I sincerely hope that security has been doubled all round. Is the new case sensitive to body warmth radiating from at least eight feet? The visitors will not like being checked by electronics before they cross that eight foot barrier, but it cannot be helped.' Silence again. 'Okay then. That should be all that's necessary unless the person whom we seek is a virtual Houdini. Thank you and tell Old Joe thank you from his PM.'

He thoughtfully put the telephone receiver back into its cradle, a satisfied look spread across his young face.

'Well fellows, we have a new development.' He stood to his

feet and walked a short distance over to the fireplace. Leaning against it with his right hand grasping the mantle, he said, 'Unbelievable as it may sound, the scepter is now back in the case! The paste replica was left lying on the floor.' He turned from the slow blaze to gaze into the surprised faces of the trio.

'They broke into the new case?' Old Blue whistled.

'Yes, into the new case!' the Prime Minister quietly answered.

'If you don't mind me saying so,' drawled Sam, the laid-back cowboy with the straight black hair, 'I think someone is just deliberately tweaking his nose at the Royal House, unless of course, the jewels in the original scepter have been removed and replaced with paste.' He sat slouched low in a burgundy chair, long legs sprawled in front of him.

'The jewels are intact including the five hundred plus carat Star of Africa diamond; and there's not a scratch on the scepter. Mystifying, simply mystifying.' The notable put his hands behind his back and walked to the center of the room, deep in thought.

'How'd they get that long thing back into the case, pray tell?' Old Blue wanted to know.

'The glass was not disturbed this time,' the Prime Minister answered, 'and oddly, still sitting directly beside it in a golden frame, which incidentally has had all its rare gems removed since last night at closing time, is the tiny portrait of a princess within a heavy gold frame.' He turned on his heel to look at Old Blue. 'Who is she, by the way?'

'Well, in searching through Hampton Court I discovered that a life-sized original oil hangs there. It is utterly beautiful. She happens to be Catherine, Princess of Castile, who was the fourteenth-century Duke of Lancaster and second wife's only issue.'

'That wife of John of Gaunt was Costanza, Queen of Castile, was she not?' the British subject asked.

'Yes, you are correct.' Old Blue stood. 'As a matter of fact it is interesting that you want the DeSilvas questioned, for when I was at Hampton Court I took a walk along the banks of the Thames before crossing the bridge to the grounds themselves. What do you suppose I found floating in the water being held securely in place by a branch of gorse?' He dug into his breast pocket and pulled out a plastic envelope.

Rick and Sam stood up as the Prime Minister approached his tall guest who was unfolding the entire zip-lock bag. All the men noticed the monogram in the corner of an expensive white, soft linen handkerchief, which Old Blue pulled out.

'How did it get into the river in the first place?' Sam asked.

'Well, it could have fallen from someone's coat pocket the day of the heist, for it was very windy, and as you know the DeSilva men are so macho they wouldn't dream of buttoning up against inclement weather. Maybe it blew out at the Tower. Maybe it blew out as he went to Hampton Court to check out the authenticity of the miniature's likeness. Maybe he was blowing his nose and the durn thing flew away mid-wipe…' Old Blue laughed at the last thought. He laughed so hard at the thought of the elegant DeSilvas losing a newly soiled handkerchief right out of their hands while in the act of using it on the streets of London, he doubled over and silently laughed until the tears rolled down his cheeks. Standing up, the laughter was contagious as all the men visualized the proud suspect's embarrassment.

'If this holds water, our job has just become easy. All we need to do is set a trial date,' Sam drawled.

'Even though the scepter has been returned to the case?' Rick asked.

'Of course, Bozo,' Old Blue wiped tears of mirth from his brown optics. 'One can't just dance into a joint and rip it off without promise of time in prison if that something happens to belong to the Crown, and to the people.'

'Maybe one of "the people" was just borrowing what already belonged to him for a little while… to see what it feels like to hold the durn thing for ten minutes,' Sam set the others into a fresh need to laugh, but they held back to hear what the PM wanted to say.

'Spoken like a true American – democratic to the core,' the Brit said. 'What are your thoughts, if you can stop laughing, Old Blue?'

'Well, yes… back to our little Princess Catherine of Castile. Thanks to her dad's skillful guidance by way of marital contract, she eventually became Queen once her Prince became King

Henry III of Castile after his father, who had usurped the original usurper! But, she was Queen of a foreign country, not England, when she gave birth to heirs. Therefore, even though her progeny was half English by way of the Duke of Lancaster's blood which coursed through her veins, the children were considered Castilian and not entitled to their grandpa's titles and lands in rich England. Remember, John of Gaunt the Second Duke of Lancaster was the richest man alive at the time, even richer than any king. Don't you suppose those facts have stirred the desires of his descendants who have been without recognition, his lands, titles and wealth down through the centuries? They are half English after all by way of their birth! English blood runs through their veins as thickly as any other.' Old Blue shook his head.

'Bet a dollar to a doughnut that someone is madder than a hornet because they are not titled, landed and endowed with wealth in Britain!' The CIA agent sat down.

'Awe, Old Blue! Now that would take a real stretch of the imagination to connect the disappearance of the scepter with such a long-lasting vendetta – something wild indeed!' Sam snorted, sitting down again while chewing quietly on a toothpick that was half in and half out of his sensual mouth. 'What about the War of the Roses?' he continued. 'It was supposed to have settled that matter.' His face was a mirror of doubt.

'Well, don't die of contempt, pal! Even you alluded to it a bit ago. How'd you like it if you were a misplaced or deposed prince... and poor into the bargain?' Old Blue looked threateningly at his peer... 'All your lands, titles, and wealth confiscated by a bit of chance? That chance being the wrong seed in the right womb, and the right seed in the wrong womb which took English lands, titles, and the esteem of other English Royals, plus your power away? Maybe had there been a few boy babies born to Costanza on English soil, the Lancasters would have won a lasting victory. Besides, even commoners fight wars which last for centuries intermittently – for instance Bosnia, Kosovo and the whole Balkans area, the Mideast... they're holy wars, Bucko, stemming from the Muslim Turkish push into Christian Europe and the Crusades – all of which took place during medieval times!'

In a moment of anger at his boss, Sam suddenly turned his teacup upside down to see the brand. Jumping up exclaiming, 'Hot tamales!' he regretted the absent-minded act and hastily sopped the unannounced refill out of his now straightened lap. Royal Albert demurely proclaimed its innocence from the carpet where it had been flung unceremoniously.

Robert Alexander Lavernson's Romanov genes which had been kicking with indignation and anger, softened as everyone offered assistance to Sam with a flourish of three handkerchiefs from three separate pockets; and one pitcher of ice water hastily dashed on his legs. After everyone settled down, and Sam was standing at the blazing hearth to dry, their host said, 'You might have something there, Blue.' He sat down, leaned back in his chair and looked contemplatively across the room. 'Our present Royal House is descended from the House of Plantagenet in part from which the fourteenth-century Duke came, and *not* through the Castilian princess born of John of Gaunt's second union with their mother.' He smiled. 'Let's go for it. Find the connection, boys. Find who it is.' He turned in his chair to look at Rick, 'For your wife and Mrs. DeSilva's sake, I sincerely hope it isn't her husband who is the guilty party.'

Again he stood. The session was coming to a happy end. 'Until we find the culprit, we cannot rest. We mustn't let it happen again, nor anything similar. A theft has occurred and just because it was a nice thief who returned his booty for some reason doesn't mean that he isn't dangerous. Only an ill person would go about establishing himself as someone to be reckoned with in such an unbalanced way at a time like this when our nation is fraught with sorrow.'

'He needs to be behind bars. Who knows what is lurking in his mind as a next step to get what he wants!' Rick decided.

'Yes. I agree. I say, let's go get him fellas! When I get my hands on the perpetrator, I'll be sorely tempted to wring his scrawny little neck for being so insolent as to disturb the Royals' peace and that of the nation! God all Friday! What's this world coming to? I thought the English and the Americans led the world in having become civilized at long last!' Old Blue expostulated wrathfully.

'You of all people should know the answer to that question…

all three of you should by now.' The Prime Minister walked toward the men with outstretched hands to shake theirs goodbye.

'We've been working hard the last fifty years to bring global peace and compatibility. But risking life and limb for democratic ideals may not be enough from us. Yes, I'd say we know what it *should* be coming to, this old world. But will it?'

Rick sighed as he finished speaking his mind, standing with a stretch of his hard chest and waist, hands on slender hips. Age had only made him more handsome, if anything. The gold in his hair still heralded his good looks by framing the integrity of perpetual kindness deep within the lavender windows of his soul. He clasped a friendly light-hearted hand on his seething friend Old Blue's shoulder and looked into his smouldering, blackish eyes. 'That murderous look is in your face, buddy, let's leave the execution of justice to the courts. We'll just apprehend the jackal, okay?'

Old Blue jerked away silently.

'Two wrongs don't make a right – that old cliché is true,' Rick sympathetically said. He didn't realize that burning in his buddy's depths was the yearning to shout to the world: 'Hate me or love me. I too am a Royal! I am a Russian Prince! I know what I'm talking about. My cousin lives in St. James Palace not far from here... and by God and all his holy angels, he shall sit upon the throne some day so help me God – or my name isn't Robert Alexander Lavernson Romanov!'

Aloud, he only murmured in a captivating, suddenly charming way, replete with instantaneously subjugated eyes, 'Old Blue at your service.' He bowed slightly to all the men in the room and walked elegantly without pretense from the room stuffing the quart-sized, neatly folded plastic bag into the faithful Harris tweed.

Rick and Sam shook hands with the Prime Minister as he handed them three fragrant cigars. 'Help yourselves, and give one to Old Blue,' he said. 'Goodbye.'

Old Blue stood beside Scar-P on the other side of the door. 'Have you seen Orange today?' he asked of the tall blond Briton.

'Can't say that I have, old chap,' icily grinned his friend. 'I thought it was you whom I saw coming from her door recently...

it certainly wasn't me,' he snapped.

'Come on. Let's get out of here,' Old Blue said as he was handed a stogie and an envelope from the inner office. 'What have we here?' He hastily tore into the paper. Pulling out a sheet of parchment, which he quickly scanned, he folded it and put it back into the envelope and stuffed it into the other breast pocket. 'According to this directive, we have work to do. We're off to White's Club on St. James Street. I'm starving, aren't you fellas?'

The three Americans appeared at White's two hours later, dressed in appropriate business suits, ties, collars, French cuffed white shirts and smart shoes. The cowboy boots had obviously been put away in footlockers. An off-duty Royal equerry met them for drinks and a little tête-à-tête and passed along a black portfolio. Ordering pilchard pie, white Chablis and Old Blue's ever-present black coffee, they settled down for a well-deserved repast.

Old Blue despised fish of any kind, except fish eggs... caviar. Hiding his disgust, everyone at the table, indeed in the room, thought he relished every bite. In his heart, he was longing for a sirloin steak, medium rare, E. coli threat or not, and a keg of Pabst... and a certain, beautiful young lady whose eyes and gracious smile seemed to beckon from the gold-rimmed, cathedral stained-glass colors of the china and delicate sounds of sterling silver against Royal Doulton. Every prism of his Waterford glass seemed to mirror the longed-for face, and dinner seemed to take for ever. He had hoped to pop by to see her in between duties, but no such luck. He also wondered how she was faring with Orange. Actually, he thought, with Angela there even though Pamela had flown back to Arizona to take care of her horses, Christiana should be quite safe. Two sisters and Orange against the unfamiliar, what could be better?

'If my family hadn't been misplaced, she'd be for me!'

'What say, Bucko?' sotto voce from Rick.

Old Blue scowled.

Chapter Twenty-Four

Often during the past ten years, Christiana had felt that the political and social climate in her beloved United States of America was reminiscent of what she had read of pre-Civil War days and years. She felt it. It was in the air, in the very fiber of the massive country as its internal, silent rebellion swelled against the rotting places of its beautiful fabric which had been woven on freedom's loom. Her own political party had returned to its post-Civil War meanness displayed after the assassination of President Abraham Lincoln when under their own censorship of the Republican vice president, newly elevated to position of President by said death, Andrew Johnson became head of the Republic. Because he was the son of a defeated state in the South, he was not trusted by many in the House and Senate as having the best interests of the shaky Union at heart. Nothing could have been farther from the truth. Hard-hearted, graspingly selfish politicians overruled his policies which followed Lincoln's compassionate example in offering decency, honor and equality not only to the newly freed black populace, but also to the defeated whites.

Christiana had always sympathized with both the factions who had been put upon by the greed and avarice of carpetbaggers and corrupt government officials who saw opportunity to line their own pockets by making it impossible for reconstruction to truly reshape the lives of all during those cruel years.

Now with resentment of all kind growing and seething beneath the American surface in the name of freedom, she often wondered where respect and dignity had fled. She loved her country, but didn't know how to strengthen its good other than by being a model citizen, kind to her neighbors and supportive to her leaders who had been voted into office. The latter took being a good sport about the democratic process at the ballot box if one's preferred candidate did not win; however, she believed that all must work toward the common good for there was good in everyone. Because of America's problems, England appealed to her for it seemed that respecting others was the order of every day, and she loved civility.

A knock came at the door. Although Orange had been with her earlier, she had disappeared long ago while Angela was taking a nap.

'Delivery. Please sign here,' the courier said as he handed her a telegram.

'Thank you.' She scribbled her name on the slip, and shut the door examining the envelope, which she tore open to read.

Please come to Oxburgh Hall, King's Lynn, pronto.
Hurry. Jill.

Christiana called a car rental establishment, threw a coat over her shoulders, grabbed her purse and a little extra cash from a cache in her drawer and hurried to answer the summons. Jill must be in trouble. I wonder where Ned is, she thought to herself as she hurried out the door.

Scared spitless, Christiana knocked on a massive oaken door after trudging across the moat's footbridge where more than once she lost a shoe when her heels got caught between the well-kept bricks. She hadn't realized how far she would be driving to get to King's Lynn near Oxborough from London. 'Thank goodness the fellow at the car rental office suggested riding the train to Peterborough, and then renting wheels! I would have been lost until doomsday wending my way through hedges and rolling hills on all sides, fens and marsh grasses once I neared the North Sea.' She smiled in the darkness – in spite of having had to walk from half a mile down Stoke Ferry Road. The car had slipped off the motorway when a flat tire pulled the steering wheel away.

The sun had gone down hours ago, and she felt absolutely beat. Thank God again, for Jill would be there to make the visit comfortable... and to explain to the occupants why Christiana had come. She pulled a metal cord hanging by the door and a bell tinkled inside as she looked around. The moon scudded behind ominous clouds teasing her desire to see what she could sense was a very beautifully kept estate with gardens that were spectacular.

Finally, the planet above made its presence known, and in that brief space of time the fleeting clouds afforded, Christiana could see the mercurial waters of the moat lying serenely on either side. There were woodlands all around, for she had walked up a tiny drive to reach the medieval castle-like home on which a plaque etched in stone declared it had originated in 1482. The brightness of the moon astonished her as it bathed the battlements and gatehouse in silver. The heavenly light hid itself and she was plunged into utter oblivion... to be blind would have been the same. If she had known that the 1530s Lady Bedingfeld had been ordered by Henry VIII to accompany his first queen's body to Peterborough Cathedral for burial, Christiana would have shuddered. For Sir Bedingfeld had been said Catherine of Aragon's final steward and comptroller who treated her well, being of the same Catholic faith, and charity of mind. In those days, Catholics didn't relish King Henry's notice as it led to confiscation of titles, lands and often times death, hence the priests' hole fashioned beneath the red brick floor in the Kings Room garderrobe of Oxburgh Hall. Notwithstanding its frequent use to hide priests from Henry's blade during that purge of Catholicism in England, Lord Bedingfeld's courage and polite service to the fierce King saved their home and selves. Catholic the family remained.

Suddenly, a crash of thunder opened the heavens in a downpour of wind and rain. Christiana knocked harder this time as the bell hadn't seemed to do any good in summoning a butler. She tilted her head back discreetly, hanging on to her garden hat of straw and watered green silk ribbon which made her eyes startlingly vibrant, so much so that they stirred with points of dark energy as do spirits in a glass of crème de menthe and soda. The rain stopped, but not soon enough for she was soaked through.

The shuffling of feet sounded from behind the door, as if an ancient one were doing the soft-shoe dance in kid slippers. The iron door handle agonized in a deliberate, unhurried way. Giving up a tortured moan, the hinges of the door started doing their work as a little, wizened old man with fragile hands pulled the cumbersome portal toward his sliver-thin, paper-faced self, which was set aglow by reflections from a red lamp. His white hair appeared as if the Biblical burning bush were atop his thin head, while the fire seemingly decomposed his features.

'Madam?' he intoned through parched lips.

Christiana could have sworn she saw a dust curl under the socket of his left eye, nestled in the hollow between cheek and white bristly eyelashes. Pale white irises eerily checked her out. A pinched, yellowy translucent nose rose majestically over a rubber band mouth stretched to its limit in kind politeness. All that was left of a formerly handsome young man was the noble brow which rose opposite, giving his sunken jawline and chin a bit of wrinkled redemption. He was five feet seven inches tall... a treasured ancestral friend of the Hall's heirs with whom he had lived most of his life.

The pit of her stomach won a knot-tying contest right then and there.

She smiled bravely, hoping that her mouth would go on automatic to save her from her faltering brain. Feeling terrified of the white-eyed apparition with the beady black pupils staring into her wide open green lights, a moan inquired from his thin lips, 'Yaaaaaaaaas?'

The door shuddered from a sudden gust of wind, which sent bits of dust and leaves up her wet skirts to her knocking knees. She clutched her hat to her head with the right hand more tightly as lightning flashed. Raindrops dripped off her black curls from another impromptu shower of cold moisture running down a sodden neck.

Say something to him, you idiot! she scolded herself inwardly. 'I... I... um... I...'

'Well! Get on with it!' the half-dead man croaked.

'I, ahem,' she choked, 'I was wondering if my friend, Jill DeSilva is inside.' Now her face was dripping rain onto her soaked blouse. Would he never invite her in, out of the wet?

'No, she is not, madam,' and the old man started to close the door.

'Oh, please! Wait a minute! I need to use your telephone, if you would be so kind as to let me in.' Desperation had made her brave.

'Great Uncle! Let the lady in, for heaven's sake. It's storming out there.' Christiana heard footsteps approaching the end of the hall where the old gent stood. He stepped aside for her to enter.

Christiana shook water from her hat as she swept it off, looking down to ascertain the watered silk skirt, which was truly watered now. She looked like an upside down daffodil that had ceased to trumpet its glory.

'Well, hello stranger,' someone addressed her.

It was not the voice she expected to hear, certainly not that of soft-spoken Jill. Looking up, she found herself looking into mean, smug eyes framed by orange hair which, from the ruby lamp, looked hellish and evil.

'Where's your car, Christiana Elizabeth Stuart?' sarcastically asked the outlandish green lips above which charcoal shadows topped the cheekbones beneath black eyes.

Shadows, shadows, Christiana thought.

'It's down the road near Pudding Bag Lane. I had a flat tire and walked in.'

'That's even better,' Orange smiled cruelly.

'Where is Jill DeSilva? She said that she would be here,' Christiana repeated.

'Oh, did she now? I don't recall seeing her here today. Do you, Great Uncle?' The old man shook his head.

An archaic clock struck the hour as if confirming that indeed no one but the three of them were stirring, and if they were, they should not be. Then slowly, and most officiously with hundreds of years practice, the clock bong, bong, bonged toward a culmination of twelve strokes.

The ancient dusty one wheezed a sneeze aiming his brittle head toward his sunken bosom of white, pressed pleats under a black smoking jacket of velvet lapels against embossed satin, clean and elegant. His whole frame shook like a dry leaf in the wind from the expectoration which followed. Without thinking, Christiana reached for the man to break a fall. Orange rudely butted her out of the way and grabbed the old man.

'He's my great uncle, isn't he?' The vicious woman steadied the little gnome until he could recoup his timorous dignity. One slipper had flown off, he had sneezed so hard. Something rattled.

Chris wondered if it were his bones. Suddenly the thought made her feel like laughing hysterically for she was both terrified and amused.

Orange and Christiana looked at each other while the troll smoothed cotton fuzz back into place atop his pate from off his forehead where the momentous sneeze had dislodged it.

Gusts of wind drove rain against the other side of the now closed door. Suddenly, a smile and cognizance transformed her host.

'Come in,' he quietly invited. 'But, of course you may use the telephone if the storm hasn't put it out of commission.' He stepped aside on the polished floor to let her pass.

Christiana followed him down impeccably kept, ancient hardwood floors which were held together by wooden pegs rather than iron nails. A high heraldic ceiling rose above her head in the West Drawing Room. How very nice and clean, she thought as she said a breathless, 'Thank you. It is so kind of you, Sir…'

'Sir Hugh… Sir Hugh Dunford of Rolling Ladle Dip-Gap Winding through the Meadows.' His mind had taken flight once more into his own fanciful world.

'Is that first cousin to Horsey Windpump which I passed en route here?' She giggled, unable to help herself. Orange was no longer in sight to intimidate her good spirits.

The old man and Christiana looked at each other, his lowering brow and her fair face suddenly bursting into laughter as his mind came back to keep her company a little longer.

'No,' he chortled, 'but we are first cousins to some who be at Peckover House on the Firth of Froth… or is it the Froth of Firth?' He scratched his head trying to remember. 'I am not the owner nor heir here,' he added.

Suddenly all fear and irritation were joyously swallowed in peals of laughter – hers as light as wind chimes caught in a delicate summer breeze, and his as coarse and rumbling as the North Sea which was battering ships offshore with gale force winds threatening to drag them onto the jetties that protruded from the bleak coast.

Weak from the unexpected exertion, he fell backward into a Windsor chair, landing as lightly as a bit of dandelion down puffed into a corner by the wind. Christiana jumped to break his fall, but was too late. Having seen a massive oak sideboard ornately carved with game birds and fruit supporting silver trays, decanters and crystal, she hastily sped down the hall into a well-lit reception room where flames were ferociously licking logs in a huge fireplace. Pouring a bit of brandy into a snifter, she dashed with it in hand back up the hall to the fatigued cadaver-like body lying listlessly in the chair. Head against the red upholstery, arms askew on the rests, feet and legs straight forward, he looked dead. Kneeling down to cradle his head in her left arm, she placed the spirits to his lips carefully.

'Drink,' she softly implored.

He took a sip... caught his breath, and proceeded to pant like a winded puppy. Christiana waited. The little fellow's respirations settled down and she helped him drink more. Eyes closed, he lay still as silent lightning played outside the windows casting blue light over his listless body.

'Enough!' he suddenly shouted, shoving Christiana and the glass to the floor. 'Are you trying to drown me, woman?'

Nervousness returned to his angel of mercy. It was obvious that he was not quite right. He started laughing again like a lunatic.

'The telephone you say?' he screeched. 'Well. Go to it!'

'But excuse me, sir, where is it?'

'Don't ask me foolish questions! Go look for it! What do you think I am? A tourist guide?' His voice lost volume like the last bit of steam from a radiator.

'No... no, sir. No sir, not at all.' She backed away from the weird little skinflint. Trembling, her inherent goodness overcame weak knees and she asked, 'May I help you to a comfortable sofa beside the fire in the next chamber before I search for the telephone? It is cold in this room.'

His white pupils looked up into hers of green, which unbiddenly reminded him of lush forests, alive and fragrant with youth and vigor in the springtime of his life. Quietness and politeness overtook him as quickly as had the rudeness.

'Yes, how kind of you,' he silkily purred like a sweet old tom cat. He docilely allowed her to help him stand up. They repaired to an adjoining room where she seated him in that which was obviously his wing chair of golden satin with shiny horsehair fabric on the pillows, so ancient it almost neighed. She wrapped an afghan of blue, red and yellow around his ankles and knees, snuggling it up to his benign, parchment-like face which was aglow with love for her. Something about her stirred old smoulders into hot coals.

I am not dead yet! he thought, and the thought surprised him.

And she thought, What is that saying – there might be snow on the roof, but there's still fire in the furnace?

Suddenly she was filled with apprehension again. His eyes were deceptively changing. Acting stoically unperturbed, she poured him a bit of hot tea from an ornate Russian samovar of silver and placed the cup and saucer on a lace-covered tea table beside him. Casting a look about the room into all the dark, unlighted corners, a huge harp lurking in the gloom assumed the shape of a giant Hunchback of Notre Dame. Christiana turned away to go seek a telephone.

A dry old claw grabbed her hand. Heart leaping into her throat, fright made her jump. Quietly came the words, 'Make your call. You must leave this place for your own safety as quickly as possible. That's all I wanted to say.' The old man sighed and dropped her hand, exhausted from the action. He sank against the golden cushions and promptly fell asleep as Christiana whirled about to face him.

'Where is Jill DeSilva? Sir! Wake up!' She frantically nudged him, his skinny bones rattling under the sumptuous jacket. She shook him. 'Sir! Wake up! Where is Jill, I asked you! I need to tell my friends where I am.' She shook him again, and out of his clothing fell a large blue gem, which cast red fire from its depths, and a rainbow of colors from the white diamonds surrounding the rock. A diamond chain rattled to the floor, secure in the clasp attached to the Hope Diamond. Christiana gasped, and knelt down to pick it up.

'I'll take that, if you please,' a hard voice said behind her. Suddenly she was yanked to her feet by a very irate Orange. Their eyes met. 'Come with me,' the hard-bitten wench gripped Christiana's elbow so tightly it hurt as the former swiftly bent down and scooped the prize off the floor. 'Too bad you had to see that,' she said as Christiana was pushed out into the hall. Orange let go of her arm. 'See the end of the corridor down there? Well, go and get out of my sight before I am tempted to follow my instincts and kill you. Get on the telephone and then get out of this house.'

The hall was dimly lit and damply chill as ancient rear corridors can become. Through large windows, the stone and wood of ancient times were caught in reflection upon the beautiful moat fed by the River Gadder which still surrounded battlements and wonderful rooms of the manor home.

Ancestors peered from their frames hanging on intricately painted Spanish leather wall coverings of crimson, gold and cobalt blue rising alongside a handsome staircase. Alone she wound deeper into the bowels of the house, becoming colder from fear with each step. She peered into the warmth of an adjoining library, alive with old books lovingly kept through the years.

'Where is the telephone?' she asked herself quaveringly.

'It's right there. Can't you see it?' the old man's voice screamed at her elbow in the darkness. She jumped a foot, for she had thought herself alone with the gnome asleep in the other end of the house. Christiana hit the floor in a dead faint.

The old man chuckled, picked a flaming candle off a hall stand a few feet away, and went tottering down the cavernous gloom of the hall, turned right proceeding through great double doors, and disappeared... totally forgetting Christiana's existence.

Christiana lay soaked to the skin, cold and unconscious. Lightning flashed into the room sporadically, the sole light signifying her incidental presence in its glow.

Two feet appeared at her head, black pants with a sharp crease disappeared under the hem of a rain slicker. Bending over, Orange and a strong person lifted Christiana into his arms.

'Shh. Be quiet. I don't want crazy old uncle to hear us leave. He will disturb his host who has treated him like family these many years.'

'What did you do with the Hope Diamond?'

'I stashed it in the priests' hole.'

She opened a hidden door, which led to the bridge from the

room in which they stood. Hurrying toward a car parked in the garden, the heavily breathing fellow asked, 'What are we going to do with her?'

Orange snapped, 'Quit panting so loudly! Someone will hear you!'

'In this wind and rain? You're crazy!' he retorted.

'Well, what are we going to *do* with her, I asked!' He reached for the door handle of a Bentley hidden in the lane under writhing bushes near a garden shed. Christiana's sodden skirts blew up over his head. 'Bloody wet clothes,' he cussed trying to disentangle himself. 'Give me a hand, would you? You and your greedy ideas!'

Orange laughed and pulled the soaked mess off his hat and face, which sent the fedora flying across the garden into the moat. Water started dripping off the man's black hair into angry eyes as he struggled to lower his burden to the level of the door, which his companion was opening.

'You're going to take us to the train in Peterborough where we will board and return to London. I just might stop at Gatwick en route and drop her onto a plane back to the USA; but as much as I despise her, I can't begrudge a woman at least one change of clothes.' He sent a scathing look Orange's way as they settled their guest across the back seat. 'On second thought, maybe she won't be needing them by the time we get from Kings Cross to the Piccadilly Line.' Orange laughed, climbing into the front passenger seat.

As her partner climbed in behind the wheel, the redhead pulled a syringe out of a pocket to check the contents of milky white clearness. The ensuing smile was terrible to behold.

Now I have the man, or shall in the very near future, she thought, and if I play my cards right, who knows what else I will possess?

The car pulled away and wound unobtrusively through the night toward Peterborough in Cambridgeshire to the south-west.

While Christiana was 'enjoying' her outing in the Oxborough area, Angela slept on from having had the flu, and the three American agents were relishing their evening on the town.

Wishing for a rare steak, Sam had been politely eating fish as well. The equerry had been entertaining and the men felt good.

'Well, here you are, Sir,' the equerry rose to his feet. Everyone looked up to see who was at the other end of the spit-polished, soft-kid shoes which had suddenly come into their line of vision as they studied the red carpet over glasses of brandy, a treat supposedly from the number one woman herself. On duty or not, everyone needed to let their hair down sometimes, she had emphasized... or so it was said.

A chess set of ivory and ebony beckoned on a glossy mahogany table before them. Firelight and shadows flickered over the kings and knights as bishops reverently contemplated suicide while pawns hated their serfdom when the queens rode by.

Old Blue looked up. There stood his cousin before the benign little group. Smiling in his hesitant, but pleasant way, the men were warmly greeted. He stood humbly before them.

Golly! Old Blue thought, as he stood to his feet grinning from ear to ear. If it isn't the man himself, my cousin who doesn't even know he's my cousin! Old Blue bowed slightly, just a smart little nod of the head accompanied by a slight tilt from the waist. The cousin noticed and extended his hand to clasp that of the man he admired probably more than any of his acquaintance. Before him stood another Braveheart – a man whose brilliance, compassion and honesty added fire to his heels in battle, be it physical warfare or mental.

'A strong man amongst men!' he had exclaimed to the mirror as he straightened his tie before going to White's. He had read everything available about Old Blue before the evening commenced. The Prime Minister had wisely thought it a capital idea and sent a brief to St. James Palace. After reading the material, the Royal had fed it to the fireplace flames, which hungrily licked the pages into oblivion. His lips were sealed in order to preserve the much admired covert agent.

And so here they stood, a mutual admiration society, security unobtrusively all around. The hours went by quickly. Ships, jets, the armed services of two countries; the caper of the scepter; and finally, pictures of an emerald-eyed beauty were exchanged and the latter tucked away in Old Blue's pocket after he shrewdly observed the quiet intensity and pleased look which stole across the face of Christiana Elizabeth Stuart's newest admirer. It drove a spike into Old Blue's heart, but never did it interfere with the brotherly love he felt for his cousin, that affection peculiar in Old Blue's countrymen for family and motherland. Beautiful and honest was that love.

It was nearly midnight when they all rose, exchanged farewells, and went their separate ways – all except for Old Blue and the British security detail who accompanied the Prince home.

When OB got into his room, the desire to talk to Christiana surged through him. One call wouldn't hurt. It'd be nice to hear her gentle voice again.

There was no answer, which seemed very odd. So he tried Angela's number. A sleepy woman answered.

'Where's Christiana?' asked Old Blue.

'Isn't she in her room? Why don't you call her directly?' her sister suggested.

'I already have,' he started to worry.

'Oh dear. I'll get up and go see if her bed has been slept in tonight.' A silence followed. 'Sometimes she doesn't sleep in the bed next to mine.' Sixty seconds passed. 'Old Blue?'

'Yes?'

'She's not here. Her coat and purse are gone, and a bit of cash. Something is terribly wrong. She would never have just bolted out of here without leaving a note had she not intended to be back before now.'

'Go downstairs and ask the desk clerk for a record of any calls or other activity in or near your suite. Hurry. I'll be right over with the guys.'

Shortly, three Americans exited St. James Palace.

Later, a few apartments away in the same building the Prince lay in his bed alone as the full moon cast a glow about the masculine room. It was a pretty night although rain clouds threatened from the east. His thoughts were resting upon a man's dark brown eyes which had spoken volumes regarding pain and sacrifice, strength and courage – and an almost broken spirit without consciously being aware of it. Above all, the future King had recognized love and fierce loyalty quietly enfolding himself into the eyes almost savage depths. Yet there had been a refined quality midst those hot, tormented coals of the man's soul. A regal bearing, a patience acquired through breeding and possibly solitude?

The cousin shut his eyes and suddenly a green-eyed brunette, exquisitely beautiful and soft-looking swam before his closed lids. The naivete was gone from her look in the pictures he had been shown, but in the countenance had been a touch of tragedy overcome by purity of soul. Love had shown from her photograph, a sweet love. He wondered who she had been observing when the picture had been snapped. Whomever it had been, she had loved that person deeply. Her son? Her divorced husband? Who?

Christiana Elizabeth Stuart, progeny of the one who was baptized Katherine; hidden child of King Charles I, give or take four hundred years. Interesting. So... we shall meet at tea tomorrow; but to what end? I'm not open to new love, he thought.

Old Blue and his men were chasing through the night in their own rented VW on Norfolk's highways going to King's Lynn. The hotel had traced Christiana's call to a car rental agency and her route had been quickly established once the contents of the one and only telegram delivered to her door had been ascertained.

Off Stoke Ferry Road, they found the lady's vehicle, flat tire and all.

'Leave the thing here, we need to find her. We'll phone the company to come retrieve it,' Old Blue said as he tossed the cellular to Sam. 'Be my guest,' and he spun out, fishtailing the VW as he sped toward ancient Oxburgh Hall and its inhabitants.

An hour later their search revealed nothing. Not a trace of her remained. Old Blue felt sick in the pit of his stomach as they headed back toward London from the ancient home. Despite the hour, the old gent and his butler had been kind enough, but neither seemed to remember a girl with black hair and green eyes having been there.

Chapter Twenty-Five

Orange decided during the train ride from Peterborough to King's Cross station in London that the groggy lady sitting beside her deserved to live – at least until she could size Old Blue up again. After all, it had been many years that they had been an item. Surely he wasn't going to throw her over for this namby-pamby piece of protoplasm! She looked sideways at the sleeping Christiana, whose head rocked against the window of the first-class compartment in which they were riding. Good heavens! He can't love her, Orange thought. But he had not been the same last time they had been together... maybe it was just because of jet lag, she comforted herself. Feeling better, she indulged in a nap for twenty minutes, enjoying sweet memories of Old Blue before there was any Christiana. In the meantime, there was Scar-P. Things weren't that tough. If she continued to be clever, his naivete would reward her and she could have both men without either being the wiser. She looked over at the gent who had carried Christiana to the car, driven to the station and arranged for the three to return by train. The female spook laughed.

Men!

Arriving at King's Cross, both ladies awakened and were guided by the same person to a taxi after deboarding. Christiana couldn't get over how civil Orange had suddenly become. They went to The Savoy by taxi and parted company from the mystery man.

Upon entering her suite of rooms, Christiana fell into her sister's arms and wept. Tight security had been placed around the floor, which amazed the tired young woman, but it comforted her instead of alarming.

As she was tucked into bed after a warm bath and cup of hot chocolate, her sister said, 'Good news, sweetie. Guess who has invited you to tea tomorrow afternoon. A distant peer who just happens to live in St. James Palace.'

'Oh, get out of here,' she smiled, shutting her eyes as her head sank into the down pillow. 'I'll believe it when I see him and the tea is served. Thanks for trying to cheer me, but I'm as happy as a clam who escaped a bake. Please, let's go home tomorrow,' she sighed. 'I miss Geoffrey... life isn't the same without my son. I live for him because he is now my sun, my moon, my stars. England is lovely, but I yearn for him, my little pond and lake... and my tiny apartment. I want to be held in the security of it all again.' Before she could finish her request, sleep had overtaken her.

As Angela stroked the black tresses from her sister's forehead, she noticed an ugly black and blue lump, which was as big as a duck's egg. 'Where did you get this, sweetheart?' she sorrowfully asked. 'I must put an ice pack on it or your eye will be discolored in the morning.' She then noticed a huge bruise on her sister's upper arm displaying finger marks.

A call to Old Blue was immediately made.

The next morning dawned bright and sunny, then mist and fog shrouded the city for a natural period of respectful mourning at 8 A.M. When breakfast was over at ten o'clock, the heavens were rejoicing with triumphant rays of golden light once more and the birds and people responded, stepping lightly as they folded umbrellas of varied colors and sizes, although most preferred the traditional black protection.

Angela and Chrissy were visited by clothiers and busily selected evening silks, velvets, satins, morning woolens of dove gray, forest green, lemon yellow, pinks piped in black, reds and warm browns. Finally, all was completed. They both went to bed and slept after the couturiers left, for tiredness lingered from illness and adventure.

Tea was planned for four in the afternoon.

Old Blue had popped by the suite in the morning before heading for Piccadilly Circus. He saw the bruises Angela had reported and it gave him a tremendous zeal to bash someones' heads together, but he contained himself, as a civilized gentleman should. It was one thing for *him* to get used for target practice, but when it came to a sweet thing like Christiana it made no sense at all. Who would want to hurt her, and why? Besides that, she was supposed to have the best protection available in a woman agent... Orange. The tough woman shouldn't have been taken off Christiana's detail and sent to the prison to watch the Kurd. That was a man's job. Who had ordered that stupid plan, he wondered. Since he had requested to be relieved of Orange as a partner, he didn't know where she was half the time. At any rate, Old Blue needed to get his thoughts organized before seeing her this morning. She was needed to find the younger DeSilva – Raoul.

Arriving at her mystic shop, he entered silently. A dark-headed man was talking in low tones to her... that it was Raoul DeSilva was unknown to Old Blue. Raoul, hidden as he was in the safety of fedora brim and the collar of his leather dress jacket, slipped unobtrusively out the door.

'How's my best girl?' Old Blue asked Orange.

She made the gum in her mouth snap over and over, an irritating habit as far as Old Blue was concerned.

'Who's asking?' she coldly responded.

'My! Are we in a snit today! What's the matter, did you lose the Hope Diamond or something?'

She visibly stiffened, mouth open for a second longer than usual between chews.

'Naw... what's the Hope Diamond?' she resumed popping and cracking away.

'Don't act innocent with me, you little liar!' Old Blue laughed. 'You probably know more about it than I.' Though his eyes were laughing, they were trained on her reactions like a mongoose on a snake.

'What do you mean by that smart remark?' she chillingly asked.

'Oh nothing. It just seems as if you have a burr under your saddle and I'm wondering why. Last time we parted, you were much friendlier.'

She handed him a Pabst from the small fridge under the counter.

'Thanks pal.' Old Blue tore the blue ribbon off, opened the brown bottle and took a disgustingly appreciative drink.

'Knock off the "pal" bit, Bucko! You're a real pain right where it hurts the most – do you know that? I wish you'd sail for the States in a leaky dingy until your hat floats!'

'Awe, come on, what's eating you?' his gorgeous deep voice purred like a cat's velvety rumble. Following her shapely derriere and slender self through the curtains into the living quarters at the back of the shop, he took another swig of beer, set the bottle on the table, and caught her in his arms, turning her around into an all-encompassing embrace, his legs wrapped on each side of hers.

'Let me go, you fickle…' her voice became smothered in a kiss which ravished not only her breath, but her very mind which was sent spinning into spirals of the pleasure she had learned to expect from this virile lover. In spite of her angry reaction to his obvious enchantment over Christiana Elizabeth, she started kissing him back hungrily, throwing her jingling, braceleted arms around his deceptively lean-looking rib cage which filled her arms before her hands could meet on his back.

He picked her up and carried her to the bed.

Afterward, while straightening his tie in the steamy little bathroom where she was still in the shower, he asked, 'Where's Ned DeSilva these days?'

'Why do you ask?'

The water splashed deliciously; he could see her form faintly through the kaleidoscopic colors of the shower curtain. She was lathering her orange and black hair.

'I need to see him, that's all.'

'He's coming to town tomorrow.'

'What about Raoul? Where's he?'

'Around.'

'Find him.'

'What for?' she asked.

'None of your business.'

'What do I do when I find him?'

'Bring him to Scotland Yard.'

'Oh, oh. Sounds serious,' Orange joked.

'Chances are he's not being invited to a tea party,' the CIA man agreed.

She laughed, and stepped out of the shower.

'Why don't you let that God-awful orange hair turn black? You could be such a beauty if you wanted to be,' said Old Blue.

'And ruin my cover? Are you insane?' Her gold bracelets, still wet from the shower, jangled as she dried off.

Old Blue had seen a similar piece of jewelry before, and it had not been on her wrist. Oh, well. Lots of women wore the same kind as that which had been stuck beneath the rubber mat near the Crown Jewels.

'Speaking of which,' she said as she toweled off, 'who stole the famous scepter and then had the audacity to put it back again last night?' She shimmied into tight black leather pants and vest – no bra and no undies – after powdering with Opium dusting powder.

Old Blue looked at her in surprise carefully masked. He wanted to ask how she knew about the scepter's return, or even its disappearance for that matter. Instead he asked, 'What scepter?'

She started applying make-up with delicate, deft movements of her fingers as she stood before the sink mirror which Blue had left to go into the bedroom. He buttoned his shirt and settled into gun holster and jacket.

She turned to look at him. 'Golly, you're gorgeous! Where are you going?'

'To see the Queen, pussy cat.' He smiled, gave her a quick peck on the cheek and said, 'Meet me at the Hyde Park Hotel for lunch at eleven thirty tomorrow morning. Bring Ned. Make sure you're both there, and on time! You'll recognize him from this photo.' He pulled a black and white snapshot from his everlasting Harris tweed. 'These are the DeSilva brothers.'

He dashed out the door. Orange lit a cigarette as the telephone rang, picked up the receiver and depressed the connection after listening a minute. Then lifting her fingertip and punching in a few numbers, waited a moment and said, 'Hi, baby. He's gone.'

She listened awhile, holding the phone from her ear as screams poured forth from the receiver. Finally, it fell silent. She put it back to her ear over which wet, straight hair had been combed in a fetching bob.

'Are you okay, little brother? What scepter?' She fidgeted with her cigarette, blowing smoke rings as she listened. 'Okay, babe. I'll come bail you out. I'll be there in half an hour.' She listened. 'Don't worry. I can get you out!' She put a fresh piece of gum into her mouth as she ground the butt of her cigarette into the ashtray.

'Listen, honey, don't be so upset. Big brother wants to see you and requests your presence tonight. Think over what you want to eat – we'll pick up a takeout on the way home and don't be stubborn about it.' Making a kissing noise over the phone, she said, 'Cheer up! The worst is yet to come!' she laughed. 'Sure. You know that you can always come here.'

Sunshine falling through her window onto the bed caused a prism of blue light to flash. Activity had moved something to the open edge of the daybed pillowcase in which it had been hidden.

She hastily removed it, grabbed metal cleats, pincers and scissors. Securing the Hope Diamond into the midnight blue curtain amongst fake jewels of all colors, Orange cut a slit into the drapery one-sixteenth of an inch below it, dropped the attached diamond chain through the opening between lining and curtain, popped the tools into her purse and left the shop.

The tea at St. James had gone very well after starting promptly at four o'clock. Angela and Christiana looked ravishing in chic suits, which became them. Angela was in shades of beige, sand and browns; Christiana in an emerald green wool jacket piped with black, which featured a soft ebony wool sheath underneath. Black suede pumps complimented the outfit. A black fedora trimmed with wide green bands of pleated wedding satin accented the emeralds set in platinum gracing her earlobes against the jet black hair which wafted a faint scent of her favorite perfume – Joy by Jean Patou.

Her face was serene with the bruise acquired the day before being unnoticeable because of the way her sister had fashioned bangs to fall softly over the decreasing lump. The bruise on her arm was covered as well.

Warm and tender in her reflections of Old Blue when she noticed him walking in, their eyes met and she smiled wishing that he had been with her the day before to save her from the scare. Seeing him made her feel more at home midst the towering ceilings, ornate mirrors, fireplaces, oil portraits and snugly arranged tea corners on richly colored Persian rugs. Deep reds and blues bravely set off the lemon yellows and snow-white accents of the decor. Chandeliers of fine crystal sparkled.

The door opened from the far side of the room, and in came the Dream Prince.

Christiana really wished she were anywhere but there at the moment. Suddenly, she felt like laughing because it seemed so ridiculous, so unimaginable. Surely she was dreaming again! Straight from Alzheimer's patients, hospice patients and other maladies, which needed tender care, she had come to this: last night's terror plus the splendors of St. James Palace! It couldn't be real.

'What will the Prince think of my work-worn hands with the white, blunt fingernail tips? Oh, Lordy. This is a mistake.' She looked up at Old Blue who was as elegantly relaxed as always he had been. If she had known what he'd been doing two hours earlier, she would have been incensed. Happily, she didn't know.

Old Blue sauntered over and sat down beside her. Suddenly he felt ashamed of his previous activity. If she knew, what would she think? he wondered.

'Do you still see Orange at work?' Christiana innocently asked. A fan came on from the furnace, blowing a mild stream of air through the room. It moved Christiana's hair enough so that Old Blue caught sight of the goose egg hidden under her bangs.

Tenderly, but quickly, Old Blue reached up and moved the hair more. 'Who did this to you?'

Smiling, she wondered why he thought someone had done it rather than receiving it from a fall, and said, 'Actually, I fell.'

'Last night? Where?'

'Yes, last night at Oxburgh Hall.' She looked down.

'In King's Lynn?'

'Yes.' She felt uneasy. Wanting to tell him about Orange's behavior toward her, she thought better of it.

'Tell me about it. I don't believe you would have fallen had someone else not been involved.' He searched her eyes.

'Oh, I became frightened that's all, and fainted. I hit my head on the floor, I suppose.' She shrugged it off.

'You seem to be warm. Here, Christiana, let me assist you in removing your jacket.' A nasty suspicion had just crossed his mind. His orange-haired partner had a reputation for more than a nasty arm hold. He wanted to see Christiana's arms again.

'I'm just fine,' she became suddenly regal and untouchable. He backed off.

'You haven't seen Orange during the last twenty-four hours by any chance?' he asked.

'Yes, I have.' She searched his eyes, wanting to tell him about what looked liked the Hope Diamond.

'I think we need to talk, come with me and we can sit in that far corner. A tea table is set up there as well.' They moved to the quiet spot.

In relief, Christiana unburdened her terrified heart.

When he had finished Old Blue thought, Well, old Sir Gork helped Raoul lift not only the scepter, but The Royal Blue!

'Raoul has been apprehended and released?' Old Blue couldn't believe his ears. Speaking into the telephone, 'Released? Why?'

Understanding that Ned was waiting with four others at an interrogation table in a side room at The Savoy, he said his farewells to Christiana and his cousin who had appeared right on time, and went to work. Scar-P took Old Blue to the famous hotel. Upon entering, the two men were taken to the conference room where Ned and Raoul DeSilva, the Kurd, the Ambassador, and Orange were seated around the table, each with their own guard.

Old Blue looked in surprise at Orange. 'What are you doing here?'

She looked at him with hatred seething from her eyes. She was steaming and hopping mad from their tryst. For as she had reflected his coolness later, distraction in a man as he made love was a slight which hot Castilian blood could not abide. In her mind, he was exclusively hers. She had nursed him to health after Vietnam and her Harvardized soul had known her match when she met it.

'Just accompanying my brothers. For once, they need me.'

Old Blue was stunned. She had family! He started shaking with silent laughter.

'What's so funny?' she asked.

He bent over and whispered into her ear, 'You have family, and here all this time I thought you had crawled out from under a rock.'

'You jerk!' She pulled his ear... hard. Your dark side matches mine, she thought, passion and fire! Your only weakness? You hate lies. I love them.

Rubbing his head, he found a chair and sat down still trying to repress his sense of humor. The chauffeur and a doorman stood inside the closed doors, hands and arms folded across their chests, moving only to admit two plain-clothes men from Scotland Yard, and another gentleman whom Old Blue recognized as the head of MI6.

Ned was dressed in an expensive chocolate-colored suit and was nervously tapping a foot on the thick carpet under the table, black eyes full of fury. Orange was sitting between him and Raoul looking brazen and contemptuous, chewing a wad of her everlasting gum – bracelets jangling every time she slightly moved which annoyed Ned even more. Plus, he was mad at his kid brother for losing a handkerchief in the Thames when, of all things, that youngest sibling had intended to heist the life-sized portrait of Princess Catherine from Hampton Court with the aid of friends, who failed to show, of course.

Raoul was slick of hair and smile, disdain and hatred pouring from his little body with every breath as he sat, still dressed in his leather jacket and fedora.

The fourth unfortunate soul looked bewildered, frightened and anything required – repentant, courteous, informative – he just wanted to go home to his Kurdish wife and baby who had escaped with him to live in the land of safety, Britain. He was truly terrified for he had done no wrong, his religious leader had told him so. When someone strikes you, strike back. It said so in the Koran. His holy man had told him that a blond had stolen jewels from America and England; and to go to Rye without his buddies where that man was supposed to trade the loot for money. He couldn't help it if he had followed the wrong blond fellow while trying to help the Queen get her majestic symbol back. And the blue plastic jewel? How was he to know that it was an exact replica of one that had been stolen in America? It had cost five pounds. Seeing it in the shop window, little Ryhana had come to mind. She would love it, a good woman his Ryhana.

When the blond man Rick had heard the true story he had laughed. So, why can't I go home? the little man was wondering. I can't help it if my idiot friends chased the ambulance at the airport to save me and we all are now in jail!

Old Blue looked at the Ambassador sitting next to the Kurd. Kind face, neat appearance, ostrich shoes; a long slender case was wedged between their two chairs.

'You want to see my new putter?' he caught Old Blue's eye and smiled. 'You should come try it sometime.' In an aside, he confidentially asked, 'Can you tell me for what reason we are all here?'

In through the door came the Prime Minister and Scar-P. Everyone stood to honor the former. Scar-P and Orange looked suddenly brazen and for some reason did not include one another in their look around the room. Old Blue didn't miss much.

Joe Bly entered quietly.

The men from Scotland Yard stood and introduced themselves. Taking charge, the Chief Inspector explained that in order to make certain all were available for questioning, the present course of action had been pursued. 'For who knows,' he said, 'which one of you would not answer an invitation to headquarters. As you know, without evidence we can't make arrests to force you in. For those who have no knowledge of the recent capers, you can relax. We don't know who that may be at this point, but in the luxury of the adjacent room we shall ask each of you, one at a time, a few questions. Hopefully, all but one or two will be able to go home in a couple of hours.' He continued, 'Believe it or not, this course of action was taken in order not to harm the dignity and reputation of you who are innocent.'

One by one, each suspect was taken into the smaller room. When Raoul was led away, Ned looked appealingly across the table at Old Blue. They had been friends for years but Old Blue had not known that Orange was the sister Ned had always worried over. Blue looked at Ned and smiled comfortingly.

'Drink your coffee,' he added to the smile in undertones, and then silently mouthed, 'For, if I have my investigative mind tucked into proper compartments, I know it's not you who's guilty of thumbing your nose at what's left of the British Empire; and you certainly have no use for a cursed diamond.'

'You know that I am not guilty in these matters but do they?' Ned nodded his head toward the interrogation room. 'Will they believe me?'

'Believe you about *what* matters?' Orange questioned innocently.

By that time, OB was standing behind Ned's shoulder. Bending to the irritated man's ear, he whispered, 'Honesty always pays off; we all know that you were in Jill's company the morning in question. Also, you were nowhere near Washington.' The comforter straightened his tie as he walked away and resumed his seat.

Raoul was a different matter in Old Blue's mind. He thought the diminutive little brother would probably end up busily twiddling his thumbs in prison until he turned gray.

Raoul came back into the room escorted by Joe who indicated that his charge be seated and OB wondered while looking at him, how did Raoul think that stealing the portrait of Princess Catherine from Hampton Court would keep us from identifying the miniature in the glass case? Stupid!

Scar-P was dispatched to escort Ned's little brother from the premises. The agents returned to the room and summoned Ned, asking Old Blue to come in as well in order that he replace Scar-P as detail for the Prime Minister. They all sat down in comfortable wing chairs. Ned was humiliated and seething with rage that his favorite location in all the world had become a place of debasement for him. Everything Lancaster had ever touched, seemed to reach down through the ages and bang him on the head to remind him that life had cheated the DeSilva half of the family out of what was rightfully theirs, including the real estate in his favorite city, which had once held the palace of Ned's dreams, the incomparable Savoy! Here he sat on those very grounds before the Prime Minister, Her Majesty's highest officer of the people, suspected of some terrible crime.

With great dignity he quietly asked, 'Gentlemen, what is it that I am supposed to have done?'

'Is this yours?' One of the men from Scotland Yard drew a small miniature of a princess from his pocket.

Ned looked at the face of his ancestress, Princess Catherine of Castile. Fierce Castilian pride colored his face, but he kept silent except to ask, 'May I see it?' He felt murderous until thoughts of the cool, honest, beautiful wife waiting for him upstairs calmed him. 'I won't disappoint you, darling,' he whispered.

'Pardon me?' the interrogator asked.

'I was murmuring thoughts of my wife, who is upstairs.'

'Which reminds me, where were you on 31st August around four in the afternoon?'

'Actually, I was right here in London.'

'Were you alone? Who was with you, and where were your accommodations?' the chief added.

'I was with my wife; we stayed right here at The Savoy. We have not checked out to date.'

'What was your business here?'

'We came on a second honeymoon to our favorite city and our favorite hotel, which you probably already know,' he smiled.

'Were you together the entire day and evening of 31st August?'

'Yes we were, other than for a few hours that morning.'

'Where did you go at that time? What did you do?'

'Well, in the morning while my wife was preparing to go out for a day of sightseeing with me, I went downstairs to the River Restaurant and had a bite to eat with Raoul. He had business to tend, so left first. I stayed to have a couple of drinks between noon and one o'clock, went upstairs to fetch my wife, and then proceeded with her to the Tower of London where we joined a tour of the castle, ending up at the Crown Jewel display.'

'What was your impression of the display?'

'My impression? Truly magnificent, every item was breathtaking. We both commented on the luster of the jewels as being full of depth and brilliance in comparison to the paste display in the Bahamas. They are lovely as well, but cannot hold a candle to the real articles of grandeur.'

'Which did you like the most... which crown, or other item?'

'I enjoyed St. George's crown; and the scepter, of course! The diamond in the latter is magnificent – the size of a large orange, cut beautifully, superbly crafted.'

'I see. When did you leave?'

'It was three in the afternoon when we left to go to King's Cross. We went to Lincoln on the train to view the cathedral.'

'Well, if we need you again, where may we find you?'

'At The Savoy, and the day after tomorrow, back in Phoenix.' He reached into his inner breast pocket to bring out a business card and handed it to the officer. 'May I ask to what these questions pertain?'

'Yes. We are trying to discover who misplaced an item on the day mentioned. That will be all.'

'One moment, please,' Ned spoke again. 'How did you gentlemen come into possession of this antiquated portrait? It was stolen from our home and properly reported as missing to the authorities last winter. I am certain this is ours. May I?' He stood, looking at the two detectives who handed him the miniature.

They nodded in approval as Ned examined the back more closely.

'The last time I saw this was during a party at our home.'

'May we have a list of your guests who came on that date?'

'Yes, of course.' He turned the picture over. 'If there is a small diamond in one hinge, and a tiny sapphire in the other, it is ours; and here they are. You see, this was handed down through the centuries after sitting on John of Gaunt's camp desk; and when he was home, on his night table. This is my ancestress.'

'We will see to it that you are given what is rightfully yours. We'll send it to this address once the investigation is over,' the agent waved Ned's business card in the air.

'Thank you,' Ned responded, unhappy over the gemless frame.

When Old Blue and Ned returned to the others, Orange was taken in for questioning instead of the Middle Eastern dignitary. Scotland Yard ascertained that the Ambassador's slim, long case held nothing more than a putter and felt he should not be detained. He had been waiting to talk to his old pal.

'What were you doing here?' Old Blue asked. 'Going back to

college?' He grinned impishly at his former hall fellow.

'No, I needed to order new uniforms for our armed service.'

'So you can blow our heads off, no doubt,' Old Blue chuckled.

'No doubt.' The Ambassador then smiled and asked, 'What do you do in between visiting London? Anything? I suppose you ride your horse in South Dakota.'

'I rarely get home, but when I go that is exactly what I like to do.'

'I like to imagine you doing that sometimes. I think of you a great deal because we had much fun in college.'

Old Blue patted his shoulder. 'We surely did.'

At the tea, things were progressing famously. Subjects in common including Mr. Stuart's vocation of restoring the eco-balance, organic farming and gardening, were enjoyed by Old Blue's cousin as it came from the above-mentioned man's daughter. The new acquaintances became good friends and had an enjoyable day.

At the end of the hour, the Dream Prince decided he would like to know her better... there was something very comforting and serene about her. He seemed to find himself talking and expressing memories of an adult lifetime spent in treasured pursuits regarding ecology which had caused sneers in the press a decade and a half before, but which now showered favor.

She's a marvelous listener, he thought to himself as he realized that she was truly animated by his narrations, and not just pretending to be so. She asked for descriptions of the pond and watered areas he had restored in Gloucestershire, and type of cattle which grazed his lands, the sheep, horses and the grains planted, about the weeds allowed to reach maturity in the forests and fields which in turn would break up soil hardpans by their root systems thereby allowing subsequent crop roots to feed deeply during drought, fiberizing and replenishing nutritious humus to enrich the soil for the earthworms and insects who make their homes within. 'Most natural plants and dirt inhabitants seem to work for the welfare of man,' Christiana enthusiastically repeated her father's discoveries. She went on to name the attributes of phosphorous and nitrogen in each weed, calling the plants by name and comparing them to those which her enchanted host said had cousins in the British Isles.

An amazed man caught the ball and responded with tales of experiments, successes, disappointments.

'Weeds, when controlled wisely, are guardians of the soil, Daddy said.' She smiled at the kind eyes of her new friend.

Old Blue walked into the lovely room of lofty ceilings, marble pillars and glowing mahogany furniture which reflected firelight from the hearths as warmly as the Prince glowed from the exuberant interest of his guest. Noticing OB's late arrival, the host stood to dismiss Christiana upon her request.

As she walked out in search of the ladies' room, he asked the tardy man a few questions, which piqued his curiosity.

'How can a woman love such things as much as I and still be so feminine?' He shook his head in wonder, adding, 'She even loves to fly and relishes architecture and design – not to mention music, horses – she's quite an equestrian, you know. At home she goes fishing... can you imagine that girl standing waist deep in a swimsuit, casting into the reeds for something she calls "sunnies"?'

Old Blue laughed and asked, 'Where does she keep the leeches and earthworms most people put on their hooks if she's in a swimsuit?'

The Prince smiled. 'In a container which she secures to a fabric belt around her waist. What a maverick. I like it! The only thing she isn't mad about is getting bitten by deer flies when she exits the water... all the "mosquito dope" as she calls it, gets washed off her skin.' He shook his head in enjoyment, watching the door avidly hoping for her return.

'You should dance with her sometime,' Old Blue commented. 'A real dream of a partner. She'd make an elephant think he was Fred Astaire.'

'Well, if she can dance as well as she discusses eco-balance and such, I can't wait to take her for a turn about the floor!' OB's cousin concluded. 'How can she do all of those things and know so much? The same way we all do, I suppose,' he answered himself.

'Because she's crazy,' the tall ex-Romanov laughed. 'But she's my kind of crazy, and I love it! She even plays basketball with her son and he has a hard time keeping up with her.'

'Does she like snow?' the Royal asked. 'Of course, that's a ridiculous question when being asked of someone from northern Minnesota. One would have to be a snow bunny to live up there, wouldn't one?' he discreetly hid his embarrassment regarding a question with an obvious answer.

'I suppose she would like to ski,' Old Blue divined the interrogator's inner thought, 'but the doctor has forbidden it for a time. No doubt, she'll be back on the slopes in a year or two if I know anything about her. I guess what I appreciate is her honesty without pretension – not catty nor vicious, nor unkind to anyone. Regal? Yes. Noble? Yes. But extremely vulnerable, trusting and tender. I call her a bunny rabbit.' With that he smiled, accepting a gimlet to replace the tea.

Before the day was done, three Americans - two sisters and their bodyguard had been invited to stay for dinner at the Palace.

It was a happy day. Their host was utterly charming in a natural sense and they all got on swimmingly.

An irate Orange jealously waited outside the Palace gates while a steaming Scar-P watched her. He had offered her everything and still it wasn't enough! There she was, lusting on Old Blue. I wonder if all women are as fickle as she, the MI6 man rarely involved with women contemplated. Too bad she isn't loyal, as is that little bird from Minnesota. Something about her fills one with peace – she even works like an opiate on Old Blue's hurting places, and he is one calloused man!

Chapter Twenty-Six

'So, Connie and Raoul were in Phoenix?' Old Blue asked Ned. They were having coffee together the next day.

'Oh, yes. Scar-P came home with them for the Christmas party.'

'I didn't know that Brit knew you folks,' Old Blue laughed. 'He must get around more than I give him credit.' I didn't know Orange, either, he thought. Here she's been your sister, Connie, all along.

'That I warrant he does,' Ned agreed.

'Sometimes I get the feeling that he and Orange know each other much more than I suspect.'

'You jealous?' Ned asked.

'Sometimes, but since I met Christiana, I am not.'

'You really like her, don't you.' Ned smiled.

'She's another Jill, Rick says and I must admit that I agree. The Man even likes her.'

'Who does she lean toward?' Ned inquired.

'Her son, Geoffrey!' Old Blue moaned. 'She doesn't know we exist. Really, Geoff's a complete thing for her – she dotes on him.'

'Well, that's good. He's blessed.'

In came the men from Scotland Yard.

'Hello, may we see you a moment?' they asked Old Blue.

'Of course.' He got up and walked away from the table, after excusing himself from Ned's presence.

'We've found the Hope Diamond and know who took the cursed thing after it reached these shores. You'll never believe it. Remember wondering where in the world your partner went?'

Old Blue thought he was dreaming. 'Are you speaking of Orange?' He was speechless.

'She wasn't the only one involved.' The guys shook their heads.

'Who was the accomplice?'

'Scar-P.'

'I don't believe it! You have to be wrong, especially about him. He's a great agent... loves his country... wouldn't embarrass...' movement near the entrance caught his attention. Three men were approaching.

'Come here, Scar-P,' OB waved toward the door. In walked Scar-P, handcuffed with Sam and Rick beside him – one on each side. The little room suddenly became smaller. 'My buddy... my buddy. How can this be?' Old Blue felt sick again. He looked at the scarred wrists in steel bracelets and wanted to tear them off, let the man go free; but instead, he looked into his eyes and asked, 'Why?'

'After we were shot up in the desert and everyone was killed except you and me, it seemed that nothing I did that night was truly appreciated by the country I serve, nor even by my own family.' Tears filled his eyes. 'I guess I've become hard. If it wasn't for you, my hands would have been given for my country. Pretty tough gift for a man who has legitimate Royal blood running through his veins. I didn't steal DeSilva's miniature for nothing. I am half Plantagenet just like Princess Catherine Lancaster of Castile who became Queen of her mother's lands upon marrying her cousin.' He held out his arms... 'can't you see?' Tears coursed down his cheeks. 'Long slender body, arms and legs... just like John of Gaunt our grandsire... and his brother Lionel.'

'So, you want recognition, and if no title, a bit of land? Man, couldn't you have bought a few acres with your military pay?' Old Blue felt sorry for the poor sucker.

'A little house on a little plot with a little garden in the back? I'm too big in size for little. At least where I am going now, I will be in what was my direct ancestor's castle in Lancaster. I'll be home, though it's been a prison for years. I'll feel his presence there, and I'll be able to look up at the gate and see him standing, carved in stone – my grandfather many generations removed, but without whom I would not have come into this world.' He stood tall, gracefully proud, fierce like Lionel, his uncle of old whom of all King Edward III's children he resembled the most.

'Like John of Gaunt, the Second Duke of Lancaster, there is only one woman who has captivated my heart,' he bowed his head and continued, 'for her I stole the Hope Diamond. She stole the scepter; I had no idea she had confiscated it nor my miniature until hours later.' Dead silence filled the room. 'But I love the Queen the most, so I returned our radiant jewels of mercy.' He jangled his shackles inadvertently, wanting to run his fingers through a shock of hair, which had come out of place, but was unable to raise his arms. 'I couldn't find Orange's bangle though. When climbing up through the hole she made beneath the case, it got stuck in the rubber mat track – she's lucky she didn't lose a finger.'

'When did you go to Washington?' Old Blue quietly asked.

Joe Bly who had walked in unobtrusively listened attentively.

'I didn't, other than on an assignment previous to the theft.'

'How in h-e-double toothpicks did you steal America's portion of The Royal Blue then?'

This time Joe couldn't keep his lips zipped. All eyes looked his way as Mr. Bly expostulated. 'Pardon me for butting in but what are you Scar-P, a genie?'

'Yeah, are you?' echoed Old Blue, eyeing his buddy and smiling for the first time since all had become tense in the room.

'I'm not an Arabian spirit. It was easy. I had a buddy pick the gem up and deliver it to Sir Gork,' the skinny blond murmured.

'Where's your buddy?' OB inquired.

'Floating somewhere in the Volga – he's dead.'

'Who killed him?'

'He swallowed a pill… killed himself.'

'Why?'

'Russian Mafia closing in.'

'Why?'

'They gave him money for the trip to D.C., and wouldn't wait for the diamond to be cashed in. You see, the jewel disappeared… I still don't know where the thing is. We intended to split the proceeds.'

Old Blue whistled. 'What a circus!' He rubbed his cheek. 'Where was it the last time you knew?'

'With Orange's great uncle. The old gent grieved because he hated her "poverty", as he called it. He was going to sell the necklace to establish security for me in order that I be able to offer marriage.'

Old Blue's eyes nearly popped out of his skull. Why would she want to marry him? She loves me! he did a quick take in his head.

'Is that right?' the startled South Dakotan looked at the washed-out middle-aged man who wanted only to cease from the hard world of espionage and hardship... a lonely man standing eye to eye with lost heritage, scarred wrists bearing heavy chains upon the hands of a previously selfless British subject.

Old Blue suddenly choked back tears. He loved this hapless jack-a-nap who had stood by him through thick and thin. What had happened to him? In his heart he knew, perceiving as surely as God was above, for had he, himself, not wept during many a tortured night when memory of conflicts warred within his soul? He, Old Blue, wanted out. Scar-P wanted out. Scar-P now had his wish, but not in exactly the manner he had intended before falling in love.

Suddenly Old Blue could see Orange for what she was. She thought Scar-P was well fixed before she stole the diamond from her great uncle; even prior to taking the miniature from her plantagenet lover!

'She couldn't marry you, so I suppose she settled for me,' Scar-P huskily said. The truth hurt, but as always he could take it, for his soul was truly full of integrity and remorse.

'What makes you think she would have settled for anything but your money?' Old Blue asked as the friends looked into one another's eyes. 'She's a cold-blooded killer, my man. Getting caught saved your skinny behinder.'

After all, she loves *me*, he silently conjectured. I'm poor in her book but that doesn't keep her from liking my lovin'. Yup! She liked *my* amour, and *your* supposed fat pockets. What a fool she is! Course it's the truth... I wouldn't marry her if I had all the riches in the world and let's face it, if she had her own riches she'd be content to remain the way we three have always been, the scheming vixen!

Looking at his peer who had saved his life many times over, a lump came into his throat. Old Blue slapped Scar-P on the shoulder and held it tightly saying, 'I love ya, man! If you were a woman, I'd marry ya!' A tear trickled down the side of his beat-up, reconstructed nose down into his beard, washing over the scars beneath. 'Get the hell out of here,' he softly choked.

The men took Scar-P away with Joe Bly following sadly behind them.

Vauxhall Cross loomed before Scar-P's mind. His home office, Vauxhall Cross would now become enemy number one. Involving the Russian sealed that fact in the grieving agent's mind.

Old Blue walked dejectedly upstairs to his room. Unlocking the door, he found Rick and Sam lounging on the bed.

'Hi,' he plopped into a chair.

'You found out,' Rick said.

'Yes, it makes me wonder if Orange was the one who took pot shots at me in an attempt to keep a sumptuous retirement plan from failing. Scar-P takes all the blame, but he doesn't even know where the Hope is. He's never seen the durn thing. What do you think?' He looked up at his team.

'I think it is Orange,' Sam drawled, 'who knows all about it. Bet she's been the shooter, too.'

'Oh that would be impossible,' Old Blue changed his mind. 'She's weird, but not insane. Course she can be an esnecca, alright,' he added.

'Yah, and a cobra at that!' Sam agreed.

'This makes me feel terrible! Hey. Let's cheer ourselves up by calling Angela and Christiana and inviting them to the theater tonight.' The very thought made OB feel better.

'Not tonight we can't unless we go with Angela alone, which is fine too,' Rick said.

'Why, what else is going on for Christiana?' Old Blue wondered aloud.

'Well, she's having dinner on the Thames with His Lordship,' Sam announced.

'Not Lordship you clown, His Royal Highness! He's a crown Prince, not a lord!' Old Blue laughed.

'Oh, who knows! He's a lordly Prince. I care but am too tired to give a fig presently... well... not quite true for I like him very much and hope to see his future secured, along with the rest of the family. But I'm one tired cowboy and want to go home,' he literally sang the last four words of the old American tune.

The three men said goodnight, and suddenly Old Blue demanded, '*What* dinner on the Thames? They weren't supposed to be going anywhere together until Friday night. This is only Thursday!'

'Can't the Prince change his mind if he wishes?' Sam asked.

'Not without everyone who matters knowing about it, and I was not informed of any changes in his plans.' Suddenly he felt adrenaline pouring through his veins and into his brain.

Jumping up, he ordered, 'Get the security guard and ask the Prince's location while I call Wise Acres in Minneapolis. Rick, find Angela's whereabouts. *Move it!* The guards will let you use their communication system.'

He grabbed the telephone, punching the buttons fast and furiously.

'Yes, man. What's up?' Wise Acres asked.

'Where's Christiana Elizabeth?'

'According to this screen, she's not in her room... hmmm... but she is supposed to be getting ready for tea with Angela to be had at four in the afternoon today.'

'Where *is* she?' Blue demanded.

'Her body sensor shows me that she is in motion, moving along the Piccadilly Underground line at a rapid clip toward Heathrow.'

'What the deuce is she doing on the Underground, and with whom?' A thought flashed in his mind. 'Look up Orange.'

'Hmmm... she's not at her Piccadilly shop... let me find her position. Well, I'll be a monkey's uncle!'

'What is it? Hurry!'

'She's on the same train. Let me bring up the other screen... yes! Both sensors are side by side in the same horizontal line. Christiana is with Orange.'

'Bring up Angela's sensor. Hurry, man!'

'Rats!' Wise Acres exclaimed.

'What's wrong?' Old Blue was almost beside himself, itching to go save Christiana from whatever an obviously demented woman had in mind for her.

'The screen won't come up... let me call the engineer to

throw the generator into gear.'

'Those things are supposed to kick in automatically, and we shouldn't even have to rely on anything other than satellite!'

'There's a meteorite storm right now. Sorry, pal.'

'Hurry!' Old Blue gasped. 'Do something. Better yet, hang on – I'll stick Sam on the line. Give him the info when it comes up and then send him after Angela with Rick as back-up.'

'Sam!' Blue shouted.

'Yeh, boss!' Sam appeared at Old Blue's elbow.

'Hang on the telephone with Wise Acres, then do exactly *what* he orders… *as* he orders.'

'Gottcha' Sam took the receiver.

'I'm going to intersect the Piccadilly line; on second thought, I'm taking Rick with me… Christiana and Orange are in the same seat, which bodes ill! See you later – and hopefully when I do, Angela will be with you safe and sound because she and her sister are *not* on the River Thames with the Prince.'

Suddenly Old Blue shouted, 'Rick! I need you with me!'

Already down the hall, the blond doctor waited for OB to catch up.

'Come on pal! We've a life to save,' Blue demanded.

'I'm with you!' Rick had grabbed his raincoat, and was throwing it on over his suit, checking security devices as he followed hot on Old Blue's heels, med bag in hand.

Instead of having to wait for transportation, the SOS had been heard by others and an MI6 agent was waiting at the door of a taxi which was opened wide.

The spooks jumped into the black vehicle and were driven with bobby escort to the end of the line. The Americans jumped out of the cab while policemen hopped off motorbikes; all running to storm the train. They poured down the concourse in a stream, shoulder to shoulder, pedestrians scurrying out of their way. The Chief was close on Old Blue's heels which one could barely see for the soles of his flying shoes as they pounded down the pavement alongside the track.

A great incoming roar and slight rumbling of the pavement underfoot announced the impending arrival of the train. Security forces spread out to cover every door of each car. Out of nowhere it seemed they doubly lined the opposite platforms as well, politely asking passengers waiting on the adjacent walkway to go back upstairs until an all-clear sounded.

'Hurry, please hurry,' the bobbies and plain-clothes men smilingly implored, belying the seriousness deep within their eyes. Always courteous, ever the British way, an endearing quality which every American visitor including Angela, Christiana and the trio had noticed.

The train whooshed up and thundered to a quick halt. Electric doors opened. People started pouring out and were quickly held firmly, albeit politely, by the second line of security guards while the first line rushed in asking everyone to freeze.

Old Blue dashed through the first passenger door while Rick bolted through the back door, both followed by a stream of policemen intent on the sting of the woman whose face had flashed across every screen and been described on every handset across Britain between the time OB and Rick left the hotel and arrived at the last subway station.

Old Blue saw the familiar shoulders he had loved in times past, shrouded in a red wool cape with a hood trimmed in black piping. She was sitting in an aisle seat, and the tortured hair that strayed via two spikes from the hood matched her cape.

The car was quickly cleared of other passengers. 'Is something wrong, dear?' Orange looked up sweetly at Old Blue.

Christiana's shoulders voluntarily shuddered as she sat wedged between Orange and the window. Rick and Old Blue noticed the slight movement.

'I think you're the one who can tell us that,' Old Blue quietly said. 'Come along. Come with us, ladies.'

But neither of them moved.

'Christiana?' Old Blue urged.

Christiana turned her face from looking out the window to look at Blue and Rick. They gasped. One eye was black and blue apparently, for extending from beneath her shades was a deeply colored bruise which extended down her cheek under the chin, disappearing into the hair which covered her ear and neck. She seemed dazed... unable to recognize them.

'Christiana?' Old Blue asked again. 'It's me, Old Blue.'

She simply gazed at him and then turned her head to continue looking out the window at the security officers lined up closely to the passenger car on the cold, gray platform.

'Orange, bring Christiana with you, and get out of those seats,' Old Blue quietly snarled.

'I can't, sweetie.' She smiled ruefully.

'Why not?' He lifted the cape from her lap. The wrap was partially spread over Christiana's legs as well, after being draped totally over her left arm and hand.

'You unholy witch!' Old Blue softly, meanly said to Orange. 'You should be horsewhipped and sent to solitary confinement where someone could teach you a lesson or two!' His eyes watered from bitterness and spiritual gall. 'To truss a mere bunny into a wrist-cuff attached to a vampire is one thing; but to make sure she doesn't try to get away by wiring a filled syringe into a pressurized straightjacket with a time-released needle poking into her arm, is vile!'

He placed the long strong fingers of his right hand around Orange's gorgeous neck seemingly to caress, but soon her face started becoming red... then rather blue. Old Blue's face stayed calm, unperturbed, smiling as he held her gaze.

'Unscrew the depressor from the needle and give me the key for that Houdini torture cuff... *now*! And, in that order!'

Her left hand went feebly to her V-necked blouse. She lifted the end of a long, gold chain which had previously been out of sight between her breasts. Old Blue took a tiny key dangling from the end of it as Orange's body sagged into a state of unconsciousness. Her left arm fell onto the train seat. The chain dropped over her black bodice as Blue took his hand from the neck which he had kissed a thousand times through the years.

Focusing on Christiana, who had also lost awareness, he slowly and carefully pulled the intramuscular needle from her lovely arm. Rick handed him a sterile gauze pad, which he held over the wound. Withdrawing it, OB said, 'The poison must have coagulated her blood, she doesn't bleed.'

'Must be venom.' Rick lifted Orange from the seat and passed her along to the next security agent. The officer carried Orange past the double line of officers who fanned left and right into each seat next to the aisle in which they'd been standing. At the door, Orange was carried out, laid on a trolley and tended by paramedics. Oxygen was attached to her face as vital signs were taken. She roused. Then, wrapping her in the blanket upon which she'd been laid and strapping her securely to the gurney, she was carried to a waiting ambulance where dispatch to the hospital took a matter of minutes.

Rick in the meantime had started administering first aid to Christiana Elizabeth.

'We have to determine what she was given,' Rick murmured as he withdrew a small amount of blood from a capillary under her thumb. While he performed the invasive measure, Old Blue hurriedly checked five little vials being held upright by a compartmentalized arrangement in the lid of Rick's med bag. Below each cylinder of solution, were two sealed bottles for each malady test; one made up of liquid, the other of powder. In a third row were various chemicals and natural ingredients to use in determining poisons, which had victimized. The bacterial agents, toxins, and biological compounds which men used in espionage were therefore quickly made identifiable by mixing and matching, and a knowledgeable person could produce multiple antidotes for multiple problems.

'Is she breathing? She's pale as death,' OB's heart was in his throat.

Rick took the stethoscope from her chest.

'Her heart is faint and slow – brachacardial. It'll hold if I can determine what was in this syringe fast enough, a depressant of some sort, it is.'

He took the syringe, closely scrutinizing the milky substance, which had been releasing very slowly into her muscle. Without wasting one second, an idea hit him: DeSilva's from Arizona! Desert reptiles. Rattlesnake venom! It seemed the most logical guess, so Rick inserted the offensive needle through a rubber seal on the neck of vial 'C' quickly releasing one-eighth of a cc into the solution. The liquid turned a color, which matched a tiny patch of red in a graduation of shades marked rattlesnake milk.

'Oh, dear God,' he prayed silently. 'Help.' Quickly taking the antidote, Rick filled a new syringe and injected it directly into

Christiana's veins to carry it immediately to her failing heart as OB applied an oxygen mask to aid her struggling attempts to breathe.

'Come on sweetheart... don't die. Come on baby, fight!' Blue's voice choked. He thought his big heart would break in two.

'Get this woman to the hospital!' Rick quietly ordered as he snapped his bag shut.

A pair of gentle hands helped lift the unconscious woman from the train seat. Old Blue took her lovingly into his arms.

'Make way, please,' he called to the men. And again they fanned aside down the entire length of the aisle for a rushing form. A stretcher was waiting as they climbed down the coach steps. Old Blue and Rick jumped into the waiting ambulance with the British team of medics, and with sirens wailing raced to the hospital.

For the first time since 'Nam, Old Blue felt himself praying, bargaining with God. He didn't care that the med team was hearing every word as he became more frantic with every promise.

'Oh God. If you will let this innocent live, I'll change my ways. I'll renounce my loose behavior, I'll make a novena, I'll return to the church and do penance for the rest of my life, I'll even become a damn priest if you really insist upon it! Just let the little lady live... and forgive me if in a moment of passion I kill the person who did this to her. If you don't want me to end Orange's miserable life, stop me!' Tears streamed down his grizzled face.

Softly a voice floated into Old Blue's troubled thoughts. It was Rick's comforting, strong words reaching out to his friend. 'He shall call upon me and I will be with him in trouble to deliver... with long life will I satisfy. Under his wings shalt thou trust, and he shall cover thee with his feathers.'

Usually OB hated Bible-spouting; but this oddly comforted his savage heart. Conflictingly, an urge to kill Orange suddenly made him salivate. He trembled, trying to pray sincerely.

The ambulance swung into the drive and screeched to a halt. The men whisked their precious load into casualty – ER.

Surprisingly, in walked a very concerned Dream Prince.

Chapter Twenty-Seven

'Potpourri! Potpourri!'

Christiana thought she was back in Minnesota. It was springtime, April first, in her delirium. The redwing blackbirds had come back from points south to serenade her as they swayed on the long, dried rushes surrounding her lovely apartment. Their little black wings wearing scarlet epaulettes blazed against a new four-inch snowfall of heavy, beautiful white, which layered every burst cattail frothing with buff-colored fluff. The wet snow hugged all bare elm branches and evergreen trees as far as the eye could see. Newly returned ducks were gleefully rising and landing en masse like children on holiday enjoying a roller coaster ride, while sampling the recently thawed waters of the western pond and lake across the gravel road. Both bodies of water sported a two-inch layer of mush, newly formed, which reached from the bank to open ripples of water far from shore.

'Daddy? Daddy?' She wandered around in the snow, barefoot, but couldn't find him. Her long robe trailed behind exposed ankles. 'Father?'

Suddenly her feet began to bite with cold. The beautiful pristine whiteness, which she had loved all her life, started to cause pain. She began shaking, quivering; the beauty was turning into an alarming, white tomb. She couldn't find the door to her warm apartment. The birds kept singing happily as if nothing was wrong but things just were not right. She touched her cheek with cold fingers, and pulled them away in horror for her own flesh felt like cold cheese and left upon her fingertips a white sticky powder that smelled peculiar and stung as if it were the hoar frost of death.

She staggered up the steps of the snow-covered deck to her locked door as the stinging in her feet, legs and chest became unbearable. Christiana pulled on her bodice to lift the cloth from herself for something was crushing her lungs into objection with every attempt to breathe. The weight on her bosom, excruciatingly oppressive, forbade respiration.

'Daddy? Daddy? Is this death? Where are you? I'm cold,' she shivered looking longingly at the warmth within through the glass of her own door, but could not get in. Reaching up to feel inside a velvet pouch hidden behind the porch light, her heart fell, for the key was not inside.

'Oh cruel, cruel death! I know now thy sting for I have felt your scorpion tail and feel it still. Where is the warmth of heaven? Father, are you there, safe and warm?'

Suddenly, her apartment door seemed to be the pearly gates, not warmly glowing but coldly mocking everything in which she had ever believed. She wept. The tears froze upon her frosted cheeks like brilliant diamonds resting there.

With bluing fists, she weakly pounded upon the door.

Suddenly the portal flew open. A handsome man stood, arms outstretched, welcoming her to warmth and happiness. It was not her father, but from the light and kindness, quietness and peace emanating from his eyes, she recognized a like spirit.

Walking in, his arms drew her into a warm embrace.

In reality, a team of doctors struggled to massage her heart while using IVs to thin her blood allowing the flow of oxygenated plasma to her brain. Hoping to prevent cell damage, they feverishly continued. While being given transfusions, her heart started to react, and all that could be done had been done; needles and lines protruded and ran everywhere.

She moaned, rolling her head to one side.

'Geoffrey? Geoffrey?' she murmured. 'Water.'

Her mouth was moistened with sponge sticks. Comforting hands acted as conductors of kind concern, life-giving hope.

Two princes, one Russian, one English, waited outside the emergency room door.

Simultaneously both asked one another, 'Will she live?'

A plane landed at Heathrow as Rick waited patiently near gate number 5. Emerging with the flow of passengers, Pamela walked into his waiting arms.

'It is good to be home again. Wherever your arms encircle me, it is home, darling,' she whispered as he kissed her. 'I wish I had not flown back to the States.'

'Come quickly, dear. Christiana has been calling for her father, you and Angela. Where's Geoffrey?'

'He flew in ahead of me, landing at Gatwick. He should be by her side right this minute. I think her son's presence will give the will to live. It did for me twenty years ago, remember?' Pamela kissed her handsome man.

'I remember, and now we must hang in there for a very sick little sister.' Rick gently ushered the now tearful Pamela to a waiting taxi while Sam gathered her luggage.

Scarred wrists were seen as the wheel turned, guiding Pam, Rick and Sam to the hospital.

Old Blue has done it again, silently Rick noticed Scar-P. Guess Old Blue convinced the powers that be to release our buddy because the diamond and the scepter were stolen by someone else, he thought. Looking out the window at the teeming traffic on London's streets, Rick felt proud of Old Blue's compassion and understanding for it always seemed to be applied where rehabilitation was truly possible. Now, Orange?

I'll be doing well to keep OB from murdering her! Rick sighed. She's a wicked woman, truly selfish, jealous, you name it. Better lock her up and throw away the key – that's all she will ever understand, I'm afraid. With such thoughts racing through his head, the taxi pulled in front of a hospital. All went inside, including the driver.

Entering Christiana's room after greeting the two Princes, Pamela turned to her doctor husband. 'Will she live?' she asked, looking sadly at her unconscious sister lying pale and still in the electric bed. Walking to the bedside, where Christiana's teenage son was standing beside his mother holding her motionless fingers, Pamela placed her hand over both of theirs.

'She will live,' Christiana's son confidently prophesied. He held his head resolutely, as if by doing so, his strength would flow into her unconscious body from his which had once been part of her own before separate life had commenced at birth.

Angela stood at the window from which she watched the bed. Her amber eyes were dark with sorrow.

The door opened. In walked the doctor accompanied by two Princes, one known, one unknown.

'Will she live?' quietly asked Pamela and Angela in unison. Angela walked over and took Pam and Geoff's hands.

A flutter outside the window caught their attention. A tiny white bird flew to the marble sill outside the window, a red bougainvillea in its beak. Suddenly it was swooping with a flutter of wings over the Princess, Christiana Elizabeth Stuart. The blossom fell upon her heart, now covered by white sheets. The scent of gardenias mysteriously filled the room.

'The promise of the Stuarts,' Angela whispered.

'How did that bird get in here?' questioned the doctor.

Angela and God smiled.

Princess Christiana opened her eyes. Aquatic green met earth tones of brown, and then of sky blue. She fell into the optical embrace of the man who had opened the door in her venom-induced dream.

In that instant, his gaze made her his own. The Second Duke of Lancaster and his Katherine, Queen Henrietta Maria and her beloved King Charles I, had come full circle. Meeting again, noblesse oblige made a bid to survive.

The acknowledged Royal pulled a miniature of King Charles I from his pocket. 'I thought you would treasure this,' he murmured to the ill woman.

Angela took its mate from her purse, 'And this,' she smiled at her sister. Charles I's Queen became another Christiana's gift.

Smouldering earthy-brown shaded by black curly lashes watched quietly. Determination to win the prize poured jealously into his jaded soul. Will I become the next pernicious teaser of the Crown in order to gain the girl? he wondered. He tucked his head down. Love triumphed over his stinging soul causing him to acquiesce to whatever fate held for them. He took the Stuart miniatures from the other Prince and Christiana's sister, placing them side by side on the bedside tray. Christiana looked at him. Their eyes locked. Both sets filled with tears. It seemed as if the silence in the room screamed in pain, and he wanted to hold her... comfort her. She yearned for that reassurance of his strength as he tore his gaze from hers and stepped back to stand beside his cousin and Scar-P.

The two Princes stood together, one tall, one of medium height, both towers of strength. The tall man moved away. Rick and Sam fell into step beside OB as he walked out the door into the corridor, exit bound. Christiana's heart dropped as she saw that her friend Old Blue – her comfort zone – was leaving.

'Don't leave us now,' she whispered.

Old Blue didn't hear her because of the hushed voices and hum of activity peculiar to hospital wards.

'I won't leave,' kindly responded the remaining Prince.

She looked at him, warmed by his sincerity and the intense faces held within the framed portraits, all oddly familiar. As the door sighed shut, everything seemed to fall into a sleep, which threatened to become eternal. The green eyes which eventually opened and gazed into those of the Prince seemed to be sparkling with Caribbean sunlight as it used to softly reflect off warm cay waters above his head when, as a boy, he would search for conch shells. Pale, finely textured sand, like skin, smooth and warm to the touch came down memory lane contrasting with the gentle coolness of tropical seas. All were mirrored in Christiana's face as a smile of exquisite tenderness beautified her face.

An intuition from long ago nudged her to recognize which man would be a perfect match when coupled with her strong, loving presence. For those same qualities in him would present themselves to her in a manner which she would find agreeable down through the years. Those attributes were the secret nourishment of the Stuarts and the Duke and his Katherine, strengths made perfect by the natural grace of emotional dedication to serve while preferring the loved one's wishes. Strange how being in love cools selfishness, the lady thought. *Noblesse oblige.*

'Thank you for your kindness,' she whispered. 'Perhaps I would not be here in this bed had I double-checked my schedule. I can't blame this misfortune on anyone but myself for being gullible and spontaneous to a fault.' She quietly laughed at herself, turning her head aside.

'That awareness is the beginning of wisdom,' Angela stepped

forward as she spoke and patted her sister's arm.

One other thought is the beginning of wisdom, Christiana said to herself, recognizing that one can be happy alone, if one so desires to remain. For the thought of never seeing Old Blue again made her heart feel heavy, while the thought of getting to know yet another, delightful or not, made her reel with mental tiredness. Suddenly, the thought of her son brought great balm as sweet as the scent of Gilead trees wafting over her father's generous acres. She needn't prove anything to Geoff. He already knew and loved her unconditionally.

A call was waiting for Old Blue at the nurses' station.

'You sure?' He listened. 'Well, it figures. Thanks.' He handed the telephone back to the nurse. 'Fellas, the Hope Diamond was found hidden in the midnight blue divider behind the counter at Orange's shop.' He told them the details, including the Russian's assist in returning Christiana from Oxburgh Hall.

'That clears Raoul,' the elegantly tall Romanov Prince said as he strode down the hall. Terrible feelings were raging in his core. He was suffocating, burning, at the thought of Christiana's vulnerability regarding his charming cousin; not to mention the sheer hatred he felt toward her tormentor, the bangled thief.

'Let's go throw the book at Orange.' Grinning to hide his emotions, Old Blue continued, 'I'm an attorney and as was said previously, the courts can handle it.'

Suddenly he chuckled, malice leaping merrily through his soul, 'Got to admit it was clever where she hid the Hope Diamond. First at her uncle's who, bless his demented soul, is safe at the home of friends with his nurses. Secondly, in the midnight-blue curtain which is the same color as the stolen jewel!'

'Yes. If she hadn't forgotten to sew the chain into the drapery lining after inserting it, nothing would have rattled when the boys shoved the divider aside during the search of her digs,' Sam laughed.

'She gave Scotland Yard and SIS a break,' Rick agreed. 'Vauxhall Cross will rejoice; they love our buddy, Scar-P.'

Scar-P had disappeared.

Old Blue threw his head back and laughed viciously until tears came. 'Losing two dames in one day... Jesu, Mary and Joseph! Who needs purgatory with a life like mine! I'm already in hell.'

'Pal, she never was intended for you,' Rick motioned toward Christiana's room with a nod of his head.

'I never intended to care for her,' Old Blue groaned.

'Act on what you found lovable in her and you won't stay in purgatory long,' Rick counseled. 'Who knows what tomorrow will bring if you clean up your act? Besides, do you feel no sense of obligation to Orange?'

Old Blue looked at his buddies, started to whistle and opened the door to the fresh air and sunshine of a beautiful English day. As long as Christiana was alive, there was hope. Maybe happiness wasn't that far off after all. He stopped, turned and looked at the men.

'Orange?' he asked. 'Never trust a liar. It's over.'

A taxi pulled curbside. Lanky legs, body and arms unfolded from behind the wheel as their favorite driver emerged to open the passenger door with a scarred wrist and hand. 'Hurry,' he said, 'I have to leave for the Bahamas at once – on Her Majesty's service. *You're* taking *me* to the airport this time.' He patted a slender case on the front seat as he re-entered the car. 'We won't be needing this baby ever again, I warrant.' His gray eyes danced.

'How so?' chorused the men.

'Because you are now looking at an earl – lands, title and a yearly allowance to afford it all. In lieu of service over and above the call of duty for decades before I blew it, a full pardon was granted; *not* to mention the gifts of appreciation.' Scar-P fairly glowed. 'I was forgiven because I replaced it.'

'Do you mean the symbol of mercy,' Rick questioned, 'the scepter?'

'Yes. My record of service had already been under review, and I had been selected for these honors before the heists.' He sighed, 'I'm ashamed... so ashamed. It wasn't for lack of loyalty that these wrists became scarred, you know.'

'You were just temporarily insane,' Sam announced.

'How so?'

'You were in love with a witch of a woman – no conscience in that one!' Sam's blue eyes squinted against serious thought.

Old Blue pulled out a cigar, offering it all around. To his delight, everyone declined… it was his one and only. Settling back against the cushion, he clipped the tip and savored the acrid haze as it rose from flame on tobacco leaf. 'Wonder if there'll be stogies in heaven,' he mused. 'If not, I doubt I'll even want to see old Saint Peter.' He paused to suck slowly on the satisfying roll, allowing the fragrance to saturate every taste bud on his hungry tongue. 'Let's go home to South Dakota and let the wind air out our brains.'

'After we tend to Orange?' Rick reminded.

'Mmm… and after we comfort Christiana,' Old Blue the Russian Prince said between one charmingly chipped tooth set amongst perfect ivories which held the cheroot as if in a vice. A smile as big as the heart of God spread across his rascally face, 'You guys go without me. Comforting a woman takes time.'

He settled deeply into the car seat.

Strength and peace wound its healing way from Christiana's resolve into her physical being. She would seek the roots of her existence to bring her son's life into the promise of his lineage. She would give him the opportunity to have the future which providence was laying not only before him, but herself as well.

Green eyes smiled into blue, promising to try. For this, she now knew, was why they had been deserted – to open heaven's gates into the majesty of self-discovery.

Chapter Twenty-Eight

Christiana awakened. Soft morning light caressed the walls of her white apartment.

'If only all of this had not been just a dream!' she sighed. 'I could have sworn we went to England! It seemed so real!'

Reaching for the television control, Christiana pressed 41, bringing LUK into the room. London was being shown with Kensington Palace surrounded by an ever-expanding sea of flowers.

A tear dropped off her cheek soaking into the satin of her pillowslip. Suddenly she sat up – there was Rick with the curly-headed cigar smoker again! She saw them hail a taxi.

The cellular telephone started ringing incessantly. Scrambling out of bed to run across the cool floor, she intercepted the fourth ring.

'Hello?'

'Christiana!'

'Pam, what's happening?'

'You'll never guess!'

'Guess what?'

'Do you remember the stogie smoker we saw with Rick on TV?'

'Yes, and I just saw them hail a taxi in London on LUK.'

'I'm looking at them, too... that's why I called – to have you turn your TV on, and to say that when Rick comes home his captain is coming along expressly to meet you!' Pamela was breathless.

Christiana felt dizzy. 'Is he bringing Orange, too?'

'Orange? Orange who?'

'Oh... no one... nothing. Well, who is Rick's captain?' Chrissy wondered aloud.

'That Cigar Cowboy Boots, that's who!' Pam laughed. 'We're supposed to meet them at the Fargo airport. Angela is giving us

her Buick to do the honors and I'll pick you up at nine tonight –
that'll get us there in plenty of time to meet their midnight flight.
Someone else will be along, Rick said. I suppose it will be Sam.'

'What about Scar-P and the Prince?'

'Scar-P? What in heaven's name is a Scar-P? Did you have a
nightmare, dear?'

'I think so.' Christiana shivered in anticipation of looking into
the captain's eyes and the blue or gray eyes of this 'someone else'.
Somehow she already knew that the grizzled man's eyes would be
brown with frustratingly long, curly lashes... sagely ancient with
depths of brilliant intelligence.

The sense of deprivation, which her dream had given as Old
Blue had walked out of the hospital room, was replaced by one of
well-being. I already know him, she thought as she started her
bath water replete with bubbling oils.

'Pam!' Christiana said.

'What, girl?'

'Has the Hope Diamond been found?'

'I don't know. Keep the telly on – it'll be mentioned sooner or
later.'

'What about the scepter?'

'What scepter? Chrissy! Are you alright? Earth calling Chris!'
Pam laughed.

'Come over for breakfast and I'll tell you of a wild dream I had
after the storm last night,' she answered.

'That was a wicked one. Okay – I'll be there in half an hour.'

'Bring Angela too.'

'Okay. I will if she's able. Bye, dearie.'

'Bye... and Pam. Before tomorrow you'll know what a Scar-P
is... and who knows maybe even a prince!'

With a shadow of a smile momentarily replacing the terrible
sense of loss she'd been feeling for three months, the dream of
blue eyes and brown made Christiana look out the window where
she saw the shattered cottonwood tree. A shiver of anticipation
coursed through her body as she cradled the cellular, slipped out
of her nightie and into the tub of bubbly hot water.

'All of our family knows we've descended from the Stuarts,'
she whispered, 'and just maybe my dream meant that dying to

selfishness in our quest to help others leads to the majesty of peace, love and understanding amongst humankind. Is that not the essence of the ancient heraldry of my ancestors and the Dream Princes' crest through the centuries – three feathers encircled by a golden coronet on which has been fashioned the words "noblese oblige"... to serve? And serve, those in my dream so steadfastly did. Everyone's good works are deserving of honor, yes? There need be no pernicious teasers of this world. Oh, let it be, dear God! Let them all be like my father... and my Dream Princes and Princess!'

Looking toward heaven with her plea, she started scrubbing her face with all the anticipation hope creates. The thought of love and forgiveness ruling decisions and saving lives from death before their time, filled her heart with joy.

Come on my Dream Princes, I'm ready for such a world! Bring them on, Rick, she exalted as her thoughts and entire self submerged in the water for a thorough rinse.

Bibliography

Merriam-Webster, *New Biographical Dictionary*, by Merriam-Webster Inc., ©1983, John of Gaunt et al (Katherine re: Savoy destruction 1384–1385)

On Lady Katherine deRoet Swynford Lancaster, by R.E.G. Cole, Prebendary of Lincoln.

Joseph A. Cocannouer, *Weeds, Guardians of the Soil, Organic Method Pioneer*

Notes and words of my father, Melvin E. Cordes, pioneer of organic methods re: farming, gardening, animal husbandry, fowl management in:

    a) Organic Garden & Farming Magazines

    b) Prevention Magazines

    c) Minneapolis Star & Tribune, Sun. Edition

    d) Private Papers

    e) Discussions and Lifestyle

Merriam-Webster, *Complete Biographical Dictionary*, 1943 etc., to present: John of Gaunt, Queen Constanza, Lady Katherine Swynford & issue, Henrietta Maria, Charles I, etc

Merriam-Webster, *Complete Geographical Dictionary*

Merrian-Webster, *Complete Geographical Encyclopaedia*, The Civil War, Cromwell House, Ely, in Cambridgeshire, England. (No quotations used.)

Assorted materials from visits to: (No quotations used) Hampton Court; Kettlethorpe Manor; The Savoy Hotel, etc., London, England. On Lady Katherine Swynford: Rectory, Kettlethorpe Manor, Lincolnshire; Lincoln Cathedral

E. Beresford Chancellor, *The 18th Century in London*, (pp. 123–124), re: Boodles Club, White's Club, etc

Hogarth, *The Rakes Progress*, Figure 96, April 30, 1733, Whites Destroyed by Fire

The Daily Current Widow White's management of White's Club after husband died.

Encyclopedia Britannica (2 sets – 1940s – and current)

Webster, *Complete Bibliographies* (1948 to current)

William Drummond of Hawthorndon, Scotland, (1585–1649), *On Lady Jane Maitland* The Muse's Library, 1894

Shakespeare (Act II, Scene I of Richard II.), *The Complete Works of Shakespeare*

Smithsonian Museum of Natural History re: Hope Diamond, Washington, DC

National Geographic Society, *This England*

Dicey, *Law of the Constitution.*

Walter Bagehot, *The nature of the English Monarchy*

Encyclopaedia Britannica, 1950: King Charles I and wife Henrietta Maria, and offspring

Alexandria Public Library:
   a) Henry of Navarre (Henry the Great)
   b) British Security Forces, M15 and M16
   c) Diamond of the Golden Fleece and its subsequent jewels.
   d) Royal House of Windsor et al, all history contained herein (and much more.)

Printed in the United States
1018800001B/31-39